CHAPTER ONE

February 1870

1

Drunken shouts from the scrubland clearing, by the sprawling Cornish roadside inn, split the night's silence, then carried away across the bleak, low-lying farmland that stretched to the ocean. The sounds were so distinct in the sharp, crisp, air that the tall, fair man walking quickly home after a reasonably productive evening spent fishing in the shadows of towering cliffs, paused for a moment.
The miner, distinguished by his trailing, surprisingly blond, hair knew exactly where the cries of alcoholic battle originated from. Grimacing slightly at the thought of yet another pointless melee outside the Britannia Inn, he hesitated for a passing moment, and then dragged on back towards the family cottage in the nearby hamlet of Biscovey, deciding he was too tired to bother any further with thoughts of a useless brawl in frost-covered mud.
A fitful moon, mostly obscured by scudding clouds, struggled to shed some light on James Rosevean's path back to the granite cottage that had served him as home throughout his life. Maybe he would have taken an alternative route, trailing eastwards, instead, through the lane of conspiratorial cypress trees to the Britannia, if he had known his eldest brother was about to be caught up in a killing. But the 'maybe' was minimal. The ties between himself and Nathan had

noticeably loosened since their father's death some months before. To his mind drink had become his brother's sole companion since then, happily selected above family.

The angry, escalating, mish-mash of voices followed James as he pushed himself onwards, but became fainter as he wearily picked his way up the steep, wooded slopes to the few cottages that constituted Biscovey. The weather had deteriorated during the evening, becoming unexpectedly cold, and he just about summoned enough energy to stamp up the icy, rutted paths in a bid to prevent heels and toes freezing.

Eventually, the track widened and Wheal Bethany rose before him, the non-stop bellow of the mine's engine almost finally drowning the noises of discontent, now as faint as a whisper, but still discernible if he strained to hear. Deliberately not glancing at the engine house and its straggly rash of outbuildings, he carried on to the home his driven father had deliberately built to look a cut above the rest. When he reached it, there was no light from the oil lamps within the cottage to illuminate the choking, dead-of-night, darkness. But he knew his way around its small rooms as expertly as he did the deep, twisted workings at Bethany. After lighting a belligerent candle, he gutted the pollock he had caught, and left them in the kitchen for morning. Then he staggered upstairs, noted that at least two of his other brothers were snoring, and crashed into sleep himself.

11

His rest was uninterrupted. Very seldom did doubts assail such a set mind during the hours that, for some others, held the most torments.

Well before James had eased himself between the sheets, Nathan Rosevean had studiously swallowed a sea of alcohol, as had most others who had packed into the Britannia, and then staggered outside when the doors had closed on them after drinking time came to a begrudging end. Hazily, he was being jostled and pushed into the heart of the fighting that James had idly acknowledged, and was gradually slipping past caring whose body he was ramming his hardened fists into.

By that time he was in no state to realise that the situation was turning from the usual bruising free-for-all into a confrontation that had much uglier connotations.

All he knew was that the havoc around him, and the swaying, cursing figures that staggered across his blurred vision, aptly matched the turmoil within him. For six months he had known no peace. His father's death the previous year, although partly expected because of his fading health, had given birth to a deep anger within him that he could neither comprehend, nor control.

As a result, it had become part of his weekend ritual, to blood-let after the beer, little matter what the cause or who the opposition. It was a way of dissipating an energy, a restlessness and a trapped helplessness that, although not unique, had perhaps reached its most dangerous in him.

And as the senseless sparring persisted his senses deadened further, leaving him struggling for breath, his slim, lean body aching with the punishment it was receiving. All coordination had vanished into a welter of violent madness.

Remnants of sanity told him to move on, but stubborn pride kept him in the midst of the raw brutality, kicking, punching and head-butting on impulse, with the rest of them. Cuts opened above his right, heavily-lidded eye, and on his right cheek. The gash, just below his eyebrow, began to blind him with trickling blood, that and the pain further affecting his ability to focus. Myopically, he stared into the mass of fists and bodies, dully accepting that he had come to enjoy smashing knuckles into the face of a fellow human. In reality it was about all he did enjoy. There was little other impetus left in his life.

During the alcohol-induced insanity someone gripped his arm. Instinctively, he went to hit out, at the last moment stopping himself as he just about recognised the wavering, pot-bellied silhouette in front of him as that of Bill Richards, a friend of his father's in the days when both had been mine captains. Bill was wracked by coughing and almost on his knees in exhaustion.

'Get me out of here, boy. This is too much for the likes of us. Take me home. I won't be able to make it on my own.'

Heavy, lumbering clouds continued to drag across the waning moon. Only for a few seconds at a time was there enough clarity of light for anyone to pick out shapes and faces. The pushing and yelling and hatred were increasing, and had become infectious.

Nathan, annoyed at the, as he saw it, totally pointless interruption, started walking away from the broken old man.

'Why the hell leave now?' he spat, seeing not an old friend of the family, but someone who was no use to him. 'I'm just warming up.'

Bill made another effort to halt him, though the continuing effects of what he had been drinking over the past hours, and his struggles for breath, were likely to prevent any hope of success.

'Don't be stupid,' he mumbled. 'This is bad. Can't you see that they're after killing each other?'

Nathan straightened his angular six foot frame, wiped away some more of the muck from around his right eye, and looked on with very obvious contempt.

'You go home if you want, I'm not. I'm sick of sticking by old men's rules, I've had them hammered into me all my life.'

He shivered. Now he had stopped moving, even for an instant, the cold was biting with conviction. Although the trees that grew behind the inn sheltered it from the wind to a certain extent, they could do nothing at all about easing the plummeting temperature.

'Just go, Bill. I'll leave when I'm ready and not at your bidding. I've got damn all to lose by staying.'

His mood seemed defiant, but a fraction of sense remained within him, insisting that he should just disappear. Surely Bill was partially right? There was an atmosphere of menace. The ingrained prejudices between different villages and mines were being whipped into much, much more - that could not be denied.

Eventually, he stayed long enough for his initial scratches to develop into full-blown, deep, weeping, cuts, then finally decided that he had little option but to retreat as Bill had almost three quarters of an hour before. By that time he was so drained of energy and emotion he could hardly stand.

As he turned he wasn't aware that one of the miners lay dead a mere ten foot from where he stood. Joel Hartford of St Blaise, had collapsed, his blood seeping into a dank, freezing, puddle, with a knife twisted carelessly into his stomach. He died unseen as his so-called friends fought aimlessly around him, a shy, retiring young man, in his early twenties, caught up in a spiral of despair he had no understanding of.

Nathan managed to stumble, then almost crawl, less than a quarter of a mile before his legs completely buckled, causing him to topple into the uneven ditch that ran parallel with the lane stretching across Par Moor in an almost unwavering line.

It was true mid-February weather. The night sky was hastily clearing, becoming as bright as crystal, allowing the stars to shine in their myriad, and the temperature was continuing to plunge. Despite the previous month being warm for the time of year, and exceptionally wet, the weather had started to alter since the previous full moon, and there had been a number of exceptionally heavy frosts in the past week or so.

Feeling the cold creep underneath his skin Nathan desperately wanted to pull himself away from the ditch, to keep on the move. For once he longed for home, but his limbs, which had revelled in such violent action only half an hour beforehand, refused to move more than a few inches. Finally, in spite of all efforts, the legacy of drink, and the previous expense of spirit, dragged him into an uncomfortable doze.

When he slowly returned to some form of consciousness around an hour later, aching in every conceivable part of his body, and with his feet and hands so numb he believed for a moment they had been chopped from his body, the sounds of battle had died completely. All that remained was the whirr of the night birds, linked with the chilly rush of a biting easterly wind which rustled through the oaks, growing at intervals along the side of the lane, and in the clumps of trees in the copse nearby. Whiteness gripped every part of the moorland landscape, and shone virgin clear in the moon's now steady rays. The beauty it gave rise to did not impress Nathan.

What a ridiculous waste of another evening, he groaned to himself as he staggered to his feet, hampered by a head, cheek and eye that were throbbing beyond belief. Annoyed, he found that he had also twisted his knee, and walking became limping as he followed the well-worn route to Biscovey, as James had done, with a great deal more agility, some hours before.

It took him twenty minutes longer than usual to drag himself through the woodland, across the sloping, bare fields, along the footpaths and up to the small cluster of homes near the towering church spire of St Mary's. As he went he swore loudly, his sharp, staccato words puncturing the silence that gradually became shattered by the pumping of the mine. The pain from the knee was not only hampering him, it also was also irritating him intensely by betraying weakness.

There was no movement near the cottage when he eventually did reach there. There was no light, and no neighbours were around to note his condition and report it, with delight, to all and sundry. For that he was greatly relieved.

As quietly as he could, he let himself in, lit the oil lamp, and realised, with a sense of gloom, that it was well past 3am. He had to be on shift just after dawn, and the thought did not please him. A born miner, for him survival underground was almost automatic - for he had been involved in the search for tin and copper since the age of eight.

But, he reflected as he struggled to pull off damp and relentlessly dirty clothes, he had not only grown to despair of life underground, and somehow life in all its generality at the same time. So deep was the melancholy that he doubted if he would have been any less disillusioned if he had been mine captain, mine owner, or the Prime Minister himself, concocting yet more taxes in his enclave up-country.

There's so little point, he thought as he fell onto his hard, narrow bed in the small room that he had long ago claimed as his own. Death's always there, always waiting, always ready to grab you. It'll rob you, in the end, of any success, or stability, you might be able to grasp onto. Father's found that out. For all those years he wouldn't rest until he'd said his blasted prayers four times a day, wouldn't allow any damned person to question his faith, and when he died he still went in fear. With such pessimism alive within him he idly felt his scarred chest for the bruises that were bound to show the following day, before reluctantly checking the time yet again. To a certain extent he was glad of the very late hour. It meant his mother must have given way to sleep long before he was able to stumble back home. He knew that he must have looked a degenerate wreck when he arrived back, a mirror image of his mental state, and he didn't want to have to endure her irritating, overwhelming, pitiful, concern.

The stupid woman's got enough worries, he

admitted to himself with resentment. No husband, that dictator she married now rotting away to dust and bones, but with five sons to care for. And me, the eldest, the one they should depend on, showing all the signs of running like hell from leaden responsibilities I don't want, and never asked for.

No refuge or comfort was to be found in bed or sleep, but then for him they seldom were. His muscles still felt as if they had been slowly shredded, with each movement, however small, verging on torture. There was no rest waiting in the wings for him either, or that he was sure. Eventually, he rose again, moving across the room to stand by the tiny, murky window staring across woods and rolling meadows to the glassy, black sea pounding on to Crinnis Beach in the same way it had done for aeons.

His bloodied and bruised eye remained closed, and the moonlight kept fading and restricting his view further, but he knew every tree, every field, fallow or otherwise. There had been so many occasions when he had gazed on the scene that it had become fused into his brain. Once it had held magic, and the ability to cheer him, years before when in boyhood the sight of a brig in the bay had conjured up dreams of discovery.

Now, he thought bitterly, it could never excite again. It's known surroundings, and because of that it's terror, and it's a trap.

When he did lay down again all that swam before him were ropes, and gags and amorphous enemies. In order to banish them, he tried to concentrate instead on sights so far unseen by himself, though known to every Cornishman by lore. The mines in the cauldron that was the Australian outback, the riches of South Africa and the mysteries and enticing stories that were being relayed of the American west.

Miners like himself had been emigrating to such bolt-holes for decades, ever since wagon trains and forty-niners had made their way to find the famed gold lying beneath the ground, and in the streams, of Sutters Ranch in the state of California.

They had been running from taxes, from poverty, from the same depression that was now gripping him.

In the past there had been a time when he had tried to leave the shores of the South West, but had been deterred almost before the dreams were made, when his father had accused him of being a turncoat, disloyal to the family. As a result, the chance had slipped by, and simultaneously his naive determination to escape the path that had been set for him seemed also to have been forever crushed.

But what the hell, he thought, it's all there still, all waiting, and there's no-one left here to call me traitor. At least no-one who matters. And nothing can be worse than where I am at the moment.

111

They were waiting for Nathan as morning broke, when he staggered, heavy-limbed and with eyes that had yet to open fully, to start his long shift at Bethany. A pale, insignificant sunrise was failing to wash the new, still rime-covered, day, and the stars were gradually fading.

A large knot of humanity was already huddled near the building that housed the mine's gargantuan steam engine, and was watching him approach in some sort of fascinated awe. Nathan himself was dazed, riddled with cramps and too beset by his own thoughts to notice any of them in any detail, or the tension that was crackling in the crisp air.

At the same time, he also didn't give the police uniforms a second glance, being too busy dreading the day ahead, hoping the spearing agony that was his left knee would soon ease.

Mining in such airless, unhealthy conditions was barely tolerable for him when fully fit. Ahead of his shift, he knew from past experience that it was destined to be unbearable with his whole body an aching sore.

The climb down to the adit, on ancient wooden ladders, called for constant vigilance because of the danger of falling rocks, and the hovering menace of explosions or flooding was enough in itself to make him aware that in order to survive, he had to be forever alert. Only those at the peak of health should be doing this, he thought wearily, as he considered the shift that lay in wait for him, like a wolf on the prowl.

Wanting only to disappear, from the trial that had become his life, he glanced up at the grey, open sky and then levelled his own grey gaze to the horizon. There the brooding sea was sucking and churning, smashing plumes of water against granite rocks at the base of Black Head. Stronger, violence-ridden winds were obviously on the way, such was the increase in the swell.

Thoughts of the hours ahead were as dark as the threatening weather, serving to deepen his belief that mining never had been an occupation for those of little faith, such as he. The desperation within was evident to anyone who studied his appearance - his skin was stretched tightly across the thin, skeletal bones in his somehow aristocratic face, robbing his complexion of any colour, while his hands, with their long fingers, were balled into bony fists. The signs were many that he was primed for retaliation of any sort, but not for work. The police officers were no strangers to Nathan, or to the large groups of men and bal maidens who had already ambled their way, as dawn strained to rise, towards the mine. In such a close neighbourhood, where few ever strayed more than five miles or so from their birthplace, all lives were indelibly entwined. So, when the uniforms eventually did edge their way into Nathan's still blurred, and disinterested, focus, he was not particularly surprised to see them.

His initial presumption was that there had been yet another accident, and some poor devil, who had picked his way down the ladders only hours beforehand, was now going to leave enclosed in a coffin. Fatal accidents were the unwanted norm in any Cornish mine in the 1870s. Only the week before seven men had been swept to their deaths in a fatal flooding at Wheal Jenny near Boscoppa, just off the track to St Austell. Nathan's surprise, and scepticism, rose to the surface when he realised they were there because of him.

'You're wasting your time, Freddie, or should I say Sergeant?' he advised the broadest of them, a bull-necked man who stepped forward with exaggerated purpose and stood full-square in front of him. 'I've done nothing to interest you.'

Freddie was not the type of personality to be diverted. Once his mind was channelled into a certain direction it could not be budged with ease. Especially when he had a ready-made audience watching on, just waiting to be impressed or, more likely, entertained.

'I wouldn't be so sure. Are you going to tell me you weren't in the middle of that fight outside the Britannia last night? If you are then I'll have to ask where you got them there bruises and scratches I can see on your face. Battling in your nightmares were you?'

The voice was sharp, detached, accusing, belying the fact that Sgt F Pentire and Mr N Rosevean had been drinking colleagues on numerous occasions. Indeed, they had as good as grown up together.

The breeze had heightened already, and was beginning to moan and whip its way through the workings and across the fields that still showed white with a frost that was threatening to deepen. Later, an uncompromising wind would be howling in contention with the whine and reverberation of the engine, and adding further to the bleakness of the day. Primroses and daffodils should have been peeping through banks and hedgerows like shy maids by then, the wet warmth of Cornwall's weather usually tempting them to open quicker than anywhere else in the country, bar the Isles of Scilly. Instead, what had been a bitter start to the month seemed to be continuing, for another day, its march across the county. Everywhere, as it had to Nathan the night before, appeared to be as cold and lonely as a lost and desolate soul.

As such thoughts crossed his mind, he looked down at his wrists and frowned as he imagined invisible bonds tightening on them once again. Then he cleared away the fantasies and gradually began taking in what was happening around him.

Brother James had suddenly appeared, and joined the crowd. and was standing only yards away. Other miners had gathered alongside him to listen, their faces strangely expectant. The women and young girls who had to sort the ore once it had been brought to the surface, hovered in the background.

For a second he believed himself on general trial. There were few, he thought, who would defend him, whatever position he was in. Of choice he had driven all close companions away.

But this was more tangible than absence of friendship. It was as if a psychological barrier had been placed between himself and the rest of the tightly-knit world he had grown up in and seemed destined to inhabit for the rest of his life, whatever his personal goals and aspirations might be.

Just ignore the idiots, he told himself, nothing they can say or do can touch you. They'll tire of baiting eventually, they always do.

He shrugged indifferently.

'I was there, Freddie, I admit that much. You're already as good as damned certain I was, so there's no point denying it. Maybe I hit one or two, and got hit a bit in return, but there was nothing worse than usual, nothing that doesn't happen there almost every night. You've even been part of fights like that yourself, even by my side on occasions, so you don't have to block my path because of it.'

With patience at its brief limits he spoke briskly, and with authority, as Tom Rosevean had taught his sons, so assiduously, to do.

With expert precision, he had hammered it into their minds that they had been born of a mine captain, and so had always to demonstrate the gulf between themselves and others. Never beg, never show weakness, always reflect authority.

The confrontation, for that was what it was, was far from being private. No-one in the large arc of gawping onlookers was talking - just standing like statuettes and taking in the stand-off taking place in front of them with some relish.

An unnatural hush gripped them, until a lone voice ventured: 'Haven't you heard then, Nath?'

'Heard what?' he answered, very deliberately, in his clipped voice, his breath snatched greedily away by the cold, swirling air as he spoke.

Up until then he had easily ignored the crowd, concentrating instead on Fred and his sidekick. Although he told himself that in no way would he be intimidated by them, against his will his stomach began to heave like the waves smashing at the cliffs in St Austell bay. Gradually, he was starting to realise that there was nothing routine in Fred's early morning visit to the mine.

Fred, himself, also aware of the watching, greedy eyes, decided to play to the gallery, raising his voice several notches in what he deemed as impressive fashion.

'It wasn't an ordinary little fight, whatever you want us to think. Joel Hartford was stabbed as you, and the others, beat each other's brains out around him. We think he died within minutes.'

The noise from pumps and pistons pounded around them. It had provided the background pulse beat to most of Nathan's life, in fact he had probably heard it whilst in the womb. Usually, he hardly noticed the din, but on this early morning it had started gradually to worm its way into his head, snaking around his thoughts like a serpent determined to make a killing.

All his remaining energy was steadily seeping away, and he still had the long haul down the ladders to face.

'Are you pulling some sort of sick joke?'

'Not at all,' Fred snapped, his protruding teeth clicking as he spoke. I don't joke about murder, even with you.'

Dear life, I didn't even see Hartford there, Nathan thought as he genuinely struggled to recall details of the previous night, but not being able to move beyond images of emerging from a frost-encrusted ditch and a long limp home.

The stares from those encircling him suddenly seemed oppressive. Was this how lynch mobs began? From their expressions he knew that they had already judged him guilty.

They're re blind idiots, he told himself. They follow each other like brainless lambs. Gossip rules their wretched lives, and they can see no further than the rubbish they spout.

If he admitted it, he had been friendly with the majority of them since childhood. He had run the wide, wild fields with many of them, when younger, in search of mushrooms, blackberries, anything they could eat. They had gleaned the meadows after hay-making and had dived into the waves, whatever the weather. Living in such a small village, and in such restricted confines, it would have been impossible for him to isolate himself completely from others.

But friends from such days had gradually been alienated as he had voluntarily started to step outside their world, a world he had no wish to return to if he could gain complete freedom.

Wanting to at least appear unnerved, he glared at those nearest him, most of them unshaven and ill-dressed, and illiterate. The majority were unable to meet his bruised, calculating eyes.

They've never understood me, or even given a second to try, he thought. Though then again, why should they worry about someone who doesn't give a real damn for any of them, the fools that they are?

'I didn't even see a knife,' he spat. 'I never saw one being used, and I also never heard one word about murder, or saw a body. In fact I can hardly believe this rubbish you're telling me.'

Fred, shorter than Nathan but about three stones heavier, shifted ponderously on his large feet.

'Would you like to repeat what you just said in front of everyone who was at the Britannia last night? From what I've been told you were definitely in the middle of the fighting. Those injuries of yours tell a tale my boy. We - all of us - know that once you get into a fight you seldom get a scratch, but this morning that eye of yours looks a real mess to me. And that father of yours isn't around anymore to keep you in order, and you're a different person now. I don't know how far I'd trust either you, or your damned fists, these days.'

Nathan, despite edging nearer to explosion point, realised he had to remain outwardly calm whatever was said.

It was gradually dawning on him, from the

expressions of those surrounding him, that Fred was right, and Hartford was dead. Furiously, he tried to recall details of the man. He had been just out of his teenage years, Nathan estimated, with sharp, foxy features that had hinted at a cunning his dull nature did not have. He hadn't been anywhere near a colleague, even at the best of times, but he was someone Nathan wouldn't have bothered to harm.

'You don't honestly think I'd risk being chucked into jail by you for Hartford's sake do you? I can't even remember him being there, just as I don' t remember a knife being pulled.'

At that, he took a deliberate move nearer the mine and much nearer the crowd, everyone of which immediately stepped backwards en masse as a complete, sheep-like entity.

Half of them must have been at the Britannia as well, he thought. If the guilt is to be laid anywhere they're surely as branded by it as I. Fred was a simple man, seeing most matters in the context of black or white, and he had never understood the layers of complexity that had long tortured the man standing before him, not that Nathan himself had ever deciphered them himself.

'Come on, Nath, just tell me exactly what you were doing at the time Hartford was stabbed then.'

Nathan's frayed nerves and sinews tightened in further protest. Maybe, he didn't place himself above the law, but he certainly did set himself above the likes of Fred Pentire and his silent colleague.

'How in the devil's name can I answer that? I told you, I didn't even know it was happening. There's little to tell about the evening anyway. We kicked, we punched, we basically hit out at anything that moved. Most of what went on after I left the bar happened in a daze. It was the same old story, known to all of us. Those from St Blaise settling old scores with their neighbours down the road, from the Gate.'

Fred was not convinced.

'You mean that you managed to ignore most of what took place there, even a murder?'

There was total anger now. It seemed to Nathan that everyone was closing in on him, willing him to confess.

Well, he silently raged, it's about time this farce was brought to an end. If they think I'm going to stand here and dozily provide them with their day's entertainment they'll have to think again.

'For God's sake, listen to me,' he seethed. 'I had no knife and I never even saw that lad there, be it inside or outside the Inn. Before we go any further you had better find some decent reason for accusing me, rather than relying on petty gossip. If you do eventually dredge anything up, and I'd be very surprised if you can, you'll find me underground. Follow me down there if you want, Fred, but remember the dangers you might face in a mine. That uniform of yours won't protect you from floods or falling rocks.'

'Is that a threat?'

'Take it how you ruddy well want.'

With his knee seemingly radiating fire with a pain which forced a pronounced limp, and his fine, wayward hair, with the darkness of jet, blowing into his eyes, he pushed past both uniforms and the staring audience, heading furiously onwards towards the depths of Bethany. No-one tried to halt him. His thin, educated face was contorted with anger to such an extent that even James, who had considered joining him as he entered the mine in some attempt at fraternity, kept his distance.

Despite the complete absence of attempts to stop him Nathan had learnt enough of the world, and what he perceived as the attitude of the common herd, to realise that his alleged part in the matter was far from over. This was just one of the wretched, unwanted problems he saw as gathering around his life, intent on mobbing him just like the gulls and terns did to any stray hawk they wanted to chase away from their territory, their nests.

This is just what they've been waiting for, he murmured to himself. They want blood. They want mine, but there's no way I'll easily let it flow for them.

1V

The green-eyed girl with the halo of auburn hair and the false air of self-possession arrived at the Rosevean cottage that evening. Nathan had known she would call. News of the murder and his confrontation with Fred had been rife, and was bound to have reached her. But, despite the love he had once shared with her, he didn't want to see Lorna. She was part of a past, and the problems he had come to realise that he wanted to lock away for good. It had been a dire day. Coping with the agony of strained, twisted muscles, as he hacked at stubborn rocks, had shattered his energy. Dealing with men who had made it plain they believed him responsible for a killing had taken him into another dimension. After finishing his shift he had walked the short distance home in the same foul humour. None of the fury from the argument with Fred Pentire had abated - if anything it had increased. Above all, he had found it hard to believe that so many of his fellow villagers could be so simply led.

One uninformed idiot claims I stabbed Hartford, and it's instantly taken as truth, he had seethed as he dodged home through primrose-absent hedgerows. No questions asked of others, no understanding of the fact that there's no evidence, no trial. Who was it said no Cornish jury convicted their own? How wrong they were.

He walked slowly, with his head bent forward of his slim shoulders. It was nothing to do with drink this time, more to do with a south-westerly which had become gale force and was tearing across the stunted February grass and through the isolated, bare, bending trees. It was then he had thought of Lorna, during a brief patch of time. Despite her trick of being able to reach depths within him, he knew even she would stand no chance of lightening his mood. All he could take was solitude.

With everything apparently against him, he didn't want the willing, gentle, sensual woman he had desired for so long, but now just sought to distance himself from. For her sake as much as for his.

Unwillingly, he had returned to Biscovey for family tea, the one meal his mother preferred they all attended, if shifts allowed. She also pressed them to be there on Sunday, the day when parish church activities had once dominated their lives. Tom Rosevean had delighted in shunning Methodism, believing that his high Christian ideals were better served by strict adherence to the doctrines of the Church of England.

Once through the cottage door and into the steaming kitchen all Nathan's appetite had fled.

He couldn't face food, and his mother's cooking had never rivalled the decent culinary standards of most of her contemporaries. His obvious reluctance to stay didn't please her, however, for she had wandered around her home for most of the day, trying to occupy herself with the baking, her mind in a turmoil as she had been made well aware of the trouble her eldest son was in. Providing for her family gave her life justification, edging in a marginal way towards keeping exhausting depression at bay, although the rumours she had been hearing about her eldest son did very little to lift the hopelessness that dampened most of her days.

'You know all I ask is that we're together for at least one meal a day,' she implored when he had said he was not staying. 'What else do I ask from you - nothing.' She rubbed her large, red raw hands through the lank, grey strands of hair. 'I know none of your brothers are here yet, but Alex and Billy will be, Samuel as well. I like to pretend that we're still close, even if it's not so. We're not together any more, and that's not what your father wanted.'

She spoke in her weak, lost voice, that was used to pile on the guilt, that was bereft of any shreds of the richness and vitality that it had borne in youth. It did not sway Nathan, who had heard the tone many times before. He was deaf to it.

'Don't excite yourself,' he said tersely as she leant over the big, black range which had so dominated the kitchen for as long as he could remember. 'You'll only have one of your attacks. Your other dutiful sons will be here soon, and you can fuss around them. I won't be here for one meal, but don't get so worked up over that. If anything it should be a relief. I bet it will be for the others.'

'But we want you here,' she persisted, straightening up as best she could, moving her hands to her hair again, then dropping them as if they were stones, to pull at the folds of her drab dress.

Hearing those words, he turned on her, all the frustrations he could not name boiling up inside him. With the anger evident, he pulled up one of the chairs with such force that she jumped away from him.

'I know, I know you want me tied to this place. You want me sitting here, at the head of the damned table, just like father used to do,' he yelled, lifting the chair up and smashing it down again on the hard floor. 'A shadow of him, an image of him, as if nothing's gone and changed.'

'What's so wrong about that?'

'You want me to be him all over again, that's what's wrong with it. But he was a bigot who loved using his power over us all, including you, and I don't want to do that. I don't have his faith, and I'll never be his double. The sooner you understand that, the sooner you'll be able to bear it.'

Mary stepped backwards again to avoid his wild gaze, tiredness and misery wearing her down.

But she wouldn't let herself give way.

'Don't go out now, Nathan. Stay here tonight,

please. I know why you're saying these things. I know you're not yourself. It's that killing they're all talking about, isn't it? It's the way all of them have been telling lies about you. Let us help. Stay here. Talk to us. That's what family is for. Didn't your father always tell you we have to stay together?'

Her eldest son automatically turned his back on her, deliberately put his coat on, while edging nearer the door. Nothing she could have said at that moment would have changed his mind.

'Don't beg. I'll see you tomorrow. I'm just in the mood for a long walk, whatever the weather. If the storm hits while I'm gone all the better.'

Crushed by his brusque reaction to her pleas, she rushed to pull him back to stop him, trembling in the effort.

'But you must talk to me, you must. Were you involved in that fight? They've been asking me questions about it, questions I can't answer. Fred Pentire was here a few hours ago and wants to talk to you. What do I say if he comes again, and you're gone?'

'Tell him to come looking for me out near the cliffs. If he really wants to find me he'll be able to run me to ground. Tell him as well that I don't want to play him around. For once I've got nothing to hide.'

Despite his attempt at denial, she shook violently, unable to control the thoughts that were busy twining themselves like garrottes around her mind, her white lips working in distress.

'Are you sure you didn't kill that boy?'

That made him turn back to face her. For a while he didn't allow himself to answer her. For pity' s sake, my own mother thinks I could knife someone without any guilt. Surely she knows, though, I wouldn't take the risk of being hung for a nonentity like Hartford?

'I'm as sure as I'll ever be about anything,' he said icily. 'Now you really need to let me go.'

With her face flushed in distress, she edged away from him, as if in agreement, but still searching for words that would touch him. But he was oblivious to that, only wanting to wrench the door open, and escape.

Lorna was standing on the other side, a living, loving spirit in the darkness, holding herself taut, with her dramatic mane of hair streaming banner-like behind her. She had been there for three minutes or more, dredging up the courage to knock.

At the sight of her he started. Initially, he noticed her bright, hopeful smile and watchful eyes, along with the welcome and the anticipation that shone from her. Then he looked further and saw, even in the pale, dull, light from the candles in the cottage, the worry that she could not disguise, and the frown that was etched on her high, delicate forehead.

Seeing her beauty and her concern, he groaned, not bothering to hide his dismay. How the hell was he supposed to think straight with her so near, making him ache for her against all intentions?

His reaction was so obvious that she bit her lip in distress, simultaneously striving to defeat weakness. What kept her there, wanting him, needing him, was the memory of love, and the warm intimacy they had once shared. The trouble was that in past weeks Nathan seemed to have abandoned all such memories, as if they were unwelcome, and utterly false.

'I'm sorry,' she breathed, holding onto the door as the wind, that had as good as blown her up to Biscovey, increased in force. 'You were on your way out. I didn't think you'd be going out so early, before tea. I thought, I hoped, you might have expected me.'
She stood within inches of him, looking upwards with her sweet, compelling expression, and with her clothes flattened against her body so they accentuated every valley and curve. Against all intentions he found himself reaching for her, and for that resented her even more. With his life as it was at that moment he didn't have the patience, or the desire, to want or need anyone.
Put your stupid arms down, he chided himself. Don't touch.
'I'm ahead of myself today, for a number of reasons,' he answered, his eyes still drawn to her thighs, her trim waist. 'But I wasn't quick enough, was I?'
Knowing she couldn't let herself be cowed, she met his lack of tact head on.
'In other words you knew I would turn up here, and you wanted to avoid me at all costs.'
'Would that have mattered too much?'
In spite of the whirling, caterwauling gale howling straight up the hill from the bay, he kept her standing there in the open, determined not to give way to those old, enticing emotions, which he begrudgingly accepted he would be doing if he let her into the cottage.
Give her the smallest of chances and she'll walk over me, he told himself. She'll make someone a good wife, I know, but not me.
To divert any possibility of succumbing to any basic needs he grabbed her arm tightly to propel her back into the night.

'Come on, as you're here I suppose that you might as well walk with me. I had decided to go out on my own, but I suppose some would say company's better for the soul.'

It was absolutely bitterly cold. Lorna had already climbed up to Biscovey from her family home in Par. Her toes and fingers had turned numb soon after she started the journey, and as they went she briefly looked back at the cottage, where she knew there would be a warm fire. At her heart she was a creature of the summer and the sun. The Cornish mizzle that would descend one morning, and often would not lift for 48 hours or more, always dulled her, leaving her yearning for July heat.

But although the hated weather had beset their corner of the world for days, she had known that the cold was irrelevant against her desire to see him, to console him, even to challenge him, that evening.

He worried her so much. However differently he had begun to treat her, she couldn't block out her own love.

'All right, as you want,' she sighed, with exaggeration.

Although she kept silent she walked alongside him, as near to him as a lover would be, clinging close. She was, at 5'8", taller than her three sisters, and her mass of hair, tangled by the wind, added to her height. But beside him she felt insignificant. Undoubtedly, he was the leader, and she the follower, as was shown in the way she kept glancing up at his lean, rangy figure, hoping for a smile of acknowledgement from him, and in her occasional need to run to keep pace with him as he deliberately tried to push ahead.

They went southwards, towards the sea, his

head sometimes bent reluctantly towards hers as they battled with the chilling gusts which stung flesh as they whipped inland.

But Nathan enjoyed the wildness, as if it was a kindred spirit, and ignored worries about the girl now shivering uncontrollably at his side. Hasn't she chosen to come? he thought. She can't hold me responsible for dropping temperatures. Gloom maybe, or betraying her, but not the weather.

The Hartford affair had grieved him more than he would admit. So Fred had been to his home and was obviously still hunting hard for evidence. The questions and wry, sly comments others seemed to delight in aiming towards him were unlikely to stop for a long, long while. That afternoon he had been warned time and time again of revenge mobs from St Blaise. And a couple of the dead man's so-called friends had gone out of their way to threaten him, although the comments hadn't come individually, only when they were present in strength.

Annoyingly, he could still hear them in his mind as he finally took hold of Lorna's flailing hand and pulled her along the Par Moor track.

'Careful Rosevean, turn your back and someone'll be there with pick in hand,' had extended to: 'Ever thought what it would be like to burn, Nathan boy?'

It's so crazy, he thought, forgetting for a moment, in his anger, that Lorna was beside him. While they're so busy persecuting me the real killer is out there, covering his tracks. Nathan was certain that the unstable fervour, the baying for his blood, would eventually cool, but he couldn't help taking it as a warning. It was as if life was just waiting for him to fail, whatever the cause of his destruction, whether earned or not. His destruction was a real possibility, he was very aware of that, but when it came he wanted it to be self-motivated.

What also irked him was that he knew very well that Lorna had arrived early because of the murder. That had been clear from the distraught expression in her shy, but expressive eyes. The news had spread like the plague, and after hearing the details at least third hand she would want the truth from him in person.

Ten minutes passed. They staggered on and turned into the lane of cypress trees where the evergreen branches swayed, bowing drunkenly above them. They half walked, half ran, until the cliff-top was only a quarter of a mile further on. By then, Lorna was beginning to limp in the same way as Nathan had been earlier in the day, because she had badly grazed one ankle, and had broken the back of her shoes. Gradually, he became aware that she was breathing heavily, staccato-like, the rasping sound heard even above the growing gale - and it almost stopped him instantly.

It did at least force him to break the impasse. Against initial intentions he slowed his pace and then halted. The sentinel rows of trees had petered out to be replaced by scrubby blackthorn hedge. After drawing her off the path, and as good as pushing her into a break between the thorns, and the bare, twisted bushes, he decided it was best just to confront her and force her to voice her suspicions. There was no-one else around, and the blackthorn that pulled at her dirtied, trailing dress, seemed to enclose them. It was as if they were on their own in a coal black, totally isolated world.

'Ask me then,' he snapped, impatiently brushing away the hair that was being swept over his eyes and into the corners of his mouth.

'Ask what?'

Dejection softened her words so he could barely hear her. Now they were closer to the sea the wind was lashed with salt. Tasting it on her previously dry, chapped lips, and feeling it settling dankly over her clothes, she quickly pulled her thin coat around her slim body for some sort of warmth.

'Don't be stupid on purpose. Ask me about last night. Ask me what I was doing, drinking myself senseless. Ask me why I was involved in a pointless murder. And ask me how on earth I can expect you to have any kind of peace while I carry on in such a way.'

'I wasn't going to say anything like that,' she answered, steeling herself because she now had an idea of what was ahead.

It was obvious to her that she couldn't spend the rest of the time she had left with him treading carefully and trying not to antagonise, disguising what she felt for him. For months she had been patient, but she had discovered that even with him patience had its limits.

'You mean you were going to hedge around the subject, pecking at it every now and then until you were convinced that I was worn down enough to tell you every little detail?

Taking a deep breath, she vowed that she wasn't going to be brow-beaten. The strong part of her deep and determined character had the upper-hand, despite the rapidly disintegrating evening, and their disintegrating relationship. Where once he had been tender and compassionate he had become deliberately ruthless, as if determined to bludgeon all her feelings to pulp. But, she thought miserably, only a fool would allow that to continue.

'Not quite,' she answered, raising her voice. Rain was now threatening to fall, simultaneously with her tears perhaps. 'But you can't blame me for worrying. Heavens Nath, not only do they think you knifed that poor man you also have the whole of St Blaise hunting you down, wanting to kill you.'

Hearing her words, he dug his hands into his pockets, lifted his long, introspective face to the now force seven wind and wanted, with all his soul, to run from her at the speed of one of the express trains that regularly steamed into Cornwall, over Brunel's Bridge from Plymouth.

'Then do you think, as well as they do, that I hurt him? Do you believe I killed him, just the same as Fred and most of my former friends do, my darling? Given the chance, dear old Fred would haul me into jail at a moment's notice, despite all the beers we've drunk together, and the lack of any evidence. Shall I give myself up, confess it all and beg them to hang me at Bodmin? If nothing else I suppose it would give the idiots a day's holiday.'

Although she deliberately ignored his sarcasm, she shifted quickly on her feet as a stray thorn dug so deeply into the back of her leg that it began to bleed.

'I was told you were in the middle of it all.'

'And you instantly believed whatever evil little gossip happily passed on that little snippet?'

His words were spoken with so much venom that she stepped even further back into the

hedge as if he had slapped her, and this time scored her hand and forearm equally deeply. Averting her eyes from him, she sucked away the blood that started to trickle down her right hand, steadied herself, and then said with as even a voice as possible: 'Why not? All you seem to enjoy at the moment is drinking and fighting, and you have to admit that the bar at the Britannia has become your first home.'
'Keep going,' he sneered, 'you're on your favourite subject - my bad habits.'
A subject for general discussion, he thought with irony.
'You're so wrong,' she insisted, shivering.
They had begun to walk again, at his bidding. Although Lorna hadn't said anything he had noticed, even in the near darkness, that she had hurt her hand, and for an instant he wanted to hold her close, to tend to her himself. That, to his dismay, had disturbed him almost as much as Fred Pentire had done. Shaken slightly by this reaction, he suddenly strode on ahead of her, stretching his long legs so he covered ground quickly, not wanting to stay so companionably close, with her breathing hot on his cheek, any seconds longer.
The headland loomed a little way on, and soon St Austell Bay, from Fowey to the east, to the fishing port of Mevagissey in the west, would be spread in front of them. Striding ahead, he walked as far as the cliff edge itself. Lights glowed from ships at anchor, waiting for high tide before slipping into the ports of Charlestown and Pentewan. The odd light could also be seen around the mouth of the River Fowey. To the left Gribbin Head slithered out into the ocean, while to the right, on a stiller, lighter night, they would have

been able to see past Mevagissey to Bodrugan's Leap where Sir Harry Trenowth of Bodrugan had apparently jumped into the sea in a desperate bid to escape Sir Richard Edgcumbe - and, to his pursuer's amazement, had succeeded.

'I wanted to know the truth,' she said when she caught him up. 'I just wanted to hear it from you.'

Despite the struggle for strength her voice was thickening with unshed tears and, to her annoyance, she knew it. Turning his back on her, he shivered himself as he remembered their loving moments spent together. Her devotion had made him feel wanted, needed. No-one else had ever needed him unconditionally. Certainly not his father, who had his ideals and his religion, or his brothers, or his mother who had utterly bound her life to that of her husband.

'You've seen me, you've said what you wanted and I've answered as best I can,' he said acidly. 'Let's finish the walk now. You're near enough home and you should be there in the warmth. You're frozen stiff, angry and unhappy, and to be honest I could do with a few hours to myself to think - alone.'

His continuing brusqueness cut her, making her brush aside immediate tears. In the dark he couldn't see them, but he sensed they were there all the same. Misery wrapped around her. Despite being within inches of him, she felt completely alone, unable to understand how the safety she had felt when she was with him had irrevocably melted away. Since his father's death he had undeniably altered. Where once he had been open, he had closed off those nearest him, and thrived on aggression.

Initially, she had reasoned with him, tried to deal with the restlessness, but she had achieved nothing. Now she accepted that he wanted no-one to reach him.

They had never mentioned marriage, but she believed that there had been the underlying assumption that they would be together for the rest of their lives. It had been accepted not only by both of them, she was sure, but by others too.

Now, as she wept silently beside him, she finally realised that any such ties had been torn apart by the person he had become. Over time he had evolved into a complete stranger to the Nathan Rosevean she had so happily given herself to, and she saw clearly, of a sudden, that she was reaching the stage where she could endure no more.

It had reached a point where she had to make one last effort to beat a way through to the man he had been, even if the loss of him was the price she was to pay as a result.

'Why don't we end it here, really finish it? Be honest with each other?'

She spoke slowly, deliberately, and loudly enough for him to hear, not wanting to have to repeat it.

For a long moment, he pretended he could not understand her, although that was a lie. His senses had leapt in agreement. Her challenge had echoed what had been hammering inside him for weeks. The truth was, she caught at too much of his heart. It had been that way since he had first glimpsed her, and he wanted to be free of such deep, dangerous ties.

'End what, this little stroll?'

Wondering deep inside herself where all her words would lead them, she bit her lip until she tasted blood again, and told herself she must not falter - as if she was a foot soldier charging into a battle she could not win.

'You know very well what I mean. I mean ending whatever there is left between us. You've made it clear over time that you don't want me holding you back. You want to be on your own without a girl who needs more from her lover than walking to a dangerous granite cliff edge in a cold gale.'

For a woman she was reasonably tall, and was no child, but her slight figure lent her a waif-like appearance in the growing storm. Her natural glamour had fled. Her eyes were black in their sockets, her hair a wild tangle of auburn.

'And how do you think you'll manage on your own?' he grunted, annoyed by the unexpected surge of deep concern that he experienced for her.

Could I bear it, he thought, when and if someone else comes into her life? He brushed aside the answer that came to him.

With some harshness, she laughed at his strained, half-hearted demonstration of a caring lover.

'How typical. Do you think I won't be able to survive without you, or that no-one else will want me now you've carelessly taken, and then abandoned, as much of my love as you felt you needed?'

'No . . no.'

'Then answer me truthfully. Talk to me the way you used to. Do you want to carry on as we are, or am I right - is it best to end it all now?'

The rain had begun to fall with a vengeance, and water ran down through the strands of his fine, dark hair and into his eyes. Impatiently, he wiped the drops from his prematurely lined forehead.

'Do you want me to be honest?'

'Of course. That's all I ever wanted. What we .. what we had was good, and lies would just cheapen it. Even now.'

She believes we were good for each other, he thought dryly, and wondered if she was right. Yes, perhaps for a while they had been.

'I couldn't marry you,' he murmured. 'I couldn't even think of marrying anyone, I don't want to be responsible for anyone.'

'And I guess that I'm probably the last woman you'd now choose to bind yourself to anyway.'

After she had said that he looked down at her, instead of ahead of himself at the lashing, boiling waves, and for a moment could not deal with the old emotions that came gushing to the surface, as if from a long-tapped well.

'That isn't true, you have to believe that.' With difficulty, he searched for an apology, for some explanation that might ease her, and salvage some of her pride.

'I hope you realise none of this, or what has happened to me these last months, has been due to you. Don't blame yourself. I've changed, and it doesn't please me. I suppose if I'm honest with myself I have to say that I've lost some sort of purpose, of direction, and I haven't a damned clue what to replace it with.'

'I'll leave you to walk then,' she answered as the rain scythed through her thin clothing, systematically soaking her. 'I know you don't want me to stay. From now on I don't suppose we'll meet just by accident. And I promise I won't arrive early to ruin your evenings any more.'

Without uttering another word as they

continued battling against the rushing wind, he let her go, surprised that it took every ounce of self-restraint to stop himself gazing after her as she disappeared into the gloom, picking her way very carefully along the cliff path that was to delve down into Par.

All his energy went into concentrating on his sense of relief, relief that she had gone ahead and done exactly what he had himself been planning. In that moment he was grateful for her courage but she, as she stumbled through ruts and puddles on the narrow track home, sobbed because of it, tears joining with the rain to obscure everything around her.

Three months later May 1870

V

A far, muffled cry, disembodied and mournful, like a spirit in an abandoned place, echoed through the workings. When it came Nathan, crawling on hands and knees like a trapped animal, had to stop and regulate his breathing to control the fear that had begun to grip him like a vice. It was a fear he hated to acknowledge, but one that was threatening to paralyse him.

It was May 1870. Three months since Joel Hartford's death and his own final parting with Lorna. Since their strained and stilted walk to the cliffs, he hadn't set eyes on her, but he had seen Fred Pentire on a number of occasions, all of them official. Up until then no-one had been charged with the murder, but suspicion still rested very heavily on Mary Rosevean's eldest. Nevertheless, matters hadn't progressed as far as a lynching, or past a lukewarm warning from Fred.

That didn't mean efforts hadn't been made to drag him to court. They had, but a lack of hard evidence had halted any real progress. An atmosphere of hatred and distrust still persisted, though, and the affair continued to nag at him like a sore that refused to heal. It was still there, in his thoughts, as he crawled in the filth of Bethany in a desperate, tortuous attempt to prove something to himself and his persecutors. He was out hunting respect - and a lost man.

Will Langdon of Polkerris, who just happened to be one of those locals who continued to accuse him of the knifing, had been missing in the mine for over five hours. The likelihood was that he was dead. Nathan had believed he was, until the cry proved otherwise. By that point he had been unsure why he had volunteered for the search, only guessing it was a subconscious attempt to show enemies, former friends, and maybe himself, that he preferred to save life rather than take it.

As he scrambled along in the dark in an unknown part of the mine that was liable to collapse at any moment, he fought off visions of being entombed forever, but he could not help thinking, while fumbling his way, that he was in a trap which, unlike the trap of Lorna and marriage, had no form of escape. Claustrophobia picked at him. Shivers of fear ran riot, and he literally had to shake them off before continuing. He yelled Will's name, and hesitated a moment, hoping for a reply. Then he tensed and tried to wriggle fast through a narrowing tunnel. It took more aching, bruising minutes before he heard a deep groan and knew he must be near.

Over the years he had become more than used to groping in the damp depths of the mine.

Starting from a young age, he had worked in Bethany for eleven years, yet as he inched further along, in the overbearing darkness, his heart twisted in what he acknowledged must be fear, and beads of sweat stood out coldly on his strong, grimed face.

When the long moments began to pass without further sound, he half expected to place his hand upon Will's body, at any time, in the dark, and that terrified him enough to make him consider turning back for the light, for certainty, for a part of Bethany which he knew as well as he did the Cornish lanes near his cottage.

Fighting back the terrors, he called out again, but this time no response came, except for the eerie trickle of the stream that ran along the bottom of the level, and the hollow echo of his own clipped voice. Then he squeezed himself through the narrowest part of the passage and, as the claustrophobia was beginning to overwhelm him completely, found his man.

Will was alive, but the fact that he was still clinging onto life was a miracle. Pinned down on his face by rocks, the only part of his body which he could move was his head, and he had to throw that back as far as possible to stop the stream water pouring into his mouth and drowning him. Nathan was transfixed in horror by the sight, just visible in candlelight. All he could think was that he was powerless to stop the man dying. The rocks were far too heavy for him to move on his own, and the constantly running water seemed to be rising every second.

What in the devil's name do I do? he panicked.

Taking off his sodden, grimy coat, he placed

it under the miner's chin. Will, far from sure about his apparent saviour, tried to smile in thanks. To warm him further, if that was possible in such dire circumstances, Nathan took out his hip flask and poured some brandy down his throat, reserving a drop or two for himself.

Then he squatted right down beside Will, with the water splashing over his boots, and was silent for a while before explaining as firmly as possible: 'I can't stay here, you know that. In order to save you I have to get more help. I can't move those rocks safely on my own, so can't move you.'

'But you'd never get back here,' Will murmured. 'It'll be worse when you go, worse than before. I didn't think anyone would come.'

Nathan could understand the feelings only too well, but knew that staying impotently to watch a man drown was of no earthly use.'

'Do you realise how many rocks have to be shifted? It's the only way to save you, believe me. I want you to get out of here as much as you do yourself, but I have to get help.'

It was enough to sway the petrified mind. Will nodded his head slightly in acquiescence. 'Go then. I'm real sorry I've thought ill of you of late,' he gulped. 'Now I think God needs to be with both of us.'

It was an apology. However, as he left Nathan doubted if there was any god guiding him, and thought that if there was, and he was the merciless, domineering god his father had worshipped he didn't want his protection. Instead, he wanted to rely on himself alone. Under what he regarded as his own skill he reached the surface surprisingly quickly, finding the terrain much easier on the return journey. Despite the speed he went with no lightness of soul. The situation seemed hopeless to him.

Experience had proved it was no simple task to work at a load of earth and rocks in a narrow level, and remove them before a trapped, helpless man was exhausted. When he finally reached the others, and explained the task ahead, most of them shared the same fears, despite agreeing there was no point discussing drawbacks. Many were fervent Methodists, however, and their unwavering belief in divine assistance visibly outshone Nathan's.

It was late in the day before they brought Will to the surface. He was pale, limp, unmoving in his rescuers' arms and, at first sight, dead. His young wife was there, tears flowing in despair, but after a host of doubts and some expert help from the doctor, the eyelids flickered and her man showed some definite signs of returning to the world.

As soon as he knew Will had survived and the graveyard at St Fimbarrus Church at Fowey or Tregaminion at Menabilly, the nearest parish churches to Polkerris, had been cheated of yet another victim, Nathan turned wearily towards Biscovey and bed. By then his limbs felt as if they were ablaze, and his grey eyes were red with strain. His mind cried for rest, but would not cease travelling in limitless circles.

In the short space of time that had followed the rescue an astonishing number of colleagues, who had shunned him since the murder, had made a point of talking to him. Their change of attitude, welcome as it was, had failed to lighten his mood, even though there had been a positive outcome to the day.

Other worries had surfaced. The sight of Will, trapped so pathetically, kept replaying itself in his brain, as if it was a replica of what was happening within himself. I'm trapped for life, he thought, by everything around me. I'm hemmed in, gasping for air, crying for a nameless saviour.

The knifing, however he tried to ignore its effect, and the fact that he hadn't even been aware at the time that murder was taking place within yards of where he had been fighting, had placed untold stress upon him. It had not been enough on its own to make him want to flee, but it had combined with the desire to break from a family he believed was demanding way too much from him.

With such matters peppering his mind, he was walking slowly back to the familiar row of miners' cottages, his angular figure silhouetted against the bare, muddy fields, when Lorna appeared in front of him in her quiet, ghost-like way. Without thinking of his reaction, she had rushed to Bethany the moment she had heard he was involved in an underground rescue and, as a result, had been there among the band of waiting, restless, worrying, relatives ever since, unable to concentrate on anything or anyone but Nathan.

It had been traumatic enough surviving without his presence in past months. While she had stood, silently praying, not knowing whether he still lived, she had realised it would be absolute hell trying to come to terms with his death. When he had been below ground she had felt some relief in joining the cluster of people huddled near the engine house for news. Sharing her fears with others had helped.

However he, when he emerged, definitely hadn't expected to see her there. Although she was sure he had caught sight of her, he had looked straight through her, and walked on. At that point, knowing he was safe, she had meant to walk away too, though was stopped from doing so as her willpower evaporated. As he neared home he saw her oh-so-familiar figure in the distance, but showed no sign of welcome, hoping ignoring her would stop her in her tracks. It didn't, and a few minutes afterwards she had closed the distance between them, and was by his side.

In resignation, he decided that the situation called for sarcasm. Staring ahead as he spoke, he was determined not to be lured by the body he continued to remember too often in the lonely dead of night.

'Well, look who it is. Darling Lorna, come to see if I'm still intact after all the excitement of the past hours. You shouldn't have worried, I thought we'd freed ourselves of concern about each other a while ago.'

'I couldn't help it,' she said softly. 'You were out of sight for so long. No-one knew what was happening down there.'

'That mine's meant to be my second home, if you remember. You shouldn't have wasted your time waiting with the others. You could have done much more with your day than hanging around a filthy mine.'

Instinctively, she put out a hand, wanting to touch him, but in the end made no contact.

'It's Will's second home too, but see what happened to him,' she ventured. 'Are you saying there's no way you could have been hurt? Are you immortal or something? You could have been crushed or suffocated like anyone else.'

Sighing, he stared at her, his complexion sallow and lined instead of healthy and unworried, one rogue muscle twitching near his mouth as he barely controlled his passion.
'I'm suffocating as it is,' he whispered fiercely. 'Surely you know that?'
Before she could react he strode away with obvious deliberation, but she ran to catch him up, and clung onto a flailing arm.
'You haven't changed have you?' she challenged, with greater strength than she felt. 'I thought you might have gone back to something like your old self once I was out of the way, and you had that freedom you so wanted.'
Despite wishing to berate her for her forthright words, he retained enough restraint to temper his reply slightly, and pause until he could speak without too much venom in his voice.
But, he told himself, couldn't she see he didn't want any interference, couldn't take her meddling, or bear her to be so near, near enough for him to feel the heat of her, to smell the light scent she wore? She didn't understand. But she had waited all those hours, patient and devoted. Didn't he owe her something?
'It hasn't happened like that,' he snapped, eventually. 'Let's say there was a problem solved, and then a couple more heaped on me.'
She wanted to say something relevant, words which would hold him permanently. Without finding the right approach she settled instead for the inane.
'What is it Nathan, that you can't just let go and be happy? Why do you have to find problems everywhere?

It gave him an easy excuse, and he pushed past her, sending her staggering slightly on the uneven ground.
'Everyone has troubles. Believe me, I'm not the only one.'
He said no more, hoping silence would be enough to drive her away. It didn't. She was still by him as he neared his home. His mother was going to be enough to deal with after the trauma of the last hours, and there was no way he could face Lorna if she followed him into the small confines of the cottage too.
With that in mind he stopped at the top of the hill and she did as well, a sweet, cloying shadow. Her questioning, beautiful face was raised to his and the concern etched there was laid bare for him to see.
It occurred to him that they were back on the cliffs, in the rain, and she was grappling again with the courage to leave him. They were retracing old ground that they should not have returned to.
'What is it you want Lorna?' he asked, slowly. 'You know how tired I am. I'm in no fit state for riddles.'
She swallowed, the saliva sticking in her dry throat.
You're pathetic, she told herself, pathetic for not accepting plain facts, stupid for trying to cling onto something you yourself threw away.
Then again, hadn't she seen fragments of desire in his expression just now, when he had thought she wasn't looking? Part of him, a hidden part maybe, still wanted her, of that she was absolutely sure.
'I've missed you, I wanted you to know that,' she murmured.
I could probably deal better with her hate than

her love, he thought in return, struggling to keep his temper. Hadn't he already explained to her the complexity of his own, personal demons?
'I understand, I really do, but it changes nothing. So go away Lorna, please, and stay away. I don't want to be tied down by you, or anybody else at all.'

VI

The rescue proved to be a catalyst. It led to the crystallisation of ideas that had been forming inside Nathan's heart and mind for a long while. When he woke the next morning he knew that every fibre within him was clamouring for him to leave. If others saw such a departure, from cliffs, and stormy seas, as cowardice, then that was their problem.
As he had factored, his mother failed to take the news in either a happy or understanding spirit. When he told her, in very direct terms, that he had finally reached a decision to emigrate her pinched face instantly turned ashen, and her clawing fingers went to grasp him.
'Say that again, you can't mean it,' she demanded after he announced in as unemotional, certain, way as he could muster, that he was planning to leave for America.
She swayed on her feet in front of him, feeling sick, imagining she was in the midst of a nightmare.
Nightmare it must be, she thought, for I've dreamt so many times that he would desert me.
When her legs buckled he didn't try to catch her, being too irked by her reaction, too hardened by what he regarded as her hysteria

to care. Without his aid she collapsed lifelessly into the nearest chair.

Looking at her, still not swayed by her reaction, he noticed idly that her clothes were old and tired, and hung from her slim frame, and her hair was lifeless and unkempt. Not a windblown but shiningly attractive halo of untidy tendrils as Lorna's had recently been, but lank and greasy. Good appearances were uncalled for now she was no longer a mine captain's wife, now her beloved Tom was dead.

'Don't look at me as if I'm hell bent on murder or treason. Half the village has been doing that for months, also with no good reason,' he tried to reason with her, despite realising that he was bound to fail to convince her that his plan was sensible, sane and timely. 'What I'm planning to do is perfectly understandable. I'm only hoping to grasp a future that has already become normal for many who originated from Biscovey, as well as from the rest of this damned bleak, windswept and poverty-stricken part of the world.'

At that his mother rocked in her chair and buried her head in careworn hands, trying not to show her reaction, but knowing that despite all her objections, he was right. Emigration was not at all unusual. Thousands of Cornishmen, and women, had flocked overseas since the early 1860s, heading for new lives and hopeful fortunes in any country with emergent mineral wealth.

Their skills were so accomplished that almost all were guaranteed work wherever they went. Mexico, South Africa, Brazil, Peru all offered welcome, as did the compelling expanse of America where the madness of the gold rush had really opened the way to the wandering tribe of Celts, and those who were happy to go anywhere for a 'quick buck'.

Nevertheless, Nathan's father, staunch and unbending as he had been, had always criticised those who had fled - accusing them of leaving their homeland behind to suffer, and struggle with the consequences. His chief argument, put forward on any suitable occasion, had been that Cornwall was being bled dry of all her best men, and most able brains and, as a result, home mines, with all they meant to their homeland, had had to pay a drastic price.

Mary, in her obedient way, had always thought his strict views would influence his sons enough to keep them home, below the earth of Bethany, and near to her, especially when she needed them. But now Nathan, with his hostile eyes alive with what she saw as contempt, stood before her intent on shattering everything she wanted to stay secure. And what scared her more than his defection was the knowledge that she had no longer had any hold over him, because she did not matter that much to him any more.

It was impossible for her to understand that, inwardly, he had kicked against parental influence since childhood.

Nathan could have torn the cottage apart in frustration. In a wild moment he had hoped she would grasp the myriad of underlying motives for his flight, especially after his brooding attitude of the last year or so. To his way of thinking it must have been glaringly obvious, for a very long period of time, that he was not content. Leaving was a step forward, a step which would see him contribute to a growing part of Cornish tradition. It wasn't betrayal.

She can't begin to accept it, he thought as he watched her. My father, her dear husband, made her so narrow-minded, so lacking in imagination that it's impossible for her to look outside her tiny world. Well blast her, her small universe, with all its fences and its rules and regulations, is certainly not mine.

But, as her grief persisted, and her sobbing carried on, echoing harshly around the room with its burning driftwood fire and once well-scrubbed surfaces, her distress began to make some impact, chafe some part of a guilt he did not like to admit to. He hadn't helped enough since his father's death.

Way down inside his soul, he felt that he hadn't taken on enough of the family's burdens, or dried the right amount of tears. His father had rammed it into his brain that he was meant to be the chosen son, able to show the others the clear-cut path, and at one fleeting time he had been the golden boy, the one who did hold within him the promise of the future. Instead, he had managed to lose himself in a maze of self-pity, and a dawning realisation that he held none of the beliefs that his father had held so dear.

Mary was not stupid, and was shrewd enough to suspect she was making some headway in the argument. Knowing that, she increased the pressure, thinking that later he would surely see that what she was trying to do was the best for all of them, for the family as a whole.

'Nathan, just listen,' implored. 'I rely on you. Up until this year I thought you were the closest of all of my boys to me. You can't leave. America is thousands of miles away. You have a home here, work, money and a family. What else do you want? You remind me of your father so much more than the others. I can see him in you now. Tall, powerful . .'

Unwittingly, she had broken the spell she was trying, against all true hope, to weave, as if she might hold some magic within her words.

'But I'm not him, and I will never be,' he exploded. 'Won't you ever be able to see that? He put himself up on this blasted pedestal, and us with him, just because he happened to be a mine captain. Well, we aren't. We might have more education than most, speak a few extra fancy words than our neighbours, and live in a decent home of sorts instead of a damp hovel, but I can tell you that, for sure, we're on the same level as everyone else.'

Biting back his anger, he ran a long-fingered, almost delicate hand, through untended curls and slowly lowered himself into the wooden, throne-like, high-backed chair that had been his father's.

How could he explain reasons when he wasn't sure of them himself? He hadn't been able to rationalise with Lorna, why should it be different with his mother? Nevertheless, he tried.

'I don't want anything else but escape. I suppose I'm running. I feel I'm chained here, like a domestic animal, I suppose. If I don't move now, and go searching for some meaning, I never will. I'll be in my forties, bitter, and on my way to dying quite casually in a fight, or in the mine, like Will nearly did. And I won't have achieved a blessed thing.'

Hearing his words with dread, she looked at him through her sore eyes, noted the set jaw, the swarthy skin made less healthy by the hours encased without light, and the bleakness of expression that dominated the whole personality.

'It was your father dying that led to all this. I thought you grieved too little, but could have misjudged you.'

Sighing heavily, he exhaled the air with exaggeration. Once again she had manipulated the conversation, brought it around to his father. If only she could understand that he was the cause of so much of the uncertainty? But then again why did there have to be a simple cause trotted out for every ill and depression?

Perhaps what he felt was just born of the unknown.

A considered retort was once more on his lips when he looked up and saw James leaning against the doorway, blond hair bright, his broad figure throwing a shadow over them from the gas lamp. That stilled him enough to hold back and let his brother talk, suddenly bored with explanations. There was no way either of them were going to alter the decision he had made.

'What's going on?' James enquired, although he had already heard enough to know the answer. The raised voices, from both, had woken him.

Mary turned to him, sorrow branded into the lines of her face. Then she lowered her gaze and fixed her eyes on the stone floor before she spoke. Never had she felt as deeply for any of her sons as she had, and did, for Nathan, and it had always been so. James, at 22, was only a year younger than his elder brother, but to her he had never had the same magical force. Physically he was bigger and taller, but he was without Nathan's presence. Her trembling fingers picked at the cuff of her dress, with its thin, trailing, grubby lace.

'Nathan's going. He's emigrating, or so he tells me. He's sailing across to America, Wisconsin perhaps, or then again California.' The names came easily to her dry lips. The towns and states of America were as familiar to her as parts of London and the north of England - maybe more so. It was true that a great many of their own 'Cousin Jacks' and 'Cousin Jills' were walking the trails of that new land, working and building new homes there. And so many letters crossed the ocean and were read to all and sundry, that such familiarity had quickly grown.

James, as fair as Nathan was dark, moved to his mother, and placed comforting, muscular arms around her. As he did so he gazed at his brother, and subconscious rival, now lounging in his chair and staring out of the window.

In truth, he didn't blame Nathan, understanding that his problems had built to such a degree that there was no other option. But he guessed the news had been broken to his mother without finesse or tact. It was his brother's way to blunder in, as an uncaring bull, unheeding and without previous thought. For a long time he hadn't been sure if anything touched the man before him. If Lorna couldn't then no-one stood a chance. Slowly, he turned back to Mary, unconcerned. Four men still remained to support the family in the future. Alex and Billy were yet to bring home men's wages, but he felt he was competent enough, together with Samuel, to ensure there were no hitches with money, even if his mother didn't entirely believe in his ability.

'You knew something like this would happen,' he said patiently. 'You understand, I know, how aimless he's been of late.'

The spoken-of third party scowled in contempt.

'You surprise me James boy, being able to notice how someone else is feeling, realise how important their dreams are to them.'

James snapped back. 'You can stop your sniping, I'm only trying to help. Eldest brother you might be, but I don't need your acid remarks.'

'You'll get them anyway. You must be able to see, both of you, that I've got to go. All I can give to any of you here is money, and I can do that equally as well from over there. And there is such a thing as the post, remember. I'll make sure none of you sink into poverty, I can assure you of that.' Stopping suddenly, he tried to defuse his temper. 'Look, just think of this - you'll be rid of my black moods, my drinking, and my dealings with the police.'

It all offered no comfort to Mary.

'But I don't want to be rid of you. I want you here, with me. Safe with me, safe in Cornwall.'

'Mother,' cut in James, forcibly holding her shoulders down as she tried to move across to Nathan, now standing by the window, looking out at the scene outside, so making sure that he had his back to both of them. 'If you let him go you might in the end keep some part of him. Let him do what he wants. We can't beat what's eating that black soul of his.'

'Well, well,' breathed Nathan in feigned amazement,'you surprise me, brother. I couldn't have put it better myself.

July 1870

V11

Nathan discovered that leaving his homeland was not to occur without further dispute, none of it - during his final days in Cornwall - stemming from his mother or James. With resignation, they had both come to accept the situation. For his part, James had absorbed the news with less regret, mainly being relieved that Nathan had taken some measures to deal with his problems. Overall, he was quietly pleased that his older brother's absence would instead give him a chance to prove he was equally able to cope with the family's needs. For quite a while he had viewed himself as much more of an extension of his father than Nathan had ever been. Above everything else, he craved leadership, and wanted to grasp it, if it was offered, with both hands and use it to prove his ability - not side-step it. The trouble was that James, steady, determined, more ambitious than even he had guessed, was certainly not the only other brother. Samuel, the third born, rather than viewing Nathan's desire to flee as providing an opportunity to leap into his footsteps, regarded his plans as treachery, and was determined to make his feelings public before it was too late.

That happened in the last moments, when the Roseveans, as a supposedly united family, were gathered at St Austell railway station to bid farewell to yet another Cornish adventurer.

Left to his own devices Nathan would have crept quietly from Biscovey, from the cliffs of his childhood, from the mile long white, gritty beach at Crinnis, from Lorna who still beset his dreams, and would have gone like the wisp of a ghost, without fuss. But his mother wanted the goodbyes to be conducted properly, and he had reluctantly let her have her own way on the final issue. As a result, he was actually on the platform, with the express to Bristol due in a couple of minutes, when Samuel, stocky and barrel-chested, stepped forward from the clustered family group, the anger he had concealed from all suddenly bursting from him.

'You're running out on us, you know that, you bastard.'

Nathan heard. It would have been impossible not to. The accusation rolled down the platform, and echoed, like a clarion call for battle, around the smartly painted brown and cream station.

What the hell is he going on about now? he thought. Ignore him, it's the only way. The train will be in within a minute or two.

Trying to shut everything and everyone out of his mind, he continued to edge away from the family group, glancing along the empty track on the opposite side to where he stood, the one that snaked westwards past rhododendron covered banks, and then disappeared around a bend was eventually to lead to the end of the line, at Penzance.

It was not Samuel's intention, however, to let him go in such quiet fashion. Rushing forward in an explosion of frustration, he grabbed Nathan by the shoulder, and dragged him back towards the shadows of the small waiting room.

'Mother needs you,' he spat. 'Look at her trying not to cry. Look at her, damn you. Your family needs you, yet you're just going to walk out on us as if we never meant anything to you.'

The assault, unlike the words, couldn't be brushed aside easily. Nathan did try not to respond in kind, bar breaking himself free, which he succeeded to do initially. Although anticipating another quick attack he then tried to tidy his clothes while studying Samuel's flushed cheeks and burning short-sighted zeal. Then he measured his answer with deliberate care.

'I'm just doing what thousands of others have done. Men have left their families here, gone to Australia, then South America, and then come back again. It's normal. Les Williams and John Trago who lived near us for years did it, and their wives just waited for them to return.'

But it had become impossible for Samuel to accept an opposing point of view on any subject.

'That's rubbish. You're taking the simple way out, being a coward, and that's what you've always been deep down inside.'

Nathan searched within himself for the patience which he had always only harboured in short supply, and which had been in such notoriously short supply of late.

What do I do, he thought, hit him hard, or ignore him, or try to talk to him?

Without further consideration he decided on the third option.

'There's nothing for me in Cornwall. If I stay I'll just ruin what years there are to come. Is that really what you want me to do?'

Samuel was far from mollified by the words, and his face reddened further as his blood pressure continued to rise.

'What the hell are you after - paradise? Grow up. It doesn't exist, and it never will. We want

you to stay. When father died you were meant to give us guidance, not run out on us like a whipped dog. And a fat lot of guidance there has been with your drinking and whoring.'
Nathan breathed deeper, but didn't put down his battered cases, which he had picked up again after Samuel's attempt to floor him.
'My future, Sam, is mine alone. It doesn't belong to you, or mother, or anyone else. Don't try to tell me what to do, because I tell you now that it won't work. I don't take orders from you, or anyone who comes to mind.'
His tone, so supercilious to Samuel, brought about the free for all. They were in the midst of crowds, and their own family members, but that didn't stop Samuel throwing himself on Nathan, fists clenched, determined to ram into flesh and bone. A corpse wouldn't be able to escape, would it?
The cases fell again from Nathan's hands, crashing to the cold floor, and Nathan himself followed them down, unable to steady himself in time. His head cracked back on the stone slabs, robbing him of breath, sending instant pain searing through him, which stunned him for a few seconds. Samuel was kicking and pummelling, a blindness in him, a desire only to gain some sort of revenge for the betrayal of his mother, even somehow for the death of his father, and for the terrible let-down of life itself.
Nathan's lip had split. Tasting blood in his mouth, he saw the station roof whirl in a daze in front of him, and took in glimpses of Samuel's crimson face.
Behind him he could see that James was standing to one side, his shoulders braced, seemingly ready to join in when he judged

necessary. For a while, Nathan fought to clear his throbbing head, and subdued his punches with the least retaliation, trying not to attract more attention from the general public than they were already doing.

But that was hopeless. Samuel had no such qualms about fighting in front of a horde of train passengers, and only seemed to be banking on beating him to a pulp, perhaps showing in his own particular way that he had comparable qualities to any of his kin.

In the heat of the scuffle the train steamed in, the tank engine chugging past them before coming to a noisy, smutty halt, and at that point Nathan knew he could waste no more time.

From a quick glance he could see that one of his cases had broken open, and spilt much of its contents. His coat, which would be more than needed on the boat, was in a heap on the floor, and one of his books was somersaulting away on the wind, its pages ripping as it went. Knowing there was no saving it, he merely watched it go. Neither his mother, nor any of his other brothers, were making the smallest attempt to retrieve anything for him. Instead, they were staring ahead at them both, as if riveted to the scene.

They weren't alone. Despite the rush of passengers to the train the watching crowd around them seemed to be increasing by the second. By then Samuel's large hands were at his collar, tearing at his shirt, trying to strangle him. Knowing that if he didn't act quickly the train would leave without him, Nathan prised the fingers away from his neck, pushed his brother away as far as he could, and then slammed a fist into Sam's round, sweating face as hard as possible.

It was the end. Samuel sank to his knees, robbed of breath, moaning in agony, blood coursing from nose and mouth.

James, sure his younger brother's nose had been broken, went rushing to him, as did Mary. Nathan, though, unconcerned now about any physical or mental hurt he may have caused, bent down, and hurriedly stuffed his dusty and dishevelled clothes, as best he could, into one of the suitcases, and hurried to the waiting, belching train. He didn't look back.

There were no weeping farewells, as envisaged by his mother, as he disappeared into the clouds of grey steam. But he didn't care, only thinking that, with Cornwall soon to be behind him, it seemed almost certain that he would eventually arrive in America, unless fate, in the guise of storms or hurricanes, had its capricious way. But after that nothing was clear.

And so, when the engine pulled away from St Austell he tried to concentrate only on matters other than the shambles he had just left behind.

Ahead was a cramped Atlantic crossing on a ship on which he was to travel steerage with hundreds of others, and provide his own food. The women passengers were to cook in stinking cabooses on an open deck, and for the man who had come to crave isolation there would be no privacy. Also, there would be no medical attention, something that made contracting any illness extremely hazardous. The captain was only ordered to provide those on board with water, which Nathan instantly discovered was rarely fresh.

What was always uppermost in his mind, though, was the problem of reaching his first destination of Wisconsin. The routes there were many. He knew he could travel by way of Quebec, a journey which was the cheapest, but also the most prone to disaster because of fog, high winds, or ice. Alternatively, he could take the long river trip from New Orleans, up the cholera choked Mississippi, or hike overland from New York, following the Ohio River until it joined the long and winding Mississippi.

Another option was to make his way up the Hudson and continue by barge through the Eerie Canal to Buffalo where he could transfer to steamer across the lake.

He thought frequently of the Wisconsin he had conjured up in his imagination, the Wisconsin he had been told about by those who had been there and then returned. Of the green woods and the blue rivers, and thousands of streams that flowed into the Mississippi.

Eventually, such thoughts allowed him to block out Samuel's manic anger, but they could not quite eliminate flashes of Lorna, hovering sensually in the corners of his mind.

V111

He left home in the summer of 1870 when there were only two sources of tin in the world, the Malayan states and Cornwall, where copper mining had gone into steep decline in the previous decade, and where tin had, as a result, overtaken it in importance. The new saying was that deep tin was to be found beneath shallow copper. That had been true at Dolcoath, which had made a fortune from it, and all competitors hoped to follow her example.

The Cornish industry was, therefore, experiencing a rosy boom, the next two years seeing tin fetch a better metal price than ever before, and mines were opened and re-opened by the score, almost by the hundred. Nearly every acre of ground in the mining districts was taken up in one way or another. A few of these were 'bubble' ventures, got up to make money by way of promotion and share dealing, but the majority were hoping to become genuine second Dolcoaths. Unfortunately for the adventurers, a third supplier of tin was to emerge in 1873 - Australia - where vast alluvial deposits had been discovered. It resulted in over-production and a tumble in the tin price. From their peak in 1872 prices were to fall dramatically. To worsen the situation, riots, which had wracked the Malayan continent since 1868 and had held up mining there, ebbed into peace.

And then a further source of tin entered the fray, in the form of Tasmania. The effect on Cornwall was catastrophic. While his brothers, all four involved in the mining industry in some respect, struggled to come to terms with the prospective collapse of their livelihoods, Nathan undertook his own prospecting in the virgin open spaces of America.

There, he no longer searched for tin or copper. Instead his inherent mining skills drew him to the lead regions around Galena.

CHAPTER TWO

June 1873

1

Although able to call upon a quicksilver mind and lightning intuition, if he wanted to use them, James Rosevean seldom took speedy decisions. Within him there was also an irrational fear of failure, which he masked with a refusal to be beaten at whatever he attempted. Mixed with this slow, determined stubbornness, was a subconscious desire not only to win, to triumph, but to destroy all those with whom he was in competition. Over the years, he had grown accustomed to the gnawing need to outshine Nathan, who had always appeared to be the epitome of confidence. In his eldest brother's long-term absence he felt partially vindicated, but the terror of taking second place could not be laid to rest easily.

On one scorching, burning, day in the June of 1873 he stood in silent mourning in front of Wheal Bethany, the mine that had provided him with a living for ten years. She was still very much alive. Machinery ground and rattled, bal maidens worked in the open, perspiration running down their leathered foreheads and into their dark brows, young children scurried around the ore that had been brought to the surface, sorting it into piles. But he stood away from all the familiar activity, closed his eyes and visualised the engine house as an empty, derelict shell, succumbing to the spread of gorse and grass with her workers gone to scratch a living elsewhere - if they were lucky.

Although he was anticipating her closure by a couple of years, he knew on that day, for a certainty, that she was in her death throes.

Severe financial cutbacks had been brought in to cope with the dramatic turn-around in the world markets. Australian tin was causing havoc with Cornish profits, and men who had worked almost all their lives in mining had already lost their jobs, whether they had been employed in the untamed wildness of West Penwith, or along the more peaceful borders of the Tamar river which divided Kernow from the rest of the world.

Shading his pale eyes from the steaming heat, he stepped back to take a wider view, and grudgingly admitted to himself that, at his young age, he was in a better position than most.

Above all else, he was strong and could still cope with the efforts mining demanded. The crisis would have loomed darker if he had been 20 years older with the best of his strength gone. Healthy, adaptable youth stood more chance of survival below ground. Nevertheless, Bethany's whole future appeared to be a sickeningly unknown quantity, and he, for his own future, wanted a safer and more secure path.

Outwardly, on that blistering morning nothing had changed. A lazy, hot, benevolent air hung over the buildings and the surrounding, stunted trees. In the far distance the sea dipped and shone, and gulls hovered high in the azure like minute white dots. The fishing fleet was out in force from Mevagissey, and the fields on the Gribbin were rippling with ripening corn. With little effort he could have side-stepped his worries and slipped into a mellow, reflective mood, but he deliberately stopped himself from what he termed as lazy-thinking.

Complacency leads you absolutely nowhere,

he told himself. It's up to each individual to save themselves, and equally make sure that their survival cannot be doubted.

One recent suggestion was uppermost in his thoughts. It was a hazy idea, put forward by a friend over more than a few pints in the bar of the Rashleigh Arms which stood on the main track from St Austell through to the port of Charlestown. But the suggestion was becoming more substantial. It involved a joint venture with himself and a friend and regular drinking partner, Ned Trevenning.

Basically, it was a gamble with china clay, or kaolin, which was gradually being excavated by the increasing ton from Hensbarrow Downs which lay on the outskirts of St Austell.

James thought of Nathan, chasing his own treasure trove in a vast foreign land. It would be sweetly ironic, he thought, if he could unearth his own crock of gold much nearer to home.

The scheme was Ned's brainchild. He had argued his case with great persuasion despite the amount of alcohol under his belt. Over and over again, he pointed out that the china clay industry had grown steadily since William Cookworthy had taken out a patent for its manufacture in 1768. Ninety years after that 65,000 tons were being produced and the figure, as Ned had emphasised, had continued rising. In that year there had been an even greater influx of money into the tips, despite most hardened miners considering it not quite proper to 'go clay'.

When James had first been approached about contributing to the prospect of opening up kaolin works in the virtual, seemingly barren isolation, of the southern slopes of Bodmin

Moor he had turned it down with little deep thought, and a whole lot of scepticism. Although Ned said he was willing to put in the major share of the required finance, it would still have swallowed every penny of Tom Rosevean's tiny legacy and James's small amount of savings. Another drawback was that that part of the moor that had been outlined as promising for kaolin was in a new area of excavation, and the nearest point for railway sidings down to the docks was Bodmin Road for Fowey, with its gentle, winding river.

But, what in theory seemed almost like easy down-grade routes to the main line had been, on closer inspection, deeply entrenched and winding ravines.

Despite such negatives, of late James had begun to consider the scheme with some seriousness, wondering if Ned's apparent rantings might actually hold some promise. Fear was partially driving such thoughts, for he was sure the tin crisis was deepening and, although some insisted the mines would recover as they always would, he couldn't see it personally, knowing that production around the world was pricing Cornish firms out of business.

With this in mind he returned home determined to explain Trevenning's idea to the family and prove to them that 'going clay' might be worth much more than their passing interest. However, in spite of his own enthusiasm, he made scant progress, even though his mother and Samuel were the only ones there to convince. So dulled was she by the rigours of merely living that she met his arguments with silence, while Samuel offered nothing but sarcasm and scorn.

After around twenty minutes of gentle persuasion James began to realise that his brother would probably be avidly against any suggestion he would have put forward.
Billy and Alex were out fishing off of Mevagissey and James ached to be with them. Staring with open anger at his other brother, he restrained an urge to hit out with fists as well as words. But that would not solve any problems, and would be totally on Samuel's level. With some difficulty he ignored the insults that had been thrown at him - from being an idiotic day-dreamer to wanting to waste every penny of the family's money, including all that Nathan had been sending them - and concentrated on what really concerned him.
'Sam, you're talking with your eyes closed to everything that's happening around us. Most of the tin mines near here won't last much longer, surely you realise that? The competition is becoming too great. There's no earthly use playing blind and hoping they'll go on for years.'
'And what makes you so damned certain you're right?'
Samuel stood in the middle of the dark, sombre room, his arms folded, his thick, black eyebrows brought together in a perpetual frown which signalled that he was at his most stubborn.
'So you think Bethany'll survive even though St Ives Consols, Wheal Vor, Ding Dong and Balleswidden are already struggling to keep going, and look likely to fold before long?' James asked coldly.
Samuel snorted in disagreement, but much of the reaction was false. Deep down he, too, had his doubts, but he wasn't going openly to

admit to these.

Why the devil should I give him support, he thought. If I'd come up with such a fancy plan, and gone begging to him for money, I'd have only been laughed at.

'We'll be fine for a good few years yet. You're bolting at damned piskies, I never thought you'd be so easy to scare.'

James switched to a different form of attack.

'What about Billy or Alex?'

'What about them?'

'I wonder what they'd think about it all. I'm sure they'd give this idea more thought than you have. They might be young, but neither are short of brains, especially Alex with all his ideals.'

'They'll think the same as me. You'll have some difficulty getting them involved in such a crazy scheme.'

'You speak for them now do you?'

Samuel literally bristled.

'Are you trying to say I go out of my way to influence them?'

'No, no I wasn't quite saying that,' murmured James, with defeatism now creeping upon him.

It had been an exceptionally hot day, and he felt drained and tired of a sudden, squeezed dry by the warmth, although it wasn't overtly hot in the house. The sunlight very seldom penetrated there. Why continue arguing? He couldn't win, he knew that from experience. After all I've done for them since Nathan's defection, he thought, shouldn't I be entitled to my family's full support?

Samuel saw him hesitate and decided to strive for a parting which might dent his brother's starched pride, as well as his misplaced enthusiasm.

'Are you sure that even if you did scrape together enough money for such a scheme the big shots running the china clay industry would happily and easily let you join them? In that cut-throat business you depend on others for a place on the railways and at the dockside. They're all-powerful those families, and they wouldn't look too kindly on you, a no-one from struggling mining stock. We may have ruled the roost here once, but our name certainly doesn't carry the same weight now as it did when father was alive. Not half the same.'

What he said achieved its aim, to a great extent because there was some truth within his brother's final, jarring, words. The jibes rankled with James for days. It was not so much due to Samuel's lack of faith in him, as that was almost to be expected. Samuel regarded life through a cloud of pessimism, and distrust, as well as a certain amount of envy.

More annoying was his brother's absolute refusal to offer any financial help, especially as his words regarding the china clay families had verged on the truth. To find the money required he needed help from those close to him, but even if he managed to achieve that his background, and his lack of status, were very much against him if he wanted to build himself a successful business.

A fortnight after his own moratorium at Bethany the vast indecision remained within him. During the intervening period he had produced no answers. There had been no softening in Samuel's attitude, or interest shown in the scheme by his mother or the other two boys. No money had materialised from the air, or from any member of his family.

As he tussled with the negative thoughts which had seemed to be pursuing him for months, he had walked to the sea, to the port of Charlestown, which lay between Duporth and Carlyon Bay. It was late afternoon and he had just returned to the surface after eight sweltering hours underground.

For once claustrophobia had been sitting at his shoulder in the darkness, as if waiting to imprison him, and now he had fled from it he wanted free open air and the sight of a restless sea.

Some of Nathan's words drifted back to him as he walked: 'There's no joy left any more, if ever there was. I get down there and I'm trapped. Haven't you ever felt that way? Too sure of yourself to do that, I suppose.'

James made his way past the majestic village church with its spire pushing up through the trees and at the end of the lane he turned left and almost ran down to the water, covering the ground with his long, confident strides. The road, widened by the convoys of carts used to take cargo down to the oblong shaped dock, stopped abruptly when it reached the quay, which had been modernised by Charles Rashleigh a century before. When he stopped too he was only yards from the beach.

The pocket-sized port was teeming with activity. Together with Pentewan, further around the coast, it exported the majority of china clay tonnage, and the dock workers were busy loading four ships with the white cargo. The village had developed strong ties with three working railways - the former West Cornwall, which passed through St Austell, Burngullow and Par; Treffry's Newquay to Hendra Downs line; and the Par to Molinnis

track which skirted the clay works on the eastern margins of Hensbarrow Downs.
James loved the place, the colour-washed cottages clinging to the harbour wall, the clank of the forge, the wide and challenging view from the headland that climbed around to Crinnis. There were many familiar faces in view, involved in loading or re-fitting, but he ignored them, wanting isolation and little else. He smiled wryly. Was this yet more shades of Nathan catching up on him?

Pausing slightly, he watched the crowded ships lying lazily at anchor as they were being loaded, their masts raking the horizon and their rigging whistling, rattling and clattering in the warm breeze. Looking at the way they were lying in the water his guess was that at least two would be ready to sail on the approaching high tide, one probably for Rotterdam, the other for Hamburg.

With his eyes continuing to avoid meeting with those of anyone he knew, he slipped past the bulk of the activity and veered off to the right of the encircling granite arms of the quay and onto the small, stony beach. The sea was rushing in fast, crashing with force onto the shingle and dragging much of it back into the waves, there being a clash of tumbling stones as it did so.

Looking southwards, he was surprised that a still day had produced such an amount of surf, even though there was a full moon due that night and he knew the tide would be particularly high. A cormorant drifted close to the shoreline, disappearing every few minutes beneath the water to search for fish. Three others of his kind stood on the rocks holding out their wings to dry, looking in silhouette like small, prehistoric creatures.

Squatting on his haunches, he picked up a handful of pebbles and idly threw them into the breakers as he stared around him. If he had come there to seek them, there seemed few answers to the questions which had begun to pepper his mind, to be found from his surroundings.

What the hell am I hoping for, divine intervention? he thought, unable to shake off the despondency that had been gradually settling heavily upon him, like a suffocating blanket, mainly generated by Samuel's valid points about the strength of the families running the china clay businesses. James had come to admit to himself that it would be well nigh impossible to create a firm which would be able to break into their tight circle.

With his broad, tense back aching from crouching down he stretched to his feet again and kicked his way along the beach. The high, rugged, cliffs that carried the coastal footpath from Fowey to Porthpean, through Duporth or the 'black cove', towered above him. As he walked into their shadows he shivered.

The sun had also lost some of its heat as quickly scudding grey clouds began to blanket it frequently, and he began thinking that the height of the surf might also be due to approaching rain.

He thought to himself that the shore was as much a part of him as a limb. Looking back, he realised that he had visited it since boyhood, whenever strife threatened, or when he ached to be alone. To think, to reason. The water, even on a storm-ridden day usually had the power to wash over even the most pressing problems. It wasn't so that day.

He spotted the child just as he was about to turn and leave the stretch of shingle to return to the quay. The small figure, probably a girl he thought, was scrambling over the rocks, and even from that distance her balance seemed awry. To his dismay, she fell as he looked on. It seemed she had jumped back to avoid an incoming wave, missed her footing and disappeared into the swirling water.

James stood transfixed for a second, watching the small body being washed back and forth against the jagged, razor sharp rocks. Then he moved, racing across the seaweed-strewn boulders scattered at the base of the cliffs, as if possessed.

Heart beating like an insistent drum, he leapt onto the rocks with the expertise of years, and scrambled to reach her, concentrating as hard as he could in such circumstances, as he went because he knew that if he fell himself her prospective survival would be severely hampered.

At low tide it was possible to walk on the boulders from Charlestown to the beach at Duporth. However, the tide was rising quickly, with waves rushing in at alarming speed. Fortunately, he realised that the small figure wasn't far around the outcrop, but the heightening sea still seemed to be doing its utmost to batter every breath from her body, making her look like a helpless doll in its swirling grip. Fearfully, he realised she wasn't struggling to save herself. There was hardly any movement.

'Swim,' he yelled into the spray. 'For God's sake, swim.'

There was no response.

To his eventual relief, once he was in the water it was relatively easy to catch her. After swimming about twenty yards out he was able to grab hold of her wet, flapping, trailing clothes and pull her into his arms, fighting hard at the same time to prevent either of them being dashed further against the granite. Immediately, he could see she was already cut on her arms. She was small and remarkably thin, so he had little trouble holding her as he fought his way back to the shoreline, though despite that and being an accomplished swimmer, he still swallowed what seemed to be a gallon of salt water as he battled to safety.

Once he had waded ashore with her, with more difficulty than he had anticipated as most of his strength seemed to have evaporated, he could see she was bleeding from several other cuts. One across her forehead was quite severe. Initially, she lay inert in his arms, her eyes closed, her mouth slackly open, but to his relief there was a definite pulse and her slim chest was heaving. As at first sight, when he had initially glimpsed her, he still presumed she was about fourteen, for although she was unconscious she was not heavy to carry. When he reached a small, sandy stretch of the beach, he laid her down gently, hauled himself over to pick up the jacket that he had thrown off before going to her rescue, rolled it up and placed it underneath her like a cushion, much as Nathan had done for Will when they were deep in the mine.

Within minutes he and the prostrate girl were the focus of attention. Men and women who had seen what had happened from the harbour wall gathered around as he tried desperately to warm her, massaging her limbs, praying his uneducated efforts to revive her would be successful. But, after a while, he realised that her heart was beating quite strongly, and he guessed she was suffering from shock more than anything else, and allowed himself to believe that the chances that she would live might hopefully be quite high.

Above all else, he kept asking himself, what on earth had she been doing on the rocks. Playing some misguided game? Surely she hadn't meant to fall, to harm herself? Knowing she still needed some expert help, he yelled for someone in the crowd that had formed around him to fetch a doctor, eventually forcing one of them to gather enough wits together to run to Dr Hendry's large, imposing house on the outskirts of the village. James kept the girl's hand in his while he waited for professional assistance, feeling as he knelt beside her, the cold starting to seep through his skin and eat its way into his bones.

The heat had fled from the day for good now. His hunch about the change in weather had been right. A woman slung something across his shoulders and that helped a little, but only slightly. Stones dug into his knees as he stayed in the same position, and then began to sting flesh. He tried to move, but cramping pains shot up his legs and wrapped him in giddiness. The trials of the day below ground, and the unexpected swim, were really taking their toll. Through a haze he vaguely heard a general discussion being aired on the girl.

'Tis strange, I don't recognise her 'tall.'

'Certainly not from the village.'

' What the hell was she doing on the beach then?'

'You say that, but I'm sure I've seen the maid here before. I b'lieve she's called Helen, and is old Matthew Courtney's niece, or summat like that.'

'I didn't know he had any family. He keeps to himself.'
'Weren't there some talk back along of a quarrel with his brother, you know the one that's got money?'
'There's bad blood there, you know.'
The debate was brought to an abrupt halt by the arrival of Dr Daniel Hendry, red-faced from the exertion of stumbling to the beach at more than his usual, painfully slow, walking pace.
Drastically overweight, beset at times by gout, he was no great advert for health. But despite that he was respected, being equally concerned for all his patients, whether they were the wealthy whose money kept him financially afloat, or among the poor who could never afford to pay him.
Once there, he barged through the small crowd, pushing all aside, including James who staggered back, his legs refusing to hold him, and was caught by a friend from Biscovey who worked at Charlestown.
'Come on Jamie, let's get you warm too. You're chilled through. There's nothing more we can do here.'
'But the girl . . '
The girl, lying painfully still in her sodden, clinging, torn clothes, still wasn't moving.
'She's in good hands. She'll survive. I've seen many more in worse state pulled out the sea, and so have you.'

July 1873

11

James folded under the concerned pressure, waited until the young girl's eyelids began to flicker, and then quickly took his friend's advice and went straight home to a very welcome bed.

After a sound sleep he forced himself to think little more of the incident. It bore no relation to the problems mainly occupying him, and as long as she had survived that was all that concerned him.

His own legacy of his unexpected dip in Charlestown waters was a nagging bronchial cold that hung on for at least a month, but which was never tenacious enough to stop him working - a fact his mother was silently, but exceedingly, grateful for. James was an expert miner and, as a tributer who worked his own pitch, earned more than most at 'Bethany'.

Over the resulting weeks, therefore, he gave the girl only passing thought, though did go as far as checking with Dr Hendry her name, which was Helen Courtney, and that she had fully recovered. When the answer was an affirmative, he decided it was best to let the matter rest.

The one piece of information that trickled down to him was that, although she had indeed been staying with Matthew Courteney, her direct family members were, as had been rumoured, supposedly wealthy and lived in grand style on the western side of St Austell. For a while he endured ribbing from his younger brothers about his heroics, though he ignored their taunts as much as he could as he pushed the matter to the furthest reaches of his mind.

He had easily succeeded in that when the 'girl' appeared out of nowhere at Biscovey. She was totally recovered and now looked definitely more than fourteen. Due to that, and the surprisingly elegant clothes she was wearing, James thought she was a stranger wanting directions when he opened the door to her.

'You haven't an idea who I am, have you?' she said, embarrassment swamping her when he showed no signs of recognition.

In response, he said nothing, only stood blankly staring at her. She, in turn, was rather astounded by the sight of him. He was so broad he seemed to fill the doorway, and the chiselled, craggy features, together with his silence, made him seem totally unapproachable. As she couldn't remember anything of her rescue, and only had a hazy recollection of the events that led up to it, she had had few preconceived ideas of him to work on.

Her rap on the door had woken him and because he was still half asleep he was perhaps more bemused, and terse than he would have been otherwise.

'Not really. Should I know you?'

Shifting lightly on her feet, she wondered if she had assumed too much. Was this the right Rosevean? Hadn't someone said there were five brothers? Nevertheless, she ploughed on.

'Well yes, I think so. If it was not for you, or someone in your family, I don't think I would be here bothering you now.'

At that, he looked at her properly, at the almond-shaped hazel eyes, at her slim figure, at the cap of short brown hair that hugged her scalp, at the thin scar on her forehead where once there had been a deep cut - and the answer came to him.

It came slowly because she wasn't the child he had believed she was. With her head high, and her back held straight, his girl from the sea had more maturity and fire than he would ever have imagined. And what surprised him most was that the clothes she wore were plain, but obviously expensive. But hadn't he been told that her family were wealthy? He had, but he had really half dismissed that almost outright.

The jewellery, which was also plain, was gold.

'But how did you find me, or even know who I was?' he asked, also thinking - and why bother to come here?

So absorbed was he with such considerations that he didn't think of inviting her inside. Shock had made manners extinct for a while. Noting how uncomfortable he seemed as the news gradually dawned on him, she gave him her warmest smile, striving to put both of them more at ease.

'It's simple when you know the right people, the doctor for one. He soon helped me, but it was handy that he is very friendly with my uncle.'

'Shut the door James, please, I'm freezing in here. You know I can't stand draughts any more,' cried Mary from the depths of the cottage, and that finally awoke him from confusion.

Guiding the visitor into the kitchen, he decided he had better rustle up some sort of refreshment for her. The task was left to him because, as soon as his mother saw there was a stranger at the door, she had made herself scarce. In the past months, she had retreated further into herself, hardly communicating with anyone who wasn't family.

Her departure left them alone. For the first few minutes there was constrained silence between them. Trying not to be too obviously studying her, he managed to notice that she had an oval, boyish, tanned face which was made darker by the pale lemon colour of her dress. There was a sprinkling of freckles across the bridge of her nose, and a wide gap between her two front teeth.

'I've come to thank you for what you did for me. I was very lucky you were on the beach that day. It was stupid and misguided of me to go slipping and sliding around like that.'

Although he was in his own environment, he continued to find words difficult to come by.

'Well, at least you'll be wiser next time,' he murmured eventually.

'That's true, I will be.'

Outwardly, she showed no nerves in his company. To her he continued to be unexpectedly thickset, especially in the confines of the kitchen which was nothing more than poky by her family's standards. Nevertheless, he was not threatening. If anything it was she who showed assurance way beyond her seventeen years, and although afterwards he could not remember what they had spoken of she stayed for over an hour and chatted amiably enough throughout.

Even the arrival of Samuel, and the surly five minutes he spent with them, did not deter her. The girl who had appeared so young and vulnerable when she was struggling in the water was, it seemed, in reality made of much sterner fabric.

When the conversation finally failed, and she made signs of wanting to move on, he felt he ought to escort her home, despite still not knowing exactly where that home was.

Hastily, she declined, saying she had defied her parents' wishes and was staying in Charlestown again for a few days, and was quite prepared to walk back there on her own. Still sure he ought to make some effort, he insisted on at least taking her to the outskirts of the village and, with minimal further objections, she agreed.

This was mainly because there was one more matter she wanted to talk to him about. Deep inside, she hadn't wanted to broach it, but knew it was an order from her father, and she had little option but to do as she had been told. From her years of living with him, she knew for sure that he would only send someone else to ask, in her place, if she did not obey him to the letter, and carry out his wishes.

'My father would like to meet you, to thank you personally,' she said, hesitantly, as they walked together down the steep, winding hill until they reached the straight road that ran across Par Moor. After the never-ending showers the hill had almost become a waterfall. As it poured down onto the track the excess water soaked their shoes and left the hem of her dress dirty and dripping wet. 'I don't really want to put you through the ordeal,' she added, 'though I must. He wondered if you would take tea with us next Sunday.'

The refusal came to his lips instantly. James didn't particularly want to 'take tea' with anyone, and he was not convinced that she, for her part, was at all anxious to have him accept the invitation.

'Tell him not to worry about thanking me. You put yourself out to come to see me today, and that's enough,' he answered sharply.

Despite the fact that he had turned down the offer almost without any consideration, she persisted, unwillingly he thought, but she persisted.

His main trouble was that he was unsure how to treat her - as a young and assured woman, or wayward child. The idea was growing within him though, that whatever her true character, her mind was very much her own.

'My father's extremely persuasive,' she stressed. 'He doesn't ask, he issues summonses.' Sighing, she then smiled at him yet again, weakly, the light never reaching her eyes that were to some extent assessing rather than innocent. 'I've said that badly, I can see you've got strong opinions too. It will make you all the more determined not to go. I have to tell you, as well, that he does have a great deal of influence. You saved my life, of that we're all sure. For that he won't send you away empty-handed.'

'So you think the promise of a reward is enough to make me trot along to your home like a good and grateful boy?'

In spite of speaking lightly and without malice, he quickly wondered if she might take the words to heart.

'My father is Richard Courteney,' she continued, as if he had never spoken. 'I wouldn't like to think how many lives he has control over. He runs a huge number of railway companies, mines and china clay businesses. I couldn't begin to tell you them all. Indeed, he has an interest in almost anything that makes money around here.'

The words slowly began to make an impact on James. In the back of his mind he remembered with greater clarity the details he had been told of her family, although he had initially thought them mostly uninformed gossip and exaggeration. After all, her Uncle Matthew didn't exactly live in sprawling and luxurious surroundings in Charlestown. Glancing down, he slyly studied her as she walked effortlessly by his side. There had been few loving phrases in her description of Richard Courteney.

'Do I read into what you've just told me that you're not utterly over-fond of your father?' At his suggestion her face didn't cloud, and nor did she turn away. All she did was shrug her slim shoulders.

'He and I just see the world in different ways, that's all. It's probably down to us being from different generations with opposing ideas, or maybe that's my excuse. I am, and always have been I think, a great disappointment to him. I'm a woman when he always wished for a son, but I also put forward my own ideas, which well-bred ladies shouldn't do. Uncle Matthew doesn't expect so much from me, so I'm happier in his company.'

'And what does your father think of Uncle Matthew?'

'That he's a gutless waster.'

'And is he?'

'If that means he doesn't particularly ache to make more money, day by day, then I suppose he is.'

When they reached the parting of the ways she said, very directly: 'You will change your mind and come on Sunday, won't you? You can form your own opinions of my father then. But if you don't come he'll only send me again, or one of his many employees in my place, to urge you to visit us. You see he hates being in anyone's debt.'

James hesitated, and wondered what he had to lose. A few hours couldn't hurt. Surely his tolerance could stretch that far?

'All right,' he agreed. 'I don't want to offend such an influential man as your father now do I?'

Relieved by his reply, she produced a piece of paper from her pocket and gave it to him.

'It has my address and a map on it to our house, 'Trevarnioc'. I was already prepared for you to accept. I can sometimes be as determined as father dear, although I trust never as ruthless as he.'

111

In the intervening days between their meeting, and the following Sunday, James began to wish he had obeyed initial instincts and refused the invitation. He was definitely not a man for tea and cakes and small talk.

Thinking about the subject, he didn't believe any of the Rosevean brothers were, except maybe Billy, the youngest. But then Billy was probably too introspective to want to spend time with people he hardly knew. James doubted if anyone truly understood his youngest brother to any real degree at all.

If he had been totally honest with himself he would have admitted it was the mention of wealth that had made him accept. Intuitively, he had decided that someone with a deep knowledge of china clay could not be casually ignored, especially when his own elusive idea of becoming a businessman persisted.

Even though, when Sunday dawned he yearned for rest, not involvement with strangers who, however grateful to him, were bound to see him as outside their class. Way outside.

As Samuel had so bluntly pointed out, despite

their father being able to rule the roost in Biscovey at one time, Biscovey was just a minute speck, even on the local map.

With his knowledge preoccupying him, he groaned as he stood in front of the cracked mirror in his bedroom and studied his reflection, which sported his best and only suit. His almost white hair was smoothed down into some sort of a style, and his shoes polished to a shine they hadn't known for quite a while, but he believed he didn't feel, or look, right. Above everything, he felt a sham.

If I had the damned money, he said aloud, speaking to his mirror image, the future wouldn't be so damned bleak. But I live just above poverty level and real prospects will always be denied me, at least in Cornwall. Perhaps Nathan had the right idea after all. He escaped from predictable tracks before he was stuck on them to the grave. America's probably different, being a new country, one which has rebelled against the rotten, unfairly protected British class system.

While grappling with such assumptions, he told himself he wanted just one chance, however fleeting.

If you could see how quickly I'd grab it, he said aloud, speaking with utter certainty to his neat, sardonic reflection. To hell with anyone who got in my way. I'd make it work, or die in the effort. Better than giving in and dying with nothing achieved.

The gold jewellery, the well-bred speech and the girl's references to her father had prepared him to some extent for what was ahead, but not completely. Helen Courteney's family definitely lived in a fashion far removed from the cramped cottages in Biscovey.

He discovered that 'Trevarnioc', with its seven bedrooms and four reception rooms, stood in a hidden valley on the Mevagissey side of St Austell, a few miles outside the hamlet of London Apprentice. Its grounds stretched for seven, lush and rolling acres, while its majestic driveway meandered through meadows that, he was later assured, were able to boast a blanket of wild daffodils in March, were covered in a spectacular sheen of bluebells in May and were lined with pink, blue and white hydrangeas in August.

After reaching the official arched entrance, with its family crest set in the granite, and a lodge house nestling at the side of it, he wandered further into Courteney land, and found that the immense scale of it staggered him. It also caused the nagging doubts to set in in greater intensity.

When he finally emerged from a forest of vegetation to see a huge, greystone building with a vast array of windows, together with two impressive wings built either side of its main block, rising before him, he could hardly credit that such a slip of a girl was even associated with the place, except perhaps as a scullery maid.

It's all a hoax, he told himself, at that moment truly imagining that it was, and that he was a dupe to have even bothered to make the journey there.

But seconds later Helen came into sight, running to greet him as soon as he emerged from the end of the drive.

By then he was so stupefied by the grandeur of the grounds that all he could manage to murmur to her was: 'I had no idea.'

This time she was wearing a dark, long smart skirt and a bodice that made her look exceptionally prim. It disguised her thin figure and added strength and a surprising maturity. Nothing had been done to enhance her short brown hair, though. There were no curls, no bows or ribbons, or bowing to fashion - and there was hardly any colour in her whole appearance.

'Why should you have had a true idea?' she answered, gazing around her. 'I was little more than a drowned rat when you first saw me, and up to very childish tricks. I was hardly in a state to give you my full pedigree. And I'm never that forthcoming about my background anyway. I hate to say it but apart from being slightly embarrassed about it, I may well take it all for granted. The money has flowed in for as long as I can remember, and no doubt will continue to do so. Father's too . . too dedicated to his, our, survival for it to fail, although that may be to the detriment of everything else.'

He heard the bitterness again, then convinced himself it was his imagination. She was bubbling with welcome. Rich girl she might be, but she was immediately as relaxed in his lowly company on her home ground as she had been in the much plainer, earthier, surroundings of the cottage. But he was soon to discover that her relaxed attitude did not extend to her mother.

They mounted the stone steps to the massive front door together, and a smartly dressed servant appeared, intent on leading them into one of the sumptuously decorated reception rooms where Eva Courteney was waiting, in all her glory, to grant him an audience.

Within seconds he formed a negative opinion of her, finding her, from the outset, gushing, overdressed and condescending. Before even having a decent conversation with her he felt she managed to make him totally aware of the yawning gap that stretched between her good self and stock such as he.

Like her daughter she was barely 5' tall. The difference was Helen just seemed to accept her height, Eva tried to cheat it. He believed the towering hair style and unusually high shoes were all meant to make her appear taller. Instead, he thought they made her seem totally out of proportion.

For a long second they stared at each other after he sat down precariously on the edge of one of the gilt-coloured chairs, surrounded by overpowering original oil paintings and tapestries.

In the strained atmosphere, so at odds with the few minutes she had spent with James outside, Helen wished herself far from her stilted home. Nevertheless, she sat quietly as the visitor and her mother assessed each other until, eventually, Eva thought she ought to seize control of the situation, and lilted in her apparently unnaturally high-pitched voice:

'Tell me Mr Rosevean, where do you originate from?'

At first he felt like answering: Where do you think, the moon? Instead he murmured:

'Biscovey, which is where I still live.'

'Oh, I'm not that familiar with where that is.'

Automatically he smiled, sure she did know, especially as her brother-in-law lived only a short distance away from the hamlet he had been born in.

However, the family, apart from Helen, apparently disapproved of Uncle Matthew, and he guessed never visited Charlestown as a result. Perhaps she was telling the truth. Eventually he decided to be as magnanimous towards her as he could find it within himself to be, and he murmured: 'I wouldn't be surprised if you hadn't heard of it. It doesn't take up much space on the map.'

'And your father? Tell me, what does he do?' continued Eva, in her artificial and imperious way.

James saw Helen, seated uncomfortably opposite him, pale at that. Aware that she seemed almost as ill at ease in her mother's company as he did, he wanted to tell her not to be worried, as the woman's cold questioning didn't bother him. All it did was destroy whatever nerves he had been battling with. Rarely did he allow himself to be hurt, or insulted.

'My father is dead.'

There were no whispered condolences.

'Well, what did he do when he was alive?'

James sat right back in the chair, now deliberately lounging instead of sitting in the expected, respectful position.

As he had trekked along the driveway and had realised how wealthy the family was, he had told himself to swallow pride and be over-polite if anything. The trouble was he didn't particularly care about adopting manners any longer.

Given a few hours in Eva's company, he mused, I could be easily tempted to strangle her. That short, thick neck with its double chins and appalling necklaces almost begs for it. Why on earth is Helen so touchy about her father when it's her mother who seems to deserve the loathing?

Finally, he, pointedly, answered: 'He worked in the nearest mine most of his life, until he became ill and had to stay at home, coughing up his guts. He became mine captain, which justified his life for him, and he was a die-hard Anglican. There were many who respected him, I have to say but from my view he had neither sympathy, nor understanding, but then I suppose many of us lack both of those qualities, don't we Mrs Courteney?'

The sentiments kept her quiet for a while and, as she grimly poured herself another drink, Helen seized the initiative. Striving to freeze her mother out of the conversation, she turned her back on her and spoke straight to James, thinking how much older he looked in his suit. Older and with an air of authority that reminded her of her father.

That disturbed her as much as did her uncontrollably fast pulse rate, though she deliberately kept her voice, and the subject matter, cool when relating the history of the house, built two centuries before by the same Rashleigh family from which Charles, the renovator of Charlestown, had emerged via marriage.

Trying to put her reaction to one side, she enquired about his brothers, especially about Samuel, the only one she had met. She asked about Bethany, and did her level best at the same time to ensure that her mother, for whom she had come to feel only detached pity, remained silent. From experience she knew Eva could create irreparable damage to any fledgling relationship, although she realised there were underlying reasons why her mother had gradually turned into the creature that she had unfortunately become. As she sat and watched James instead of her mother, and saw for the first time the slightly cleft chin, while also noticing the guarded eyes that would suddenly blaze with humour, she understood that this was the one relationship she really wanted to protect, even after such a short period of time.

Richard Courteney made a brief, hurried appearance, which was nevertheless long enough for him to make an indelible impression on James, an impact that was to colour his life for years. Richard's unique strength of character was apparent as soon as he charged through the door, eyes sweeping the room to assess what was happening. A big, burly man, he was obviously full of muscle rather than flab.

Absolutely self-possessed, he radiated a dynamic energy that would have taken an age to dim. Even Nathan, James thought, would fade into mediocrity within five minutes of meeting this man.

As it was his wife and daughter, although there in person, paled into nothingness as soon as he appeared. Richard made it undeniably evident that he was head of the household, the almighty provider. At his unuttered bidding they became nonentities. He was sharp-eyed, effusive, critical and immaculately dressed. Under his influence his wife's social veneer and confidence could be seen to ebb away. Helen sank lower into her chair, tried to hide her face in her hair, even though it was so short, and said nothing in a way of greeting. Her father didn't seem to expect anything else from her, seizing on the introductions himself.

'You must be James Rosevean,' he said, grasping his guest's hands together in a tight grip. 'I'm glad Helen was able to lure you here. At least it proves she can accomplish something. I'm afraid I won't be able to spend as much time with you as I had planned. Business dictates otherwise, and I can't afford not to be in quite a few places this afternoon. Sunday it might be, though for me it is no rest day. However, there is long enough for tea, and thanks of course.'

James went to say something, but the host just ploughed on.

'It was extremely lucky for Helen that you were in Charlestown that day, although it was her own foolish fault. I've tried to keep her away from there, but she will insist on going. I'm just sorry she caused you so much inconvenience.'

His guest could very simply have backed away and, like Richard's family, been swallowed up by the man's dominant personality, but pride kept James standing there at eye level, made him pull himself to his full height and meet Richard Courteney's disturbing, unwavering gaze.

'I couldn't let her drown.'

'I'd have been tempted to, but then you weren't completely aware of her stupidity and obstinacy were you?'

James immediately experienced a shaft of sorrow for Helen. With concern for her in mind, he turned around to look at her. She had lifted her head and was looking out of the window, her face elfin in silhouette.

It seemed to James that she was striving to make it appear that she was unconcerned by her father's attitude. Suddenly, he realised she had yet even to acknowledge that he had arrived.'She was stupid to go around so far on the rocks' James agreed, unwillingly speaking of her in the third person when she was but feet from him. 'I must admit that those rocks further out from the base of the cliffs are very slippery. And there was an exceptionally high tide due, though I doubt if she realised that.'

'I doubt it too, but she should have found that out before she went slipping and sliding everywhere. That would have been blindingly obvious to me, and I imagine to you as well.' With his unsympathetic words hanging in the air, Richard then turned to his daughter, who eventually tore her eyes from the outside world, to the inside of the home she hated.

'Take note of what this young man says, girl. Those words came from the lips of someone who knows, and who is obviously wiser than your precious Uncle Matthew could ever be, even if he lived to be a thousand. Now let's move into the other room and eat. As I said I haven't got much time to waste.'

During the meal which, to James, was more like a feast than tea, Richard ate only moderately. Despite keeping his sentences to a minimum, he still succeeded in interviewing the young miner with precision. This was because he went about the task with much more finesse than his wife had done, and before James realised what was happening all the relevant details of his life had been neatly, professionally, extracted from him.

Even the depths of his ambition, which he had kept well hidden from most, were laid uncomfortably bare.

Helen had described her father as ruthless. As he assessed his answers, James soon accepted that with little encouragement, and the right chances, he could probably be too.

Unbidden, he found himself describing the now almost abandoned plans for opening up clay works on Bodmin Moor, as well as talking with cutting regret of the lack of finance and the short-sightedness of his family.

'It was an opportunity,' he said, with more

feeling than he liked to betray. 'A real chance. But it's been thrown away. I shouldn't even be mentioning it. It stirs up too much resentment, all of it unfounded I know, but there all the same.'

It seemed that his host was actually taking note of what he was being told, and James allowed himself the belief that not only was Courteney absorbing his words, but that he was actually interested in his paltry tale, although there was little time for him to expand further. As soon as they had finished eating his host abruptly left. Work, it appeared, ruled most waking hours.

I bet the schedule is welcome though, James thought. I guess he finds little pleasure in the women in his life, he's already made that plain enough.

After the servants had set about clearing the table Helen, released from the restrictions that both parents seemed to place upon her, showed him around the house and extensive, manicured grounds. As they walked, he could fault nothing except, perhaps that a few could own so much while so many struggled.

But if I was handed all this, he asked himself, would I ever have the strength to turn it down? Never. That would be stupidity.

The delicate, unmistakable scent of honeysuckle pervaded the air, and martins and swallows acrobatically skimmed the fields that were 'Trevarnioc' land. As he watched them, he envied them their freedom, and Helen the acres that stretched away into the distance. Also, he envied her the power that money evidently gave her family, though he tried to keep the green-eyed monster firmly under locks.

When he did speak he ensured, as she had

earlier on, that his voice was toneless, matter-of-fact. This day was just a one time occurrence, he reminded himself, which meant that there was no point letting his surroundings influence his feelings, his hopes, his plans.

After reluctantly returning inside he studied the paintings, the china, and the fine furniture with detached interest, at the same time refusing to enthuse over them.

She, in turn, didn't seem to expect him to rant and rave about the quality of her family's possessions, the inlay on the tables, the marquetry on the book cabinet, the ormolu clocks, the John Opie paintings.

Gradually, James formed the impression that she took it all for granted, treated it almost dismissively. Hadn't she as much as admitted that herself already? Would that I could as well, he raged silently.

In the end he stayed for most of the afternoon, then made his excuses to leave as soon as he thought it appropriate. In his mind was the fact that he was due at Bethany at five the following morning, still forced to work there despite its closure becoming more imminent. He thought it ironic that, with the proceeds of just one of the fine pieces of art on show, he could probably buy into clay and secure himself a decent future. Then bitterly accepted the paintings were not his to sell, nor ever would be, so rendering the thought useless.

'I'm glad you came,' she said as she took his coat from one of the maids.

At that point she was smiling, but as soon as her mother walked into the room her expression dulled, flattened again, making her so different from the animated girl who had visited him at his cottage.

James realised, as he saw her expression change, that she had been unsure of herself for most of the time she had been inside her own home, or at least when near either of her parents. Although she tried another smile for him as he reached the door, she failed in the attempt, her mouth remaining as prim as her clothes.

'Father was pleased to be able to thank you personally.'

'I was pleased to meet him. He impressed me a great deal. He was full of energy, and of fire.'

'Oh, he's all that,' she answered slowly, playing with her hands. 'My father is tireless when it comes to business, or money. You know - all that matters, or apparently matters.'

IV

Later that July

It had been a strange day, a step into another world. One he would very much have liked to inhabit, but nevertheless a definitely alien one, and he took it as the end of the affair. Instead it was to be the beginning. Helen reappeared at Biscovey a week later and, at her insistence, he visited 'Trevarnioc' once again, this time to have a longer discussion with Richard Courteney.

'He told me he enjoyed talking with you,' she tried to explain, evidently not happy about coercing him back to her family home. 'You weren't frightened of him. You said exactly what you thought, and much of it he felt was very sensible. Believe me, with him such praise is not usual, or expected.'

'But we hardly spoke at all . . '
'It was enough for him to form an opinion. He was impressed by your confidence.'
You weren't affected by . . . '
'By all your family has, that mine hasn't?'
'If you really want to put it that way, yes.'
She bowed her head so low that he could see the hair parting at the back of her neck. It was a shy gesture which, again, made him think of her as a child.
'I don't think your mother relished my company as much as your father apparently did,' he said with an unrestrained grin, knowing full well that the woman had absolutely abhorred him. Lack of money, and of social status, had as good as branded him a leper.
'Don't take any notice of my mother,' answered Helen, recovering slightly from the effect that the grin had had upon her.
'Unfortunately, I never do these days. The people she pretends to like are in general worthless idiots. The more my father ignores her the more she seems to cling to empty beliefs that I know aren't really hers.'

V

October 1873

'There's no chance now of me having a son, of course,' explained Richard to James who wasn't quite sure why he was becoming privy to so many of the man's regrets. 'I can't have a boy, at least not a legitimate one within this sterile marriage of mine. Eva's too old and, besides, the desire I had for her dried up a long time ago.
'I suppose I could spread these wings of mine,

tie myself to someone younger, which I can assure you is not hard when you have money behind you. But, believe me, if I went as far as divorce society, hypocritical as it is, would frown upon me. And I do rely on my social position for business purposes. Helen may tell you that I revel in it, but that's not true, it's just a necessary part of existence.'

James shifted uneasily in his chair, not really wanting to hear Eva being denigrated, no matter how much he disliked her. He was still a relative stranger to Richard, and being his confidante was not a position he felt he should be able to enjoy, or even be privy to.

How do I handle this, he asked himself, still uncomfortable, as well, in the opulent surroundings. I don't want to alienate myself from him. I have a real feeling that he's someone I want on my side.

Richard carried on with his soliloquy and his regrets, totally unaware of his guest's dilemma.

'I shall have to hope Helen chooses a son-in-law for me who I can trust, but so far there's been no-one who impresses me in the least. If there had been I would have very forcefully pushed her in his direction. The men, or should I say boys, she meets through social channels, are usually weak fools, with no craving for success. They've inherited money and gone through life with everything handed to them, so that the hunger to achieve more has never been born within them.

'And don't stare at me like that. She may look like a baby to you, but I can assure you she's a very opinionated young woman. It is just an absolutely damned pity she's not male.'

They were in the reading room, or rather Richard Courteney's private retreat where only he usually set foot. Certainly no-one else ever went in there on their own. Its contents were entirely masculine. Charts, some tanned and curling with age, were spread on the table, while a wide variety of maps littered the walls. There were umpteen diagrams of Cornish mine workings, various quite detailed outlines of proposed railway routes, graphs of profits and loss. And a Turner seascape haphazardly hanging above the bureau.

'Is having a son so important?' ventured James, trying to insert some of his own opinions into the conversation. 'Helen's not male, there's no denying that of course, but it seems to me that she's bright enough. I'm sure, in fact, that she's more able and intelligent than most.'

'Maybe, maybe. But business doesn't interest her, especially mine. Even if I involved her in my affairs I know she'd hang back if it came to the kill. She wouldn't fight for money, which I'm sure you'd do if you had the opportunity. I can sense the zeal in you. Tell me, how does your own little scheme progress?'

There was a short silence during which James wished that particularly telling question hadn't been raised.

'If you want the truth,' he said eventually and apologetically, 'the idea's still there, but that's about all. I still haven't enough funds, despite starting to save, nor can I find enough from elsewhere, to make it work.'

'And what of your friend who had the initial idea and wants to go into partnership with you?'

'I'm afraid his savings go down by the day. Drinking and gambling see to that. We haven't the same social position as you, sir, or the same often very handy business acquaintances.'

Any confidence that was in his voice gradually faded away because he knew very well that he was making excuses, and Helen's father allowed that impression to stay with him.

'Can't speaks too much of defeat, surely? There's no use hanging back. Barge into the fray. You won't achieve anything otherwise. And play by no rules but your own, I can tell you that. For pity's sake don't be timid because you're afraid of hurting someone. Drum it into that thick-skulled family, and those friends of yours that you need the cash, or else it's a case of them eventually having to scratch around because you, and they, will be without work.'

James had little idea why the man even bothered with his company. There was nothing he could offer Richard Courteney, or his various wealthy and expanding companies.

Nevertheless, the Sunday afternoon invitations kept coming, and he kept accepting them. Although he repeatedly told himself that he should bring a halt to what he saw as a charade, the other world of high finance and apparent opportunity drew him like a materialistic magnet. It was where he wanted to be.

And 'Trevarnioc', with its richness and possessions, was inordinately compelling. Once inside its walls he was taken way out of his mundane existence and propelled into one that liberated his mind.

The only drawback was Helen. It came to him gradually, as he was drawn deep into the Courteney web, that the initial gratitude that she had shown him was being replaced by something deeper. If it wasn't love then he imagined it to be infatuation.

Her small, oval face lit up visibly when he was near, with the almond shaped eyes misting in expectation. Whenever possible it seemed that she edged towards his side, held his arm, approved of his ideas. And it slowly dawned on him that if ever he looked down there she was, staring up at him with total, rapt approval in her steady hazel gaze. He knew it was a development he should halt. Both of them were indulging in acts of escapism. For him 'Trevarnioc' wasn't real, nor were the dreams that Richard Courteney tempted him with. They belonged to a privileged world that wasn't his - although he still clung to them as Helen had begun to cling to him.

Certainly, he didn't reciprocate any feelings of love. Maybe he liked the girl, yes, but that was all. Perhaps he enjoyed being with her, appreciated her wit and young laughter, but he didn't physically desire her. When he looked at her body he still saw it as belonging to a child, as he had done when he had dragged her, apparently inert, from the waves.

There had been sexual games available with certain girls from the village since he had turned the age of fifteen, and he had actively sought the infrequent, illicit nights spent with a willing partner in isolated coves or long abandoned cottages. However, nothing had developed past fleeting attraction and the panting, sweet lust of the moment. And independence was something he had always treasured.

When he asked Helen to marry him he was almost in a trance. The voice did not seem to be his. It came from the unknown areas within the subconscious where his materialistic need burned so bright. It was egged on by the belief that, by some miracle, he was within reach of a solution to his persisting dreams. The girl herself played little part in the decision.

But, despite choosing to step into the future with her as his wife he continued to regard her as gentle, but easily forgettable, quiet although not retiring, undemanding and easy to please. A partner, he presumed, who would give him very little trouble, and who would fade into the background without argument and bring, as a dowry, some exceptionally necessary advantages.

The proposal was made, as well, because he knew that her father didn't disapprove of him and, above all, was able to offer him opportunities which otherwise would be beyond his grasp. He asked because, although his pretence at wanting to make Helen his wife was a sham, it provided him with a future he could not resist striving to win for himself.

Eva objected, of course, but James was initially not too concerned about that, believing that her opinion counted as less than nothing in the Courteney household. And as for Helen, she was seemingly more than content with the situation. Not only did she want to be with James, she also frequently told him that she desperately needed to escape from the confines of 'Trevarnioc'.

James, himself, was hoping to bind himself to the family because of his prospective father-in-law's overwhelming social influence, but his future wife saw the marriage as a means of self-imposed exile from it - and escape.

One fear James did come to harbour,

eventually, despite his previous belief that she was irrelevant, was that Eva would, eventually, find a way of wrecking his route to wealth, knowing she at least had enough insight to see his marriage proposal for the calculated move that it was. But he had not learnt enough of the Courteneys to take into account Richard's absolutely overwhelming influence. Nor did he quite grasp that the master of the St Austell mansion, and owner of the riches, saw matters from a very different perspective to those of his wife. From the outset Richard had sensed raw talent in James, a talent he believed he himself had harboured aplenty since youth, this being the ability to seek out success at all costs. He itched to mould the young miner's drive and ambition, to harness it and watch it work for monetary and personal gain. To bring it into the family and under his control.

His understanding was that he had found in the young, basically simply-influenced miner, a new line to pushing, burgeoning, very pliable youth, an ingredient he and his expanding companies needed. And Helen could at last do something worthwhile and tie such energy, and lack of real guile, to the family for him.

For a while he had been afraid that his daughter, in her desire to oppose him, would link herself to someone like his brother, devoid of motivation - or someone who had taken life so easily up to that point because of their wealth that they wanted to be cosseted and little else. Matthew, content to waste his life observing wildlife around a small china clay harbour, dismayed him, as did the coterie of most of his friends' so-called eligible sons. When James finally did understand Richard's views he felt a mixture of elation and guilt. Overall, he wished, if only to enhance himself in his own eyes, that the driving reason behind his decision to marry, hadn't been greed. Nevertheless, in the face of all the doubts, as well as his own mother's disapproving silence, and Samuel's wry, depreciating remarks, he avidly carried on with the deception he knew he was playing upon Helen.

December 1873

V1

They married at Holy Trinity Church, in St Austell, during December 1873, three days after the bride celebrated her 18th birthday. James had recently turned 26.
The church stood, grand and grey, in the middle of the bustling market town, its inner and outer splendour a fitting backdrop to any public occasion. And the wedding was very public. The day passed amidst a flurry of wealth and pomp, and the large gathering of guests enjoyed a spectacle that was celebrated in a style that was way beyond anything either the bride or groom, who were both anxious only for anonymity, had envisaged.
James had hoped for a quiet ceremony, over almost before it had begun. Those ideas, however, had fallen far short of Eva's plans. Helen, despite trying her utmost to talk her parents out of interfering too much, eventually and reluctantly, as if to pacify her mother's horror at the match, left all the organisation to her. As a result, it became a bloated extravaganza. If nothing else was to go right for her daughter then Eva felt at least she had

to be feted properly.

There were flowers by the bucketful, lines of bridesmaids, choirs, ribbons and bows, a coterie of Richard's wealthy associates and laden tables lined with more food than anyone could gorge.

The Roseveans wilted under the vast public pressure. Half-way through the wedding breakfast Mary slipped home, unable to take the sly glances and remarks any longer. Few, it seemed, approved of Helen's choice of partner, or rather what they saw as the choice that had been made for her. Reasons for that, though, may have included jealousy at James's good fortune in stepping, in one genius move, from obscurity into a rich and prospering family.

It was generally agreed that James himself had been won over by money rather than love when it came to the betrothal. And he, himself, heard much of what was being said, but stayed guiltily silent, knowing the truth of it.

Samuel almost stirred up a fight after overhearing one disparaging comment about his family, and the younger brothers swallowed too much beer and threatened to bring it back, along with their meal, in front of a clutch of guests. However, the 'almosts' never quite became the actual. The near incidents were lost amongst the overall melee created by Eva's apparent desire to outdo any wedding that had gone before, or would come after.

There were moments when James felt like disappearing from the circus of the day and admitting to all and sundry that, indeed, he was making a gigantic mistake, but those moments were fleeting. In reality, he went through with his avid social climbing game. Standing in front of the minister he made the right responses, trying at the same time not to look too frequently at the trusting girl by his side who was blithely offering not only herself, but much more besides.

And that much more is unfortunately what really matters to me, he thought as he placed the ring on her finger. Not that childish body of yours, nor that shy, trembling smile.

The strategy paid off instantly. For a wedding present her father had bought them a home standing in half an acre in the wooded hamlet of Tregrehan, just over a mile from Biscovey. James had already been there and investigated every square inch of his new property. To the east of its boundary lay Bodelva and the local mine workings, while to the west were the sprinkling of cottages and the chapel which constituted the village of Bethel.

A twisting lane linked the rather impressive driveway with the nearby main Plymouth road which was under increasing use from horse-drawn traffic, while the garden was completely private, overlooked by no neighbours.

Cornwall was slowly, and to a great degree unwillingly, being dragged out of its isolation and away from the cherished and definite belief that it was a Celtic nation wanting to stay forever apart from the rest of England. Brunel's impressive railway bridge had been built to span the River Tamar, and the way into Kernow from Devon was well and truly open.

It was to the house at Tregrehan that the groom and his young bride went when the overblown celebrations were finally finished. As he walked into the impressive house that was now his, but which he had paid no money for, the unwanted guilt suddenly bit hard. James found himself critically surveying the furniture, and the little luxuries that had been provided even since his last visit there.

It's all coming too simply and quickly, he panicked. Surely I'll have to pay for it in the long run, one way or another? It's inevitable. Slyly, he glanced at Helen, realising she had been quiet and reclusive, and had been since the crowds and the guests had closed in on her. Also, the idea was growing on him, that she was also wiser than he had given her credit for, and had probably assessed his motives for the marriage almost as soon as he had quietly asked her to tie herself to him for the rest of their lives.

Later, as they both moved hesitantly towards the largest bedroom of the three, the one she had chosen for them, she caught him by his right arm. By then, she had changed out of her ivory silk wedding dress, with its dramatic train which had given her small figure so much impact, and all that he saw was the extreme youth of her, coupled with the inexperience.

'Don't bother to pretend any passion. It really won't be necessary,' she said with a boldness that startled him.

At her blunt honesty guilty shivers ran riot down his back and he instinctively looked away from her so that she could not read whatever was showing in his eyes.

Has she seen through everything? he thought. But he still continued trying to play out the charade.

'What does that mean?'

Gently, she sat on the bed, and put her head in her hands for a while, so her newly washed hair fell in front of her face like a small, brown curtain, and then she straightened up to regard him with a soft, yet unwavering gaze. 'It's obvious you don't love me, in fact if I was pushed I would say that you're not even attracted to me.'

'Helen.'

At that he had caught her arms, and tried to protest but in reply she laughed him down. It was a gentle laugh, not at all melodramatic, and as such it affected him more than any dramatic tears of self-pity would have done. 'Don't look so offended. I've known from the start you prefer me as a friend more than anything else, such as a wife or lover. I'm not a glorious beauty, nor is my personality so wonderful that I charm everyone around me.'

As she spoke she sunk further back onto the bed, pulling herself upwards so that her back was lying against the cushions. After the very many stresses of the day she was exceptionally tired. She had just kicked off her silken wedding shoes, bought after much searching by her mother in a store in the heart of Bristol. They were the last vestiges of her finery. Watching her, he decided that he needed a few moments to assess the situation with some clarity, and wandered to the window. On the way he touched her shining hair with his fingers.

Outside night had fallen on the surrounding woods. It looked a different world than it had done an hour before - mysterious and powerful. The exact opposite to his wife. Bereft of her expensive clothes she suddenly seemed to him to be more inconsequential than ever. Although her bold words hinted at a character with hidden depths.

'Why do you think I married you?' he asked.

Finally leaving the window, he sat on the bed too, wanting to be more on her level. While standing he felt as if he had been deliberately dominating her.

At his question she smiled into the growing blackness. They had yet to light the lamps fully.

'Escape, in the same way as I have taken escape,' she answered softly. 'Nathan took one way out, you took another. You wanted life outside Bethany, but you couldn't work out how to create a new existence for yourself. You wanted to buy into that china clay venture of yours, but you didn't have enough money, or your family's support. I provided the answers, or rather my dear father did. And besides, I have a feeling I'm likeable enough for you to put up with.'

The bed was tidy. Complete with her nightgown and his night clothes laid out upon its pink counterpane. Waiting for them to be joined beneath its brand new sheets. But at that moment the bride and groom were most definitely apart. When this moment came he had expected her to be scared, sketching for himself a mental picture in which she was trusting, timid beneath a brittle exterior of being blase. It was a picture coloured by Richard's throwaway comments on her personality.

Instead, she had tackled what he had expected to have been a forbidden subject head-on, and was astonishing him again with her unexpected self-confidence. At her words, he stared openly at her, briefly wondering how much her father knew of her strengths, or her soul.

'Good God, and you went ahead knowing, or rather thinking that?'

'Of course. Here I am with a ring on my finger officially announcing that I'm your legal wife. I do believe, though, that whatever happens to us in the future you'd never purposefully hurt, or deceive, me.

To sound so certain, and yet be so naive, he thought as he stifled an unwanted yawn. It had been a long, tiring and trying pantomime of a day, made all the more ridiculous by the pomp surrounding it.

'Face up to reality, Helen. I've already deceived you, haven't I? In fact you've already told me as much.'

Wishing to emphasise the fact he leant forward towards her as he spoke, moving so suddenly that his white-blond hair fell into his eyes. As if in challenge she also moved towards him, edging so near he could smell the natural freshness of her. Instinctively, she pushed his fringe away, letting as she did so, her clean, scrubbed nails gently brush his brow.

She's too young to be married, he reproached himself, remembering how he had thought her about 12, or only slightly older, when he had lifted her, sodden and limp, from the sea. Too young to cope with all I want to throw at her, perhaps to accept that if her father had not garnered so much influence I would not be here.

Although she had an idea of what way his thoughts were turning, Helen manoeuvred herself into his arms, enjoying the physical contact, the feel of his flesh on hers, his breath on her face. She ached to let him know how much she adored him, but the pride she had inherited from her father refused to allow her to.

'Not really deceived me. You've never told

me you love me. I know, but I'm positive you'll come to care as much for our marriage as I already do. I suppose I've gambled on that, on you being not half as much like my father as he evidently believes you are. I haven't walked into this with my eyes closed, please believe me.'

After those words their love-making was shy and awkward. She was a virgin and although she insisted she wanted him to take her, he couldn't quite overcome the somehow fixed conviction that he was forcing himself upon her.

'You don't have to tonight,' he had whispered hesitantly. 'I know . . I know it's your first time. I can wait until you're sure you're ready. I don't want to make you do anything you don't want to do.'

'You mean you've taken me as a wife in name, supposedly bound yourself to me for the rest of your life, but you don't want my body?'

Staggered again by how forthright she was, he could only mumble in reply: 'No . . no, I don't want you to believe that either.'

As she had taken them off, she had neatly folded her clothes, and then stacked them on a chair by the bed, glancing at him every now and then to see if he was watching. He was. Despite everything he had said, and thought, he couldn't help himself. It seemed incredible to him that this boyish, slim girl with the taut thighs and still ripening breasts was completely his. Now a girl of eighteen, to have whenever he wanted.

He slid into her as slowly as he could, not wanting to hurt her but at the same time finding it almost impossible to contain his mounting excitement. But he could not prevent her eyes widening in reaction as he thrust between her legs, though, despite all intentions to take everything calmly and slowly.

Seeing that he tried to withdraw, but she clutched tightly to him, winding her legs around him, determined not to let him go. As if striving to encourage him she arched her body and moved with him, though he could feel she was still trembling and tense. He wasn't convinced by the show of enthusiasm and his conscience, when it surfaced above the rutting desire, remained uneasy. But eventually he was lost inside her small, soft body and could concentrate only on the wanting and the brief, amazing ecstasy ahead. When their senses returned to normal, and they lay side by side, both damp with sweat, moving but not touching, he knew for sure that the act had come as a shock to her. She could not disguise the truth that was there in her eyes, in her far from relaxed movements. Instinctively, he tried to reassure her, but whenever he tried to form the words she refused to let him apologise.

'I asked you to make love to me. I wanted you,' he whispered. 'It gave me pleasure. Please believe that.'

After all the trials of the day, and the emotions that had been stirred, tiredness overwhelmed him. Although he fought against it, sleep was creeping up on him, and the exertions of the past hours were telling. The darkness was complete now.

Turning towards his new wife, he could hardly see the unbearably trusting face on the next, freshly laundered pillow. There was an owl outside, not far away at all, and something seemed to be moving stealthily through the undergrowth that stretched right up to the bedroom and needed to be cleared. A fox?

Perhaps I could cultivate a quarter of an acre or so, he thought blearily, but that's in the future. Then he wondered what she was thinking, and whether she had truly meant those words of hers. However, he quickly and deliberately pushed the guilt aside, something he had become very adept at doing. Ruefully, he accepted he had never felt deeply enough about anyone or anything to experience real, heart-searching guilt at any hurt he had caused.

If she wants pretence, like me, then she can have it, he concluded.

But one annoying image did remain. That of Uncle Matthew, so much older and more decrepit than he had imagined, confronting him at the wedding.

'I know Richard's using you,' he had said, 'and so do you. That doesn't worry me too much. You two can play as many nasty games as you want. If you hurt Helen, though, then the situation changes, and I won't just sit by.'

Well if Helen herself and her father are on my side, James thought fuzzily as he drifted into slumber, I'm sure as hell not going to worry about Eva or Uncle Matthew, especially as he looks as if he won't be wandering this earth much longer.

January 1874

V11

The summons to appear before his father-in-law came three weeks after the wedding. By then both he, and his new wife, had settled into a kindly, ultra polite routine. There was no constant passion, at least on his part, no real highs, but immense consideration for each other.

When he allowed himself to think in depth about their relationship James supposed that she was content with him. It took painfully little to make her small bow of a mouth curve into a grin, and her arms stretch out to greet him, although what was most obvious was the gleam of freedom that constantly lit her liquid hazel eyes. By then he could understand why it was there. There was no mother to pacify continually. No father to avoid because she so diametrically opposed the views he demanded she should hold.

In bed they remained tentative with each other, despite James no longer regarding every aspect of lovemaking as an assault on her. In a short while he had come to terms with their slightly strained intimacy, and believed that, personally, he couldn't really ask for anything more physically earth-shattering than that. For his part sex was a duty more than anything else, a fraction of the bargain he had taken on. And if there was little burning desire within him as he caressed and kissed her, how on earth could he complain?

He told himself it would be optimistic in the extreme to expect an explosion of the senses. What did annoy him was that he had not yet managed to quit Bethany, a situation which also depressed him in spite of the vast changes in his personal life. In a bid to shake off the discontent, he told himself he had more than enough with a new home and embarrassingly wealthy in-laws without wanting more.

But he did. Deep in his mind he knew he wanted money, he yearned for social status, and above all he wished both of these would flutter to his feet without the need to beg, or sell his soul. The extent of his dreams did worry him. They had never been quite so evident before he had met Richard Courteney, but since then he had had to accept that they had become a vital part of him that he couldn't defeat, or ignore.

However, until the note arrived from Richard, he had gone out of his way to avoid 'Trevarnioc' since the wedding. Helen had shown no wish to visit her parents, so the prospect of even travelling near the Courteney mansion had not arisen. James was still taking stock of his new existence, discovering what barriers he could safely push himself through. With luck, and the right moves, he knew there was much more he could achieve, but he understood he had to progress with some tact. Surely he couldn't barge in demanding cash from his father-in-law for this and that, just because he had married a rich and impressionable young girl. Could he?

The truth was he still had to absorb exactly what kind of man Helen's father was, and what kind of attitude he respected. However, he was to learn much more when he was finally alone with him again.

After being summoned to 'Trevarnioc' James was instantly struck again by the vitality of the man. The magnetism permeating the air around him was infectious, giving the younger man the impression that he only had to breathe in some of the same oxygen in order to equal Richard's impregnability.

Helen's father was bulky, fearsome, and over 6'4", but in no way ponderous. More than anything else he impressed. The strong, bearded face with its deep, etched lines, the critical gaze, the beautifully cut dark clothes demanded attention. Typically he came directly to the point. There was no waste whatsoever in his life, particularly when it came to words or emotions.

He spoke quietly, but distinctly.

'It's been a while since I saw you. Too long. I meant to arrange this earlier, but I've been too busy. The wedding was a wash-out. Too much of a petty nonsense to be able to carry out any business after the ceremony, but then that was entirely Eva's fault. Tell me, are you still hoping to go into partnership with that friend of yours, or have all the plans fallen through?'

Strangely James had only been speaking to Ned a few days before. A chance meeting again, that had taken place outside of the Rashleigh Arms, had developed into a full-blown discussion which had served to refuel his enthusiasm. The difference was that this time he had been able to talk of the future knowing that money was so close to him. It was only a question, a demand away. Something Ned, who had already drunk more than a few pints of the local Walter Hicks ale, had forcibly reminded him of.

'It's the reason you wed the maid,' he had said, and not under his breath despite the throng around them. 'Surely it was? I know you're more than interested in being your own boss, you don't have to tell me that. Now that money is as good as in your hands go and grab it. Wrastle it out of her old man. Dig it out. You can do it well enough with the ore.'

'All right, don't push me, I'll get there d'rectly,' James had answered roughly, wishing Helen hadn't been mentioned, wanting to keep her separate from the rest of his world.'

'D'rectly isn't good enough in this case, and you know it,' Ned had protested. 'The chance won't be there long. It's bound to pass. Maybe we've frittered away too much time as it is.'

They had moved deep inside the Rashleigh by then and James was staring fixedly into his own beer, as if the froth or the dark liquid had held all the answers.

'You're sure I didn't marry 'cause I loved her then?'

Ned, wed to long-suffering Beth for over 20 years, had tittered at that, baring his yellow teeth as he did so.

'I've seen youngsters lost to love in my years. They moon and they mope and turn stupid. None of that's happened to you now, has it? But then I s'pose you're no real youngster. None of you Rosevean boys ever seem to have been them. Except Billy. Now he's different to the rest of you.'

No, there had been no such signs James thought as he stood uneasily before Helen's father, annoyed that he was so far from being relaxed. He wondered if he should ask if it bothered Richard that although he'd married Helen, if the truth was known, he had no deep feelings for her.

Instead he answered: 'I'm still talking about the idea, but I've got to admit that talking is all there's been. And dreaming. The more so as the price of tin plummets and my job, and those of my brothers, are put further in danger.'

Richard Courteney smiled, although the slight movement of his facial muscles was masked by a new growth of steel grey beard. It was not his daughter's smile, given freely to lift the spirits of herself or others. There was no warmth there.

'I must say even though I was lax in sending for you I had expected a visit from your good self before now. I thought you'd be hammering at my door as soon as you were officially part of this family. Don't try to tell me that the prospect of coming face to face with Eva kept you away. Surely you know how to handle her stupidities by now?'

James shifted. For some reason his ankle was hurting. He couldn't remember knocking it. The pain nagged at him as his feet sunk into the soft, plush, pastel coloured rug.

I'll soon have no control over the conversation, he thought, if I ever have done. I ought to be open with him, tell him I didn't want to rush too quickly in case I overplayed my hand.

'I didn't want it to seem I was begging for your family's help,' he ventured, nervously pushing back his hair. 'After all, you hold the purse strings and I already live in a house that is mine only due to your charity. I don't particularly enjoy crawling on my knees, even though I do enough of it in that blasted mine.'

Richard moved to the drinks cabinet, quickly surveying the line of bottles before deftly pouring each of them an expensive brandy. Notably, he didn't bother to ask James what was his preference.

'I must say your reticence surprises me. I'd

expected a harder approach, I would have wagered a good-sized sum you would have come to me asking, demanding, or trying to trick me out of a loan by now.'

James took a tense gulp of the brandy to strengthen his nerves, and warm the icy pit in his stomach. He was beginning to grasp the fact that Richard would never have condemned him for asking for money, as long as it was tied to ambition and sound business sense.

Hell, he told himself, taking another sip of the French Napoleon and this time letting it roll comfortingly around his tongue, he's encouraging, guiding, almost rebuking me for not doing this earlier. Poor Helen, what with her father and me both pushing for our own needs I b'lieve she had little choice at all on our marriage. We both went for what we could get, and he's well and truly got me.

'Begging came harder than I thought it would, that's all I can say,' he tried to explain, accepting that it sounded lame.

Richard began pacing the room, which had been made to appear larger than it was by strategically placed mirrors. It was in fact small by 'Trevarnioc's' grandiose standards. With his beard and explosive energy Richard reminded James of a caged lion, inside bars totally against his will, anxious only to be outside stalking prey, hunting for warm blood.

'Then you'd better start applying yourself to tackling all those things that you find difficult, whatever the cost. Cheat, beg, go out and flatten everyone else, but make sure that you're feared, not ignored. I don't want a run-of-the-mill out-of-work miner as a son-in-law. I don't want anyone like that even associated with my name.

'You must know I have faith in your ideas. I've shown enough interest in them, and I had understood that Helen and I had ensnared someone with desire, and stamina. I want you to go ahead with your scheme. I've told you before that when you want something you should apply yourself to getting it, no matter what the opposition, or expected opposition.'
Eventually, he stopped striding and halted in front of James and, with great emphasis, placed both hands on the young man's shoulders, feeling reassured that they seemed gladiatorially strong and rippling with muscles. A true young fighter.
To the newest member of his family his touch was heavy, compelling.
'I trust this will only be the start. In fact I'm sure this will only be the start. Let's say that this is just to test your business ability.'

V111

And so the money came, almost in a way of challenge. It was what James had wanted. It was the root cause of his marriage. But on the day he left Bethany and her so familiar, tortuous maze of levels and adits, for good he was bombarded by doubts. The worries had soon surfaced.
Helen hadn't enthused over his partnership with her father when he had outlined the bargain they had made between them to her. In fact she had retreated deep into herself after he had arrived home, boiling over with news about it, unable to stop bombarding her with information.
In spite of the fact that he had tried to convince himself that all would be well with their joint scheme, her barely concealed

misgivings began to unnerve him. So had the realisation that what he was doing was looking as if it might contribute to splitting his own family - just as Nathan's decision to seek a new life in America had done in the past.

This time the raw bitterness had not come from Samuel, however, despite his previous harsh words on the subject. The vitriol had stemmed from Alex instead. Nevertheless, it was soon obvious that while the accusation came from a different brother, his crime was still apparently the same one, that of betrayal.

'You're selling out, that's what you're doing,' Alex had protested, immediately after he fully grasped what was happening - his intense, deceptively pale face signalling every thought.

'What on earth are you talking about?' James had argued, confused by the reaction, so certain that what he was embarking upon was bound, in the long run, to be approved by everyone. 'I'm buying in. Buying for the future of all of us, and you can have a great part of whatever I achieve.'

'You must be mad. Become a boss. I want none of what you've got to offer. I intend to stay on my own level, fighting for my own kind. I don't want to go round pandering to those who already have most of the advantages going.'

Alex had the slightest build of all five brothers, carrying none of the bulk of his father and, as a result, James still regarded him as little more than a youngster. There was no hard sinew evident in his chest or shoulders, his face was smooth and completely unlined, his waist as trim as a vain young woman's. But the fire of maturity did blaze from his open, blue-flecked eyes and there was a determined set to the straight, sharp nose and the wise, thin-lipped mouth. There wasn't enough, though, for James to take him seriously. With Nathan gone he regarded Samuel as his only worthy adversary.

'What do you think I'm doing, turning my back on you and running as far as possible as Nathan did? I'm staying here among my own kind, staying to set up business, create jobs, help.'

The statement, made with obvious irritation, didn't impress Alex. As he watched James in full flow, breath rasping from his powerful torso in obviously suppressed anger, it only succeeded in making him think that eventually, with the money he now had access to, his brother could become not only a bigot, but a bore.

'How benevolent of you,' he sneered. 'And while you're on your way to making a fortune for Samuel, Billy, mother and I, how are you going to repay your workers? Do you intend to give them the best wages and conditions you can?'

James blinked at the unexpected turn of the conversation.

For pity's sake, I've got to prove the company viable first, he thought. Damned well prove a few things to my father-in-law, carve out some self-respect. High wages are miles from my mind at the moment.

'If I can - eventually,' he answered, sharply.
'Then you're plain stupid. Making money is a disease, James. It becomes compulsive. It hardens your heart to the rest of the poor souls who are battling away to make a paltry living.'

James couldn't believe what he was hearing. It was late at night. All his mind, and muscles, wanted was bed, not an inquisition on a subject he had initially thought rather straightforward, although in retrospect he accepted he had probably been naive in that assumption.

'What rubbish. What the hell have you been reading? You haven't had enough experience of life or money to know what you're talking about. And remember I'm not alone in this. I'm only a partner, and a minor one at that. I can't go around handing out cash here, there and everywhere. I have to abide by what the others think, to a certain extent at least.'

'Oh yes, there's Ned Trevenning to consider. What an upstanding citizen he is. A womaniser and a drunk. If he treats those who work for him the way he does his wife they won't even be on survival wages. And then of course there's your great backer, Mr Richard Courteney. Since you married I've been hearing a few tales about him. It seems to me that he represents all that I've just been talking about.'

That exhausted James's already strained patience. By then his pulses were beginning to work at triple speed.

'Look, I'm not interested in your dumb opinions. I've come to tell you what's happening, that's all. I don't want a load of criticism. I was trying to be open with you. Now I've got no reason to use the Rosevean money in this venture there's nothing my family can do, or say, to stop me. I've silenced Samuel, which usually takes some doing. I trust I'll eventually prove to you that what I'm doing is for the benefit of all of us.'

Alex remained unimpressed, and didn't bother

to hide it.

'And what about Helen?'

'What about her?' James snapped. An unexpected twist again.

'Does she approve of all this?'

That made James hesitate slightly. The one surprise at his wedding, apart from the fact that he himself had actually gone through with the ceremony, was that Helen and Alex had bonded noticeably well. Somehow, she had made his brother laugh, made the pale mask of his face crack, and that had been an achievement in itself. Despite Alex not harbouring the gloom that so encapsulated Samuel, it sometimes appeared that he was perpetually serious, another Rosevean bound up in some sort of grudge against his existence.

'As a matter of fact she does approve,' he murmured after some while, trying to emphasise that she and he were of one mind. 'She only has one reservation, and that stems from the fact that I can't start the company independently, entirely with my own money.'

Alex always saw deeper than anyone gave him credit for. He watched, and he absorbed. 'In other words she doesn't want you completely beholden to her father. She's afraid of what might follow. Helen did strike me as a clever girl, and it seems I wasn't wrong. It's a pity you aren't so wise, but then as far as Courteney is concerned, as his daughter she knows exactly what he's capable of. She's got around an 18 year start on you.'

1X

When James's last day at Bethany finally arrived, and he strode away from the workings that had been part of his family's life for decades, he tried to force purpose into every step.

It must be for the best, he thought. No longer will I have to work in blackness, or climb never-ending ladders, or use a pick and shovel while worrying about roof falls or flooding. Nevertheless, in spite of outwardly sweeping aside the doubts openly expressed by his wife and brother, he couldn't totally ignore them. When it came to it, instead of feeling jubilation at turning his back on the mine, he discovered he was only faced by a blanketing depression.

He had come to believe that because it had been so simple for him to get so far, the rest of the route to success was bound to present him with a much tougher struggle. Over the years he had come to accept that his Celtic soul dealt heavily in fate, and his mind was telling him that all his senses were pointing to difficulties ahead. The depression had not lifted by the time he reached home, despite the fact that he took himself on a five mile detour in a bid to walk it off.

And when it comes to basics, what do I know about china clay anyway, he thought on arriving home, with an anger he hadn't expected to feel.

March 1874

X

The impenetrable darkness and fear that

surrounded Nathan, and tore at his guts, was worse than when he had slithered through Bethany in desperate search of Will Blackwell. His head throbbed unbearably and his lurching stomach was tied in a thousand knots.

Above him, as he crouched below deck with a stinking hoard of equally terrified passengers, the sea pounded and roared like a swarm of she-devils. He longed to be sick again, but in such diabolical conditions he forced himself not to be. More than anything, he didn't want to parade his weaknesses for all to see, from the scruffiest child, to the oldest, most helpless grandmother. Not that anyone would have bothered to notice him.

Around him unwashed, untended children screamed and attempted, with minimal success, to play in the midst of potential disaster, and women who were well past trying to pacify their youngsters, merely sat and stared sightlessly ahead, waiting for the worst to sweep them away.

Up above, in the teeth of the horrific, freak weather, the crew fought for the survival of all. At one stage Nathan had tried to join them, wanting to face the dangers that threatened to overwhelm the ship, rather than hide from them, but he had been sent below decks again.

One of the masts had already gone, smashing onto the deck with such a devastating crash that every cringing passenger had thought it was the end, certain that within minutes there would be no home, bar the chillingly cold bottom of a merciless ocean.

Damn this wreck of a boat, damn myself for being here, for running from life and the girl who at least loved me, he raged bitterly, and felt the sweat prickle on his forehead again, due to the terror surging through him, and the bile rise. Why such paralysing fear?

It's because I'm not in control, he told himself, the saliva bubbling out of the corners of his trembling mouth. This isn't underground among rocks in a narrow level that's become as natural to me as a Cornish sky. This is mid-Atlantic on a bucking, powerful, sea I believe I've always partially frightened of.

Thinking back in time for an instant he accepted that there had been enough wrecks along the stretch of coastline from Looe to Veryan Bay to teach him that the ocean was far from being a passive creature. Over the years he had fought with waves off Porthpean Beach in a vain attempt to save doomed sailors from a barquentine which was breaking up too fast, and he had seen bodies washed up at both Crinnis and Charlestown - a few fresh, but others bloated or even stripped horrendously clean to the bone.

'Oh God help me,' he stuttered, shaking as the gruesome images from his youth flashed in front of him, not sceptical any more about the reality of an almighty power. At that moment he didn't dare to doubt the existence of one. His heart was accelerating at a pace, his pulses quickening further - and then with a disjointed, primeval cry he came to.

The cry echoed and then stilled suddenly in the warm, morning air. Gradually, he was able to cling onto the realisation that he was not even within sight of the sea. The storm, despite being terrifyingly real once, had blown itself away years before. Instead, he was reliving it in a nightmare that, to his dismay, had wracked and wrecked his nights since he had first landed in America in 1870. The present time was now California in March 1874. The ship, although crippled by the vigour of wind and waves, had somehow managed to limp into New York, complete with cowering passengers who had felt they had looked the Grim Reaper in the face and only just managed to evade his retribution. Nathan sat up slowly, pulled the blankets around him, and strove to steady himself, angry that he had put himself through such horrors yet again. Trying to reassure himself that he was on safe and secure ground, he blinked at the perfect azure sky, the rising circle of sun.

But the fact that he was waking up to a scorching, hot day hardly affected him. Inside, he was frozen, and knew from past destructive experience that a residue of the panic he had experienced once more, would cling to him for at least an hour or so. It was as if the storm had been sent to convince him that however much he fought and battled with life he was still desperate enough to want to embrace it constantly, with a pathetic need.

He had made it to his New World. He had left Biscovey thousands of miles behind, and had discovered in those years since landing on American soil that memories, even unwanted ones, were difficult to erase. In the odd optimistic moment, he had to admit that the restlessness within him had waned slightly. Not enough, however, for him to find the need to settle. In the vast land of a million complexities he had kept on moving, aiming to reach the next town, the next state.

Nathan was not alone in such a nomadic existence. There was an army of others, from a welter of countries, descending on the plains, the mountains, the arable land, and reaching for the ranch, the farm, the nugget that would change their lives, the strike that would make them reach beyond dreams. Still staring at the sky, he lay back on the baked Californian earth, a lean, athletic man, rough with beard, and strove to banish the nightmare by facing once more in his mind the beginning of his journey, one he had sometimes thought would never end, except maybe in tragedy.

For almost four years he had been wandering, and he had only managed to discover that answers remained as stubbornly elusive as ever.

At the start there had been the lead mines of Wisconsin, and the Cornish cottages and Methodist chapels in that land of blue rivers. After landing at New York he had made his way to Buffalo, and then taken a steamer to Wisconsin along the canal linking the Hudson River with Lake Erie. It had been a slow, but reasonably cheap journey which had given him the chance to unwind from the trauma of the kicking, diving six week crossing with its fetid drinking water, unhygienic conditions and final, fearsome storm.

The steamer, simple as it was, had provided absolute luxury in comparison with the ship. There it had been impossible for him to think straight, or even keep a grip on nerves that had become stretched beyond anything he had ever experienced before, even during the hideous weeks that had followed the murder at the Britannia, when at one moment he had imagined being caught and lynched for an apparently random killing he hadn't committed.

While he was crouched below decks, his skin

clammy again with anticipation of imminent death, the idea that he could have tied himself to Lorna and settled for a life hemmed in by the screams of his own children, did not seem to be the 'prison' he had once convinced himself it would be.

Anxious to prove to himself that he had made the right choice to turn his back on what many would have termed a 'normal' life he sought strength so that he could begin to find the certainty, within himself, that whatever America held it was definitely better and more satisfying than the existence he had so determinedly thrown away.

Once in Wisconsin he had come to understand that the farmers had settled to the east, and the miners to the west. So, with mining still thick in his blood, he went west to Galena to search for the lead that had never been mined properly until the Cornish had stumbled on the scene. The first to find minerals there had been Indian squaws who had used only fire to break the rocks. Their successors had been the emergent Americans themselves who also harboured only basic mining knowledge. Gunpowder and the art of sinking shafts had been unheard of. So, when the Cousin Jacks had arrived with their wealth of experience, it had been almost like virgin land for them. Opportunities abounded, east as well as west. Nathan was told that the farming land was as productive, so fertile that the maize crackled as it grew in the perfumed stillness of a summer's evening.

For a brief while, he had stayed in one of the old miners' cottages which looked as if they had been transplanted from Cornwall. Cut from local stone and complete with their own landscaped gardens they had walls 18 inches thick, deeply sunken windows and two rooms up and two down, with a staircase in the middle. Nathan had worked hard, exploring the brown bluffs and rolling pastures before deciding, like so many before, that he hadn't yet travelled far enough. As a result, he eventually drifted away, not caring too deeply where he went just as long as he had both food, and space to think in.

In the end he had journeyed north, to try his luck in the harshness of Dakota, Montana and Idaho. As he travelled, he ignored lands that were to become huge spreads for the cattlemen, and headed for the wilderness where there was none of the softness of his native county. No green meadows, or soft mizzle, or hidden inlets and caves. Only untamed country with wide open horizons and opportunities.

With the passing of time he reached the stage where he ceased bothering to shave or dress with any thought. Beard and moustache grew, his tall, spare figure shed all vestiges of fat, and his skin turned leathery brown from a sun which burned like a brand. He lived rough, and the acquaintances he made were individuals, characters formed by the unforgiving harsh nature of the country they were struggling, daily, to come to terms with. They were a dying breed, throwbacks to the mountain men who had trapped beaver a generation or more before the cowboy came into his own. They belonged to a time when buck-skinned fur trappers searched for beavers in the streams across the Rocky Mountains, and the first frontiersmen were found in the high regions of the wilderness. Of Anglo-American, French or Spanish stock these had spoken mountain talk, which was of mixed tongue, and had earned the name 'white Indians' because they lived and dressed so much like the native Indians. There were times of great loneliness for Nathan, when he really believed he was following in the exact footsteps of Kit Carson, Joe Meek, Hugh Glass or Grizzly Adams.

His respect for the men who had gone before, and those few he ran into in the depths of his isolation, became complete. Of necessity, he caught his own food, learnt to enjoy his own company rather than merely seek it and, along with thousands of others, came to master the art of panning.

With experience behind him, after weeks of trying, he became expert at filling a wasp pan with pay dirt before swirling it around in the water to wash out the lighter gravel.

Frequently, he found small particles of gold with the heavier metal and stone left at the bottom of the pan. Not a great deal, but an encouragement.

Winters were a different matter. As temperatures plummeted he had to suffer a depth of coldness he had never come near to experiencing before, especially in the middle of nights when any exposed piece of flesh was frozen to the ground. For the sake of mere survival, he came to know how to dress for warmth.

His usual attire comprised two pairs of wool socks, a pair of socks that came up to his knees, moccasins, overshoes over the moccasins, two suits of heavy underwear, pants, overalls and a heavy shirt.

Striving to ensure that he definitely beat the killer temperatures, he also made sleeves out of women's stockings, wore woollen gloves and mittens, a blanket-lined coat and a big sealskin cap, and while wearing all of those he was just able to feel a slight edge of warmth. Often, against his will, his mind would switch to Cornwall and dwell on regrets he had only now begun to open himself to. Regrets that he had left his mother far from happy, regrets that he had quit in anger, regrets even, in the midst of a long night, that he had denied himself Lorna's sweetness and loyalty. His image of her, trapped in a squat cottage with a brood of unkempt children and old before her time, had started to fade. But when the clarity of day came he dismissed all softenings of the heart as the inevitable results of his self-imposed exile.

Entertainment, when it did come, was in the form of the shanty towns that had sprung up whenever the words 'gold rush' had been whispered. The saloons were shabby places at the best of times, full of drunks, whores, and gamblers, and open door to those who wanted to cheat the innocents of every penny.

So many had arrived with hope, but once trapped there had lost not only the optimism but even the pittance they had travelled with. In the end they stayed on like lost souls, unable to return home, if there still was one to go back to, and admit defeat.

It was neither hope nor defeat that took Nathan to the saloons. Above all, he was grateful that while there he could at least get a decent wash, and scrub the grime and parasites from his body.

The cowboys claimed that those who lived in the mountains, as he had chosen to do, revelled in the filth that came hand in hand with surviving in earthy conditions. He for one denied that, discovering that a good soak in the tub did wonders for his morale, although one drawback was that it also brought him back to reality, and in shanty town bars reality was very heavily dominated by drink and casual violence.

After a while, he understood that a cowboy on the loose after weeks or months on the trail was as unpredictable as the longhorn bulls he herded, apt to use a knife or gun at the least provocation. A misunderstood word, a stray glance, could cause bloodshed.

To Nathan the cowboy seemed to exist on a diet of whisky and tobacco, and lived with the overwhelming compunction that he had to fire at anything that had the temerity to move. He also never went far on such nights of freedom without one of the saloon 'hostesses' by his side.

Like most of the others the girls in the shanty towns were out to make as much money as possible within the least amount of time and, like their male counterparts, their morals seldom got in their way. They were from every race and every social class and each one of them, in wide skirts, layers of petticoats and fine kid boots, never went far without a jewelled pistol or knife to hand.

They didn't interest Nathan. Since his exodus from Cornwall he had found out that his solitary life had robbed him of any desire to jolly along with seething humanity. He could take the company of one or two other drinkers, but if he found himself in a group of any more he wanted to back out. Also, he discovered that he was consuming less alcohol than in the final dissolute days in Biscovey. And on some occasions he even managed to come to terms with the black, raging anger that had so easily welled up inside him.

Few would have recognised him at first sight. Although he had remained slim his shoulders had expanded and his thighs and legs gained in strength. Moustache and beard obscured all hints of youth. Deep within himself he felt he had undergone a necessary metamorphosis, but he was terrified that with just a few setbacks, the process could revert.

Although at times it had seemed to him that reaching California would be impossible, eventually he dragged his aching body into the golden state of the far west, lodged between the foothills of the Sierra Nevada and the surging Pacific. Under Mexican rule until 1846, when John Charles Fremont and his guide Kit Carson arrived, he soon found the truth in the claims that it was blessed with fine weather, fertile land and mineral wealth.

Nathan was just another traveller. California had been a haven to thousands of seekers since James Marshall had struck gold while building a sawmill on the south fork of the American river at Coloma. Certainly his journey, although arduous and terrifying to start with, hadn't been so treacherous as that of the first Anglo-American settlers who had made the great overland trek from the Great Salt Lake in Utah. For the most part Nathan, too, had walked, though it hadn't been entirely essential. The country's giant railroads, the Central Pacific and the Union Pacific, had joined to link east with west. And so it was that when Nathan awoke, shaking and sweating from one of his recurring nightmares, it was to yet another state, on this occasion his destination of the land of the Redwood tree and the condor. The land of live oak, sycamore, blue oaks, digger pines and tarweed, where the Mother Lode stretched from Mariposa to the Feather River. Groaning, he leant forward and shook the dust from his now long dark hair with its wayward curls like corkscrews. Where to go from here if here was not the mythical end of the rainbow?

Tired in bone and sinew, he told himself that he had run as far as he could, at least for some time. From England to New York, and then from there to the west, he had fled to bury loss of hope and desire. It could be said he hadn't made San Francisco as yet, transformed by the gold rush into one of the busiest ports in the world, but after that there was only the ocean again. The oceans, however, did lead to Australia and also to South Africa.

Stretching his taut, aching muscles, he took a swig of water and briefly wished it stronger. It was time, maybe, to slot himself back into the populated masses.

Another few isolated years, he thought, and I may never want to return to the mainstream, and I've a vague idea I didn't come here to bury myself in my own little world forever. There are some chances for me out there, surely, if I can endure so-called normality again.

While considering the options that now lay ahead for him, he stared around at the country that had once been the settled home of the Modoc, Mohave and Yuma Indians. But it was also where they had gradually died of disease, starvation and murder by the white man.

Well nothing's going to defeat me, absolutely nothing, he whispered to himself as he stumbled to his feet, gathered together the few belongings that now constituted his world, and set off for the next, unknown, stage of his self-imposed exile.

CHAPTER THREE

Summer 1874

1

Mevagissey Feast week in Cornwall. Crowds excitedly thronging the inner and outer harbours, locals hanging out of the sail lofts to watch the luggers racing for the wind out at sea, the smell of pilchards laying thick in the summer air. Sideshows, wrestling matches, the sounds of marching bands and streams of banners and bunting rustling in the wind.
It was Saturday, a general day's holiday, an excuse to gossip and drink and make the most of freedom. The cacophony of noise and colour swirled in unison with the distinctive

cries of the seagulls, hovering in the briny air. Samuel was in the midst of it, bare-headed, tanned, sober and smug. For a change he was in a contented mood, and it showed. His eyes were not brooding, his scowl was absent. The reason trailed reluctantly behind him. Lorna. She was walking with her head hung low, her auburn hair, which she had cut short, curling to a vee at the base of her neck. There had been no effort from her to match the jubilation of the day, such was the despair that had started to develop deep in her soul. She wore an unflattering grey and white striped dress that so merged into the cluttered surroundings that she was barely noticeable. In a far happier frame of mind, and anxious that she would try to share his happiness, Samuel turned around, caught hold of one of her limp arms and pulled her nearer to him.

'You look tired,' he said to her, trying to raise his voice above the yells and laughter of those pressing hot and sticky around them. 'Are you feeling fine? Do you want to leave? We've been here over an hour, and you've hardly spoken.'

'No .. no, I'd rather stay here Sam. There are the wrestling matches to come yet, and you love watching them.'

'But I know for sure you'd prefer not to see them.'

'Maybe not, but you certainly do. After all, you've been talking about little else to me all week.'

In response, he placed a thick arm around her waist. Initially, she was in half a mind to pull away from him, but eventually gave in with very little struggle and let herself be handled. She thought maybe it wasn't the right time, or the right setting, to begin an argument.

Instead of moving away from the quay towards the wrestling matches, where she had expected him to head, though, he pushed her in the opposite direction, deeper into the crowd, and it was then that she did start to protest.

At no point in her life had she been a lover of cooped, cramped places. Neither had Nathan been, especially towards the end, unless he was drunk. She winced at the thought of him. Four years had gone and her inner longing for him showed no signs of decreasing, although she never let such feelings slip. It was like loving, with a secret passionate intensity, a ghost.

'Where are you taking me?' she shouted, ducking and twisting as she went, trying and failing to avoid rushing feet and elbows.

'Believe me, we're going somewhere quieter, where we can talk to each other sensibly, without having to scream above all this noise.'

'Oh,' she whispered, hiding her face from him, something simply accomplished in such conditions.

She didn't have the energy to feign enthusiasm. Then she admitted to herself that her acting ability couldn't have been too bad during the last months. And if it had been terrible, then he had been too wrapped up in himself to see through the lies.

Walking at some pace, he guided her around the left side of the inner harbour, and then up steep granite steps to the grassy slopes at the top of the cliffs. They were still not completely alone, despite the crush of humanity easing.

For both she was grateful, as well as for the view. It was a clear day, a sunny one with only the merest hint of cloud in the wide sky, although the breeze was remarkably stiff and made her shiver as she stared across the choppy sea, with its wavelets lapping and sucking hungrily at the base of the cliffs at Bodrugan's Leap.

It was much fresher on the cliffs. True, she could breathe much better now she had more space. Unfortunately, she also felt more exposed.

Samuel put his other arm around her in a gesture of possession rather than protection, and she leant tautly against him as hopelessness bore down on her. While they stood together, she kept glancing away from him, and nervously biting her lower lip as if she was a worried child.

For eight months now she had been playing a game of pretence with him, and occasionally with herself. She should have been used to the rules. Somehow she wasn't, and didn't think she ever would be.

'You've changed me.' he told her, resting his square chin on the top of her head, the wind teasing his black hair out of its usual neat, and uncompromising, style.

'Changed?'

'Yes, you know damned well you've altered me. And I have to admit that it is all for the better.'

In spite of the swirling air around them oxygen suddenly seemed in short supply to Lorna. At his words she gulped, like a fish fighting for life long past the time when it knows it has been well and truly caught.

'I . . I'm sure what I've done has done little to alter you.'

Responding with a smile, he hugged her even tighter.

'Don't be dense.'
'I wasn't intending to be,' she murmured.
There had been an increase in weight, maybe. In the explosion of well being that he had said he had experienced since becoming more than friends with her, there were times when he had been relaxing, and drinking more.
He looks like Nathan's elder brother, not one four years younger, she thought as she glanced at the stomach showing between waistcoat and trouser belt, and the set face reddening from the exertion of climbing the narrow, winding steps. But then she was comparing him with the Nathan she had loved and known all those years before, the young man who had awoken emotions she hadn't felt before or since.
What changes had time wrought on him? Would she even recognise him, even if her heart cried she would always do so?
Definitely, she hadn't remained unaltered, she admitted that. There were lines now around eyes and mouth, and a dreaded realisation that youth could never be recaptured.
Samuel's mind was far from the subject of Nathan. Since the humiliation of the fight at St Austell station he had tried to erase, for good, all memories of that particular brother.
'I so enjoy being with you, especially this close,' he said gently, stroking her hair, twirling the small curls around his fingers. 'I like being seen with you. It feels so good.'
'I'm flattered,' she answered softly, her heart racing not because of the sentiments expressed, but because she was absolutely terrified of what was coming.
Alex, seeing what was happening to Samuel, had warned her three months before that his brother was scheming to marry her.

Samuel was equally tense. Four years back he had thought such a moment would never come. Now it had arrived he didn't want to make a wrong move. But . . . but ... if he hung on too long, without spelling out exactly how he felt, he might miss the opportunity altogether.

'I want to be seen with you always,' he ventured. 'I want you by my side always, so there is someone of mine I can depend on.'

From racing her pulses stopped beating in an instant.

What the hell should I do, she thought numbly. Play dumb, or come straight to the point as I did before on top of other cliffs with another Rosevean? That decision nearly killed me. This one will only deaden me still further, though I do think I've nearly lost all ability to feel any real emotion.

'Is that a marriage proposal?' she asked, choosing the direct method.

Shaken slightly by her bluntness, he slackened his hold on her, and shifted uneasily on his heavy feet.

'You know it is, and it is genuine. I haven't asked you because of greed - like dear James when he asked Helen. I need you Lorna, believe me, I really do.'

They had been meant lovingly, but his words prompted her shivering to return again, and on this occasion she couldn't blame the heightening breeze for the reaction.

'Give me a while to think about it,' she answered in a strained voice that he could barely hear. 'Please give me time. I mustn't rush my answer and make a mistake both of us would regret.'

Determined to make the situation work to his advantage in the end, he had enough empathy within him to know that he had to show understanding of her feelings in order not to scare her.

'Be kind, though. Don't keep me in suspense too long. I've already ordered the ring. I hope you don't mind. I have to live in hope on this occasion. Such hopes have been keeping me buoyant for a long, long time.'

Samuel's pursuit of Lorna had, in truth, begun even before Nathan's acrimonious departure abroad, back to the moment when she, and almost everyone around them, had realised that her love for Nathan was heading for heartache.

Samuel had always envied his brother for possessing her. To him she epitomized all he wanted in a woman, with her gentle good looks, neatness and dignity. He remembered that Nathan had once hinted there was fire beneath her quiet manner. Such passion had never emerged while he had been with her, but in truth, he didn't want it to because he did not relish living with a woman whose emotions were difficult to deal with.

In love, as in everything else, he still regarded matters in jaundiced fashion, expecting pitfalls, holding back.

But with Lorna next to him that attitude could disappear for hours on end. Not only that, he did find her fascinating and compulsive, but also had to admit to himself that the thrill of having her linked to him was intensified because she had once been Nathan's.

A few years before she had been utterly unobtainable to him. When Nathan had left he had plotted ponderously, but deliberately, to ensnare her. At the beginning of the campaign, he realised that there were obvious differences between himself and his eldest brother. Nathan was athletic, commanding and, when he felt like it, undeniably charming. Nevertheless, Samuel had convinced himself that he could undoubtedly show Lorna far more concern, as well as appreciation and sympathy, than his brother had done.

As he planned his strategy for marriage, he was sure that if he applied his qualities wisely he could win her around. And, of course, he realised that he was more likely to succeed with her while the turmoil which Nathan had caused within her continued to shred her confidence.

Lorna was a silent battler, and had striven not to let the pain of rejection show, but Samuel had known it was there all the same, gnawing, grinding, seldom letting up. And, over the years he had come to know all about rejection. He definitely had insight enough already on that particular matter.

From her point of view, Lorna was not attracted to Samuel. She had never been. Thick set, domineering and impatient, even when going to the utmost extremes to appear otherwise, he never seemed able to bury the moroseness that was an integral part of him. Bearing that in mind, she closed her eyes to the cliffs, the bright view of the teeming Mevagissey streets winding below them like colourful snakes, and to his talk of marriage, and tried to think back.

Throughout the years he had never been actively easy to like, always being the pessimist and the downcast, never the shining knight. For a while it had been so different with Nathan.

Looking back, she accepted that at the start of their relationship loving him had been such a joy.

Despite all that she had been a simple and easy target for Samuel's clutches. Losing Nathan had thrown her into a void, and when Samuel entered the picture she just saw him as a Rosevean, a tenuous link with the man who had once wanted her with all his soul, but who now had no need of her. So she had let him play his courting games, with no real thought to where they would lead.

There had been nothing dramatic at first. She had allowed him to take her to chapel on Sundays, and had gone home with him now and then for tea, prepared absent-mindedly by his mother. Eventually, without any real effort on her part, they had fallen into a routine which she had regarded as purely mundane, but which he had seen as a precursor to something much more permanent.

Almost a year, or more, had been spent either ignoring his talk of a wedding, or side-stepping it. Often she had tried to laugh him out of his ideas of domesticity, but on other days, when she had no laughter within her, and she could only see the emptiness of her future, she had found it hard to keep tears of despair at bay. Over time she came to discover that, if nothing else, Samuel was persistent. It seemed he seldom left her in peace, and whenever she gave way on a small, apparently minor matter, he kept pushing for more.

In the end, a few weeks before their trip to Mevagissey, she had admitted to herself that his overbearing attitude was forcing her into a trap. In her mind she saw herself as an animal fighting to free itself from a craftily structured cage. Her driving instinct was to run away fast, to make her excuses and bow out of his life with as little blood spilt in the process as possible.

Standing on the humped granite outcrop, with the wind rippling with some strength through her clothes and the terns hovering daintily above, she was given the opportunity to do so. Nevertheless, she couldn't find the words to reject him. She hadn't the energy to do so. Just one letter, one word from Nathan might have given her the necessary fire. The trouble was that, to her ever-developing dismay, since leaving Cornwall he had never once stirred himself to contact her. Not one single envelope had arrived for her bearing an American postmark.

On the day after Samuel proposed, she took a long walk, to Crinnis beach where she and Nathan had been heading on the storm-ridden night when she had made the final break from him. The white horses were no longer visible at sea as they had been at Mevagissey. In contrast, the water lapped calm and serene by the side of her as she trudged the mile along its white, gravely beach.

Oystercatchers, resplendent like little entertainers in their black and white plumage, picked over the offerings left on the shoreline, and then flew into the air, piping in alarm as she neared. Away in the distance, above the sounds of the birds and the waves, she heard the clanking and pounding of Crinnis mine, one of the first great copper mines opened in the area. Abandoned in 1840, re-worked in the 1850s, the word was that it was nearing the end of its usefulness for good.

Well, she thought, perhaps it and I have both arrived at the same ending, one without hope. The trouble was she had grown insidiously dependent on Samuel in so many ways.

Undeniably, he was reliable, he protected her, he obviously felt deeply about her, and he was Nathan's brother. Of course there were no erratic beatings of the heart, or longings, when she was with him but, she asked herself, would they have lasted even with Nathan? If he had stayed with me, if he hadn't totally changed, would our love still have burned itself out anyway? And wasn't one of the lessons learnt, as life progressed, that the partial had to be accepted. That it was a tumultuous waste of desire wanting the perfect?

Before she knew it, she had reached the end of the beach, being blocked from walking further by the cliffs that wound their way along the coast to Spit Head and then to the sandy stretch of Par beach.

When she turned for home she could hardly see where she was going because her eyes were so obscured by tears. What she would have given for the perfect just then.

Summer 1874 California

11

The temperature rose to a searing 120 degrees Fahrenheit. Through his pouring sweat, and the darkness, Nathan groped half blindly for the ice water. By then he knew that if he didn't drink some quickly his toughened, perspiring body would quite literally begin to cook. The necessity was at its greatest because he was working in the lowest levels of the Empire Mine at Grass Valley, toiling in the hottest conditions he had ever had to contend with. The winter had been harsh enough with its never-ceasing cold, bitterly freezing winds and the constant fear of frostbite. This was something different entirely.

Although the months in the wilderness had hardened him, the cold remained an element he hated. Cornish winters, despite being wet, had usually been mild. The scorching days of Californian summer had proved to be a different, more dangerous, creature altogether. They produced shattering, oppressive heat that sapped all strength and left him tottering and weak, like a new-born infant. And, he discovered, it was a heat that didn't come in waves, but which was continuous and unrelenting. Above all, he not only had to survive it, but also to keep working through it as well.

If the weather conditions had been taken away, however, and there had been mist swirling in from the sea instead of a searing sun directly overhead, he could have believed he was back in Biscovey itself.

Most of the voices that could be heard from the levels originated from Kernow, and he believed the Empire Mine could have been hewn from a corner of Cornwall too. The way her waste rocks were used as wall props, and her narrow metallic lodes dipped and faulted in unexpected ways as they bored through bad, metamorphose 'country' rock seemed as Cornish to Nathan as the ubiquitous tre, pol and pen.

The water, which he liberally poured down his throat and also over his head so that it ran into eyes and trickled down his neck, helped him. By trial and error, he had found that if he began to dehydrate he started hallucinating. He wondered if Ted, a colleague from Truro who was working even deeper in the mine, needed ice too, and loudly called to him. Although he was out of sight Nathan knew he must be only a matter of yards distant, hidden by a bend in the rock. No answer came, so he called again, but more urgently, his voice rising to a screech.

If nothing else his first taste of high summer in Grass Valley had taught him it was an absolute necessity to drink ice water by the gallon, and even have it poured over the whole body, an experience verging on the sensual as well as the necessary. It was one of the only rules he had encountered in his life that he had instantly adhered to without wanting to test or criticise.

There remained silence from Ted's part of the level, so Nathan crouched down before slowly crawling towards where the miner had been working, his jumpy nerves warning him that all was not well. As it was, he stumbled on the other man in minutes. Ted was lying on the uneven floor, clutching his stomach and rolling from side to side in pure agony. He had cut his back and upper arms on rocky debris and was oozing blood, though was unaware of that. Instead, he was shaking uncontrollably, and jabbering incoherently. Nathan knew immediately what was happening, froze in panic for an instant, then unsteadily yelled for help, his voice echoing mockingly around him.

'For God's sake, someone help. There's a man dying here.'

The sounds rebounded into the darkness, and he swore because he thought no-one had heard. Luckily, he was wrong. Other miners, weary and grimy, began to appear out of the blackness, seemingly aware without anything else being said of what was happening.

Nathan, in a flash of recall, saw the adits of Bethany instead and Will Blackwell, trapped with the water rising around him, his eyes full of fear because he was certain he was near death. This would not be a drowning accident, though. Ted was roasting. His symptoms were obvious. His perspiration had stopped, he was wracked by stomach pains, and delirium had begun.

'Get the bloody ice, buckets of it,' someone barked.

'What the hell do we do now?'

'Pack the ice around him. Then get him to the surface as quickly as possible.'

'That's impossible. He won't hold still.'

'Well we've got to try, or he'll die right here for sure. He needs the doctor, and quickly too. We have to get him out, and try to take his temperature down at the same time.'

It was a difficult process with Ted fighting them all the way. As they stumbled along, trying to carry him, he was talking wildly, screaming his wife's name one minute, calling for his father, dead for more than 30 years, the next. One look at his distorted face and every one of them felt ill. It was a risk they all ran. At the hottest peak of the year the temperature never wavered, and the fear of such an attack lurked in every niche and corner.'

Nathan had seen a store of death and injury in mining accidents and, since his arrival in America, in gunfights, but the sight of Ted chilled him more than all that had gone before.

In his heart he knew that, on this occasion, the man he had gone to save, would not live. Later, he berated himself, because it became clear that Ted might have survived, if they had reached him earlier. If, maybe, Nathan had called out to him five or ten minutes sooner there could have been a chance that they would have found him with time to spare. But, looking down at the writhing man as they kept fighting to carry him back to the light, Nathan had a vision of the eyes already closed for good, and the final mask creeping upon him. His Celtic spirit knew very well that death was hovering near.

Ted lived only twenty minutes more, and after he lost his battle against the spectre of death, his dispirited fellow miners took the rest of the day off, turning their backs on the mine that stood so resolutely on Ophir Hill. Bosses or no bosses, captains or no captains, they couldn't face returning to that Dante's hell-hole quite so soon, as if no tragedy had ripped their clique apart.

Nathan, devastated, and angered, by the waste of a good life, took a solitary walk in an effort to recover at least a shred of his hard-won equilibrium. Despite being among his own kind again, and there by choice, he remained a loner. The recent, solitary years and the harshness of the land he had travelled through had moulded him into a definite individual, an even sterner man than the one who had come to alienate so many in Biscovey.

It often appeared to him that he had become an onlooker and little else. Seldom did he take part in actual, real, life, unlike others with their clamouring families, their money worries, their petty disputes. He had abstained from alcohol to a great extent, and since the scrap with Samuel hadn't raised a fist in anger, not even in the bars he had visited where fights came quick and without prompting. Instead, he merely watched, never becoming emotionally involved with people or events. It was a way perhaps, although he never saw it as that, of protecting the Achilles heel that he regarded as his soul.

Nevertheless, despite such aloofness, Ted had certainly edged close enough to him to be a friend. In a short while the Truro man had dented his defences more than most, which meant his death had been unexpectedly shattering.

As he walked in the scrubland, thinking hard and bitterly long, it seemed to him that the world had become extremely tenuous again. Nothing can ever be taken for granted, least of all the fact that come tomorrow you'll still be kicking and breathing, he muttered to himself. If it had been my body on that makeshift stretcher what achievements of mine would remain, what memories of me would live on in the minds of others? Blasted well none, he told himself fiercely. None at all.

He stared up at the narrow gauge railway that curved into Grass Valley from Nevada City over high, slim trestle bridges. For many a glimpse from a railway carriage was the first they had of this part of the country, with its plane trees, oaks and sycamores. What greeted them at that precise moment, following the hot, drought-ridden summer, was more like the dusty Australian interior. Nathan looked around, his eyes still full of the horror he knew he wouldn't forget for an age. There was no gorse or heather to tread on as he walked, only parched grass and stunted shrub that reminded him of the most desolate parts of Bodmin Moor after an equally dry summer - parts where one stray spark would set a fire raging across acres of land.

Already he had seen gold rush towns in all stages, from burgeoning spring to the midst of fall, but on that day nothing he had ever experienced seemed as depressing as the empty, sizzled waste that spread in front of him. Stunted trees gave no shade. There were no birds. He could spy no shelter, no beauty. And what is Ted feeling now, if feeling is at all possible where he is? Does he now know what the purpose was behind his short span on earth? Had there been any point to it at all, or has he discovered that his existence was little else but one long, tedious joke? It surely can't amount to much more.

Beset by such thoughts, he closed his eyes, blotted out the Central Pacific Railroad, and thought morosely of what had happened in his brief time at Empire.

Miners with legs and arms severed in cave-ins and by premature blasting, a Chinese worker so mutilated by a runaway truck that a friend had shot him in compassion after finding him twisted, bleeding and crying for mercy, and an Irish woman a month away from childbirth killed after falling down one of the shafts.

In all the events it seemed to Nathan that the lack of justice added an almost absurd touch. To him, as he stood in the midst of the incredible, strength-sapping heat, everything he had done, or had yet to achieve, seemed without purpose. Pointless and damned. The age old, impossible question of 'why' prodded and taunted him, although he was too weary to bother trying to dredge up reasons.

And hadn't he already spent long enough attempting to do just that, on the wretched boat journey to New York, in the depths of the mountains, while he streamed for tin and panned for gold, and even in the bar of the Britannia?

Once he would have solved the dejection by

making his way to somewhere like the 'Daws Union Saloon' and throwing himself with cold-blooded relish into one of the long-running brawls between the Cornish and Irish. The difference was he no longer believed that answers could be found in a bottle. The fatal night when Joel Hartford had died had made its mark.

After a couple of brooding hours he finally turned and picked his way dejectedly back to his lodgings. By choice he would have stayed on Gold Flat, in the complex of boarding houses built for bachelors, but he had taken a room with a family from Gunnislake who had already been in Grass Valley for three years. Joe Trembeth suffered from an intermittent illness of the lungs, and when he was off work the rent money was much needed, a factor Nathan was very aware of.

It was to the Trembeth home that Nathan went, later to lay down on his uncomfortable bed and drift off to sleep without bothering either to wash or undress.

With his mind already so disturbed the old nightmare returned to torment. He was back on the boat, in the storm, and the terror of drowning tore at him, forcing him to cry out, bringing the sweat to his brow. Then he was pitched to the bottom of an unknown mine where there was no-one else to be seen until, out of the blackness, Ted appeared, half alive still and half skeleton, the grinning, bony figure laughing at him, mocking him.

'You think you're so tough Nathan Rosevean. Well, you've never amounted to anything worthwhile, and you'll never have a chance to alter that.'

Nathan could see himself cowering in fright, whimpering. The whimpering turned to sobbing, and in his ravaged thoughts Lorna came and stood by him, and within moments he was more at peace with himself than he had been in an age.

In the morning he could have wept for real. In his dream come nightmare, he had seen her so clearly, he could have held her, touched her, loved her. After all the years, all the efforts to erase the past she was still there, in the back of the subconscious. And he had thought forgetting would occur naturally, with no problem at all. It was he who had forced the break between them after all, so why was such an insignificant girl still trailing through his mind?

It is just another dream, he seethed, like all the others that have hounded me since the storm. Later, though, when he sat down to send money back to his mother he also wrote a longer, and more exacting letter. Even as he composed it he convinced himself that he would never post it, that the therapy of writing the words would be enough.

But he did.

111

Lorna became Mrs Samuel Rosevean in the Methodist chapel at Charlestown, which stood only yards from the bustling inner harbour and snuggled behind the Rashleigh Arms, the second home of Ned Trevenning. The wedding had none of the outrageous pomp that had surrounded that between James and Helen, a matter for which Lorna was immensely relieved. She didn't want there to be too many witnesses to the fact that she had finally allowed herself to become so firmly trapped that escape had proved to be impossible.

In contrast, it was a day of triumph for Samuel, his satisfaction showing beyond doubt in his smug expression. His delight was in stark contrast to the bride's emotions, with her quiet despair lacing every moment. Admittedly, it could be claimed that she had made it. She had become a Rosevean. The trouble was it was via a second-hand route, by giving herself to the wrong brother. Not that any of the villagers, lining up for a sight of the newly-weds, believed she had made the wrong move. She had chosen a near enough local whose father had been a mine captain, both facts making it a highly-acceptable match.

The arrival of Nathan's letter twenty-four hours before the ceremony had contributed mostly to the havoc that Lorna's nerves were in. During all those years he hadn't contacted her once and it seemed, to her, bitterly ironic that he should do so on the day before her wedding, when feelings that had never been fully free of him were already tugged and twisted enough. The letter's effect was compounded by the fact that he had asked for her continued friendship, and a sympathy he had once shunned.

He had written: 'I thought I'd reach a point where I could keep to an even path, and walk the line between depression and happiness, but I can't. This latest death has brought all the old blackness on. I could always talk to you in the past, at least until those last months. I know talking isn't possible now, mainly due to my own desire to run, but just writing this has helped, has let me look at the situation in some sort of sane way. Would it be asking too much for you to reply?'

Asking too much, she had thought, as she stood and stared at the paper and the oh so familiar neat, sloping letters. He damned well is. Writing as if no time has passed, as if we argued and he pushed me away only yesterday. Assuming there is no way I could have forced myself back to some sort of normal existence, and started to make a different life with a new man.

As she later stood before Rev Desmond Polgrean and slowly, half-heartedly, repeated her marriage vows, her mind was straying far from what she was doing, from the moment that was meant to be all-important to her in its significance.

What would be the harm in one reply, she teased herself? I'll tell him all about my new life. The idea of me being married to Samuel of all people must at least jolt him. If he is hurt at all by that then it can only be for the good, at least from my point of view. He's hurt me enough, much too much.

One part of her, the calmer part, had told her to burn the letter and forget it had ever arrived. What he had written had hinted at a resurrection of feelings that could only cause distress. But simultaneously the rest of her, the stronger and more determined character, couldn't let the matter rest. So when she tilted her face to allow Samuel to kiss her publicly for the first time her eyes were shining for once in his company, and her pulses racing. But it was not from the excitement of the moment, more from thoughts of revenge which were shooting through her mind.

Of course, she wasn't present to see the effect that her reply, crafted in the initial weeks of marriage, had on Nathan. On the surface her terse words made little impact. There was virtually no-one else close enough to him to notice that on the day he received the letter he was even more tense than usual, that he broke routine by stopping for a whisky on the way home from the mine. Except for one person. His landlord saw no change in him. Joe was too immersed in the all-consuming illness that was draining his strength, and the uncertainty surrounding the Idaho-Maryland mine where he worked, when fit enough, as a carpenter. His wife was equally enwrapped in problems, these basically being her family's chances of mere survival, but their daughter had the germ of an idea that something had upset their quiet, morose, almost satanic lodger. And that interested her to a great degree, as everything about Nathan did.

Suzannah Trembeth was her father's reason for living. He doted on her, to such an extent that within days of moving into their home Nathan had realised that he was expected to do so as well. It should not have been hard to be mesmerised by her. Suzannah was nineteen, with a wide, eager beauty that constantly attracted male eyes.

Her golden hair gleamed intoxicatingly, her skin was dewy and clear, her lips generous, and, when she walked, her lithe body swayed in an alluring, knowing fashion.

And it evidently pleased Joe to see his non-drinking, non-womanising lodger escorting his adored daughter to the town's functions, to the typically Cornish brass band concerts and the chapels at Red Dog and Caribou.

To keep the peace Nathan occasionally did just that. Undoubtedly, he liked Joe, respected his dry wit and simple, basic kindness, and frequently wished his own father had harboured within him equal humility, and such pure love, for his offspring. It was because of this affection for the man that he accepted it would not hurt him if he pandered to his daughter now and then, so he played along with both of their wishes. Over the years he had gradually moved that far from what he regarded as his previously complete self-indulgence.

Nevertheless, he knew there was nothing within him he could give Suzannah besides company. He still recoiled from involvement with any woman, although there was no doubt that whatever face he presented to the outside world the news from Lorna had shaken him. Despite realising his reaction was unwarranted, thoughts of her with Samuel not only shocked but sickened. At the time he had left Cornwall he had given up his claim on her with barely concealed euphoria, and even now he did not particularly want past love reclaimed - though simultaneously he hated the idea that she had gone into the arms, and the bed, of his brother. Especially that brother. It won't work, he thought. It can't.

While he was struggling to come to terms with the few sentences within her letter, those which had served to stir so much inner turmoil, he knew he did not want to have to deal with Suzannah's wiles as well. It was thoughts of her, together with ragged memories of Lorna, that had made him detour into the saloon, later pausing before turning the corner to the Trembeths' timber homestead.

The house looked very different from Cornish moorstone and thatch, but inside the old influences remained in the form of rough, home made and makeshift furniture. As in Cornwall, boxes and packing cases served as cupboards, tables and seats. However, an American stove had replaced a cloam oven, and this stood alongside rocking chairs and Yankee clocks. It was basic but cosy, too cosy perhaps for a man who had not minded nights spent living in shacks, or even out in the open. He wasn't sure he had enough patience to deal with Suzannah, but she was hovering at the door as soon as he came into sight, waiting for him. When she first glimpsed him, relief streamed into her face - and then she rushed to greet him, her hair flying, her flowing dress billowing out behind her. It was like being confronted by Lorna all over again, only on this occasion there was little gentleness and tact, just an amazingly overpowering rush of exhausting ebullience.

'Oh Nathan, I've been so worried about you. You've been gone so long. You're never usually so late, you always come home straight from shift.'

Mutely, he nodded, resisting the impulse to shake her hand away from where it had come to rest on his arm. Compared with the undoubted understanding and quietness of Lorna she reminded him of a leech, although he had to admit she was a glorious one. Her looks, and her personality, could perhaps stun most men, and with no real effort on her part.

'Come inside, I've made tea for you. Mother's gone to the Carlyons, but she won't be long. Betty Carlyon pestered her to be there when she's measured for a dress which is meant to be an exact copy of the latest Parisian model.'

The chatter flooded over him as he took off his coat prior to slumping down at the table, still dazed. In his mood irrelevancies made him rage even more inside. Ted's death continued to oppress him, despite it occurring months before, and that morning an Irishman had been badly crushed whilst underground. Although he wasn't dead, it was likely he would be paralysed.

Just as Lorna will be slowly paralysed now she's Samuel's wife, he shuddered. For sure he'll make her as joyless as he is.

Such thoughts helped him ignore, to a great extent, Suzannah and her gossip, as he considered that when there were such matters of living, of existing, of dying, to tackle what the hell did it matter what the vain were currently wearing in Paris?

He had thought he would find it impossible to eat anything and keep it down, but surprised himself, for when it came to the meal he was ravenous. Avidly, he consumed everything Suzannah placed in front of him, from pie to pudding. She sat and watched while he ate, her small mouth parted slightly, a covetous expression plastered on her heart-shaped face. He recognised it, so tried to avoid looking into her eyes.

'I met Ted's wife again today,' she said as she cleared one set of plates away. 'She's such a little scrap, smaller than me I'm sure, and she had those three noisy children running alongside her, rolling in the dirty street. Mother doesn't think she'll be able to survive on her own much longer. It's such a pity there's no close family she can look to.'

Nathan closed his eyes and leant backwards in the chair, not particularly wanting to have to think about Ted's widow. They had started a fund for her weeks before, but he knew that whatever was raised, it would only ease short-term financial suffering. It could go no way towards compensating for the loss of a good, loving husband.

With such thoughts chasing around his mind, he didn't answer, hoping his silence would encourage her to be quiet as well, but she wasn't yet wise enough to let perception, and not tongue, win.

'What do you think will happen?' she pressed. 'Looking back it's such a pity you didn't find Ted sooner. You might have saved him. Do you think there would have been a chance?'

Her words cut him, but he sought composure. Mention of the whole incident always created a hard ball of fear to rise within him. Did she really believe he hadn't asked himself that exact question over and over again?'

'I don't know, how can I tell?' he whispered, the food he had eaten suddenly feeling leaden within him. 'I'm sorry Suzannah but I can't, I mean I don't particularly want to discuss Ted's death.'

'Oh, don't get me wrong, I wasn't blaming you or anything like that,' she said, hurriedly moving next to him, stroking him. 'I know, in fact everyone knows, you did the best you could.'

'Suzannah please,' he mumbled, trying to slide away from her, and not in any way succeeding.

Sensing that he was deeply upset, she had gone on to grasp his upper arm, and was smoothing down his wild curls and kissing his still dirty forehead. Her perfume, welcome as honeysuckle, enveloped him, her soft, perfect body was pressed against his and, against all instincts, he almost relaxed his grip to let her soothe all the cares away.

The trouble was he had used women before to help himself forget, in much the same way as he had used alcohol, and knew this was no permanent solution.

Nor did such actions make him proud of himself, certainly not when all was based on pure lust. Eventually, he prised himself away, and loped towards his room.

'Nathan,' she called after him, her voice cracking with hurt. 'Nathan, please don't turn away from me. I'm sorry, I talk too much, I know I do, I'm sorry.'

Generally he would have answered. Over the years he had mellowed enough to do that. This time, though, he couldn't force the words. Instead, he shut the door firmly behind him, then sank onto his narrow bed. Solitude encased him again, and he welcomed it as a friend and a balm.

1V

James took his gamble and, with the backing of his father-in-law's considerable wealth and influence, and his wife's diluted assistance, it seemed to him that it might lead to some success.

It was a rosy situation that initially surprised him a great deal. He and Ned had haphazardly opened the pit at the right time. The price of clay was high and overproduction was irrelevant. Within three months he was so optimistic regarding the future that he was channelling all his muscular, raw energy into his new way of life, determined to achieve something lasting in his own right. Power, even the minimal drop he was experiencing, provided inspiration.

Within twelve weeks he had travelled a long way towards understanding Richard Courteney's blinkered, driven ego.

After the first months of production, which proved that big profits might eventually be theirs at the end of the day, he took Helen onto the moors to show her exactly what he owned. By then he was bristling with confidence, and awash with embryonic euphoria.

'I still can't believe it,' he said as they stared down at the small chunk of bleak woodland and gorse with its heart ripped out to make way for the Rosevean/Trevenning enterprise. 'I'm the owner of all that. I don't have to bow to anyone.'

She glanced up at him, at the striking, blond hair, at the strong, carved features, caught a glimpse of a buzzard soaring regally above them, and smiled.

'You're co-owner, my love. Remember Ned is involved too. After all, this was his idea, his vision.'

In reply, he put his hand over hers, so much smaller in comparison, and tried to show the affection he should have felt instinctively. She hadn't mentioned her father.

He, surely, is the real owner, James thought, for he put up more than three quarters of the money, and contributed almost all the contacts and the know-how.

Ned had played a less dynamic part. In the past fortnight or so he had been too ill even to visit the works. For years the doctors had warned him he was drinking himself into the grave, but he had ignored all advice, including passionate pleas from his wife, so used to being outshone by the bottle. Instead, he had kept his consumption of beer and spirits as high as always, never grasping that such indulgence might really exact the ultimate price. As a result, his liver had been badly damaged and was determinedly telling him so. However, he continued to insist it was a slight breakdown in his health, from which he would soon recover.

James believed otherwise. He had visited him twice of late to discuss business matters, each time finding him confined to bed with skin white and clammy, eyes glazed and breath hard to come by. True, Ned had also caught a fever which had not helped, but a smell had pervaded the room which reeked of long-term illness. In fact the whole house, with poor Beth riddled with worry, had taken on a brooding, waiting air.

On the second occasion James had baulked from walking into the musty atmosphere. He didn't like having to face the prospect of mortality at the best of times, and especially not when new life was surging so unexpectedly into his own body.

At the memory he shivered involuntarily, then suddenly remembered where he was - miles distant from Ned and sickness - and he shook the images away. With relief, he concentrated instead on the view from his vantage point. Ahead, he could see the pits, and the workers scurrying around like dots on the land that was his, and he allowed a sense of achievement and well-being to suffuse his thoughts.

Feeling positive with his achievements so far, he turned slightly towards Helen, who was finding it difficult to stand against the force of the gusting wind.

'I'm so lucky,' he said, half to himself. 'I've so much to be thankful for, and it's mainly due to your family.'

She hadn't expected to hear thanks.

'Just remember to count that luck in the future, when you're striving for the moon and all the stars hiding away up there,' she answered quickly, taking off the hat she had been wearing, which hadn't suited her, and letting the breeze blow through her lengthening nut brown hair. 'And don't ever try to out-do father. Please promise me that. If you ever did try to rival him it would be to the exclusion of everything else, and I mean everything.'

'At the moment I really believe I could reach the moon if I set my sights on it. No height could stop me,' he said, quite seriously.

He hasn't heard me, not one word, she thought. What I say to him doesn't matter in the slightest.

She didn't say anything like that out loud, instead stifled a gasp as a few cold and warning fingers of foreboding clutched her heart. Although there was no direct reason for them, they were there all the same.

Had her mother once felt like this, when her husband had started his massive business affair, or had she backed him all the way at the beginning, pushing him to achieve as much as he physically, and mentally, could? Whatever had happened, the benefits she had reaped since that decision had only been hollow, based purely on money.

'You mentioned Ned,' James carried on, unaware of her growing unhappiness. 'I've been thinking of him a lot of late. Even if he does recover it will be a long time before he's fully fit. I'd thought of buying him out. Poor devil. I know this is all his idea, but I can't see him ever being able to carry out his responsibilities.'

Helen tightened her small grip on his hand. She swallowed.

'Don't you think you should move a little slower, see how this all really works out in the coming months, even years, before taking on everything just by yourself?' She hesitated slightly, before ploughing on. 'Remember that you're a tiny, unheard voice at the moment. The china clay industry is mainly owned by some rich, supposedly important families who, at the moment, don't see you as one of them. Being up there with them is something you have to aim for if you're serious about all this, and you don't want to have to tackle all that alone.'

'If I believed I was only a small voice, as you so quaintly describe me, then I'm sure I'd never be able to achieve anything,' he snapped, annoyed that she could try to diminish him. 'I know there's a fight ahead, there must be if we're to get properly established and join that group of people you so obviously know so very well. The trouble with Ned is he is stuck in bed, hardly able to move, so what use is he going to be in any such fight? I need just myself, and my own wits and determination, and remember I didn't go into this unaware of what the business is like. Samuel delighted in telling me all the pitfalls way before you.'

'You're jumping in so quickly,' she persisted, taking in deep and steadying breaths. 'If you wait, if you take things at an easier pace I'm sure the results will be longer lasting. All I'm saying is don't rush, all this is so new to you. Why don't you give yourself time to learn first, alongside Ned?'

At the last moment she checked herself from saying: you rushed into marrying me, of course, and the reasons were the same.

'Well I've never had power before,' he answered her, thinking at the same time how plain she looked. Her dull, nondescript clothes had somehow merged into the stunted, wind-ridden surroundings, and there seemed, to him, to be nothing about her that stood out and shone. How had someone so impressive as Richard Courteney sired her?

'Now I've got authority, I have to admit that I like it. And I'm not alone, remember, my darling. Even if Ned does agree with me, that perhaps it's best to give up his share, your father is still there, right behind me.'

'But surely you shouldn't consider splitting from Ned quite so soon, even if he does agree to it? For pity's sake concentrate on establishing yourself as a co-owner before you try to become a sole owner. Forget my father. He wants to stand back and watch to see if you have enough guts to make it work. If this goes wrong he won't help you. He'll make sure he lays the debts, and all the reasons for any failure, at your feet, though.'

Trying, and failing, to fight back the growing anger, he took everything she said as blunt criticism, which served only to wound his paper-thin confidence.

'Are you trying to hold me back? Because I would swear you are. Coming from a family like yours, with such a reputation for succeeding, can't you even begin to understand how I'm feeling? Surely you've got a little scrap of faith in me? Everything's just starting. Unlike your view of matters, it seems to me there are really good times ahead.'

In desperation, she bit her lip so hard she almost made it bleed. Why was this marriage proving to be so difficult? Ahead of taking her vows, she had thought she would be able to be flexible, and adapt to whatever he wanted, and all difficulties would fade away in the face of her devotion to him. She had certainly over-estimated the faith she had in herself.

'I'm not trying to discourage you, really I'm not. I suppose I'm only trying my best to be a steadying influence.'

'Why not be more honest about it? You're trying to stop the poor boy who's suddenly married into money letting such a fortunate turn of events go to his head.'

'That's unfair,' she whispered, her hurt words almost whipped away by the increasing breeze that, with its additional power, was teasing and rocking the gorse bushes, that made sections of the moorland seem as if it was ablaze, and the scent of the wild, pungent clumps of herbs and heather swirl around them.

'Unfair maybe, but true.'

At his cutting words, she winced, and could not disguise the pain his retort gave her. It was also reflected immediately in her tight expression, and the over-bright eyes that threatened tears.

He reminded her suddenly of a small boy who had been told by his friends he could not play in their games any longer, and was kicking out against those nearest to him in his anger. James, for his part, realised he was being unfair to her, and against his will was touched by guilt, the same guilt that had never been too far away since their wedding day. This prompted him to squeeze her tight in an unuttered apology, but he would not allow his regrets to divert him from the topic of their conversation. It helped that he was absolutely certain he had the backing of her father, which was all the security he required. Ned was actually a side issue to him, one that he could pretend to discuss with her.

'I may also be investing elsewhere.'

In immediate response, she stiffened. Every joint locked, threatening to turn her to stone. In her heart she didn't want to anger him further, though found it almost impossible not to look concerned.

'Go on, explain what you mean.'

'It's your father's idea basically, he suggested it to me.'

Silently, she cursed her father. When young she adored him but he had always held back with her, even then, as if never quite able to forgive her for not being born male. Later on, when she realised that the only affection he had ever shown her was for the fruits of his own successes, she accepted that what he felt for her, however little or great it was, no longer mattered to her. True love could not grow in an emotional desert. And now, more than ever, she didn't want him turning James into a mimesis of himself.

But she said nothing of those thoughts. It was not the moment for James to be able to understand. Instead, she tried desperately to smile.

'I'm intrigued, carry on.'

With his anger dissipating, he continued looking with pleasure at the figures rushing around the works that he, himself, had brought into being.

'There's a new passenger train service to be introduced, hopefully next year, or at least in 1877, between Newquay and Fowey. It's due to pass through Luxulyan, close to here. I was asked if I would like to become a shareholder, and I agreed.'

To her despair, she found that, from being almost completely numb, she was now trembling.

'Why didn't you tell me about this before you made the decision to go-ahead, or at least discuss it with me when it was first suggested? You've never as much as mentioned it before.'

As she spoke, he kept his gaze on the scene ahead, deliberately not turning towards her.

'I said nothing because I honestly didn't think you'd be interested.'

Almost defeated, she shrugged her thin shoulders, not trusting herself to say too much more.

'But the money, where is that to come from?'

This time it was he who stiffened.

'I hadn't expected such a bank of questions. You willingly gave me access to your money when we married. Do you think now, that you're actually my wife, that I won't act wisely with it?'

'I'm sure you will,' she mumbled, thinking how all the light had fled from the day, how the moorland, despite the bright gorse and jewelled heather, had become a barren wasteland.

'I had just thought . . . well it would be nice if we could make decisions together, that's all.'

'It was your father's idea. He's putting money into it too. I can't possibly see how you could have any objections.'

In jaded response she nodded her head, and followed his fixed gaze down into the valley, now seeing neither greenery, nor purple or golden tints, nor men chasing around a Rosevean pit, or hovering birds of prey. It was as if her system had seized, and all she could concentrate on was future misery.

V

Summer 1875

Samuel gleaned almost as much satisfaction from building his own cottage as he had done from the 'winning' of Lorna. It, too, had helped him prove himself. He had selected for himself, and his new wife, a plot of land for their home which lay to the east of Biscovey, with vast views over the ocean. It had been owned by a colleague of his, a captain at Bethany who, after tough and sustained persuasion, had finally bowed to pressure and let him have it at more than an acceptable price.

Despite the definite bargain, that managed to lift Samuel's spirits for a while, the raising of capital to build the cottage, had still proved a problem. His own small amount of savings had been spent while courting Lorna, a period in his life in which necessity had almost made him generous. With that cash gone, and the need to break away from the family home strong inside him, he had spoken to his mother, and managed to procure some of Nathan's monthly instalments with more ease than he had imagined possible.

A small part of him knew it was ironic that he should use his brother's hard earned wages, especially as he still felt so much bitterness towards Nathan. Nevertheless, he talked himself into believing that both he and Lorna were owed it. Hadn't they both suffered because of his brother's callousness?

It took him six weeks to construct the stone walls, during the hours when he wasn't below ground, and another five weeks to complete the building. Although admittedly very basic, he felt it was enough. Samuel was an excellent carpenter, and able to fashion much more than passable furniture out of the meagre wood they were able to salvage from the shoreline. Anxious to help in some way, to make some contribution to this obviously important project of his, Lorna had spent hours scavenging Spit Beach, sandwiched between Crinnis and Par, for reasonable 'finds'.

It was no hardship, except perhaps for when she had to drag an extra large piece of wood home. She enjoyed it on the beach. It was an isolated spot visited only by the occasional dock worker, local villager, or flock of turnstones, and she felt able to relax in the resulting peace. It gave her the chance to think, to recharge the strength that she was using up at a frightening rate in trying to make her marriage work.

Undoubtedly, she knew she had gone into the partnership with completely the wrong attitude, but now that she was committed she felt it was her responsibility to stay and fight for some joint happiness. Above all, she had to convince herself that she must not run, for really there was no place else to go. She had lived all her life in that pocket of land, and the world outside of it was a mystery, as it was to many of those around her, except, of course, those miners who had travelled thousands of miles to carry on their trade. To some America seemed nearer than the land on the other side of the Tamar.

The disturbing letters were still arriving from California, sent to her via the family home and read in secret. They only confused her search for equilibrium, though not enough to force her to put a stop to them, or destroy them unread.

In fact, on long days when any natural

optimism was notably absent, she found they served to lighten the hours, together with her mind. Over time, she had tricked herself into thinking that as long as Samuel never found out about the letters they could not do much damage. They helped restore some of her lost self-confidence. They meant she had not been utterly discarded after all.

After reading them carefully, she believed that Nathan had accepted her marriage, or at least that was what she deducted from his written words. Also, she felt that in absorbing the news he had sent her, she had now come fully to accept that he was now forging a life thousands of miles away and was physically lost to her. There would be no revival of old loves. The letters were just words, all that remained of a passion that had scarred her.

The cottage, despite its simplicity, and maybe because of it, delighted Lorna when it was finished. As she stood in front of the front door, on the day they moved in, watching the sun dancing blithely on its walls, and gazing across fields and grazing land to a distant sea, she admitted to herself that she had underestimated Samuel. Especially his determination, even though that should have been glaringly obvious during his pursuit of her.

The idea of building his own home had been mentioned before their wedding, but she had doubted it would ever materialise. Since the break-up with Nathan she had expected the bare minimum from everything. It seemed the best form of protection.

In the weeks after they moved in she also came to realise that she no longer begrudged the fact that she didn't love her husband. That realisation helped her take the first, small steps towards accepting the status quo.

The lack of love was not a fault that lay with him. She saw that it was to do with herself, and with a past that was unalterable.

Lorna also bowed to the fact that Mary Rosevean had virtually come to live with them. The pattern was set almost as soon as she and Samuel stepped over the threshold. Mary arrived in the early morning, stayed at the cottage all day, only returning home in the evening to attend to the

younger boys. Lorna could sense that her mother-in-law basically did not want to be alone, and could not feel comfortable with anyone who was not family, or who she saw as 'superior'.

James and Helen had tried to stress that she would be welcome enough at their home in Tregrehan, but Mary had never set foot in there. She was confined by her own attitude, firmly believing she was a daughter of the village, and could never attain anything 'higher', despite her years as a mine captain's wife. James and Helen were Courteneys, and those of the Courteney ilk were way above them. She held them in awe, even Helen who wanted no so-called 'respect', especially from her mother-in-law.

But Mary remained a prisoner of her mind, and to her James was now as lost as Nathan. He had decided to desert her, not for another country like his brother, but for another class. Her perpetual, and prolonged, visits did not upset Lorna, who had known her for years and found her restful to live with. Mary barely spoke, and was happy enough to spend hour upon hour engaged in whatever chore she could lay her hands on. Her desire for conversation of any kind had deserted her.

Instead, she was enwrapped in the past - when her husband was alive, before Nathan had left, before the seeds of hopelessness had set themselves in the ground.

Three months after they moved into their cottage the inevitable happened, and Bethany closed. James's predictions proved to be correct and the machinery which had kept generations in work, and food on tables for decades, ground to a silent, sickening halt.

It should have shattered the unnatural calm Samuel was still experiencing, but it didn't as he managed to find alternative work within days. With that accomplished he felt himself on safe enough ground for a little self-congratulation. Since marrying Lorna, he believed he had coped well, in fact unbelievably so. Being superstitious, like all miners, he now looked upon her as his taliswoman.

The alternative work was at Boscundle, close to Tregrehan. It was near James and Helen's home, although Samuel had no intention of calling in on them. Not because he was like his mother and regarded them as 'above' him. It was because, to him, James had turned his back on his family and his trade.

This time, even in his heart, Samuel felt that his new company, Wheal Eliza Consols, had a chance of survival, despite the dire years that probably lay ahead for the industry. The mine was continuing to pay rich dividends in the face of the falling price of tin. They were developing the same ground as a former mine, West Par Consols, and their shafts lay south of Parkenwise, immediately beside the St Austell to St Blazey road. When laid in 1849 they had been on the only piece of unworked land in the district.

What Samuel saw was that while companies elsewhere were cutting back and claiming defeat, at Wheal Eliza they were expanding, which gave him unswerving hope for the future, an optimism way out of character. Encouragement came from the fact that he could see the progress which was being made, with his own eyes. They were extending beneath the grounds of Tregrehan Manor, and laying tram-roads underground, while at the surface they planned to equip the mine with a railway and then use a small tank locomotive to haul ore between the shafts and stamps.
He rarely said anything about work, or his hopes, when he returned home. Often, he meant to, but although intending to try to explain everything to Lorna, the words never came. On the whole, the two of them rarely spoke to each other at length, and if he was honest with himself it was a situation that benefited him, for he had never properly opened his soul to anyone in his life before. Tom Rosevean had regarded passion and intensity with distaste, and his third son did so as well. Anyway, he regarded himself as no conversationalist, happy to apply short, blunt, phrases rather than anything intricate.
Even Lorna now needed a certain amount of prompting, or goading, before she was in full flow with words. Her vitality, once so evident, had dissipated, and though she failed to realise it she was turning inward with the same inevitability as Mary had done.
Despite his reticence with words and oft bleak outlook on humanity, on one early September day in 1875, when all was still and sweetly scented after a blue-skied, hazy afternoon, when his mother, who had shared their meal, had left for home, and they were alone,

Samuel felt oddly at one with the world. If he ever looked back he probably was to see that moment of complete contentment as a high which was followed by nothing by troughs.

'Happy?' he asked, putting a hand on the muslin of Lorna's sleeve. 'Do you approve of your new home?'

'It's magnificent,' she laughed softly and naturally, knowing how he liked to be encouraged. 'I can't really believe yet that it's ours. I think I've settled down really well.'

His arm went tentatively around her, and she leant awkwardly back against him, nearness still not coming easily to either of them. They could not utterly relax with each other, but Lorna quietly praised herself on the way she was overcoming any signs of aversion.

'So you're pleased with your new husband are you? Do you think I've done you proud?'

'Absolutely,' she answered, unsure how best to demonstrate her thanks. Eventually, she stretched upwards and kissed him on his pale lips.

He smiled in response, feeling she was acting more warmly towards him than he could ever remember. They chatted idly for a while, mainly about Wheal Eliza and James, and what Samuel had come to regard as his brother's betrayal of all the traditions in his blood.

'Going clay will never work,' he stressed. 'He's only just started up, and he's pushing too hard already. I've even heard his name bandied about as a backer for a new railway project. Who the hell does he think he is, the biggest businessman that Biscovey's ever produced?'

Lorna winced at his attitude.

'Give him a chance. He'll settle, as I've done.

He's got to learn by experience. I know that sounds as if I'm a schoolmistress, or something, but it's true.'

'He's asked Alex to join his damned company, did you know that?'

She didn't, and she lifted her head in surprise. The weak sun was managing to burnish reddish lights into her rich auburn hair.

'I had no idea, but then I suppose he's been out of work since Bethany closed, and Alex with all his energy hates kicking his heels and doing nothing. It's rather lucky for him.'

'Lucky,' Samuel snorted, 'not for either of them. He'll probably have to work twice as hard as the others because he's the boss man's brother. And James won't have a simple ride either. Alex has a head full of ideas, most of them to do with the so-called rights of the working man. Not that he's been a working man that long.'

Almost subconsciously, she grinned, and her face lit up as if an inner radiance had suddenly been re-lit. She kissed him again, spurred on by a sudden, wayward hope that maybe their joint future wouldn't be as grim and loveless as a cold, grey November morning after all.

'I've never heard you say so much before, at least all in one day,' she teased.

They said nothing more for a while, merely stood and watched the house martins skim the fields and then soar back into the sky in quick, pure flashes of white. Another month and they, and the swallows and swifts, would be gone.

Then she asked, instinct telling her that there was more to his story: 'Did James ask you to work for him as well?'

After a quick intake of breath, he hesitated slightly, unsure of what her reaction would be.

'Yes, maybe he did.'
'And what did you say?'
'Let's say I declined, but not too bluntly.' With a smile, he took hold of her hand. 'You probably haven't noticed, but I've become a little less rash since marrying you. I just told him that Alex was welcome to bear the cross of being an extremely close relative of the Big Boss, but at the same time I didn't intend to be placed in the same position.
'James wasn't too upset?' she asked, apprehensively, wondering how abrupt Samuel had been.
'He wasn't happy, I'll admit that. Of course, he thought he was doing me a big favour and then believed, for some reason, I was throwing it back at him. But there's no rift between us, at least I don't think so. If there is one it's nothing like the row there was between Nathan and I before he left.'
As they stood there, both trying to relax completely in the other's company, he stroked her hair, silky and fine and warm with the sun. The delicate, but heady, scent of late flowering wild flowers, growing on the shadowed side of the hedgerows, drifted across to them.
'I wonder now why I was so worked up when he left. It was a blessing, really, and I've been able to wipe him from my mind since then.'
After an hour it began to get cold. Their tiny but cosy sitting room with its polished brass, glowing like copper jewels, and its bright cushions, was beckoning her.
Admit it, she told herself, he has done well. She was aware that, compared with many of the cottages, it was a palace, although she worked hard to keep it that way. Most miners' wives could work wonders, even with barely

existent money and paltry possessions.
Idly, he rubbed her shoulders as the sun finally disappeared westwards, leaving wavy pink streaks like unravelling satin ribbons behind it.
'You're shivering. Come on, let's go back inside.'
Later, when he was sitting in one of the chairs he had made, and she was on her knees by the carefully swept hearth, flicking through a newspaper a friend had left behind that morning, he added: 'By the way I saw your mother today. Our paths crossed as I was walking home. She said a letter had arrived for you and wondered if you would collect it. Any idea who it's from? We've been here three months now. You ought to tell whoever it is that you're married and have moved on, and don't live with your family any more.' Proudly, he looked around the four walls again, still unable to accept how successfully he had built the place. Although she could read his thoughts, she didn't say anything for a while, very relieved he couldn't read hers. While keeping as open an expression as possible, she tried desperately to quell nerves that had decided of a sudden to leap into quivering life.
'Thanks, I'll call around tomorrow and pick it up,' she said ingenuously. 'Whoever it's from I'm sure it's of no importance.'
He let the matter drop. No more was said about it. But the slowly emerging camaraderie she had begun to feel in his presence started to slip away, leaving her once again cursing Nathan for filling her life with a sense of foreboding.

V1

It was three o' clock at night and there was no sound. Outside moonlight slithered across the landscape of Grass Valley, picking out the hills where there would be sound, as the mines continued their seemingly never-ending toil. The light slunk its way through the dusty streets like an intruder, illuminating well-tended gardens which had only recently been hacked out of the earth, and straining through a parlour window with its curtains still pulled back.

With an effort it outlined the silhouettes of the two men inside. Their heads were bent closely together over a makeshift table, untidily covered in scattered charts. Litter lay strewn around their feet, and the congealed remains of a half eaten meal solidified nearby. The faces, one in late middle age, the other much younger, were drawn and hollowed. Both men were longing for sleep but were being kept awake by a puzzle they could not solve, and by Celtic stubbornness.

Nathan was in a worse state than Joe. His eyes ached unbearably, his eyelids, heavy at the best of times, kept closing involuntarily. Every muscle was reminding him of a day's work that was behind him, and of a shift that lay ahead. But he refused to go to bed, at least until the problem that was confronting them was part-way solved. He hated being defeated. The paranoia of failure that had been instilled in all Rosevean brothers since birth nagged at his subconscious.

Over and over again, he tried to tell himself that it wasn't even his problem. Joe had been handed it after speaking too loudly, and too long, of his 'vast' knowledge of the mines back in Cornwall. In essence, a pump needed to be installed to drain a level in the Idaho-Maryland mine where he worked. It was a level which was extremely difficult to reach and, despite months of research and experiment, the answer had proved elusive to all the experts.

After speaking of his Cornish experiences, Joe had been promised promotion, and extra money, if he provided a solution.

With these promises, he had been given a week to come up with viable sketches and in the event it had been Nathan, with a quicker and more able brain, who found he had been left working against the seven day clock. Since living with the Trembeths he had come to realise how much his time in the mountains had changed him. The urge to run from responsibilities remained, but he was now able to summon up enough resilience to overcome it. And he felt responsible for the Trembeths - for Joe, slowly coughing his life away but still working whenever he could, for his quietly determined landlady, and even for Suzannah who had been brought up believing that everything she ever wanted would eventually be thrown at her dainty feet.

Nathan knew beyond doubt that he had some chance of cracking the riddle. On occasions, when he had defied his father and left home for some respite from the highly-charged atmosphere they had all lived in, he had worked at both St Just in Penwith and Perranzabuloe mines and had learnt the most practicable methods of timbering shafts and levels, and therefore of greatly reducing the dreaded threat of rock falls.

But no inspiration was to come to him that night. It reached the point when his eyes would not focus for more than a second at a time and, furiously disappointed with his lack of stamina and the tardiness of his usually incisive brain, he had staggered into his room and fallen asleep in minutes.

Exhausted, or alive with energy, he found the enigma would not go away. It was there, tugging at his mind, as soon as he woke the following morning, and it continued to haunt him hours later when he was underground covered in sweat and grime. He was still up, but barely awake, at three o' clock the next night, but on this occasion he was much nearer reaching a breakthrough.

'Strike me, I bloody well underestimated you,' Joe murmured as the answer unfolded before him. 'I only asked you for an opinion, I didn't expect all this work. After all, it was me who stupidly went shooting his mouth off about things he could do.'

Nathan kept his dark head down, anxiously double checking all his figures before showing any signs of celebration.

'If I've put my mind to something I need to finish it. A legacy from my father. There have been times, though, when I've run from problems hoping they would disappear, and I regret that now. I've come to the conclusion, too late perhaps, that it's best to hit things head-on, not sweep them out of the way, because they never really do disappear, whatever you may think, or hope.' Then he added, with a grin he could not contain: 'And anyway, when it comes to something like this it's rewarding to be able to show them that no hard-rock miners can whip the Cornish.'

While Nathan dealt with a few lingering details Joe brewed some tea, put a drop of whisky in each mug, and carefully re-lit his pipe. Then he sat back down beside Nathan and began a conversation that killed a good part of the quiet elation that the younger man had been feeling.

'I can see why our Suzannah is so taken with you. She's usually a hard one to bowl over, she's much tougher than I am, or ever have been.'

It was the first time his daughter's growing devotion to Nathan had been openly mentioned. Nathan nearly coughed up his tea. Certainly, he didn't want to discuss Suzannah, and he didn't want to hear Joe's approval of the 'match'. This was one rapidly escalating problem that had presented him with more than enough headaches already.

Of a sudden, he realised he should take note of his own words, and face the matter head-on. Tell Suzannah very decisively that he did not want her, despite her undeniable beauty, and tell Joe as directly as he could that he was not interested in his daughter.

I would have done once, he thought, and felt no regret for any sorrow I might cause. But it's different now. Since hurting Lorna I think I've lost my way with women, or at least how to deal with them, if ever I was successful in that regard.

After that his concentration went. The figures and drawings merged into a multi-coloured haze that would not clear. He could do no more, and the final details were not inserted onto the sketches for another twelve hours. And by that time, the disturbance of his mind, that memories of Lorna had caused, had been carefully and deliberately set aside once more. The solution, hatched during those long nights, brought Joe and Nathan closer, and eventually worked. Its success made the two men reluctant local celebrities. Nathan expected little reward, bar a few words of acknowledgement. However, in appreciation of his commitment, the Idaho-Maryland owners offered him an extremely lucrative job, one even his father would have congratulated him on attaining. Surprising himself, he took it, but he gave no assurances to his new employers that he would be around for years to come. He had no wish permanently to settle yet.

The pump, which went down vertically at first, took a right-angled bend and eventually dipped by 40 degrees to get to the level it was to drain. It was installed without major complications and on the day it was started the miners were given a holiday, although no-one stayed away from the mine completely. The local workers, whether Cornish, Chinese or Irish, turned up to mingle with folk from miles around who had arrived to see the new wonder put through its paces.

For Suzannah herself the day was a supreme moment of achievement. The two men in her life, one important to her, the other not so necessary to her future, were acclaimed by all and sundry, and she ensured she was in full view, in the middle of them.

On that morning her mother awoke ill, with a wracking cold and unable to attend the celebrations, which allowed Suzannah to bask happily alone in the glory, however reflected. She had always regarded her father as much of a fool. Too besotted by her to peer beneath the surface to see the true character. Too blinded by her blossoming beauty to acknowledge the faults, the darkness in her that she wanted to destroy but doubted she would ever have the willpower to overcome. Too easy, as well, to trick or bring to heel.

Nathan was different, and that excited her. He was strong and he was a challenge. With him in her house, and by her side, she was aware that she drew envious glances from most other women in town.

Throughout the afternoon she stuck close to him, not deterred by the throng that gathered around him wherever he moved. As the moments ticked by he discovered that whether he watched one of the well-contested wrestling matches, or stopped to speak to someone about the angle, or efficiency, of the new pump, she was there, by his side, as if welded to him.

It was impossible for outsiders not to think they were an established couple, especially when adoration burned from her honey-coloured, cloying eyes. When others came near she brushed her body against him, her scent heady and threatening, against all the odds, to entice. Also, he noticed, as they watched the impromptu events springing up around them such as the singing of Cornish choirs, how eyes followed them, and the looks of his colleagues gobbled up Suzannah's swaying hips.

He cursed himself for not having had the foresight to imagine what would happen. In fact, in the end, he had only attended because he had promised Joe he would be there in person, and the man he had become had instilled in himself a moral code that had been absent before.

'I'm so proud of you,' she whispered as the speeches were made. 'Have you any idea how much?'

Determined not to look into her eyes, he didn't attempt an answer, merely nodded his head and prayed for some unearthly force to transport him elsewhere.

Damn the pump, he thought, and damn your own pride for making you draw up the best plan possible. You're digging a rut for yourself all over again, and this time round it really is a rut. With Lorna the trap was an illusion. What she was offering you was unconditional love.

Eventually, he blanked his mind to what was happening around. With surprising ease, he shut out the chattering, pushing people clustered in bright, shouting groups, smoking, cursing, drinking, and eating everything the shareholders had provided in the way of refreshments. Instead, he concentrated on the land that lay in the distance and spread away from them all, stretching into natural quiet. There was a deep longing within him to return to the months he had spent in isolation. With that uppermost in his mind, he stood in the midst of the cavorting crowds, wishing himself back in the heart of the Sierra Nevada, the 430 mile range that lay in Eastern California and stretched from the Tehachapi Pass in the south to Feather River in the north. While people swirled around him, he thought back to the shack he had lived in while in the mountains, as well as the winter's night when the snow had fallen so hard that the only escape had been through the roof. It had been harsh, sometimes beyond belief, but he had discovered the compensations.

Although he had explored only a minimal part of the lower slopes, covered as they were with fir, pine, cedar, oak and scattered groves of sequoia, in the stretches of land where he had walked and lived he had found only peace. It had been part of the sprawling, diverse country where there were more mountain goats and sheep, mule deer and brown and black bears than humans. To him, it had been glorious.

In Grass Valley, among those of his own kind, he was not so very far away from the Snowy Range, but it felt as distant from him as Biscovey. He had hunted the animals there in order to survive. As he looked down at Suzannah, at the sensuous body that deviated towards him whenever the chance was there, he felt that it was now he, himself, who was experiencing the traumatic taste of being hunted.

Then again, what is wrong with me that I mind her persistence, he thought. She's every bit as glorious as the peaks, the lowlands, the seclusion were. But I want more than just beauty, though I always want more. Surely that's been the root cause of all my restlessness? Would life be less complicated, and simpler to understand, if I could accept what is offered and stop yearning for more?

It worked out that he and Suzannah walked home together, with dusk falling in around them like a translucent shadow. To his dismay they became slightly separated from Joe and the colleagues he was conversing with, and although he tried to hang back to rejoin the group the gap remained between them. As they ambled along, moving more slowly by the second, she placed an elegantly clad arm around him in a gesture of proud possession. At her touch, he was tempted to shake himself free, but with Joe walking behind he didn't. Instead, he held himself taut and leant away from her, making it obvious he didn't relish such close contact.

Much like a terrified virgin, he thought with derision. All I'm achieving is managing to be pathetic in the extreme. What the hell's wrong with me? I should be revelling in this.

If his less than pliant attitude did deter her, Suzannah refused to allow any disappointment to show. When they reached home, and she had reluctantly released him, she stretched upwards, pushing her wand-like waist into him, and murmured into his ear:

'You do realise what you do to me, don't you? Bear in mind the fact that I can be very, very patient.'

The following morning Joe closed the net still further, adding to Nathan's sense of futility. Since he had joined the Idaho-Maryland they had walked to the mine together on those occasions when Joe was fit enough to complete a full day's work, even though, since his promotion, less had been demanded of him physically. It was usually a contemplative, near silent stroll, but on that day Joe broke the soothing atmosphere with talk of the one subject now occupying his mind.

'Suzannah really enjoys your company, I b'lieve.'

'I believe it too,' Nathan answered, sarcasm sharpening his voice, but Joe didn't catch the inflection, being too concerned by what he wished to tell the man who seemed to have affected their lives so dramatically.

'I know she's very young, yet. However she may act, though, she's very unsure of herself, and most of all the maid's unsure of you. You're a deep one, you know. It takes some effort to work out what you're feeling.'

At that, he patted Nathan on the back, almost paternally.

'Don't get me wrong lad. I don't want you to think you've got to tell me your whole life

story, or let me know what you think of that daughter of mine. What I want you to know is that if it ever happened I would be proud to have you marry her. You're near enough family as it is. I hope we've made that clear.'
Nathan kept grimly quiet. Please stop the rambling, my friend, he thought desperately. I don't want to hear any of this, I really don't. But there was more to come.
'We all admire you, you know, and what Suzannah feels is even more than that. And she is lovely. Believe me, no man could have a better daughter.'
Nathan did not trust himself to answer, aware that he didn't trust the girl entirely. She wasn't devious but, given a few years, he had the idea she would be as cunning as hell. Nevertheless, after a while he mumbled some sort of reply, striving to ignore a stomach that was nervously heaving.
The nightmares were still with him. That evening, for the first time in aeons, his mind conjured up visions of chains and bars. And then, even more disturbing, sensual pictures of Lorna.

V11

November 1875

Helen was joyous when she discovered she was pregnant. Her first response was to want to announce the news to the world. But telling James would have to come first and she was very aware she would have to choose the right moment for that as she had no idea what his reaction would be. They had never discussed the likelihood of having children.
Although no-one else knew of her condition,

bar the doctor, she began to regard herself as a different person to the girl who had, not long before, walked down the aisle with James. Almost immediately she began to draw an unseen veil around herself, becoming even more introspective, as if revelling in her secret.

From the outset she felt all-powerful in the knowledge that new life was growing, almost mystically, inside her, and was amazed that no-one else noticed the changes within her, both mentally and physically. She believed even if her belly was not revealing signs of approaching motherhood her eyes, her skin, her mannerisms, were betraying it.

In fact the pregnancy finally ended her transition from girl to woman. She had matured since her marriage. Although the still slight figure belied it, her 18 years were an anomaly. Overall, she looked, spoke and acted like someone with much more experience of living.

A baby can only be a positive achievement, bringing more warmth into the home, making us focus on what is really important, she thought in the hours she spent alone, wrapped in her personal dreams. Hours alone seemed to have become the sum total of her existence. James was perpetually away, kept immersed in interests that appeared to become more complex by the day.

Helen's contact with her parents had also become minimal. Her father never visited their house. Despite being constantly asked to drop by he could never spare enough seconds to call. And her mother, perhaps afraid that her daughter had forged a more enriching life than she had ever attained, resolutely stayed away.

Once she learnt she was pregnant such 'inconsequentials' failed to bother Helen. All she wanted was to bear James's child, to have it growing inside her body, becoming part of her in a way that he never looked likely to do. Eventually, she did carefully select her moment to tell him. It came five weeks after she initially saw the doctor, when they were, for once, together in the house. There were no business associates about to arrive, and no meetings for James to rush out to.

Only half an hour or so beforehand, he had devoured an extremely good dinner and seemed in an indulgent enough mood. One reason was that he believed he had good grounds to feel self-satisfied. The works were continuing to prosper, and so were his long-term plans.

Ned, still ailing and now weak enough to succumb to persuasion, had as much as agreed to hand over full control to him. James had put to use on his partner much of what he had already learnt from his father-in-law about convincing, and unremitting, pressure.

The guilt that had nagged him at the start of his marriage had now disintegrated. Success was becoming a reality for him, and he was invigorated by the energy it gave him. He had decided to regard his 'merger' with Helen from Richard's viewpoint, and as a result had begun to believe that an injection of his youth and raw enthusiasm had been badly needed by the family.

His vision allowed him to see a future in which he would never be a lackey, however indebted he was to his father-in-law. It also allowed him to visualise himself as eventually being able to stand on his own, both independently and successfully, in the business community.

Despite Helen's words of warning he had snapped up the offer of shares in the new railway company. If anything he had been egged on by her quiet criticism. Only that morning there had been a meeting of prospective shareholders in Fowey. It had been held at the King of Prussia, an inn on the town quay named after a Cornish smuggler of ill-repute whose contraband had been brought to shore at Prussia Cove. The room they had booked overlooked the river. It had been recently refurbished in dusky red and gold, and reeked of wealth and good living. Afterwards, when business had been discussed and put away, he had come away extremely pleased with himself.

The other hopeful shareholders, most of them elderly and battle-scarred, had known that he personally lacked money, contacts and experience. It was no secret that a year previously clay pits and railways had been as good as foreign creatures to him. Ownership of either had been utterly out of reach.

In spite of that he had been treated as an equal and the benevolence he had experienced in that room had encouraged him more than a flush of profits could ever have done. Such undiluted camaraderie made him proud that he had been rapidly and readily accepted by such men.

There had been a liberal sprinkling of JPs among them, and a generous slice of MPs. The majority had roots deeply embedded in Cornish history. There were Trevanions, Edgcumbes and Carlyons sitting on one side of the shadowed, smoky room and Rashleighs, Thynnes and Bodrugans on the other. All men whose ancestors had carved out the county's history and achievements for centuries.

Every day he found himself striving harder to lay the ghost of the former poverty-trapped, down-trodden James Rosevean. When he was with Richard there was little hardship in the struggle. With Helen, who he believed just didn't want him to change, it was exceptionally difficult. Her attitude riled him - he just could not grasp why she preferred to cling onto the image of a blinkered no-hoper from Biscovey who had plunged into the waves to bring her back to Charlestown beach.

But over the previous weeks he had discovered, despite Helen's negative response to his rise in the world, that the harshest criticism of all was stemming from his brothers. He wanted Alex and Billy to follow his example and try to better themselves, but instead discovered that both seemed to derive malicious fun from the strides he had taken, both financially and socially.

The jibes were directed at him most of all by Alex, and that annoyed James intensely because, after a great deal of exertion on his part, he had persuaded his younger brother to join the Rosevean company. And he expected loyalty from employees, not ridicule, but that was all he received when he returned to his former home.

Eventually, mainly because of the seemingly constant fraternal criticisms, his visits to Biscovey became as good as non-existent. He decided he could no longer afford to waste his precious time on an ungrateful family. This meant that on the few occasions when Helen did walk up to his home village, following the same rutted route she had taken on the evening she first went searching for James, he never once accompanied her.

Nor did he ever enquire about his mother or the home life of his brothers. But, undeterred by this, she forced herself to keep in touch with them, even though Mary could never seem to relax in her company.

Helen liked Alex. They had struck up a relaxed, affectionate relationship since first meeting at the wedding. And although Billy was quieter and a much deeper, apparently colder character altogether, she believed she had made some progress with him as well. If he kept her at a distance it was part of his usual approach to others. To her, he was the silent, unfathomable Rosevean.

Personal achievement was all that was preoccupying James after the meeting at Fowey. Once home, he had budgeted on only sparing minutes for Helen because, basically, he wished just to sleep. But his schedule was shattered. When she broke through his smug thoughts to announce news of the baby his broad, uncompromising face immediately froze in horror. His self-satisfaction deserted him in an instant, and as she watched his reaction she knew the years ahead were going to be as difficult as she had started, subconsciously, to fear.

Nevertheless, she strove to quash the searing disappointment that welled up inside her. It had been a gentle, happy enough evening until then. They had sat together watching the sunset wash the sky in a coloured orange-dipped brush stroke, and had shared the glory of the dying day in seeming affinity. Instead of standing there wrapped in his own thoughts, he had at least chatted to her, even answered her questions.

But, she reflected, he had barely listened deeply to one word.

His mind had obviously been dwelling elsewhere, taking him back to the King of Prussia, lounging around a highly polished table in a more refined atmosphere, watching sailing ships glide down a still river, and seeing himself as part of a thrusting, thoroughly capable clique, one that held the real power in the county.

And indeed he had been concentrating on the previous events of the day. The village of Polruan had basked in sun on the other side of the water, its tiny streets of colour-washed houses in crisp view, and Richard had been at his shoulder, opening even more doors to a wealthy future.

While Helen had been deriving almost spiritual elation from the sunset and had hugged to herself thoughts of the coming life, he had been dwelling on matters far more pressing than the wants and needs of a wife. Not the least of them being fixated on Richard Courteney, and others, for it was they who offered the route to success and wealth.

It was when the full impact of her whispered announcement sunk in that he almost dropped his freshly filled drink on the new Indian rug.

'Are you saying this baby is actually on the way? That what you're talking about is fact, and not just wishful thinking?'

Lights from the flaming fire picked out the whiteness of his hair, and as she looked at him all in the room turned to ice. Compared with her husband, how could she ever have termed Billy as cold?

'There are only seven months to go,' she said quietly, but with emphasis, trying not to be upset by his horror.

It's an unexpected shock, nothing else, he'll get used to it, she told herself wildly. It will take a day or two for him to absorb all that I'm saying, and after that all will be well.

'But damn it we've only now got ourselves settled, Helen,' he retorted, putting his glass down as his nerves twitched in dismay. With difficulty, he made an effort not to let his temper take control, but an appeal was surely justified? 'I . . I mean it's taken a lot for me to adapt to this changed way of life, and now when I think I'm succeeding you try to foist something else on me, and without warning. I had no idea.'

'Hardly foist,' she answered, battling with a sudden fury. 'Besides that you could equally well put it the other way. That you foisted the baby upon me. I could hardly have done it all on my own.'

The answer came automatically.

'You could have with another man.'

She was speechless. Her rage and hurt increased to such an extent that her throat closed, and tears welled up instantly.

As soon as he had spoken he knew he had crossed an unseen line. This wasn't playing the game by the right rules. He had asked her to marry him. A child was the natural consequence.

Despite that, he had never once thought of having a family of his own. Because he didn't love Helen, he consequently hadn't expected her to fall pregnant. Admittedly, he saw this for an ignorant and naive assumption, though he couldn't deny that that was how he felt. Looking at her stricken face he scrambled to right the situation, to ensure that, before it was too late, he was able to conjure up an apology that was able to calm her despair.

The first instinct was to try to hold her hand, still small and childlike, but she shrunk away, refusing to let him touch her.

'I'm sorry . . I'm sorry, that was uncalled for. I know you wouldn't be unfaithful. Understand that what . . what you've told me has come as a thunderbolt. I wasn't expecting it, not yet.'

Fighting back tears, she stared out of the window, at their small valley that stretched away into a dark distance, and at the compact village of Tregrehan, now barely visible in the night, and searched for some spark of hope from within herself.

It's no use both of us over-reacting, she thought. If we both speak too rashly, too honestly, where will it all end?

'I know we've never spoken of having children,' she whispered finally, running a hand over her still-flat stomach, wondering where on earth her love for this man had led her. 'And from what you're saying I don't think you ever really intended having any.'

'No, I suppose I didn't,' he accepted, haltingly, unsure of his ground.

Depression, and a fear he had never experienced before, were about to clamp down on him. He could sense the mocking voices in his mind were waiting for him to make one more deviation from what was expected of him - before striking. Sighing audibly, he tried to wish black thoughts as far away as possible, not wanting to admit that anything could shake his new found belief in himself. He wanted to be strong, be seen to be strong, whatever happened in his life.

'My mother had five children and now look at her, as a result, old way before her time. Defeated long ago. It ruined her life, and father's to a lesser extent. None of us came up to his high-minded, ridiculous standards, and that made him so bitter his last years were nothing but wretched. I don't want my energies so bound up in other people. I don't want some little scrap depending on me.'

With speed he tried to amend his word when he saw his own dismay mirrored in her doe-like eyes.

'Or on you. You're young yet, too young to raise a family. You need to live a bit, enjoy yourself.'

'That's stupid,' she countered. 'Some women have had two babies by now. They marry at sixteen. I'm old by some standards.'

'Now you're talking rubbish. You look about ten. I can hardly believe yet that you're pregnant.'

'Well we didn't do anything to prevent it. It is something that happens rather naturally.'

'And it's slightly too late to start preventing it now I suppose.'

Unable to stop himself, he glared at her, and she glared back, her gaze level and accusatory. When it came to the bald truth, she was as much a stranger to him, as he was to her.

'I suppose there might be a final way to stop it,' he carried on, in a whisper, realising full well he was ploughing through their unwritten agreement again, but being unable to stop himself.

He was speaking from the heart.

I'm only being honest, he told himself. I don't want the child, it surely would be wrong to pretend otherwise?

Even the wan colour that remained fled from her complexion. For a second she hated him.

'Are you suggesting that I find some way to

kill our baby? If you are then there's nothing left for me here. Nothing left between us, if ever there was anything worthwhile.'

So consumed by anger was she, that she couldn't be still. When the reality of his 'suggestion' sunk in, she sprung to her feet wildly, as if to run, and he caught her back by the shoulders. And eventually, despite her violent struggles, he managed to push her into a chair, and quieten her.

'I said nothing about killing.'

'That's what you meant.'

'I don't know what I'm saying, I'm not talking sense. Give me a chance to take in what's happening.'

'It's not so unusual. Having children is about the most understandable thing that could happen to a man and wife, which is what we are.'

'Not in my world, not at this particular moment it isn't.'

Again, she sought to steady herself.

It's only the initial reaction, she tried to convince herself. He'll mellow in time. He must, or our future will be as black as the sky outside.

'I'll have to pray for some guidance, I suppose, and put up with it then,' he said with as much conviction as he could find, knowing he could go no further, and collapsing into the chair beside her.

Still shaking, but by now desperately anxious to defuse the situation, she knelt uncomfortably down beside him, and lay her head against his knees, although she couldn't relax. Instead, she stayed rigid, striving, and failing, to drive away the devils chasing in circles around her mind.

With patience she managed to dredge from

the depths of her being, she forced herself to wait until her anger had really run its course, as if she was passing through an unexpected squall, and then she hugged him as closely as she possibly could, taking in the clean smell of him.

James was dressed immaculately. His clothes sense could not be faulted. It never failed to amaze her that he had become so different from the young, unworldly miner who had hesitated on his own doorstep when she had, against her will, trudged up to Biscovey to confront him on her father's orders.

'I hope against all hope you'll want it when it arrives,' she murmured, as much to herself as to him. 'It's not his, or her, fault.'

After a while, he made himself glance down at her, but through her, deliberately not seeing her face, or her expression, or even the barely concealed desperation.

'I won't hate it, if that's what you mean.'

She couldn't stop herself protesting.

'I think I'd prefer real love, or hate, rather than indifference. I rather think the baby will as well.'

'Well we'll just have to wait and see then, won't we?'

'I do think you'd rather I gave birth to a batch of shares in another promising company than to a child,' she said in an effort to lighten the situation, but being completely serious all the same.

'At least I'd know how to cope with them,' he answered dryly. 'Remember they can be bought and sold and neatly disposed of any time you choose.'

Then he left her alone in the darkness, to stare blankly into the leaping, licking, writhing flames in the hearth, while he took the stairs to bed alone.

VIII

March 1876

Little had changed six months later, in March 1876, when the baby was nearly due. If anything, James was in a less receptive mood. Helen, now almost unbearably pregnant because of her slim frame, found herself preparing for the child totally on her own. Without any attempt at deception, he had continued to try his utmost to ignore the unsettling evidence of coming life, finding it irritating to look at her heavy stomach, the huge bulge meaning that a responsibility, he did not want to accept, was growing day by day.

They continued to sleep in the same bed, but he hadn't touched her since the evening he had heard he was to become a father. Helen, who ached to shout, scream and shake him into a different frame of mind, managed somehow to hold her silence. She bore all the worries alone. Her parents offered no backing. Her mother hadn't the interest to care, and her father's only comment was that he hoped it wasn't going to be another female, another disappointment.

Only Uncle Matthew had come through with congratulations. At the start of her pregnancy she had walked to Charlestown pretty regularly to see him, to spend a day in what she considered sane company, but walking such a way had become an impossibility in latter months, when merely strolling in her garden, and striving to tend her plants served to exhaust her.

James had other concerns, and they held him under siege. The highs that had come in the first months of production at the Rosevean pits were showing drastic signs of tailing off. The Franco-Prussian war of 1870-1 had kept European china clay rivals out of business for a while, but the war was long over and those rivals were threatening to re-emerge. The Cornish over-production, so carelessly carried out while Europe was virtually closed down, was now rebounding on home markets.

There were indications that not only were large stockpiles going to build up, but that the price of a ton of clay was going to drop. It was all in the future, but both emerging situations were setbacks, and James could see no way of avoiding either of them.

His troubles were to be passed onto the men who worked for him. In line with other owners he had, within weeks of opening, given his employees a rise which had brought their wages of 1s 10d for an eight hour day up to 2s 6d. But with the prospects for the next year looking so dire he couldn't see the rise holding.

With some patience, he tried to explain as much to Alex when his brother, and employee, called at Tregrehan unexpectedly one morning. The two of them never mixed socially. And at work the in-born differences between them had become clear.

Alex had slowly emerged as spokesman for the workers at the Bodmin pits, a responsibility he had accepted with relish. He certainly hadn't held back when tackling James about what he termed appalling wages, or lack of safety precautions. Blatantly, he paid scant respect to the 'master' who also happened to be such a close relation.

Although he had never visited James's house before, Helen knew who it was as soon as the determined, compact figure of a man came into view at the end of their meandering path. Man he had become. He hadn't Nathan's height, nor breadth. Muscles continued to be undeveloped and his waist thin, but his sharp, watchful features denoted an inner strength, and his hypnotic ice-blue eyes were those of someone who had left innocence and youth way behind.

Helen, who enjoyed his sharp wit and the consideration he had always shown her on the few occasions they had met, didn't disguise her delight at seeing him. He was seldom at the cottage on the rare occasions when she went to see Mary. Usually, only Billy was present, and he preferred to remain unseen, locked in another room with his books and precious sketch pad.

When she rushed to find James to tell him that Alex had arrived she knew there would be conflict ahead and, as a result, tried to make a play for tolerance. By this stage of their marriage she knew full well that her husband did at least feel more at ease with Alex than Billy, who now also worked very begrudgingly at the Bodmin pit.

Billy remained unknown territory, harder to understand even than Nathan. It was as if, being the last born, he had been blessed, or cursed, with a mainly negative trait from everyone else in the family. There was Samuel's melancholy, and their mother's surface timidity, mixed with a blind stubbornness which came, James thought, either from himself or from Nathan.

Besides that there was a zeal which was not, it appeared, being channelled in any deliberate manner, as was the zeal that Alex harboured. However, it was occasionally revealed in quiet, but still passionate ways, as through his painting which he carried out in almost obsessive secrecy.

In childhood Billy had always appeared almost feminine, with his halo of fair curls, long, long eyelashes, perpetually pink cheeks and large, brooding eyes. His voracious compulsion to sketch and paint had developed from the age of about five, a pastime which had brought only scorn from a father who had no time for the aesthetic.

The scorn had been merciless, and James felt it was that which had probably prompted Billy to retreat into a shell from which his true character seldom emerged.

Alex presented a slightly different proposition. With him James believed he still retained a few gut beliefs in common, although the few dwindled with each passing day.

On Alex's arrival Helen considered disappearing for a while. Anticipating trouble ahead, she wanted to avoid any fraternal crossfire, especially as she feared she would be more sympathetic to Alex's point of view than James's. Besides that, she was tired. The birth wasn't that far away, and her initial joy in pregnancy had faded. Her distorted belly was making her feel ugly and cumbersome. The baby was an active one. Its butterfly kicks, which she had loved feeling at five months, had become hammer blows which made sleep impossible.

Despite her good intentions she was dragged into their fight. Morning mizzle had slowly developed into more persistent, soaking rain, the type that so often swept across the Cornish peninsula like a ragged sheet, for days on end, so she reluctantly chose to remain in the warmth and shelter of her home rather than settling for a walk on her own. After letting Alex indoors with the brightest smile her low spirits could muster she retired quickly to the kitchen while the two men sat elsewhere and talked clay, though from different perceptions. One from that of survival in ownership, the other from what he regarded as survival of a soul, or collective souls.

'You're asking for even higher wages?' snapped James after Alex had fully explained his reasons behind the unexpected visit. 'But I can't see how we can even continue to keep paying what we are doing now. We've given far too freely for too long. It can't go on. Stocks are increasing, the price of clay is threatening to plummet. The next few years, I fear, will break a lot of owners.'

Alex hadn't made the journey to be browbeaten. Maybe he was in enemy territory, but he wasn't going to be tricked into defeat because he had given away home advantage. After all, he had walked into the confrontation willingly, being very aware of what was likely to ensue.

'But you're speaking of owners, like you, who have gone into business during the boom and apparently expected nothing more than a rosy, trouble-free life ever after. You should have foreseen that such problems were going to occur.

'You're not blind, or stupid. After all, the French and the Prussians were hardly likely to keep fighting for blessed eternity and made peace some years ago. Other markets were certain to open up again. Your overproduction has been a result of greed and nothing else. Too many people took too great and too many a chance, making the most of good fortune, and now some'll have to pay for it.'

'Including me you hope,' broke in James bitterly, thinking that Alex should be grateful for, and not derisive about, the business sense that had led to the pits being formed successfully in the first place. After all, it had provided both he and Billy with regular pay packets.

Alex sunk further back into the chair he occupied, pausing to take in the subtle elegance of his surroundings. All around him was white, light, and perfect. Flowers and greenery tumbled out of vases which adorned every nook and cranny, adding exuberant colour. Flowers were Helen's delight, bringing shades and tints of the garden into corners of the house that would otherwise have been dingy.

He did consider briefly how well James had done for himself, and strove to remember the last occasion when his brother had left such cushioned luxury to seek the plainer surroundings of the home where he had been raised.

'I can't place the last time I spied Mr J Rosevean, pit owner, within a mile of Biscovey,' he mused. 'I don't want to see your venture fail, but I would like you to be a decent, caring owner, not one out to destroy the ordinary worker and keep him in his place. Ye gods, you were where I am now only a year or so back, and you still would be if you hadn't had the luck to save a young girl from a rich family from the rocks.'

James was up in a second, primed to pull Alex out of the chair and smash a fist into his annoyingly perfect array of teeth. What irked him most was that he had spoken the truth so openly and with such contempt. James's temper had been threatening to explode for weeks, and he itched to give it full rein. But he was forced to check himself in mid-punch. Helen walked in at that precise moment.

It's almost as if she's been listening at the bloody door, he thought violently.

She seemed alarmingly unsteady on her feet as she struggled across the room with a tray on which she had perched their drinks, bringing in the refreshments as if she was a shy maid, and the men were about to partake in a genteel Sunday tea. Alex, thinking that she must be at least carrying twins, such as her size, was immediately by her side, helping her.

'For heaven's sake, Helen, don't struggle alone like that. Hasn't anyone told you to take it easy? Neither James nor I know the first thing about babies. What the hell would we be able to do if anything started right now?'

James, who hadn't sat down again, or moved an inch to help his wife, said nothing. He merely tried to smother the hope that if she fell down the baby might well arrive a few weeks early, so lowering its chances of survival.

Guilt snaked into him. What in God's name am I doing, wishing for my own child's death? There's not one damned excuse for that.

With Helen sitting beside them they both made a conscious effort to calm the conversation, and did succeed to some extent. Not completely, though. Each was too wound up to drop the discussion completely, especially Alex. After debating what was best to do for a couple of long days, he had called, determined to ram a few truths into his brother's apparently closed mind, despite also realising that nothing seemed able even to dent James's new ultra ambitious view of the world, or at least his little part of it.

In his view James was standing stubbornly in the way of an Eden in which all were well rewarded for their work. Admittedly, he felt it was a very simple perception, aware that the Rosevean pits were a tiny cog in a huge industry, but he couldn't shake off the hopeful belief that if one company paid fair wages the others might be forced, or shamed, into similar measures.

James was not, however, to be convinced. 'Can't you see it's the workers at fault? They only want to disrupt and destroy. We can't give into your demands for a wage rise. In fact, as I said, we'll probably finish up cutting the rate.'

Being well aware that he was resurrecting their argument, he did attempt to neutralise the tone of his voice to appease Helen. The tone was scything enough, despite his bid to temper it, though, to make Alex gasp with incredulity.

As a result, his instant response was to resort to a stream of verbal abuse. With difficulty he stopped himself completing such a form of attack.

Instead, he pounded the arm of his chair with his fist, and breathed: 'Have you any idea what a cut in wages would do to most workers, any inkling of the poverty it would create? But of course you have. You've bloody lived among those men nearly all your life, or has there been a convenient loss of memory along with the gaining of that wealth you so obviously enjoy?'

James knew, deep within himself, that Alex was right. The consequences of trying to live on too little money were well-known to him, although at the same time he could not envisage the impact of them as well as he had once been able to do, mainly because he was living a different life now, one where there were no monetary problems. If he was going to consolidate a social position then that had to come first, with worries about the grinding poverty endured by others, unfortunately perhaps, relegated lower down his list of concerns.

And, after all, he thought, I've clawed my way out of the mire. They must be able to do the same if they apply themselves properly. 'The workers will survive if there's only a small cut in wages, and they'll feel happier about it if they could just see it from my point of view. By paying them less I'll be able to pour more money into making the pits richer for all of us. Eventually, when the company grows larger, we'll all benefit. If the pits are forced to close instead then there'll be no jobs, no money at all.'

There was a vital meeting of owners planned within the coming week to discuss the wages problem, and Alex had fostered some hopes of enticing his brother onto his side by then. His aim was to make certain there was at least one voice among them who would speak for the men who supplied the muscle, the ingenuity and the long hours to keep the pits in full flow. As he glanced at James and saw the closed, unapproachable expression, the futility of his hopes became obvious.

Seconds afterwards, he looked across with a softer gaze at Helen, and she shot him a sad smile in return.

What a shame the husband doesn't have a fifth of the compassion of the wife, he thought with venom. It should be the other way around, but she cares more about those of his kind than he does.

'But can't you understand, James,' he persisted, 'that on 2d or 3d less a week a man will hardly be able to provide for himself and his family? Remember that work is impossible during heavy rains and unheard of on Sundays. Those restrictions already cut out a real slice of much-needed money. Even with matters as they are, with 2s 6d coming in a week, warmth and food can still only be bought if women and children work as well.'

The 'boss' poured them both another, stronger, drink. He managed to find a moment to think how comforting it was, the luxury of scotch always on hand rather than home brewed beer. Helen remained in the room, saying nothing, sipping her tea mutely but taking in all that was happening around her. Irrationally, James was certain that in her heart she was cursing him, and agreeing with everything Alex said. Despite the soothing, silky feel of the scotch sliding down his throat such thoughts only compounded his bubbling annoyance. Never one to miss much, he had noted the glances passing between them. With his mind clouded by disillusionment he saw her loyalty as deliberately misplaced. She, of all people, should understand that businessmen like myself and her father keep the country afloat, he thought, wanting to confront her openly. Without us there would be no work for the weak, or the strong. It's something Richard definitely believes in, so she must have heard him mention such truths many, many times.

'You're crying for the moon Alex if you're determined to push up wages from the level they are now,' he said harshly. 'I'm afraid your unexpected visit has been totally wasted.

Their visitor was unbowed.

'Not this year, perhaps not even the next, but sometime in the future we'll be paid a decent, living wage. You can't have it your way forever. Without the men you employ you'd be absolutely lost, and we're never going to let you forget that.'

'If you weren't my brother I'd take that as a threat.'

'Take it however you want James, but I warn you, it's you and the kind you've chosen to become who are drawing up the battle lines. All we want is fairness. And by the way 'your kind' doesn't include Helen.'

1X

Suzannah appeared from the bedroom naked. She had thrown her slip of an azure blue nightgown on the floor, and it lay there in a seductive puddle behind her. Then she advanced defiantly towards Nathan, her soft, clean, satin skin aching for his touch, her tiny waist and thrusting hips and nipples beckoning him to take her, to hold her, to love her.

Nathan, until then idly reading the weekly paper at the home-made dining table, froze when he saw her. Recently, he had been working non-stop, sparing himself little, and for a fleeting second he thought he was hallucinating. Then she smiled her wretchedly delicious smile, and he knew he wasn't. She was as real as the paper in his hand was, as his dismay was.

As he watched her slink lithely towards him his own skin turned cold and clammy, his heartbeat accelerated, and in spite of his horror he again found himself responding to the sight of her.

She had timed her seduction with infinite care, making him curse her for her cunning. Her parents were away from home, and would be for another five hours at least. It was their wedding anniversary and they had decided to travel to Nevada City for the day.

It was a rare outing for Joe, who was seldom well enough now even to reach the mine. Nathan had only just finished early morning shift, returning to the lodgings to prepare himself some kind of lunch. Nothing more had been on the agenda, bar food and recuperation, but it was obvious Suzannah had other notions.

'Don't look so disapproving,' she whispered, walking nearer to him with a feline grace that raised the hairs at the nape of his neck. 'I know I'm not that repulsive, and I also know you aren't as passionless as you make out to be. A few questions asked in the right quarters and anyone could discover that you haven't been entirely celibate since you arrived here.'

'For both our sakes put your clothes back on,' he said hoarsely. 'Your father'll be back any second, and you know that he'll hardly close his eyes to what I'm seeing at the moment.'

She laughed her low, tinkling, musical laugh, its apparent innocence jarring with her seduction routine.

'Don't clutch at straws. It's only midday and with mother on his arm and with money for once in her pocket he'll be away until night falls. She'll want to visit every shop they spy.

No-one will disturb us, and I've taken the precaution of locking the doors, and closing the curtains. Didn't you notice?'

Nathan was gradually recovering some mental balance, slowly recovering from his mind seizing, like an old engine freezing to an ice block in the depths of a seemingly never-ending winter.

'Get dressed, please,' he said, resorting to pleading. 'Look Suzannah, I like you. I've watched you grow up in the past months, and I think you're a lovely young woman. But there's no more to it than that. Your father trusts me. Taking you to bed would hardly be the best way of returning his hospitality.'

She wasn't to be sidetracked.

'Father knows how much I like you, and as you must know by now, he likes me to have what I want.'

Nathan slowly put the paper down, as he was still holding it, clutching it tight and crumpled in his scarred hands. He couldn't remember any of the articles he had read. Before she arrived he had been too tired to concentrate. Now he was suddenly fully awake, but reading had been pushed off the agenda.

Up until that moment, he had always seen Suzannah as young but, he thought, Lorna was that age when we first met. Although she was cool and demure on the surface, there was fire underneath that consumed us both.

And I matched her need for me at the beginning, and loved those snatched hours we spent together. I've been fooling myself ever since I left Cornwall, and even before then, that Lorna pursued me, that it was she who clung on just as Suzannah is trying to do right now. It wasn't like that at all.

Over the past months he had begun to think

about Lorna rationally, and had come to realise that he had duped himself. Despite insisting that it was otherwise, he had wanted her body, her spirit, her caring, desperately. It had only been after the darkness had settled upon him that he had sought to break free from her. Now that depression was purging itself from his soul, he began to regard his life, his hopes, his dreams, from a vastly different perspective.

In this clearer light he accepted that he wanted good things to hold on to after all, and he yearned for deep, honest love back. Irrational as it was, because she was thousands of miles distant and now married to his brother, he wanted the impossible, not Suzannah.

'Your father wants me to marry you,' he said to her, 'not thrust myself between your legs and then roll over and leave it at that.'

The words were spoken bluntly, in the hope that they would make her realise that what she wanted from him was based on lust and little else. But if anything it excited her more.

She had reached him, moving in her undulating, inviting way, and was pressing herself against him, rubbing her hands and limbs along his legs, his thighs, his entire body. It was the hottest part of the day. Through a gap in the curtains he could catch sight of the sun searing down outside, determinedly throwing a suffocating heat haze over the dusty street. In such temperatures, and in such a situation, he had begun to sweat, mostly from fear that someone would peer in through one of those interesting gaps, to see exactly what was happening. What they would see as a result would be impossible for him to explain away.

'Marriage can go to hell, I want you first,' she

said, grinning, shaking her fair shining hair so that it fell onto him in fragrant, intoxicating, strands. 'The rest, if it's to happen, can come later. But if it doesn't then that's what's meant to be.'
What Suzannah wanted was gradually edging within her reach. Her tongue, pink and beckoning, darted enticingly between her parted lips as she spoke, and he suddenly longed to cover those lips with her own. She was no virgin. Joe's pure white princess didn't exist.
Nathan was very aware she knew exactly what she was doing, and then started questioning himself. She's right, why should I decide to suddenly become so puritanical?
'No-one's around,' she purred. 'There's only you and me. It would be our secret, our special time together.'
By then he wasn't hearing her. Only seeing and feeling. She smelt glorious, and her body so easily surpassed those he had used in the last years when the strong and urgent need was within him. There had been hours that he didn't want to remember, spent making thoughtless, tasteless love to strangers in dirty, cobwebbed rooms.
Groaning in defeat, he pulled her to him, and ground his lips into hers, wanting the contact, though also raging at himself for giving way so weakly. But wasn't he already having what other men had surely had, as she was tasting someone who had had other women?
In immediate response she wrapped herself around him, kissing him back, now darting her tongue inside his open mouth, placing her clean, scrubbed hands inside his shirt and caressing his chest before moving lower.
'Not here,' she whispered when she finally

broke away, when she believed she had led him on too far for him to have the willpower to turn back. 'Come into my room, I've lain there so often wanting you. Now I can show you what I was doing with you in those dreams.'

His mind whirled, and he shivered with a desire laced with inner fury.

She's not going to lead me, he seethed. It's me who'll have her.

At that, he grabbed her hand and pulled her into her room, angrily kicking her discarded clothes out of the way as he went. Then he slammed the door behind them, before picking her up and literally throwing her onto the bed. She smiled at him, knowing that her wiles had won, baring her beautiful white teeth in delicious anticipation as she lay back and waited for him.

Past caring, he ripped his own clothes off, throwing them to all four corners of the room, and leapt on her, intent on hurting, on being so hard with her she would scream for him to stop, and would realise that there was no future for them.

I hate myself, he thought as he did so. I hate her for bringing me to such a frenzy. She's just another person determined to play with my emotions.

Her stomach was a completely flat plane, her breasts were soft, alluring mounds, her legs were long and perfect. She yielded to him the instant his flesh made contact with hers.

And then, as quickly as it had flared, his overpowering need of her evaporated. At the second he was about to enter her, as she was lying waiting for him, when he should have been so consumed by lust that nothing else on earth should have mattered, his balance

returned. For an instant, he understood that she wanted to be hurt, wanted him to be as rough as possible, to bruise, draw blood, pummel her, anything as long as she had her way.
And that sickened him. It was placing their mating in the ranks of despair, and he didn't want to be part of it. Not with Joe's daughter, and not for his own sake. So instead he groaned, not out of passion, but as if he was shouldering the whole weight of his life, before deliberately rolling away from her.
The room and its contents stopped moving and shunted into focus. The pretty, girlish, coverlet and the faded pictures on the wall took shape, while the bright, defiant colours of the curtains became clear. Until then he hadn't noticed anything of his surroundings. He had been existing in one giant, hallucinatory blur that was a long way from reality.
'It's all wrong,' he spat as he moved even further from her rosy, ready body, feeling exposed and childish. Nakedness, he thought, can definitely drain you of your bravado. 'I'm sorry, but this is wrong, all of it. Most of all it's me who's out of place. I can't offer you anything Suzannah, there's nothing within me to give.'
In furious reply, she tossed back the slightly damp mane of curls that fell down her slim back and across her suggestive shoulders.
'It wasn't wrong a minute ago. Sixty seconds past you had a hell of a lot to offer, and you couldn't wait to give it to me.'
'It may have seemed that way. In the end the mind overcame the body.'
Knowing that he had not acted with any real restraint, he started gathering his clothes

together, dragging them quickly, blindly, over his tanned, leathery, sweating skin as he found them.

Suzannah looked on. stunned. Then, when he was nearly dressed, she finally realised she had let him slip. Defeat rammed into her pride. Still naked she slid from the sheets and followed him as he made his way around the dimmed room in a desperate hunt for shoes and socks.

'The real reason for all of this is that you know that you can't make it with me,' she sneered in disgust. 'I do b'lieve the real tough man is as limp as a sponge inside. I should have known in the beginning, from the very first. You're afraid, that's the true answer.'

'Think what you want,' he retorted, anxious only to escape the room. 'I don't particularly care.'

Having found them, he pulled on his shoes and then fled to his own room, away from the coverlet, the curtains, and her, though escape wasn't to be that simple. She followed him, made straight for his bed and lay there, preening herself, smiling her hard, bright smile, determined not to show that his rejection had hurt her. Trying, in response, to act with a calmness that he was a million miles from feeling, he didn't look at her. Instead, he studied the time.

Her parents would still be away for a good number of hours, and he wanted to be well gone before they returned. With a racing heart, he tugged his few remaining clothes out of the basic chest of drawers where they lay, and stuffed them into his one, now extremely battered, suitcase. It had travelled a long way with him since the fight with Samuel on the station. It had seen a lot, as he had definitely done. It just didn't have the ability to tap into emotions, which made Nathan very envious at that precise moment.

'What are you doing?' she said, suddenly realising that winning him round again was not going to be straightforward.

'Leaving, what else does it look like?'

'All because you drew back at the last moment She was incredulous.

She really has no idea, he thought, but then why should she? I can barely understand my own mind, why should I expect her to, she's her own problems to solve and mine are too complex even for me.

'I told you - think what you like - it doesn't concern me. I was going to move on anyway, I decided that before all this happened. You deserve someone less complicated than me, perhaps more honest, you really do.'

At that, she leapt from the bed and stood in front of him, pushing her body towards him again so he couldn't avoid touching her.

'I'll tell my father you hurt me. I'll tell him . . . '

Blackmail, he supposed, had to be the next step for a fixated, indulged mind. He opted for being harsher, wanting to destroy further her distorted view of him as some sort of local hero.

'I don't give a fig what you tell me. You know the truth of what has happened between us, and so do I, and in my view that's all that matters. In reality what use have you of I, or I of you?'

CHAPTER FOUR

May 1876

1

The pits were idle. Discarded shovels lay where they had been hastily thrown and barrows were still. An unseasonal wind swept over the poor moorland, rushing through the workings and onto the coast in a hurry to be elsewhere. The overall undoubted impression was of bleakness, a bleakness which wormed its way inside James as he stood, his gaze fixed on the quiet valley below.
It was May, but at that moment he looked upon the world as if it was trapped in the grimmest February day.
The men had walked out three hours before, abruptly shattering his conviction that they would never dare venture as far as taking strike action. Along with the majority of other owners he had thought that their threats were as useless as his pits so obviously now were. Alex had warned him on enough occasions that the men weren't playing games, that if the employers persisted in their decision to lower wages then everything would firmly grind to a standstill. Nevertheless, James had gone his own way, ignoring him, believing his brother was speaking for himself and a few hot-heads, certainly not for the majority.
It had become James's general policy, to discard everything that Alex said, including his many arguments about money. If the advice he had been given had been slightly less self-opinionated he might have given

some thought to the reaction of others he employed, which could have forced him to make his latest moves with more caution. Instead, there had been no sense of negotiation, the quiet pits testifying to his lack of tact or true insight. Without warning he had cut wages by 3d a week.

The first sign of the anger that his cut in wages had caused had become obvious when Alex, who was helping coordinate walk-outs throughout the whole industry, stormed around to Tregrehan once more. It was two days before the actual strike and 24 hours after the discovery that the wages had been lowered.

Helen had only recently given birth to a son. On his previous visit there, with a visibly pregnant sister-in-law present, he had fought for control and understanding, restraining his language and his emotions. On this occasion the rage was in such full flight he could not bring himself to see the man he was confronting as a brother, or seek for restraint due to Helen's presence.

'What the hell have you done?' he yelled, storming into the house, pushing past Helen without even really seeing her. James was in his study, his head with its white-blond cap of hair, bent over a swathe of papers.'Didn't I warn you? Weren't you listening to one word during those bloody discussions of ours?' James, unsettled enough already despite efforts by Richard to calm him, did not hold back. He had not been seeing the papers lying within inches of him. Instead, his brain had been swimming with un-crystallized fears of disaster. Taking a short, sharp breath, he glared hard at Alex before speaking. He wanted no trouble in his company, yet here was one of his own family trying to instil mayhem.

'I listened,' he snapped, 'I have got ears, but having the patience to listen doesn't mean I had to agree with such clap-trap.'

Alex looked around then for signs that there was a newly-arrived baby in the house, not wanting the confrontation to turn too ugly if the boy was nearby. There were none. The child, if he was in the house, had disappeared along with Helen.

Despite being one of his uncles, he had yet to see Glynn, having not been invited to the christening, which had taken place soon after the birth. In fact, none of the Roseveans had attended. Instead, after the church service, there had been a gathering of Courteney associates. To Helen's dismay the celebrations, as a result, had been quick, cold and formal, turning to hard business discussion as soon as the religious aspects had been dealt with.

When planning ahead she had stipulated that she wanted all of James's family there. It was he who had decried the idea.

Alex, aware that Helen had wanted her husband's family present at the Christening, felt he had a number of reasons for not holding back when it came to arguing with James, so he happily attacked him when discussing the silent pits and absent workers.

'You knew what poverty you'd cause,' he accused, 'and yet you still ploughed ahead with the cut. That staggers me. The owners' decision is likely to wipe out some of the men financially. And heaven help Billy now he's working for you as well. By your actions you're depriving your own brother. I'm not speaking for myself, you understand. I can look after myself.'

James already had a pounding headache and this was worsening matters. At that moment he wished Alex to the furthest and darkest reaches of Hades. His study was his one retreat from the world, a place where he liked to relax, where he felt he should be completely left to his own devices. Silently, he cursed Alex for just barging in, and Helen for allowing him to do so.

'Don't concern yourself with Billy. I'll see he comes to no harm, though it wasn't me who pressed him to take the job after he had the gall to turn it down in the first place. It was Helen.'

That was it. James didn't want to have to take any more. Although preferring to remain ice cool in the face of provocation, restraint was too much to demand of him that evening. He exploded.

'Get out of my house. Get out before I boot you out, and enjoy watching you bleed, you bastard.'

Alex hadn't expected to arrive, or leave, quietly. Despite seeming to be slight by the side of James, the expression on his youthful face was all powerful.

'It's not me who should be called that. I haven't done anything grand enough. It's most definitely you.'

James rammed a fist down onto the shining, mahogany table, sending the charts slipping to the floor.

'I told you to get out of here. I don't know where Helen is but I sure as hell know that if she was here with us you wouldn't be so bloody rude. Remember, I employ you, I hold the strings and I'm going to make sure you dance to them.'

'Helen's wisely made herself scarce. But if you cared enough about her, if you had one grain of an idea how she thinks, I'm sure you'd see that she's got more sympathy with the workers than you and your cronies.'
Knowing that he would with such words, he immediately realised that he had indeed hit a raw nerve.

James needed no reminders of Helen's lack of total support. Automatically, his fists also readied themselves for fight, rather than flight and he smashed them down onto the table a second time, skinning his knuckles and this time sending the inkpot tumbling to join the papers on the carpet, where its contents began leaving a blue, weeping, stain.

'I'll kill you if you don't go this minute.'
Alex had started backing away, holding up his hands in mock surrender. His skin had darkened considerably since leaving Bethany and starting to work in the open air, and his body had begun to bulk up. As James looked at him he didn't see a Rosevean any more. Instead, he saw a meddlesome stranger, someone who needed to be stopped at all costs.

With a racing, furious mind, he thought if Alex said much more he really wouldn't be able to stop knuckles smashing into flesh rather than wood. His brother sensed as much and turned for the door.

'Surprising as you may find this, I don't believe in violence,' he said in a deliberately quiet voice. 'Because of that I'm going my dear, tough, James. But they'll strike for a long time, you know. They will, and then where will you and your precious, scheming friends be? For Helen's sake I only hope your son won't grow into anything like the

blinkered idiot his father is fast becoming.'
The words seared back to James those days later when he stood, coldly immobile, above the quiet moorland valley, looking at the empty, long, granite slated sheds where the clay was dried, and then across at the static rail trucks and tracks.

His thoughts were of Alex, of Helen, and of a baby. His son. Glynn. An active, healthy baby with a doting, indulgent mother, but with a father who could no more love him now he was pink and round in actuality than when he was a growing, unseen embryo.

He's come at the wrong time, by far, he thought. And he had. His arrival in the world had signalled such a dip in his father's plans that James couldn't avoid bracketing the child with impending disaster.

It remained an ugly truth that he still didn't want the boy, and the coolness that he felt towards him, that he couldn't seem to overcome, was drawing him even further away from Helen. Some days they hardly spoke.

Nothing, he panicked, least of all my marriage, is working.

After taking in the sight of the lifeless workings he couldn't face returning home to his wife's forced smiles and attempts to cheer him, and the boy he would rather not acknowledge. Neither did he relish the thought of calling in on his father-in-law, which was a change from normal. Richard, unlike James himself, seemed to have no nerves. Adversity only increased his energy. The latest, dramatic, price-slashing had meant that, even before the walk-out, many works, chiefly those producing common clays, had either gone into liquidation or been sold or closed. Faced with such an unwanted, colossal slide in their luck some directors had disappeared overnight, among them two from the Trevanion Treverbyn company. A third man, David Cock of Roche, had fled to America after being heavily pressed by his creditors, joining an expanding band of exiles who had run from the troubles before they escalated even further.

Emigration was a highly tempting way out, and in some respects Nathan had already paved the way in the Rosevean family, but still James's pride and determination, and the subconsciously remembered voice of his father, were keeping him in Cornwall, fighting and angry.

He wanted to win to spite everyone, telling himself that he needed to do so to prove to himself that he could make it alone without Helen's money. Eventually, he wanted to repay every penny that Richard Courteney had given him and be able to stand alone with his wealth, won by his own hard work, labour and battles.

It reached the stage where the cold was seeping unbearably into his body, and he eventually accepted that there was little option but to return to Tregrehan. He did so after convincing himself that given another day the situation could only improve. The men would have had an extra twenty-four hours in which to grasp the folly of their position, and would surely be ready and willing to capitulate.

11

By the end of the week, when the position remained unaltered, panic had mainly overtaken anger. The workers were holding out across the industry, the pits were staying deathly quiet, and liquidation and failure were haunting his every thought, like grim spirits he could not exorcise.

An urgent meeting had been called among owners, to be held at the White Hart Inn which stood in the middle of St Austell, the King of Prussia at Fowey being reserved as a venue for mellower occasions. The grey-flagged Inn rose solidly opposite the parish church in St Austell where he and Helen had been married, and James was among the ranks of suited, bowler-hatted, nervous men who made their way there for the morning session. Richard appeared slightly later than the others, still unconcerned by the turn of events. He seemed to be alone, however, in his conviction that the resolve of the rebels was bound to collapse. Most agreed with James's conclusions during the previous long, unsettled night, that a compromise must be reached. The owners were united in their disgust that the men should have taken such steps, but they fully admitted that the status quo could end up breaking them.

The unseasonable spell had broken and it was a hot, muggy day, with thunder rumbling around the clay hills of Hensbarrow, starkly white and visible from the South Street entrance of the White Hart. That, and the tense atmosphere inside, served to give James a sickening headache before the meeting had hardly begun.

And the close proximity of the church did not help him. Whenever he looked out of the window he could visualise Helen, in her virginal dress, walking shyly and slowly to the altar.

A lot has gone right for me since then, he

thought, stubbing out a cigar with some force. On the other hand it could be said a hell of a lot has fallen apart. Even I can see she's suffered through my lack of care. There was a time when I promised myself that, even though I didn't love her, I would never make her unhappy.

The air was thick and choked with stale smoke. His throat was uncomfortably dry, and sweat was beginning to trickle down the back of his neck.

James wanted only to be gone, but he broke away from his depression to hear one member, John Polglaze from Sticker, declare: 'It's no good, we'll have to give way to their blackmail. I don't think my finances can take another day without anything being produced.'

'You're not alone,' came a sympathetic reply from someone at the back of the room who knew that their own assets were also dwindling by the second.

'The only way to get them back to work is to give in,' countered one of the owners of the Great Vallen pit on Hensbarrow. 'To restore the 3d. And believe me, although that seems to be the sole solution, paying that much extra while the costs to me are so high will cripple me in the long run.'

'At least it's in the long term, and not tomorrow,' said Courteney, on his feet and speaking for the first time. Everyone immediately took note, James being far from the only one who followed Richard's every lead. He had been in the business for decades and his experience, and his extensive interests elsewhere, gave him almighty influence. 'We shall at least have breathing space in which to consider other strategies.'

'Such as what?' countered James, surprised at himself for publicly challenging the man.

'Making promises that perhaps won't come to fruition,' said Richard slowly and deliberately, letting his words take root inside minds with less determination and staying power than his.

James's headache suddenly intensified as he had a rush of insight. If what his father-in-law was suggesting was accepted by all then it would lead to all-out war with Alex. Part of him relished a fight but another part. that he was only just beginning to admit to, didn't. Not with someone so close to him.

'You mean agree to give them the 3d and then drag our heels over it?' came a whisper from nearby.

The cigars, fat and ostentatious, were out in plenty now, causing the smoke cloud to become deeper and denser. The table was fast disappearing under finished glass and partly eaten food. The staff of the Inn, primed to be willing and subservient, were doing their duty and cosseting their guests well. But James found himself retreating from excessive drinking, eating, or smoking. Visions of Helen continued to pound his imagination. He thought it ridiculous. When he should have been giving his complete attention to the meeting, itself an unwanted distraction, previously well-buried feelings of her were beginning to pick at him. All he wanted to do was eradicate them, certainly at this particular point in time.

He vaguely heard a babble of raised comments, and shouts of assent, above which Richard acknowledged: 'It's a definite possibility.'

'A promise would certainly get them back to

work,' murmured Bill Tremodrett from Penwithick. 'I firmly believe that the great majority of men have been led into this. Left to themselves they wouldn't have dared attempt such a thing. There are only two or three idiots behind it, trouble-makers set on breaking us.'

'And by this time tomorrow the pressure would be off us. We would be giving ourselves time to think rationally,' someone else chipped in.

'But we underestimated them last time,' said a more hesitant owner, not quite sure of his infallibility. 'We thought that they would do nothing, but they walked out on us. What do you expect them to do when they realise we've got no intention of keeping our promise, shrug their shoulders and do nothing? You must be blind stupid if you do.'

'The lay off must have affected them badly too, with no money coming in. They haven't been in clover, and most have families to support,' insisted Richard, his compelling expression half-hidden in the gathering smog, his words still failing to succeed in swaying the timid.

'They still won't accept it. They won't have gone through that for nothing. They'll demand that the wages are restored on the first pay day, and when they see they're not getting the 3d they'll walk out again. Remember they're also asking for lost pay for the days they've been out, and they've warned us they won't return without it. I've been reminded of that on more than one occasion.'

'They'll ruin us. That's what they're out to do.'

General panic was emerging along with the indigestion.

'But we need them, always remember that. If nothing else these last days have proved it.'

It looked for a while as if no decision would be made, but eventually they edged towards what they thought might be a tentative solution. James, afraid suddenly of the lengths Richard might go to, played some part in formulating it.

It was agreed that the 3d would be restored with no snags attached. However, the majority of the owners, anxious to be allowed to keep some degree of dented pride, fundamentally refused to pay the men for the last days, before the strike, for which wages had still not been distributed. It was decided that on the face of it they would agree to pay the back wages, but they voted to renegade on the deal on pay day itself, and not be forthcoming with the extra.

It was hoped that any resulting anger would gradually seep away once the pits were in full production, and families were receiving full pay packets again. They were adamant that the men couldn't win all the way round. It would be too much of a boost to their morale.

When he heard that the wages had been returned to their previous level Alex went out celebrating with friends, secretly amazed at how quickly their pressure had brought dividends. If he had known the full extent of the day's decisions he would not have been so quick to claim victory. The tussle was a long way from being over, as was his own fraternal battle.

111

Samuel and Lorna's honeymoon period lasted until the past, in the form of Nathan, reared up enough to poison minds and introduce violence into their lives. Although, of course, he didn't appear in the flesh himself to shatter the uneasy peace within their newly built home, the letters he couldn't prevent himself from writing, because they helped assuage some of the fury and the despair within him, were destructive enough to cause the damage. They had passed between America and Lorna's family home for many months, but she had never stopped worrying about the effect they might have on Samuel if he ever did discover that she was still in contact with his eldest brother.

Nevertheless, despite her intuitive reasoning that they would be bound to bring heartache in some form or another, she hadn't taken steps to halt them. She had kept answering, and waiting for replies with annoyed impatience, as if it was no concern to her if an emotional storm did consume them, for by then she was caught in the same compulsive trap as Nathan was on the other side of the Atlantic.

The overriding truth was that she needed the contact. She knew that she loved him, she always would, and if the letters stopped arriving she would be devastated. Gradually, insidiously, they had formed a prop for her self-worth, even to a certain extent for her sanity.

The storm erupted without warning one evening. Both Lorna and Samuel had eaten their meal, cleared away with precision, and were preparing for another passionless night. They had spoken little, only mentioning in passing the present state of the china clay dispute.

Such lack of warmth in any depth, was

completely evident to Lorna, who knew from treasured experience how both her body and soul could burn for so much more, but Samuel never seemed to notice the shallowness of their relationship. Instead, it was evident to her that he was content with the routine he had carved for them.

Above all else, he had the woman he had always yearned after, as well as his own home. He wanted for nothing else. It was enough that Lorna was there, tied to him by name and vows. After a heavy, sinew-straining day, he didn't have the energy, the insight, or the inclination to strive to develop their marriage any further.

That evening he wasn't even going to mention the letter, and when he did it was almost as a second thought, to break the thick silence between them.

The words came when he was struggling into his night clothes in the dark and the quiet was becoming oppressive, even to him. They never undressed in the light, in full view of each other as he believed that flaunting nudity in front of such a sensitive woman as Lorna was not appropriate. If she had mentioned skinny dipping in the River Fowey, as she had at dusk on warm summer nights with Nathan, he would have been utterly unable to handle the implication.

Neither of them ever mentioned sex. The lack of it between herself and Samuel had been one of Lorna's more pleasant surprises since their wedding. Before the church service she had been steeling herself to the idea of his coarse hands on her skin, and his tight, thin lips on her mouth. But it seemed now that he had merely wanted to own her, to have her bear his name so that he could declare to his whole, restricted world that she was his prize. His words stunned her when they came.

'Who did you hear from this morning then? Your mother gave you another of those envelopes with an unusual postmark on it. I've meant to ask you before who they're from.'

She froze. I'll bluff it out, she thought. He's tired, and I don't think he's that interested. Anyway, he's too blinded to think that I'd lie to him. But amongst such instincts and intentions the truth still came out. It was as if she had made a deliberate decision to place herself on a path to destruction.

'It came from America,' she said softly, shivering not from cold but from the knowledge of what she was doing. Slowly, as she spoke, she pulled the sheets right up to her chin and slithered further down the bed, as if retreating from him.

'America, who the hell do you know there?'

Hesitating briefly, she questioned her sanity, and then ploughed on. After all, she told herself, the letters were innocent enough. Full of news and views but little else. Nathan had never mentioned their past involvement outright, or hinted at any lingering feelings for her, at least overtly, since she had written of her marriage.

More than anything his words had been informative, and they cheered her up. Nothing more, nothing less. In fact she had continued to be amazed at how good and entertaining a writer Nathan had proved to be. His correspondence did literally lighten up her extremely dull and protected life.

'Someone we both know. Your brother.'

Her voice was muffled, and she spoke as nonchalantly as possible to emphasise that the

subject was of no importance to her. Within moments she discovered she had misjudged. Samuel had come to a point where he found it impossible to think about Nathan impassively.
'That bastard,' he exploded, the silence shredded beyond redemption. 'How in damnation did he know of our address?'
Instinctively, as if retreating from his reaction, she rolled over to the far side of the bed, taking most of the sheets with her, wrapping them tightly around herself as if they could protect her.
'He's been sending them to my old home, remember, not here. That's why my mother has to give them to me.'
Her heart was tumbling, her limbs were being leached of strength.
To hell with Nathan and what he can do, even from so far away, she thought. Why haven't I ever been able to hate him?
Samuel could only see that in the space of seconds his carefully constructed world was crumbling about him. Although he didn't want to lower himself to the point of asking what Nathan had said, he couldn't bite back the words. He had to ask. It was a compulsion.
'Why write to you, and more than once, after all this wretched time? There's been hardly anything from him to his real family, those closest to him. Just money sent to mother, as if that could make up for all the trouble he caused. And now this. He always could stir up misery for others, it's something he's always, always, been excellent at.'
Wondering how best to defuse the storm of emotions she had just stirred, she swallowed, very slowly.
'I didn't realise he was stirring up any trouble

at the moment.'

She could hardly distinguish Samuel in the gloom, only make out the broad silhouette hunched at the end of the bed, and hear his quick, rasping breathing.

'You haven't told me yet what he wrote to you, and what he said in all those other stupid letters.'

Always, she thought of the letters almost protectively. Nothing had been mentioned in them that could hurt Samuel directly, but she knew so much had remained unwritten, or could be read into them.

'He only told me about the ordinary things in his life,' she murmured, hoping to soothe but not able to bring herself to reach out to him, to hold him and physically stroke away the pain. 'About California, and the mine he's now working in. You can read the one I got today if you want.'

'But why have the nerve to think you might be interested?'

Beset by teeming, jealous, thoughts he tried to concentrate on buttoning his frayed bedclothes, though eventually gave up, fumbling in the effort. Ten minutes beforehand he had been reasonably warm. Now he was chilled.

'Perhaps he missed home,' she answered after a while. 'I think he does miss Cornwall. He started writing when a friend of his from Truro was killed in a mining accident. In that letter he only mentioned the incident briefly, but I think it upset him a lot. Maybe he merely wanted to be able to share his thoughts about it with someone.'

'Well if the great man wanted comfort, why not write to James, or me, or mother? Now that would have been more understandable.'

'He wouldn't have been treated with much compassion if he'd contacted you,' she snapped, unable to stop herself, resenting his imperious attitude. 'I've a sneaking feeling you'd have thrown the letter on the fire, unread.'

'Which would have been the only place it would have belonged.'

Giving up on any pretence of trying to sleep, he leapt from the bed and began to pace the tiny room, hardly able to look in her direction. Her words had wounded him to such a degree that he couldn't consider rest of any kind. Instead, he wanted to slam doors, throw furniture, kick out at anything that was in his way. The stubborn, bull-headed anger, which was very much a part of his personality, but which he had subdued for so many months, was on the boil.

Lorna, watching him, felt her own irritation rise.

'He is your brother,' she reminded him harshly.

'And was your lover,' he snarled. They were words which shouldn't have been said, but which pumped out of him as if having a life of their own, as hers had when she had made her initial confession about the sender of her letters.

'Are you suddenly condemning me for that?' she yelled back, sitting up straight, back rigid, her hair in a fair, uncompromising halo. More than anything, she was determined not to be brow-beaten. 'You've no right. You might have if I had been your wife first and his lover second, but it didn't happen that way around, and you know that.'

What she said, although factually true, didn't help him, it only antagonized, though he struggled not to let that show. However, he did manage to see through the vitriol for one moment, long enough to grasp the fact that he was being unreasonable, and to reply in what he saw as sensible fashion.

'Just don't write any more replies to that bastard again, that's all. I want to see no more of his rubbish in my house.'

Lorna didn't reply, and after a while he began to think that at least he had won something. Perhaps he had made her understand the error of her ways, by laying down the law firmly enough?

The trouble was, he didn't realise that she was marking time, knowing she had to calm herself before speaking again, for if she allowed herself to give full rein to her emotions she was aware that she could sweep away their tattered marriage for good.

In her bid for silence, she kept her lips shut, so tightly pursed they were drained to parchment as she strove for self-control - which held until he blindly sought for confirmation.

'Do you understand me?' he demanded, leaning so far over her in the bed that, despite the late evening gloom, she could detect the mad whites of his eyes.

'Of course I do,' she retaliated. 'I understand that you're trying to deny me the freedom to write to whoever I want. I thought you had more respect and regard for me than that.'

In anger, and some fear, she threw herself away from him, threw herself out of their bed with its cluttered, discarded covers, and tore through the contents of the chest of drawers he had made for them. Finally, she pulled out three neatly folded pieces of paper.

'Read his letter, read it. There's nothing in it

to make you rant or rave half as much as this.'
At the crux of his fury was the fact that he didn't want to see her as an independent spirit who was not tied to him. He didn't want her dependent upon anyone else, especially Nathan, and he could not endure the thought that she could even bring herself to contact his brother. His jealousy was live and unbearable. Knowing he had to give vent to it before it ripped him apart, he grabbed the letter from her hand and destroyed it without reading one word.
'You bitch,' he screamed, his voice no longer deep but anguished like a woman in the agonized depths of labour. 'You dare to talk to me like that. I own you. I'll tell you who to visit, who to write to. Nathan isn't on that list.'
'You can't make such conditions, you can't.' Her fury was as vindictive as his.
'Just watch me,' he spat, and before he himself knew what was happening he had smashed her across her upturned face with his fist.
Ten minutes later, when she had staunched the flow of blood from her nose and the corners of her mouth, he was cradling her in his short, muscular arms, blubbering and begging forgiveness, swearing that he had been tired, out of sorts, and would never overreact in the same way again.
Lorna said nothing. By then she was so devoid of strength she lay unmoving against him. But her mind was travelling like lightning, panicking.
The worst of it all was that she was certain it was the beginning of an end which held within it nothing but emptiness.

IV

After turning a less than decisive back on Suzannah's tempting body Nathan had no fixed idea where he was heading, although that held few worries for him. He was on his own again, something which suited. The relief of embracing real freedom once more was balm in itself.

The weather had been fair enough to make sleeping rough tolerable. Money was no problem as he had earned good wages in the past months. As he travelled, he worked for a week here, a couple of days there, spent a month or so panning in pure, clear streams, and ended up south of Nevada, in Arizona. His travels led to him straying into ruggedly beautiful cowboy territory. A country of great variations, of green cattle lands and arid desert. The home of the Navajo Indians, a once warlike nation, but warlike no more. About thirteen years earlier, in 1863, Kit Carson had been ordered to round up all the Navajos and confine them to a reservation in New Mexico, a task he went about with ruthless efficiency, razing cornfields and peach orchards and starving the people into submission.

So, despite great resistance from chiefs such as Delgadito and Manuelito, 8,000 Indians had been led into New Mexico, later only allowed to return to their homeland after signing a treaty that put away their weapons forever.

Despite Indian trouble being quelled from the usurpers point of view, it didn't follow that peace reigned. The miners and the cowboys, Chinese and Cornish, gambler and innocent immigrant, could not co-exist in those 'tamed'

lands without some blood being spilt.
Nathan eventually reached Tombstone, a haphazard and depressing frontier town, far removed in splendour from the Grand Canyon, Petrified Forest and Monument Valley, landmarks which also formed part of the territory.

When he arrived he was not alone, for the area had yielded both good gold and silver, though the rumour currently sweeping town was that diamonds had been discovered as well. Once within its town limits, he decided to stay around for a while at least, not because he seriously believed in fortunes any more, but mainly out of curiosity. It seemed to him that if so-called fortunes were to be won they were just as quickly lost or thrown away. Inhospitable as it was at its heart, the place did offer the chance of rest, and he felt drained enough to want that. One bonus was that it had developed into an area where there were a good many fellow Cornish also striving to settle down for a while, although he had to admit that the majority were, like him, single men.

Few families had settled, which meant it hadn't yet been turned into a little Kernow, as a number of other towns had, with a string of brass bands, chapels and schools.

On his travels Nathan had discovered that all raw mining towns had the same appearance before women and children, and permanent families, arrived to haul them into some sort of decency.

Homes included frame shanties and tents made from any discarded rubbish, such as old shirts or potato sacks. There were chimneys fashioned from empty whisky barrels, hovels made from mud and stone. Tombstone was, however, on the verge of acquiring some brick or stone buildings with false fronts. Not only that, but it had a bank and an eating house run by a Chinese owner plus, of course, saloons and gambling venues. But the opera house was certainly yet to arrive, depriving it of any air of true refinement.

Nathan stood, shaded his eyes from the blazing, unrelenting sun, watched the main street, unkempt and unclean, seem to dance in the heat, and remembered how an acquaintance had once described Bingham, a copper town in Utah, as 'a sewer five miles long'.

Tombstone, sad and sorry as it is, isn't quite in the same league, he thought with irony. For one thing it doesn't stretch as far as five miles.

He was to find himself bachelor quarters in the aptly named Tough Nut Street, and then he settled down for a short stay. Against instinct and a loneliness he had been trying to ignore, he was then drawn to the saloon that evening.

As he walked the short distance there, he told himself that he would only stay for a short while, enough time for one drink, as there was no telling what arguments, what violence, might break out among the clientele that evening. But this conviction wavered when he noticed there was a large contingent of Cornish clustering around the bar.

Instinctively, he was drawn towards them, and into their conversation, despite a previous determination to keep himself much to himself.

In the smoky, close atmosphere that definitely possessed more than slight shades of the Britannia, he discovered that he didn't have the energy, or the nerve, to play at being the loner.

The first whisky for some while burned into his throat with a welcome warmth which encouraged him to have another. During the following two hours he went on to drink more than he had for years, memories of his debacle with Suzannah, of Lorna with Samuel, of the unsure mess of his life, driving him on.

Within a short while he discovered that the overriding subject of the evening ebbing around him was not the girls, nor the gambling, but the mini-boom that had obviously been created by the diamond discovery. Money was flowing from the pockets of excited and exhausted newcomers, talk was rife, and there was undoubted expectation in the air.

'Has anyone actually been lucky enough to find any of these supposed gems?' he asked when alcohol had dissolved the reticence that had built up since his self-imposed exile.

'Of course they bloody have,' said a voice from the midst of the unshaven, unwashed crowd. 'This place has been bursting at the seams ever since. There've been murders, knifings, fights every hour or so over them. Not that there weren't before, but the madness has got worse recently. Too many greedy eyes, and thoughts of riches just lying out there, waiting.'

Nathan's dark, uncut curls hung in an unkempt mass. Drink had blotched his skin, reddened his eyes and made his mind less sharp. Against his numbed instincts he was ensnared by the gossip.

'So are there any diamonds left, or have you lot pinched them all? I bet all of this is down to someone's imagination, like half the drivel that I've heard since arriving here.'

'The few stones that have been found were in some fortunate pockets, but I'm sure there won't be any more,' answered the well-spoken, but scruffy individual who was packed so close to Nathan that he was almost drinking with his rather meaty arm wrapped around him. 'There's been talk of a three million dollar programme being set up to develop the so-called diamond fields. I think they'd be pouring their money down the blasted drain. There's silver around here, that's been proved, but I'd put a wager on there being no diamonds.'

It didn't impress another near neighbour. 'You talk well, but talk rubbish. Course there's gems out there. Didn't old George come back with his pocket full the other day?'

After a while, despite his emerging interest in the situation, Nathan knew that he had to escape from the crush along the bar before claustrophobia revisited him. With nerves jangling, he edged his way over to a customer sitting alone in the one corner of the saloon where seething humanity wasn't completely pressed together.

Clarence King, a small, wizened man with unnaturally pressed and pristine clothes, who appeared distinctly out of depth in the swearing, pushing company, worked for the Federal government. It seemed to be general knowledge that he had been sent to Tombstone to investigate the diamond fields. As a result, he was alone because no-one particularly wanted to talk to a government representative, whatever his business might be.

Nathan, always wanting to be different to the herd, deliberately headed over to him as soon as someone told him who the solitary drinker was. If the others weren't interested in the sober truth about what was happening Nathan did, even if it was just to satisfy his mind and escape the crush of customers and nothing else.

Also, with a sudden insight, he had begun to understand that if he kept drinking he might not be able to stop. The depression, that was showing signs of eating away at him again, liked nothing better than to be permanently awash with alcohol.

Diamonds don't particularly send my blood racing, he told himself. Little does any more. Only a few basic comforts that I once took completely for granted.

Surprisingly, though, the man from the government was more forthcoming than Nathan had expected.

'I still believe the same as I did when I was back in civilisation, and not in the midst of this hell-hole. It's not possible for diamonds to exist here.'

King looked around him in distaste as he talked. The beer-swilling, fetid atmosphere unsettled his clear-cut mind.

'So how did the bloody things get here then?' Crumpled and tired as he was, and as half befuddled and distracted as he looked, Nathan still retained a modicum of incisive thought. King, sensing as much, stared quizzically at the Cornishman before saying: 'Come with me tomorrow and see. A companion would be ideal. You weren't here last time I came. I can tell you I had a pretty rough ride. I know it sounds as if I'm panicking but I'm afraid there's a good chance I'll be shot in the back if I go alone. If they don't think I've got diamonds on me, then they think I can lead them to them, or destroy this little boom they've got going. They may not talk to me here, but they'll stalk me tomorrow.'

'How do you know I don't want to shoot you as soon as you've found something? It shouldn't be too difficult for me if you take me out into some God-forsaken piece of scrubland.'

King attempted a smile, but the effort was hidden by his luxuriant, but extremely neat moustache.

'Blind faith,' he answered.

V

They met again early the next morning. Nathan, who had woken up with a raging headache, had been unsure whether or not to take up King's offer, but in the end had decided it would be a decent enough way of exploring part of the new land he had ended up in.

He soon discovered that the government expert was a man who not only amused him with his dry wit and sceptical outlook on life, but was also able to make him feel at ease. That wasn't always simple. Nathan found it difficult to relax in the company of the vast majority of those he knew, or had ever known.

The sun skewered into their necks and shoulders as they walked out into the arid, dusty and unattractive landscape. Nathan fished in his bag for a hat, knowing from unwanted experience how the heat could turn into a killer. Bearing that in mind he had packed plenty of water in his bag as well. He kept out a constant look for 'followers', but could see no-one around, seeking to tread in their footsteps.

Above all, he wanted to pump King for information about the diamonds, as for some reason he was extra curious about them, but he decided not to prompt his companion straight away.

In the end he discovered that there was no need to be reticent. King was not backward in telling him, in his clipped, matter-of-fact voice, how he had found some of the gems a few months beforehand and had then sent them to experts to be studied.

'As I told you I didn't have an easy time of it,' he said with barely disguised bitterness. 'I wasn't welcomed here. They were all totally convinced back then that a marvellous discovery had been made. I'm sure that they thought I'd arrived to cheat them out of the further riches that were coming their way, either through finding diamonds themselves, or making money out of those who came to look for them. They were, still are perhaps, too dumb and blind to realise that someone else is busy doing the cheating.'

The sun continued to burn, leading Nathan to button up his shirt to protect himself from it as best he could.

'Is it any different this time around? They weren't exactly rushing to buy you drinks in the saloon last night, but then again they weren't marching you out at gunpoint, or threatening you either.'

'Well, it's slightly better this time, I think. I feel a few people, though they might not say it outright, are beginning to see that I might just have been right, that diamonds don't play any real part in this particular area of Arizona.'

Nathan laughed, although his expression could have been seen as a grimace. Pure joy was forgotten history.

'You're quite sure, are you, that there's no use me looking for gemstones? If you are so sure then what the hell are we both doing out here, dry and dusty as we are, and seemingly miles from humanity?'

'I want to be absolutely certain about it. Coward as I am I still think I'd rather be shot in the back than made to look a fool.'

'Your reputation means a lot to you then?'

'Unfortunately my pride does.'

They walked in companionship for a while, kicking up the earth as they went, King prodding around in the dirt here and there. Eventually, hunger pangs set in and they found some shade, sat down and shared their food. Without either of them trying hard they had forged a bond in a matter of hours. It staggered Nathan. It was rare that he was able to relax so quickly with someone who would have been termed stranger less than 24 hours before.

'You said you sent away some of this soil for testing,' he murmured, laying back and resting his head rather uncomfortably on a rock. 'I wonder what those experts have come up with.'

He sank his teeth into his pasty, one hand made by a fellow Cornishman who had set up shop in Tombstone, and squinted into the shining azure above. His eyes were no longer puffed and reddened, as they had been in the saloon, and his brain was fully functioning again. 'What if they disagreed with you. What would that do to your pride?'

'I know what they say,' mumbled King slowly between mouthfuls.

'You've had a reply?'

'Yes, I had it yesterday morning. They took

their time, you might say, but it eventually came.'

'And?'

'I was told to keep this to myself, at least until the government lets me know I can tell everyone officially.'

'For pity's sake the whole of the town, or at least those in authority, know by now. Your letter is bound to have been steamed open at some stage of its journey. And don't these hours I've spent sweating needlessly alongside you require some reward? All this searching is a sham, and you've known that all along. You've just been going through the motions. No wonder you weren't as scientific about it all as I expected you to be.'

'You would lay odds that the letter has been opened?' asked King, his expression serious, but his mocking tone saying otherwise, suggesting a greater lightness of character than Nathan had first imagined.

'Heavy odds.'

King sighed, then grinned. 'The experts are certain the diamonds I found only a couple of hundred yards from this very spot came not from Arizona, but from South Africa.'

Nathan took a cooling gulp of water from his flask. A few minutes earlier, he had moved into the shadow of an extremely large rock, but despite being in the shade perspiration was now dripping down his back as well as into his eyes.

'How do you explain that then? I presume they didn't fly here, or bore their way through the earth.'

'You want my opinion?'

'Well it would be a sensible and informed one. I wouldn't mind knowing. So far curiosity has led me to follow you through desert and scrubland for little reward. I've found no diamonds to keep me in luxury for the next few years.'

'After what I've seen today I think those gems were fired into the earth with a shotgun.'

Nathan let out a long, monotone whistle that pierced the quiet, hot and humid, air like an arrow.

'Ye gods, and those fools were planning to invest three million dollars in this place on the strength of those finds.' With a sudden thought in his mind, he turned to his companion. 'Some locals who were hoping all this new business would continue are going to be very upset with you. Once this gets out the treasure hunters will be going elsewhere, and these local investors will be left high and dry. Do you think they'll believe you, though, not only here but in Washington, where it really matters?'

'I should certainly hope so. What's the point in employing me if they aren't going to believe what I tell them? Anyway they'd be stupid if they ignored the report I'm going to write. You'd have to be greedy or blind, or deliberately stupid, not to see this is a hoax. One of thousands, admittedly, taking place, but one which could have been real costly.'

'You expected all this from the start didn't you?'

'I may have done,' answered King, stretching out a hand to his own water bottle, also being aware it was essential equipment.

'Go on then,' goaded Nathan genially. 'Tell me your theory, or theories. Who did it, and why?'

King had already decided to take Nathan into his confidence, and so had no qualms about continuing with his story, although he wasn't usually so forthcoming. But from being an aggressive, abrasive character who others naturally retreated from Nathan had subtly changed, without realising it, into someone who invited confidences. His strength had grown quietly inwards, but also revealed itself outwardly. King felt at peace in his company.

'On that first trip I found both diamonds and rubies. I think they were probably bought in London, smuggled into this country over the Canadian border, and then sown in a specially chosen area topographically similar to Kimberley.'

Nathan picked up a handful of earth that had become dust, letting it trickle slowly through his fingers.

'Impressive in some ways, I suppose.'

'Impressive enough to bring people here in their thousands.'

'I suppose some greedy, devious little man had the future of this territory, and his own pocket, firmly in mind. Someone selling the land here, maybe, or wanting to dominate local trade.'

'Tell me,' asked King after a while, 'you puzzle me. You're slightly different from most of the rabble that come to Tombstone. Was it the thought of the diamonds that brought you here?'

'Nothing drew me, and the only thing that brought me was my feet.'

The answer came glibly. No mention was made of Suzannah or the real reasons for flight.

'So what are you, more wanderer than prospector?'

'I like the description,' acknowledged Nathan after giving it some thought. 'Let's leave it at that.'

'Money didn't, or doesn't, interest you then? And don't invite my contempt by saying it doesn't.'

Nathan shrugged his bony shoulders, the skin underneath his shirt like leather after so much exposure to all weathers.

'Well it doesn't particularly. I came to America with the idea of getting rich, I suppose, although there were a lot of other reasons for my leaving Cornwall. I've lived alone since coming here for the majority of time, though, and I've lived hard, and I think I've worked out that you don't need loads of money, not to any excess. I've sent most of what I've earned back to my family. I think I believe that money makes you soft if you have too much of it.'

King stared at the man by his side. 'I think I have the beginnings of a philosopher on my hands.'

'Hardly.'

The next question threw Nathan momentarily.

'Miss your home do you?'

'I wasn't aware I had one.'

'I mean England, Cornwall.'

Nathan paused.

'It's strange, but if you'd asked me that a year ago, or perhaps even a month ago, I'd have said no.'

'And now?'

'Now, I'm not so sure.'

'Anyone to go back there for?'

'A family. A mother and four brothers, though I wasn't that close to them in the last years. I send them money now and then, as I told you, but not many letters. I think I'd cut myself away from them before I left. For a variety of reasons we didn't part on very good terms.'

And now Samuel would border on being an

enemy, he thought. Because of Lorna he probably now thinks I'm the devil himself. As for me, I want to vomit every time I imagine her with him. What a wretched waste.

'I meant more romantic ties,' King was saying. 'Is there a woman? You didn't seem very interested in the bar-room girls last night.'

'No . . no there's no woman. I was stupid enough to push away the only one that came near to meaning anything to me. But there's no way I could have married her then, I know it. All I wanted to do was break all the ties I had. I think I was trying to prove something to my father, which was ridiculous because he was dead by then.

'As for the bar-girls, they do little to excite me. It's routine for them, and I'd like something more than that. I haven't had a woman for a while now, and sadly it doesn't really bother me.'

King, a married man and an unusually happy one if he was to be believed, raised his thinning eyebrows in some sort of wry amusement.

'Most men wouldn't admit to that.'

'I'm not most men, and I haven't got much pride left, unlike you. It's a fact of life, little else.'

They wandered back together eventually, Nathan feeling that the hours they had spent in constant companionship and sporadic conversation had helped him. They had somehow enabled him to look at both himself, and his situation, in the right perspective.

There would be no time wasted, searching for solutions that would not come, in the saloon that evening.

He was to find himself work in a mine in the

following few days, where a Cornishman was one of them 'boss' miners. And while others around him searched for wealth and the occasional mindless confrontation their lives appeared to him to be a kind of 'normality' he wanted to avoid.

He felt that Tombstone, or rather America in her entirety, had affected him the opposite way around. On his arrival there he had been a drinker, and a fighter, and now neither mattered. The isolation of the mountains had moulded him into someone different. Or maybe helped him discover the true soul within him.

With so much going on around him, he took to writing about the exploits in the town in his spare hours, penning a few letters to Billy who had surprised him by contacting him on a number of occasions in the past year. His youngest brother's letters from Cornwall had been almost poetic in their content and they prompted him into remembering how Billy had painted when young, at least until their father had burned all the home-made brushes he could lay his hands on. Despite that irrational, almost vicious, action, it seemed the sensitivity had survived.

Nathan also deliberately remained in close contact with Clarence King and as a result of that wrote, on impulse, an article about the bogus diamond fields which he sent to the local paper. Once he had sent it, he expected it either to be thrown straight into the nearest bin, or for the resulting story to be tucked away on an inside page.

Instead it made the lead story. More features followed, all given equally prominent treatment. Mark Twain he wasn't, but he came to derive as much satisfaction from such penmanship as he was sure the great man did from his own.

Later in 1876

V1

Alex Rosevean was angry, and to his intense dismay it was an anger he could barely control. Although inner fury had become an essential part of him since he had come to regard life as one battle against injustice, he liked to channel it into some useful action, to be able to direct it. On this occasion it seemed that it ran so deep it would eventually control him. And most of all it was caused once again by one man. James his employer, James his brother.
The men had been back at the pits for three weeks and it was becoming obvious that the promised strike pay was not forthcoming. They had been cheated by false assurances. And he was not alone in his fury. The same, harsh, unforgiving, hatred had spread quickly when the realisation had sunk in that every man at every pit in the county had been betrayed. Feelings ran so deep that the most energetic and hardened of the workers had seemingly come to believe that they had to make the most of the discontent while it was potent - use it and form it into something extremely effective.
With this in mind they organised themselves within days, finding no problem in arranging a series of meetings. One of the first was at Roche, where Alex's already bubbling temper was to be stoked up even further. When he was among over a hundred of his own kind, many worried out of their skulls by the never-

ending, gnawing battle with poverty and survival, he was certain that positive action was called for.

When they were sick the need for wages meant that pit men could not lie in bed until they recovered. They had to work. When they were exhausted beyond reason they still had to force themselves to finish extra long shifts. The money was never enough to provide peace and security.

Why can't James see it? He asked himself the same question repeatedly as he recognised the desperation in so many faces. James should know. He, of all people, should know.

The workers packed out the dark, cramped inn that stood within the brooding shadow of Roche rock, a huge granite tor which rose majestically towards the sky about half a mile distant. It had long been surrounded by mysticism. At one time a hermit had supposedly lived there, the cell he had built for himself still to be seen, at one with the granite. The wildness of the area which stretched away into the starkness of Bodmin Moor seemed to have seeped into the hearts of many of the men who stood shoulder to shoulder in the dusty bar and outside garden area.

The discussion was heated from the outset, with talk of a follow-up strike raised from the first moments.

'Aren't we being a bit hasty?' one of those present, from the pits at Hensbarrow Downs, asked after a while, when a number of those present had put forward their thoughts on the matter. 'I mean we'm only just back at work, with a bit of money coming in again. Shouldn't we wait a bit before we come out again?'

'I hate to say it, but that might well be what the owners are hoping you might think', butted in John Bourne, who was on the same shift as Alex and had travelled with him from Bodmin town. ' In fact those kinds of thoughts are what the blasted owners are banking on.'

'They well know we and our families are too worn out to start it up all over again,' came another voice.

'So we have to do something different,' spluttered Alex, trying and failing to quell his passion.

After listening to the string of speeches, he was speaking for the first time, his voice quavering so much it was obvious to all that he was losing the battle to appear collected and assured.

'Such as what?' countered another Hensbarrow man. 'We're left with no options. The owners have the upper hand. They always have had, and they always will have. Your wretched brother is among them. Because of that you should understand how they think. Ask him.'

'But aren't you already admitting defeat before you start?' came an instant reply. 'We've got to fight. We've got to go for their throats and keep going.'

Alex whirled around as much as he could in the crush to see who was speaking, but couldn't identify him. Nevertheless, the defiance was plain. The impassioned retort had been spat.

Alex had gone to the inn to say much, much more, although with the chaos screaming around him on all sides he wasn't sure if he would ever succeed in being heard again. But he took his chance when he was pushed as far as the bar, thick with grease and wet with spilt beer.

With some difficulty he lifted himself onto it, then with little hope called for some sort of quiet. Incredibly his tactics, rudimentary as they were, worked to a point.

'I've just realised that the answer as to where we go from here is simple,' he yelled, forcing himself to stop short of bellowing. 'The owners have stuck together and that, as well as their money, is their strength. We might not have the money, but we can learn from them and become united in our aims.'

'You mean start a union?' said someone in what sounded to Alex like absolute disbelief.

'Precisely.'

There was an instant pause, followed by the stirrings of a prolonged hush. To his surprise, without much effort he had won the attention of the majority. There were, of course, a few who had already drunk so much they were past silence, but for a moment they seemed to have been outgunned.

'A union wouldn't stand a chance,' was one dismissive reaction, though.

'Why the hell not?' Alex fumed, his impatience obvious.

'The owners'll do their level best to stop you before you start. They'll do everything to halt you in your tracks, that's if you ever get one up on 'em.'

'That goes without saying,' John Bourne cut in. 'We all know that they won't just sit tight on those fat backsides of theirs and let us get on with it. But should we always give in without trying because they're so powerful? We'll never get anywhere if we take that attitude.'

Boosted to some extent by John's words, Alex

fought to stop himself sounding as if he was pleading. Pipe smoke was wafting into his eyes, making them smart, and the smell of so many unwashed bodies was rising into his throat.

'What my friend says is true. And if we're strong enough to stick together whatever happens then surely we must get our own way in the end? The idea of a union isn't mine. I've heard it talked about by loads of others over the last few days. Together we could make it work. I'm a single man, I know, with less to lose than most, so single men like me would have to bear the brunt of whatever they might try to throw at us in retaliation. Those with no wife or children behind them will be able to suffer more. We've only ourselves to think of.'

'Nice idea,' the doubter at the back yelled again, 'but how many think like that? Wouldn't it be best to ask us rather than tell us? Ask the men in each pit what they feel before dragging us further into poverty.'

Most of those who had managed to remain sober appeared to nod in agreement with this view, making Alex look on with sinking hope. He knew that to give a union even the slimmest chance of working he had to convince a host of men that it was the right move. The pitfall was that they had previously had to force a strike, and the men already walked in living fear of their employers.

If they're allowed the chance to think about what they're doing, he panicked, then they'll be cautious. I can't see a union being born of a free vote.

Gradually, he noticed a sea of uncertain faces looking upwards, towards him, waiting for him actually to voice his opinion. Go easy, he warned himself, now more than ever you have to use your head, knowing very well how the Cornish could not be rail-roaded. In essence they were a stubborn, individualistic, self-contained race.

'What's been suggested seems right enough,' he said eventually, his mind rebelling against the words. 'But I urge all of you, when you return to your pits, to put our case as strongly as possible to every single man. Don't be unsure about what you're telling them, because you'll be in the right. Let them know this is something we must do to survive. We must keep some sort of pride and self-respect.'

Even as he spoke he knew he had capitulated, and the doubter had won the day, but he told himself he had had little option, though, if he wanted to retain any power over the matter. There was a vocal minority who, like him, had wanted a union formed there and then, and they went home fuming, filled with the ill-feeling that the 'soft' meeting had led them nowhere. They had gone to Roche for bitter revenge, for action - to exact successful retribution for the owners' abandoned promises in the most dramatic fashion possible.

Together they had openly talked of causing damage at pits, of blocking pit railways and using as many delaying tactics as possible. Alex suspected that some were tinners who had not even 'gone clay', but had descended upon Roche because they could smell trouble. Well they, like him, hadn't got their way. Despite that he had more than a hunch that, in the future, if James and his cronies didn't come to heel, such die-hards would have to be watched carefully.

During the following days he began to suspect the nerve of the quiet majority, believing still that in a ballot the idea of forming a union would be gently buried. With pessimism, he expected such a dramatic idea to frighten a good many of them. From talking to them over many a pint of beer, he knew that a few of his friends would cling on through any dispute, and that certainly those who formed the nucleus of the angry and the disillusioned would stay strong. The others, however, the vast majority, were an enigma.

In the end his closely-kept, pessimistic, fears were allayed. The solid backing they so desperately needed was surprisingly given to them. After hearing of the results he started to allow himself to believe that those who thought as he did, who also wanted to change the order of a previously set way of life, might just be able to begin to push for their dreams.

It was the autumn of 1876 when the owners came face to face with the results of the Roche meeting. James was, by then, amidst troubles both at home with the wife and child he still refused to feel any love for, and work where disturbing realities had surfaced in their hordes.

Talk of a union demanding unheard of rights from companies such as his was among realities. Like others, he had paid little heed to the threat of further combined action by the men, convinced the strike had drained all energies. When the talk of a union eventually threatened to become fact he felt unbelievably betrayed, seeing the decision as one huge conspiracy in which Alex was a key player. His brother's treacherous actions were, to him, beyond reason.

For a few days after receiving the embryonic

union's written demands he didn't trust himself to see Alex, or even go onto Bodmin Moor. Instead, he tried his utmost to view what was happening to him - what the men were apparently hoping to force upon him - in perspective. He failed.

A fury that would not be diluted eventually did draw him to the pits. Despite being scheduled to ride to Plymouth with his father-in-law that morning, he chose instead to appear at the works. This meant that Alex had no inkling of what was brewing. Believing his brother elsewhere, he was near the settling tanks when James arrived, and was head down, absolutely engrossed in the problem of the moment.

In that instant his mind was far removed from unions and disputes, at least until he looked up and saw his 'boss' about thirty yards away, closing in on him.

The sun, although weak, was slanting down on James's white-blond hair. His clothes were expensive, fit for Paris rather than a china clay pit, and his every movement exaggerated his power.

In some eyes it might have been that he looked almost like a deity, but Alex held no reverence for him. The fact that he was flushed scarlet with anger and seeking vindication didn't bother him either. Alex believed himself a greater survivor than James. Being without money or many possessions didn't particularly bother him, whereas he knew a reversion to poverty had begun to scare his brother witless.

It was Alex who spoke first, who opened yet another round of ill-feeling between them.

'Not a bad day for late September is it, in fact it's quite brilliant. Isn't it strange how in

Cornwall, when we're in the midst of a real dreary autumn or winter, how the clouds can clear and sometimes give you a day every bit as good as summer?'

James came to a halt only inches away from him. His jaw was already clenched, his eyes cold.

'The blasted weather doesn't interest me in the least, as you well know. I've got more pressing matters on my mind.'

'Such as what?' inquired Alex, smiling as he enjoyed the game.

'Such as why scum like you are trying to ruin me.'

'Surely that's an exaggeration?'

'I don't think so,' exploded James. There was enough ice in his heart to freeze over all the unexpected warmth of the day. 'I consider banding together to disrupt your work for me, and to demand money I don't have, enough to ruin me.'

'We're only asking for money you've already promised,' Alex said slowly, striving to stay calm, realising that civil war between them would benefit no-one.

'Talk of a union must stop. I warn you now.'

'Why be so terrified of the idea? A union must happen, surely you can understand that?' Alex murmured, continuing to try his best to avoid a disastrous confrontation, appealing to any rationality that remained. The threats got him nowhere.

'What happens when all the men are members you fool?'

'That day'll never come, and it's you who are the idiot if you think it will.'

'As I said,' continued Alex, as if his employer had never spoken, 'what happens when everyone joins? Do you go without workers then for the sake of your meanness and pride?'

James's limited tolerance snapped. It seemed to him, in that moment, that Alex's sole plan was to destroy him.

This has nothing to do with the rights of clay workers, or back pay, he thought, it's all because he's jealous, jealous that I'm in power and he's below me. I have to prove who's the tougher, I have to show him.

Alex was unprepared for the attack. James rammed knuckles into his stomach and he fell instantly, twisting his back as he hit the ground. But once the confusion passed he sprung back on his feet, all too aware of what was taking place. He hit back, not afraid to hurt, his own frustrations surfacing fast, as his fists pummelled flesh.

Basically they were well matched, each being of equal ability when it came to brawling. James had a height and weight advantage, with Alex being quicker on his feet. They were no experts, as Nathan had been, but were both able to look after themselves and hold their own in the wrestling ring.

In the heat of the moment, James had totally forgotten that he had brought along his family with him. Work had dominated so much in the past weeks that he had hardly been home for more than a few hours at a time and, with that playing on his conscience slightly, in previous days he had forced himself to be more conciliatory towards Helen.

That included paying her a modicum of attention and promising to take her shopping in Bodmin, although he hadn't bothered asking her if she actually wanted to go. Also, he had decided to carry out some work while trying to treat her, and he had stopped at the pits on the way, leaving both her and the baby waiting for him at the entrance

It was she, carrying Glynn in her arms, who stepped between them before they badly injured each other, she who found them, both smothered in drying mud and clay dust, locked together in a clasp of despair, rolling on the earth, battling for supremacy. The scene didn't particularly upset her. James had been irate enough in the previous days for her to know that a physical fight with Alex was what had been brewing all along. What did worry her was that she had a baby with her, and that didn't seem to affect the way he had decided to act.

'What on earth are you doing?' she yelled as the blows threatened to connect with her and the child. 'Stop it you two, you're scaring Glynn.'

As soon as he heard her, Alex tried to back away, though her concern made no difference to James. As if ignoring her entirely, he carried on with the same ferocity, ensuring that in the end Alex had to tear himself free.

'I'm sorry Helen,' he panted, blood pouring from a cut above his eye and making tracks down his grimed face. 'I didn't mean for it to get this bad. I would never have wished you to see it.'

Sweat was streaming from him, soaking his clothes. He may have looked fearsome, but he sounded far from it. James, aware at last that combat was over, at least for the present, said nothing, although his expression told the all. Helen, glancing at him, felt that if pushed further he could probably do murder.

Helen bore Alex no malice. She had always thought him kind, decent, reliable. Staid qualities maybe, she mused, but mixed with his fire and beliefs it seemed that they had become potent.

Unhappiness and ferocity hung starkly in the air between the three adults, with Glynn starting to cry in the middle of them, as if sensing the tension. After some minutes Alex nodded curtly and walked away, feeling slightly awkward, thinking that he had acted like a hot-headed child rather than someone with twenty odd years behind him. Before trailing away in retreat he had tried to explain his regrets to Helen.

'Look, I'd like to talk properly, it's a while or more since we've had a decent conversation but, in the circumstances I think it's best that I just say goodbye and go and clean myself up. It's obvious that James and I both need some time apart, to cool down.'

After he had gone James turned his still bottled anger on Helen.

'Well did you have to interfere like that? That was important.'

'That . . that brawl was important?'

'I was proving to Alex that he can't walk over me, that I'm much tougher opposition than he ever bargained for.'

'You were both just proving that you've never grown up. Each of you was acting like an ill-tempered brat.'

Whatever she said, he couldn't take her seriously. She was a mother now. Her girlish figure had filled out, pushed her into womanhood. Her waist had remained wand-like slim, but her hips had widened and her breasts, since Glynn's birth, had become curvaceous. Never had she been overwhelmingly shy, but now her self-confidence, alive and growing in spite of his continual rejection of her, was evident in the tilt of her head and her whole spirited manner. James chose to see only the 'negative' changes.

Richard Courteney had so coloured his view of Helen that he saw her solely through her father's eyes. She was an encumbrance, a child with unworldly ideas of her own who refused to be put on the right path. Above all, she was someone who could never be relied upon to offer total and full support.

'Keep your opinions to yourself woman,' he snapped. 'I don't exactly put much store by them.'

'No, you never have, have you?' In reply she spoke the words quietly, almost to herself, acknowledging the great and malicious chasm that now stretched between them. 'What would you have preferred me to do, watched on quietly while you killed each other?'

'I would have liked you to keep your nose out of it. Let me get on with my own life, let me choose my own paths.'

Her throat constricted. Does he go out of his way especially to hurt me, she thought. It seems he's determined to. And he never, ever looks at Glynn. He isn't paying him any attention now, even though his son is crying in my arms.

With such thoughts tumbling through her mind she spoke again, fighting with her nerves, anxious not to let her marriage be destroyed beyond salvation.

'I care for you. I can't suddenly stop worrying about you. How can I react coolly when you're in the midst of a furious fight?'

The shopping trip was cancelled. Neither of them were in the right mood to attempt it, afraid of how much worse the day might become. Helen wasn't at all bothered.

Generally, she tried to avoid Bodmin. The town oppressed her. Everything and everyone seemed to be overshadowed by the jail, rising grimly about a half a mile from the main street. Its grey, heartless walls somehow dominated her spirit while she was there, besetting her with thoughts of the public hangings that they had been witness to, and still were witness to.

That night was one of the lowest points. Lying in the beautifully decorated bedroom that was now entirely hers, that she hadn't shared with him since he had moved out on the transparent pretext that he had paperwork to complete most nights and didn't want to disturb her, she wept for hours, until dawn was in the wings, waiting to break through the darkness. Despite her changing physical appearance she was still very young. Hopes of finding some kind of contentment in the coming years were still bright in her idealistic dreams, but she wasn't sure she could keep enduring the indifference and the malice, and continue keeping the facade intact.

One of the real problems was that she knew James was falling further and further under her father's influence, something she found it impossible to blame him for, for she knew how mesmerising her father's personality could be. What was worse was that his hollow standards of self and profit were becoming James's too, which frightened her.

Over the past months she had struggled to stop the process, and fought to make him see that he had to retain some identity of his own. But she had lost at every turn. The fear was that the need for power and money would eventually smash away the nucleus of kindness and understanding that she believed was naturally within James.

More than anything, she wished she could confide in someone, though that was an impossibility. Uncle Matthew, who had always been someone who would offer her consolation, had become too frail and she was anxious not to worry him.

In the end she decided that perhaps she might visit Lorna, deciding that even merely mentioning her concerns to another person might be of some benefit. Also, she believed that, overall, a woman would be a better listener in such a situation than a man, especially one who was married to a Rosevean as well.

Eventually, she had come to the conclusion that someone who had seemingly loved two of the brothers must have some idea what she was facing.

V11

The blows rained down so hard on Lorna's back and shoulders that she almost collapsed on the floor, although she wouldn't allow herself to fall. With gritted teeth and as much determination as she could summon she grabbed a nearby chair and forced herself to remain upright, willing her body to absorb the savagery.

If I go down he'll start kicking, and then I won't be able to breathe and there'll be no escape until his temper's run its course, she thought desperately. I know that from experience.

'Bitch,' he was screaming, his voice unrecognisable. 'You lying slut. I saw you talking to that idiot from Holmbush. I saw you flaunting yourself in front of him . . simpering, showing how available you are. But I'll end those games, you whore. I'll bloody end them.'

Her breath came in ragged gasps, the trembling increased, but she said nothing, knowing there was no use trying to reason with him when he was in such a destructive, manic rage.

Since discovering the secret of Nathan's letters he had ceased being reasonable. All the old, festering envy had pushed its way to the fore, not only obscuring all sense but tearing apart, and beyond repair, their uneasy peace. At times, when he had been drinking, he seesawed to the other side of sanity. He had, through inflicting numerous beatings, discoloured and scarred her body.

With a ragged, rasping groan she struggled to upturn the chair in front of him, so she could delay him for at least a few, precious seconds. Realising instantly what she was attempting to do, he tried to send her sprawling, and almost succeeded. Her muscles felt as if they were on fire, which made her doubt whether she could hold him off long enough to save her skin. Despite that, though, she was able to draw on the final vestiges of her fading strength to use the chair to pin him down long enough to allow her to reach the door.

The handle turned, and she nearly passed out with relief. Then, taking one last, brief, flailing glance at him, she fled. He stood and watched, his face contorted with despair as his prey disappeared. All he could do was scream into the air.

'Come back you useless piece of dirt, come back here now.'

But she was running by that time, as if there were a thousand spectres behind, past caring how many pairs of watchful eyes were taking stock of her as she fled through the village. As she went, she told herself that she wasn't going to allow herself to become a dumb victim of his stupid, senseless envy and his dangerous temper again.

Seeking solace she walked to Crinnis beach, taking steadying breaths as she slowed down, and gradually made her way as far as the grassy headland. The tide was low, the sea was sluggish and the mile and a half of white, gritty sand lay before her, beautiful, hazy and undisturbed.

Within minutes she was at the sea edge, taking off her well worn shoes to walk the tide line, not heeding the water as it lapped in and soaked the trailing ends of her dress, wincing only slightly as her bare toes discovered sharp stones under the rough sand and smooth pebbles, but limping as she went as the beating she had endured started to take its eventual toll on her muscles.

The wavelets were cold, though not icy enough for her to retreat.

She had found, over time, that the ocean always soothed her. It had done so many times during the painful last months with Nathan. It did so then, when her mind was wretched and reeling. It helped her see events clearly, sort them into her own perspective. With clarity, she realised that, despite the terror Samuel had unleashed upon her, a terror that had led her to miscarry weeks before, she had still clung to the unreal belief that the beatings would run their course, and he would stop them. By making conscious efforts to steel herself mentally, and endure, she had as good as voluntarily kept herself in the danger zone.

She had tried, and secretly failed, to convince herself that she hadn't wanted the baby. After the furore over Nathan's letters she knew in her heart that living with Samuel had become too much of a strain to introduce a child into their turmoil.

But, once she had known about the pregnancy, she had accepted the inevitable, forcing herself to come to terms with her husband's spite. Hoping that she could fix their relationship before the nine months were completed, she had gone out of her way to try to let him see that her past was buried, and that there would be no resurrection of it - no more letters, not one more thought of Nathan. All such good intentions had dissolved instantly on the day he had punched and kicked their baby into oblivion.

It had seemed to her that he had intentionally killed their child, and that belief had not altered. She had run out of making excuses for him.

As she idled in the waves, staring out across the water to Gribbin Head and at the distant dots that were china clay ships sailing into Fowey harbour, she also wryly admitted to herself that in his warped, unstable, almost manic way, Samuel believed still that he loved her.

In trying to annihilate her, as he had the foetus she had been carrying, he was doing exactly the same to himself. Pointlessly, he had wept after the baby had died, in the few moments when he had at least accepted the irreversible damage he had caused.

He always cries for forgiveness afterwards, she thought viciously. Well he won't get any forgiveness, any understanding, any compassion, one moment longer, and nor will I put up with his vile temper ever again.

As she stared out to sea a cormorant skimmed the sea on its way to search for lunch. In front of it a flock of dunlin rose in a small, brown, clattering cloud.

Nathan knew I had some intelligence and a little bit of inner strength, but Samuel sees me just as a woman that he 'owns' and as his home-maker, even slave, nothing else. No person in her own right, with her own thoughts, her own mind. Well this is the moment when all of that should change.

With such thoughts tumbling inside her mind, she walked until the trembling inside her had settled, despite the bruises that were now hampering her.

Thinking still of the deep reasons for the disintegration of their relationship, she told herself that she had continued writing to Nathan because their correspondence gave her a sense of identity. Within her letters she had never really touched on any truths, never mentioned Samuel's increasing tendency for violence, or the lost baby, while his replies remained full of matter-of-fact news and little else, which had suited her.

Lorna knew she had certainly never given a hint to him about the maelstrom he had caused merely by putting pen to paper from what seemed to her to be the other side of the world. Basically, she hadn't wanted to admit so openly that yet another member of the family had hurt her.

Damn the Roseveans, she thought, for the umpteenth time as she replaced her steps, edging back to a home that she no longer felt safe in, damn each and every one of them.

As soon as she reached the cottage door she knew exactly what she had to do. By then, he was sure that his rage would have run its course, leaving him drained.

With her head held as high as possible, and as composed as she could make herself, she walked into the bedroom where he was asleep, slumbering away the effects of the day's alcohol and physical exertions. For a short while she stared down at him with an expression of disdain, at his unshaven face, his slack mouth with the saliva dribbling down from the corners, and her distaste for him intensified still further. Then she turned abruptly, walked quietly into the kitchen where the rickety table was still lying where she had upturned it in utmost panic during her bid for flight.

A broom that had been hurled across the room, lay with its shaft smashed amongst a pile of shattered plates. Debris cluttered every corner. After staring at the chaos for a full minute, she turned, not bothering to tidy any of it.

Lorna picked her way out to a ramshackle hut that had been on the site when Samuel had bought the land. From one of the drunkenly hung racks on the wall she carefully took down a shotgun he used for rabbit hunting. Methodically, sure of what she was doing, she checked to make sure it was loaded properly before walking back into the bedroom, and aiming it at her dozing husband. She stood there for a full minute, assessing him with apparent dispassion, then dug him roughly in the ribs with the barrel.

He came round slowly. His head hurt, his eyes were heavy. The quickly gulped alcohol had made him feel ill.

Gradually, as consciousness settled upon his brain, there came to him the dawning knowledge of what he had done before collapsing on the bed. The devil had taken him over again. Restraint had deserted him, he had done his utmost to beat her to pulp.

'Oh hell,' he murmured as he struggled upwards thinking, in his blurred state, that she was in the kitchen, nursing her wounds. Dimly, he accepted he would have to go and beg forgiveness again.

But when he fully opened his eyes he realised, with a jolting shock, that she was there beside him, within inches of him, and so was a gun. He was looking directly into its cold, clean barrel.

'What on earth?' he groaned, quickly returning to full, unbelieving, awareness and the ability to grasp, fully, something of the threat that faced him.

'Just stay where you are,' she ordered, her voice clipped and controlled, her face with the dark smudges of bruising beginning to show, expressionless. 'Don't move, don't twitch, don't blink. This thing is loaded. I checked it a moment ago, and after what you did to me earlier today I won't hesitate to use it.'

'Have you finally gone senseless?' he gasped, not moving because he understood all too well that he wasn't able to trust her.

Deep inside he knew how much he had hurt her, mentally as well as physically. As much as she had gone and hurt him. 'I know what I did was wrong, but you have to let me explain.'

'There's nothing to explain. We've been through it all before. You had too much to drink, you let your anger and your stupid, stupid envy get the better of you. You love me really.' Concentrating on her trigger finger, she then added tonelessly, 'You never meant to hurt.'

She was barefoot. Her hair was loose instead of caught up in an uncompromising bun, in the way she had started to wear it, and tendrils hung in a fair, exotic haze, making her seem as wild as her somersaulting, despairing, heart.

For a brief second he guessed it must be all a hallucination. Then the shivers attacked him. He stared into her eyes and realised for sure it wasn't.

'I didn't mean to go half as far. You've got to believe me. I didn't. It'll never happen again, never,' he rushed, nervously, sweating as his gaze constantly jumped from her face to the gun.

The gun hadn't moved. It remained pointing at his temple. He could feel its danger. Simultaneously, a voice in her head was urging her to use it, pull the trigger, stop his lies forever. With utmost difficulty, she fought it away.

'I don't intend to kill you right now,' she said eventually, unsteadily, 'but that doesn't mean I never will. So help me God, if you lay one more finger on me I shall go and fetch this and I will use it. I will send you, blast you, to kingdom come. I should have done it when you killed our baby but I was weak. I backed away. I could do it now, though, because it's reached the point where I have to accept that either I survive or you do.'

'But . . ?'

He could hardly credit her threats, her challenge. The spirit he had never given her credit for had exploded to the surface, more than unnerving him, frightening him in a myriad of ways. He couldn't face losing her. Lorna was his one prize, a prize his pride couldn't afford to let slip.

'No buts,' she snarled, annoyed that he could even have begun to try to explain away the harm he had done to her. 'I'm telling you now that, although you might have believed it differently, I'm not one of those wives who'll suffer throughout their lives from their husband's moods and tempers and fists. I'd rather be dead than a whipping post for you. That's why from now on I won't ever be afraid to shoot, whatever the consequences.'

As her words sunk in, he looked up at her again, his ruddy complexion for once pale, his eyes dead in puffy sockets. The bitterness, the ferocity had fled. He appeared defeated.

For a moment she pitied him.

'You won't leave me will you?'

The desperation made her cringe.

'No, no, fool that I am, I won't. She put the shotgun down with care. 'I'll try to live with you as peaceably as possible, if that is achievable, but I can't take any more of your insane violence, and I won't.'

Afterwards, she believed that she was more at peace within herself. It was as if she had regained a necessary part of her spirit.

Basically, she cared little what he thought any more. Any true warmth or companionship she had ever felt for him had been entirely obliterated.

V111

Tombstone began to be more than another town that Nathan merely happened to be passing through. The lodgings in Tough Nut Street started to take on a too familiar air. He discovered that lethargy had started to settle in. The compunction to keep moving was in the throes of fading.

Since the two great railroads, the Central Pacific and the Union Pacific, had met on Utah soil at Promontory Point the area had become much more than merely the geographical centre of the western United States. Above all, it was the home of the Mormons who had arrived there in 1847 with Brigham Young, and stayed.

The railroads had brought with them prosperity, and now the miners were making the most of the opportunities, even though they no longer included making a fortune from diamonds.

As the weeks passed by there were more than a number of occasions when Nathan decided that he ought to push on, when he saw his life as increasingly pointless. He went down the mine, he earned decent enough wages, he returned to the light again, his eyes hurting in the brilliant sunshine, and then he sat huddled in his small, poky room and he read, or he wrote.

And he came to accept that those moments, of reading or penning feature articles for the local paper, provided him with the greatest peace his current life could offer.

Despite remaining a miner his former love of the occupation, which had been tarnished beyond saving whilst he was in Cornwall, had dulled forever. The freezing conditions he had during the winters, and the stifling, searing days of summers spent underground, had wearied him alarmingly. That and too many deaths.

The initial lust for the gold, or the gemstone, that would provide an opportunity which would springboard him to a wonderful future, had evaporated, if in truth it had ever been there. It had fled like a sprinkling of late April snow.

During his sojourn in America the knowledge had come to him slowly, that although the great, empty land had offered him escape, and for that had his eternal gratitude, it couldn't be regarded as home in the truest sense of the word. Not for him. Talking to King had helped him understand that.

Maybe it might be home for those who've got school and chapel to build their lives around, he thought, and those who only want to drink and fight. Or for the farmers who've settled on the plains. For them there's enough, and more, but for me there's nothing permanent.

Because the majority of his life seemed to be settling into such a furrow of depression the offer from Henry Sears came like the darting sight of an English summer's first swallow. It caught him off balance. He'd written quite a few more articles for the Clarion, submitting them after penning the words in his room's confined silence. At the time he had thought them idlings and little else. Some were based on Cornish memories, some mere thoughts about the land he was continuing to discover. Others were descriptive sketches of the men he had worked with.

Sears, as owner and editor of the newspaper, had always accepted them, although Nathan saw that purely as a gesture from a man who had space enough to spare because the number of shootings had fallen short of the usual quota that week.

The editor had arrived at the down-at-heel lodgings on one of the wettest evenings that Nathan could remember since crossing the

Atlantic. The rain was falling completely vertically, washing in rushing rivulets down the street, and he was vaguely wondering whether the mine's drainage system would be able to stand up to the onslaught. His visitor, an exceptionally tall and alarmingly thin man with a grey pallor and dominant hook nose that resembled a bird of prey's beak rather than much else, didn't seem to notice the extent to which the heavens had opened despite his sodden clothes that clung to each hollow crevice of his body. He was equally unconcerned with the lack of hospitality that Nathan's stark room offered.

As if anticipating that his host would have little to proffer him, he had brought over a whisky from the saloon, and although most of the glass comprised rainwater he sat down, stretched out his bony legs and drank it down in seconds. Then, in his surprisingly deep and rich voice, he had come straight to the crux of the matter.

'Do you realise how good a writer you are?' Nathan didn't reply, because what had been said had been so unexpected. When the knock on the door had resounded around the room, he had been ready for bed, having to be up by four the following morning. It seemed to him that he had spent his entire life needing to be up by four the next day.

'That's something I've never thought about,' he said eventually, frowning because he was puzzled by the direction of the conversation and, in truth, only wanted to be between sheets.

Funny, he thought, how you change with the years. Before coming to America I would have had to have thrown a gallon of beer down my throat before beginning to entertain going to sleep.

'I write because I enjoy it, not because I'm any good at it.'

Henry, his hair receding fast and his sunken eyes magnifying the size of his nose, winced as he changed position. Despite his tiredness Nathan was alert enough to notice the pain which flashed like a moving shadow across his visitor's features. He was obviously a sick man.

Henry, who would admit nothing so adverse about his health to himself, said: 'Well, believe me you certainly pass. You use strong, direct words and you don't mess around with what you want to say. I've liked reading and publishing your articles.'

That's good,' yawned Nathan, meaning it. 'I'd thought you might have put them in because there happened to be more space in each edition that you could usefully fill that week.'

His guest thought about that for a moment.

'I never print rubbish, though why I bother to be selective I don't know. The Tombstone readership isn't of the highest quality. I think the majority of the papers are used to mop up swilled drink. I have to say that I certainly use the occasional copy that way myself.'

Nathan's eyes were prickling with weariness but he managed a grin.

'Don't underestimate the general public. I'd wager only half your circulation is used for such a worthwhile cause.'

It was then that Henry appeared to change to another tack, and Nathan assumed the split-seconds for compliments had passed.

'Have you ever been a drinker my friend?'

Nathan thought back to the hours spent in the Britannia.

'Once, yes, a heavy enough one I suppose.

Before I came here, that is, to America. All it gained me was an increasingly vile temper and police suspicion of murder. Their suspicions were unfounded, I hasten to add. A man from a nearby village was stabbed. I wasn't involved. I didn't really even see him there. But many people, some I had counted as friends, thought I ought to have been put behind bars for it, even hung. My temper had gone before me.

'Since then I haven't derived a great deal of satisfaction from drinking. I don't abstain when I do so on religious grounds, you understand. Wesley hasn't gripped me too hard, although perhaps we see more eye to eye, or soul to soul, now than we ever did before. I'll drink whisky, to socialise or maybe kill a cold, but that's really as far as it goes.'

It was a long speech for him, and it exhausted him still further.

Henry nodded. He didn't say that in recent years, since being a widower, alcohol had proved the only comfort for him.

'Always been a miner have you? From your articles I'd say you've quite a wide knowledge of the industry.'

Nathan rubbed his forehead with the back of his long, thin hand. Black curls hung down into his eyes, annoying him, and he brushed them away impatiently.

'I've been a miner almost since I first opened my eyes, like almost everyone here who's made the trek from Cornwall. I can't say I enjoy it any more, I'm too used to the harsh realities of it, but like the others I know no other true way of earning a living besides burrowing in the ground like a blind mole.'

Henry stared into his empty glass.

'I could offer you another way of making money. One above ground, although it probably also has its harsh realities.'

'Oh yes,' murmured Nathan sceptically, shadows now playing on his slightly cadaverous face, making him seem satanic. 'And what might that living be, planting fake diamonds to start another round of greed, and then reporting on it?'

'Not quite. I wondered if you would write for me, on a permanent basis. Or would mining have too strong a pull on you, despite all you've said, for you to accept such an offer?'

That pole-axed him.

'You mean working permanently for the Clarion?'

'That's the most direct way of putting it. Yes, there's a vacancy. My staff move on as often as all others in this land.'

'My stars, that was the last suggestion I expected to hear this evening.'

'I'm well aware of that. What I want to know is, is it one that meets with your approval, or at least interest? I know that I haven't a great many friends around here. I keep myself to myself, a strange attitude for a newspaperman, and that breeds suspicion.'

Nathan didn't have to think hard. The answer was within him. His spirit immediately reached out to accept. But the offer had come too unexpectedly. He asked for time to consider. His Cornish character was basically dour, suspicious of anything that seemed to be too good, unused to the sudden.

'When do you need your answer?' he asked slowly, unwillingly, wondering what Lorna would think if he wrote and told her of the opportunity he had been granted, one which would mean him taking a diverse change of direction.

'Would two days be enough?'

'I would think so.'

Henry stood up, stretching his thin, skeletal legs as he did so.

'I don't think I've ever felt like this before. I feel much like a hopeful groom asking a shy young girl to marry him. With my wife I was absolutely certain she would say yes. We were always so sure.'

Nathan suppressed a grin.

'I'm no shy young virgin wanting to marry you, believe me. And you shouldn't be asking me. I should be begging for the chance.'

'If that's the case why aren't you instantly grabbing at the job, giving me an answer straight away? Why are you hedging?'

'Uncertainty I suppose. I'm a miner born and bred, as you've already made me point out. Really I'm no writer. I didn't come here to find work on a newspaper. It's never entered my mind before. That does hold me back.'

Henry turned to the window to look outside. It was so dark, and the rain so intense, he could only distinguish a few odd shapes. For once there were no distant gunshots peppering the silence, no streams of bodies spilling out in all directions from the saloon.

'Look, this is only a small, insignificant paper in a town that may be bursting with people now, but is equally likely to be derelict in five or ten years' time. I'm not after quality reporting, and remember life never does stick to a pretty pre-arranged pattern. I must admit, though, I'm amazed that you haven't asked me the most important question.'

'Which, I suppose is; will you keep me in the manner to which my family would approve?'

'Something like that.'

'Funnily enough the amount of money you'd pay doesn't particularly interest me. It may have meant something once, but now my needs seem to be so few it doesn't any more.'

'Won't your family back in Cornwall feel you've abandoned them, or at least partly turned your back on them, if the amount you send back takes a tumble?'

'I'll send them the same, keep less for myself. Not that there are many that depend on me any more. I think the youngest, Billy, shows little interest in mining, and he might end up on this side of the Atlantic as well. He writes to me, which is more than any of the others do and, reading between the lines. I think he's after the same sort of escape that I once was.'

'Many are now heading for Kimberley and South Africa. You haven't felt like following?'

Nathan sat back in the gloom and was quiet for a while. The shouts and screams of a petty argument could now be heard from the street outside, even above the drumming of the deluge, and from the saloon came the unmistakable sounds of furniture being smashed. It wouldn't be such a dull night after all. The social life was warming up.

'No, I've run far enough. It's a pretty awful place here, but here is where I might just start to turn myself around.'

1X

Lorna noticed Helen's growing frailty as soon as she set eyes on her. Her sister-in-law's exuberance of youth had melted away, as had her healthy energy. There were worry lines picking at the corners of her pursed mouth, while her eyes were unnaturally wide, and watchful.

She was too thin, and her baby clung to her too intensely for his need of her, and hers of him, to be normal. There was beauty evident now, but Lorna saw it as a wan beauty that appeared as if it could be buried by cares in an instant, as a false spring can be devoured by a voracious winter.

It seems James is far from being the ideal husband, in just the same way as Samuel is, she thought. Would Nathan have caused equal misery if I had married him? Perhaps the Rosevean men are doomed to torment their women.

Despite her life with Samuel being definitely far from the contented neutrality that she had once aimed for, since the incident with the shotgun he had kept his distance from her, and for that she was extremely relieved and grateful. Almost as a bonus she found that, because she had stood up for herself with such alarming determination, she had recovered her self-respect, a welcome by-product. Also, she was dressing smartly and with more care, going out by herself, and emerging from a shell she had inhabited since realising she had lost the man she truly loved to an angry rush of hopes and strange ideals.

Over the past weeks she had steeled herself to tolerate Samuel, as if he was merely someone who happened to live in the same house as she did. She cooked for him, kept his home clean and washed his clothes. Occasionally, they shared the same bed, but not out of love, more out of their equal emotional emptiness and primeval needs. And if her limbs and the very core of her being still cried silently for Nathan's once loving touch and hard, muscular body then she told herself it was just a physical torture that would gradually become an acceptable, everyday part of her existence.

More importantly, she was in the throes of beginning her own dressmaking business. For a long time, since childhood almost, she had loved selecting materials, feeling their varying textures, stitching them into something worthwhile, be it petticoat or old man's shirt. There was little scope, of course, to indulge her interest to a great extent. She didn't have the money to finance making true finery, but she had a good enough eye and a deft enough touch to bring out the best in every fabric.

At the start of her 'romance' with Samuel, she had been asked to sew a new outfit for one of her few remaining friends and since then, to her mild astonishment, her name had become reasonably well known. Taking on small orders had lent her a sense of achievement and given her a tiny crumb of independence.

When Helen arrived she immediately tried to make her at home, guiding her, with Glynn still held tightly in her arms, into the uncluttered, tidy and vaguely stark living room. Compared with Helen's own house the surroundings were simple and crude, and beside the richness of her childhood home, the place was little more than a hovel, but nevertheless as she looked around Helen wished fervently that it belonged to her.

Over the previous months she had become certain that if James had stayed rooted in the world that was truly his, which she saw as a basic but honest environment, they would have a more stable marriage. A tiny cottage as a home, she was sure, would have helped him keep life in perspective. Yet without her money, without the opportunities her own family ties had offered him, he would never have contemplated marrying her.

No, she told herself miserably, there's no going back, no altering the situation.

Such thoughts were bombarding her when Lorna, who had disappeared to make them both a drink, re-entered the room.

Lorna looked at Helen again, noted the stricken look on her face, and felt she had to say something.

'What on earth is wrong. You look terrible, are you ill?'

'I'm fine, really, please don't fuss,' whispered Helen, striving to banish any traces of pleading from her thin, strained voice. 'I put weight on after Glynn was born, but in the past weeks it seems to have fallen off me, but not because I'm ill or anything like that.'

They had already gone through a round of platitudes when she had first arrived. Nothing of consequence had been said, although both knew she hadn't arrived on the doorstep idly to pass the time of day. Such visits, despite the joint respect they felt for each other, were abnormal.

But even with Lorna's attention and sympathy Helen could not even start to put into words the reason for her visit. To her dismay, she found she couldn't even contemplate talking about the disintegration of her marriage over a cup of tea and a slab of cake. Instead, she made a valiant effort to turn the conversation around.

'How are you and Samuel? I have to say I was worried about you two at one stage. I heard, through the general tittle tattle, that all was not well. James thought things weren't too bright when I asked him, but I suppose most of that was gossip. You'll never stop that.'

At that point, she was uncomfortably aware that she was gabbling, and no doubt mentioning a touchy subject that wasn't easy for Lorna to discuss either. But Lorna merely smiled and dismissively shrugged her shoulders.

'I ignore gossip, but I would probably have to admit that most of what you've said is true. Samuel and I tolerate each other. We can now live in the same house without coming to blows, just.'

Helen took stock of the quite stunning woman sitting opposite her, with the wide, sensual mouth and the sleek, auburn hair. The talk had been that she was quietly falling to pieces, but to her she appeared to be exceptionally settled in herself, and controlled.

'You seem happy, though, as if all is fine. I wish I knew your secret.'

'I suppose everything is now fine, for me. I can't speak for Samuel. I took some pretty drastic action to make sure I didn't sink too low. I've now got the freedom I want, when I want. I've started earning my own money and I have an independence of sorts. In a strange way I'm happy. Not as happy as I could have been, perhaps, but then I'd like to know how many people are.'

'What if you'd settled down with Nathan? Do you think your life would have been exceptionally different?'

The questions shot out so quickly that they even took Helen by surprise. Straight away she wished she had kept quiet instead, as she knew she was obviously straying into emotional quicksands. But this new Lorna, this ever-smiling, immaculate woman, looked as if she could take the intrusion.

Much more than I could have taken such a

prying comment, Helen accepted.

Lorna had blanched only slightly.

'That's an impossible question to answer. I don't honestly know how it would have worked out between us. But then with the way he was at the end perhaps I can hazard a guess that together we would have been a disaster. For a few months back then he put me through hell. I felt his cruelty much more than I've ever felt Samuel's because Nathan was the one man in the world who I've loved. I couldn't have shrugged off his hate, and turned to such an idling thing as needlework, and been happy with it. If he'd stayed in Cornwall I'd still be yearning to try to share a life with him, not straining to live apart from him.'

'I take it from that that you still think of him?' Helen couldn't stop herself. Confronting someone else's troubles was so much easier than dwelling on her own, though even as she talked, and interrogated, her selfishness appalled her. Lorna stared across the scrubbed table and out across the bay to where the waves sucked greedily and continuously at the jagged black rocks showing like unhealthy teeth at the base of Gribbin Head, the spume crashing on them flashing white in the sun.

'In the middle of some really awful nights I do, but I tend only to think of the good times, and that's wrong of me. It's deceiving myself. There were so many times that were bad, when I cried myself senseless.'

Needing to do something with her hands, she stood up abruptly and started clearing away the crockery.

'But enough of things that are well and truly in the past. Tell me about yourself and the baby here. He's my nephew, yet I've missed so much of him. And tell me what brought you here today, not that your visit isn't pleasant. I enjoy seeing you, but there must be reasons. You've so seldom been here.'

'I only wanted to talk,' said Helen truthfully, 'sit down and talk to someone of my own age and sex. I feel isolated sometimes, and I begin to talk to Glynn as if he's already grown.'

She hugged her son even closer.

'And James, what of him, can't you talk to him?' said Lorna, turning the conversation around as Helen had been doing earlier.

Helen visibly tensed and knew of a sudden that small talk may have proved easy with this self-assured woman, but sharing hidden fears wasn't going to be so simple. Not on this occasion.

Bringing them out into the open will make them all the more true, she thought, and I don't want to have to think about them so clearly. Not yet. I can't admit that my marriage was a mistake, that James doesn't love his son, that I've practically given up believing that he will, one day, come to love me. I can't explain how quickly we've gone different ways.

'Samuel mentioned something about the clay workers getting together and forming a union,' Lorna said, filling in the sudden silence. 'He took great delight in the fact that Alex was in the middle of it. Is that right? I never quite know how many of his bitter ramblings are true.'

'Well yes . . yes, he's right. Alex seems to be among those who've formed this union. I suppose I would be surprised if he wasn't.'

'And how is James taking that?'

There was no use lying about everything. Helen stroked Glynn's tiny hand, feeling some comfort in that.

'Badly, they fought about it the other day. Fought and, I'm sure, would have almost killed each other given the chance. They're both so certain that their side is right. Both so stubborn, and so blind.'

'That's not quite the right way to solve differences, beating the opposition's brains out,' murmured Lorna, thinking that it was probably as effective as threatening them with a shotgun.

'But that's the way of the Roseveans, isn't it? Sometimes their tempers seem uncontrollable. Their ideas are so rigid. The only one who's different is Billy, and he seems to be caught up in his own dream world.'

'It wasn't always that way,' answered Lorna, her voice thickening with nostalgia as her mind wandered back to childhood. 'I think their father's death affected them more than any of them would admit. I think they're all still trying, striving, to prove themselves, and come to terms with their freedom from him and also from his strict rules and ideas.'

'James is definitely still out to prove himself to the world,' sighed Helen, her words barely audible.

Lorna was tempted to say more, but checked herself instead. It didn't take much to see her visitor was nervous, deeply worried and devoid of her usual quiet optimism. Any deep questioning about James, and Lorna was sure he was behind all her worries, would probably scare her away completely. Meddling would not help.

She had to know more, understand more, before questioning in depth. So she kept to talk of the union.

'But do you think this new movement, or

whatever it is called, will work? I wouldn't have thought Alex would let himself be caught up in anything that doesn't seem worthwhile. He's much more practical than many would think, despite some of his wild ideas.'

Helen shook her head, the opaque sunlight catching the naturally blonde streaks in her brown hair. Her voice trembled slightly as she spoke.

'Do you know, I'd really like to see it work. I agree with Alex most of the time. What he thinks is usually the complete opposite to what my father believes, but maybe that's the attraction for me. The trouble is my father and the others like him will never stand back and let a union grow. They'll want to weed out every man from every pit who becomes a member, and smash both the group and them. I really don't think now is the time for Alex to win. Those with the money still have too much power and influence.'

With careful deliberation, she hadn't mentioned James, but it was a fact that he would never have agreed with what she had just said. It almost accounted to a subtle admission of what was wrong, irrevocably wrong, between them.

As evening closed in they went for a slow walk together, and because Lorna took the initiative and Helen followed they went down to the water. Lorna, hoping that such a companionable stroll might help her sister-in-law, was however, to be proved wrong. Helen walked along with her head down, sheltering Glynn who had been wrapped in a blanket and ignoring the waves and the heaving sea, seemingly unaware of any fascination.

The scene drew Lorna as it always did. As if

in awe of nature, she stood and watched the rushing, dashing foam, and nothing seemed to matter any more. Deep inside her, she felt that the whole scene was full of mighty, undeniable truths. The cliffs, the ocean itself, the beach, had all been there long before her forebears entered the world, and they would be there long after her death.

They prove, she thought, that nothing material really matters, especially not squabbles over money that amounts to a pittance.

Helen, though, seemed unreachable that day, too buried within herself and the cares that were eating away at her. And such truths defied trite explanations, so they made their way back to Lorna's home, both wrapped in their own thoughts, still with the unseen wall between them.

Helen eventually returned to Tregrehan feeling the afternoon had helped her slightly, despite knowing that if she had allowed herself to open up a little more it could have also been constructive as well as restful. As it was, she remained battling with fears for the future.

She consoled herself with the thought that at least Glynn wasn't yet old enough to know of the gulf that lay between his parents.

CHAPTER FIVE

Spring 1877

1

The ricks burned like fury. Sparks from them corkscrewed into the night sky, crackling and spitting like fireworks. The fields glowed red, used as symbols of the rioters' hatred, and the grass and hay steadfastly refused to be quenched by the water thrown via the line of tired, filthy men trying their utmost to bring the flames under control.

Those fighting the fire were desperately using what water could be found, and were even tearing off their jackets in a bid to try to beat out the spreading blaze, despite all the time knowing they were engaged in a fruitless battle.

Biscovey did not burn alone. The rioters had raced across the now flaming fields to St Blazey and the grass, tinder dry from a spell of exceptionally fine June weather, was sprouting flames too, from belligerent torches that were putting light to anything in mindless, indiscriminate violence. Anger was running amok.

Stunned villagers huddled inside their homes, bolting themselves and their children inside if they could, fearing the anarchy outside, terrified of the men whose furious frustrations had finally given way to days of upheaval and threats. They were men whose reason, and care for others, had been shattered.

The union had been officially formed, eventually, three months beforehand, just after the turn of the year, a move which had prompted constant witch-hunts. As Helen had foreseen, any man at any pit, who had joined the new organisation had been systematically sought out, and sacked. James himself had gone as far as paying employees not to join, and had offered extra cash to those who would spy on colleagues. That measure, more than anything else, had prompted deep resentment and vicious accusations, in the long run achieving its aim of splitting the men's resolve. The fact that colleagues who had been thought to be trustworthy were pocketing money for playing traitor, had given vent to unrestrained rage.

Alex had expected to have been the first to lose his job but James, out to cause as much unrest among union members as humanly possible, had kept him on. Although he regarded the struggle at his own pits as a personal one, he wanted to be seen as a victor by being able to destroy the union itself, rather than his brother. And there were advantages to keeping Alex on the payroll. In that way his younger brother was deprived of the ability to play martyr, and he also lost a great deal of respect from colleagues. Others who had been forced out of their jobs were left asking why he hadn't received the same harsh treatment. Was it because he was closer to his brother than he had ever admitted to, or because he was accepting those tempting payments, turning his back on those he was claiming to fight for?

Basically, the campaign the owners had waged had been utterly ruthless. Men who lost their employment were given no chance of appeal, and had zero hope of finding alternative clay work. Initially, the employees had continued to believe that they had the strength to hold fast. They were sure that if they could just stay united they would triumph. However, one by one the union members, through despair or greed for extra money, had broken away.

Once the ranks were depleted morale began to take an irreversible dive. As a result, with the situation turning from hopeful to desperate, lawlessness had seeped in, created in the main part by those who had been advocating physical force as far back as the meeting at Roche. Isolated incidents, such as the breaking of windows in owners' palatial homes tucked away in idyllic pockets of the countryside, escalated until the hard-pressed local constabulary discovered that they had full-scale unrest on their hands.

Alex, understanding the emotions driving the agitators, nevertheless tried to stop any minor or mass destruction. He knew his authority was not as strong as it had been two months previously. Many, because of James's refusal to sack him, believed him a turncoat. The obvious solution to that had been for him to walk out of his job, but despite that being at the forefront of his mind he had hung on believing that he could cause more damage, sway more hearts and minds, from inside rather than outside the pits.

His main belief was that if he could just organise a complete walk-out among the stragglers in the St Austell and Bodmin works he could deal the owners a body blow from which they would not easily recover. But he soon discovered he was battling against overwhelming disillusionment. Many felt a great deal of sympathy for the union but, after seeing what power their employers continued to hold, shied away from becoming part of it. Alex, confused and depressed himself by the mess that had become of their plans, had been amongst a band of workers who had gone out that evening in peace - but had ended up with torches in their hands. The initial intention had been to march to specific owners' homes to state their case, and demand a fair hearing. It soon dawned on many of them, though, that this had been a naive intention.

No owner had wanted to listen to their outpourings of passion, and each had made it plainly obvious that they had no time to devote to the workers' side of the argument. The utter futility of the evening had just fortified tempers, and from then on there had been no holding back for a furious inner core of them. In the end the ricks had taken the brunt of the bitterness.

Alex, deeply worried by how quickly the terror tactics had snowballed, knew only too well that the destruction would not lead to any form of victory. Feeling that all sanity had seeped away, he stood in the middle of the flickering fields, the moon outlining the distinct planes of his strained, sweating face and distorting them to such an extent that he looked almost devilish - and pointlessly tried to restrain and bring reason to those screaming around him.

'Look for pity's sake, enough is enough. You've burnt some hay, but be sensible and stop it now,' he yelled, indiscriminately pulling at some of them, grabbing their coats, which were blackened and dishevelled, and urging them to return home.

'You're all right, you've got a job still,' someone yelled, unrecognisable in the mob. 'You've got money still, and no family to support. You started all this damned union business. Now you're turning your back on us when we need you most.'

'Don't be dumb,' he shouted back, his voice already hoarse, his mind telling him that he was beginning to be afraid, as well as desperately angry.

What had it been like at the Britannia when Joel was knifed? Most probably only half as crazy as it is now, he thought. With such thoughts pounding at him, he ran along beside them.

'Look, I'm with you all the way, but not with putting lives in danger. You're in such a state you're well on your way to lynching someone.'

'That's bloody right,' came his answer. 'Are you volunteering to be the first victim? There's enough with a grievance against you.'

'Yeah, whatever happens you'll have to show where your loyalties lie,' someone else joined in. 'Your dear brother's house is next on our visiting list. We'd love to put a noose around his fat neck, and if you've any sympathy left for the cause, so would you.'

Real horror gripped Alex then, not for himself, because he still had friends enough around him if protection was needed, but for James and for Helen and their baby, and maybe for his own ideals.

It could not be denied that every hope of his would be in ashes if murder, especially the killing of members of his own family, was done apparently in the union's name.

And it was clear to him, as a whole crowd pushed past en masse, that there was nothing within his power to control a single one of them. Violence and a rushing, spreading hysteria were holding sway. Only himself and a smattering of others, John Bourne and Joshua Wyndham among them, seemed to have remained untouched by the insanity which was swirling around them, and were seemingly fully aware of what could ensue.

In sudden, utter, panic, he grabbed John, the stench of burning filling his nostrils and making him reach.

'I'm scared stiff of what they'll do if they get to Tregrehan and find James. God knows if he'll be home, but Helen will be. There's her and the boy to think of. This isn't their fight. If anything Helen's with us, but they're not rational enough to think of that, or spare her.'

'You can't even start to talk to this lot,' wheezed John, fighting for breath. Smoke had caught in his throat and swirled into his eyes, stinging them raw. He, too, could have wept at what was happening around them. 'There's only one thing we can do if you want to give James a chance. Cut through the copses to Tregrehan and warn him, but we'll have to move quickly. It'll be hard finding the paths in the dark and avoiding the old shafts. I haven't been that way since I was a tacker.'

Alex put his arm around his shoulder in gratitude, knowing how little respect John really harboured for James. But he was a decent man. Bloodshed dismayed him, more than ever when it was wrongly spilt.

Alex was choking too, which meant it took him a while to answer.

'That's the best idea by far. If I cut across that way I think I could reach their house about four minutes at least before the others.'

'We're coming too,' interrupted Joshua. 'That mob may think they're on my side but at the moment they're scaring the daylights out of me.'

All three slipped away into the welcome darkness, lit now and then by ragged red sparks and a flitting moon, as stealthily as they could, anxious not to be seen. They were well aware that if any of the rioters knew what they were intending they would be liable to be strung up too.

John's route took them through hedge and ditch, though thankfully the dry weather of the past weeks had ensured there was no sucking mud to hinder their progress. Gorse and blackthorn remained in profusion, however, and they scratched and tore at their flesh as they stumbled desperately on.

There was no avoiding the thorns. At any other time they would have slowed their pace or stopped to inspect their wounds, but the shouts and calls of the following, baying pack seemed to be growing louder, and more animalistic, by the second. Fear drove Alex on, fear that twisted the gut and weakened the limbs.

'James must have heard them and seen the fires, surely?' panted John, trying to convince himself that lives weren't dependent upon their blind, desperate, trek across country.

Alex wasn't so sure.

'He might be aware,' he answered, dragging back a long, vicious briar from his face, 'but he's so stupidly stubborn. He'll stay put and fight. That blasted money of his has made him think he's invincible.'

They were filthy from the fire and earth, and also scratched raw when they reached the house, Richard Courteney's gift to his aspiring son-in-law, but none of that mattered. The torches could be spied marching across from the sea, nearing rapidly, and every moment was of the essence.

Alex hammered on the door, but met no reply. He swore, then kicked and battered it until he thought the wood was about to splinter.

'I bet they've left and they're far from here by now,' gasped Joshua, his cheek cut, his clothes ribboned. 'They've been warned already. James must have known.'

'I hope to God you're right. It would mean all this has been for nothing, but I hope you're right.'

Alex hammered again, determined not to turn away quite so soon, screaming for an answer. 'James, Helen, open up. It's important. You must open the door.'

Heightened sounds told them that the mob was closing fast, and the three of them knew they would have to move pretty quickly, or it certainly would be they who would be swinging from the nearest tree.

In haste, they were just turning to fly in search of cover when the door slowly moved, creaking on the hinges that remained. It was only opened about six inches.

'Alex, did you say it was you?'

Urgency filled every sinew Alex had. He flung the door back and propelled Helen, clinging to it on the other side, into the hall. With pulses pounding, he grabbed Glynn from her arms, and then grasped her with his other hand and pulled her back further inside. John and Joshua followed him.

'What . . . ' Helen stammered, staring from one to the other, her brown hair dishevelled, her wary eyes enormous and luminous. She was obviously petrified. Womanhood had fled. She was the unthinking girl struggling in the waves again, only this time James was nowhere to be seen.

Alex shook her.

'What's been happening? You look scared beyond reason already.'

'I . . I've been watching out of the window,' she gulped. 'You can see across the valley. See the lights and hear the voices. I didn't think they'd bother with us. I thought burning a few ricks would be enough for them, but it won't be, will it? They're coming here . . to us.'

'I have to say yes,' spat Alex, rushing his words. 'They're not sane out there. Where's James?'

'Not here.'

'Where is he?'

'At a meeting somewhere. More battle plans. He's been gone all day. I just don't know when he'll be back.'

'Right. You and Glynn. We must move. Grab anything near at hand and valuable - jewellery or anything small like that - and then we have to go. You can't stay here and face them.'

'I can't leave . . .'

She knew precisely what was going to happen. Her home was going to be broken apart by manic hands. Her dearest belongings, and even the everyday bits and pieces, like Glynn's toys, were going to be smashed and wrecked by strangers.'

'You must go, and right now. If you don't we'll forcibly drag you out. You've been watching them, you must know the danger.'

Outside the thudding of feet, the whipped up curses were almost upon them.

'All right, yes, yes I do.'

They scrambled out the back way, pulling themselves over the stone wall which separated the property from the surrounding woodland. Alex kept Glynn clutched to him, thinking they would move quickly without Helen taking him, constantly checking on him. John propelled Helen in front of them, hauling her roughly to her feet whenever she tripped.

They clambered through the woods, gasping for oxygen through dry, rasping throats as they went, not keeping now to any particular path, just dragging themselves higher and higher and deeper and deeper into the rough undergrowth until they were almost certain they wouldn't be followed, so they could relax a little.

After fifteen minutes Glynn was sobbing in terror, and Helen, her legs lacking in strength before they started, had reached collapse. Alex, thinking that they might have been lucky enough to have made a decent escape, allowed them to sink down into a cushion of cool, lush ferns and huddle together as they stared down at the house, now below them.

Its white and grey granite walls were visible enough in the moonlight. To the distraught, shivering group, the building seemed tiny and insignificant, almost as if it was part of a toy town.

Helen hadn't realised until that moment how isolated it was. She found it incomprehensible that such a small, white square held all her treasures. She had stuffed a few of James's papers into a canvas bag, though she was sure she had probably taken all the wrong ones. How was she going to explain the events of the evening to him?

'Oh God help us,' she whispered, as the torches became very clearly visible in a ragged, weaving line.

Alex hugged her, trying to give her some comfort, although he felt he needed some himself.

'Just be grateful we're up here, away from it all,' he answered.

She, never giving a second thought as to why he was hiding with her and not storming the

fields with his fellow workers, spluttered:
'But perhaps I could have pleaded with them.'
'Never. Believe me, they're not thinking straight tonight. They don't want to listen. You'd never have stood a chance.'

After a short, tense wait they heard the distant, chilling sounds of glass and wood being smashed and watched on, drained, as stark moonlight combined with the torches to illuminate the mindless and senseless attempt to decimate a building which once had been a home.

Being so far from the heat and the hatred, and almost in their own, necessary, cocooned world, it was difficult to believe that the scene they were witnessing was really taking place and not a mere hallucination. Nevertheless, in their hearts all of them knew for sure it was reality.

'What will James say . . what will he say?' murmured Helen, so shocked it took painful concentration before she could speak again. All my nerves have seized, she thought, and I think that I'll never have an easy mind again.

'Who gives a damn?' answered Alex automatically, not hiding his own all-consuming distress. 'If it wasn't for him and his kind and their ridiculous decisions . . all this would never be happening.'

'And he certainly should have been here', he seethed under his breath. 'He should never have left you two alone. Doing that was almost as criminal as what's happening below us.'

The sparks continued to shoot into the air in ill-disguised triumph, and the shouts and yelps of jubilation, animal-like in sound, could be heard for around thirty more long minutes. Then, as the clouds began to cover the sky completely, with light rain starting to fall, they gradually quietened. Mania had run its course and leapt on elsewhere to cause more pure destruction.

While the remnants of the miniscule figures below them took flight, to run back to their own unharmed homes and recollect, in the sane light of day, what they had allowed themselves to do in the name of mass hatred, Helen watched mesmerised as the plumes of smoke spiralled up from the smouldering remains of her family's possessions to reach them through the trees.

11

At the same time as Helen was crawling amongst ferns and undergrowth, fighting to keep absolute horror at bay, James was spending a comfortable evening in the company of his father-in-law. While a great many pit owners were being scared into selling their companies because of thoughts of bankruptcy Richard had decided it was the ideal opportunity to buy cheaply into clay. Over the past months he had come to believe that the future of tin and copper industries in Cornwall was doomed in the long term. Although conceding that there might be mini recoveries ahead, he was sure there would be nothing major. Indeed, he was firmly of the opinion that the emerging kaolin industry had the prosperity of that part of the South West in its grip.

Once he had formed them his beliefs were always inflexible, which meant he flung his entire energy into backing them. This had led to him already selling his own interests in tin and copper, unable to remain interested in them after he had written them off in his mind.

The only trouble was he was getting older, and he had reluctantly started to admit to himself that he had begun to reach the limits of any empire building he could personally undertake. The hunger was not what it once had been. So who better to tempt with the deals, who better to draw into the Courteney perpetuation than his son-in-law in whom he saw a mirror image of himself as a young man?

'I'll give you the finance,' he said quickly, sensing some doubts inside James. 'I know you're struggling at the moment and not happy about what's happening, and I'm sure you're thinking that worse will come before your current business life improves. Now, though, and please believe what I say, is the time to buy.

'There are pits at Greensplat, Lanjeth and Bugle going begging. There are a host of other glaring opportunities elsewhere if you bother listening in the right places. An acquaintance of mine, Henry Pochin of Salford, is thinking of buying Higher Gothers works. Now he is a chemical manufacturer and is talking about producing some sort of aluminous cake from china clay that can be sold to paper makers.'

'Have you really that much faith? Do you actually believe I can win in business?' asked James, uncharacteristically seeking necessary reassurance in a very open manner.

'You've got all the qualities needed for it. Ambition, determination, a refusal to bow to unreasonable demands.'

'You still agree with our stand over back pay then - after all that's happened you still think we shouldn't have paid up?'

'Most certainly,' Richard laughed tonelessly, his muscular, but slightly failing body shuddering in the effort. 'Those scavengers should be grateful we're able to give them a decent weekly wage packet. They shouldn't be in the business of trying to kick us into the ground.'

James was heartened a little by that. Helen's attitude had started to unsettle him. Recently, she had been telling him constantly about what she saw as the unfairness of the situation. She had been so sure his employees should have his total sympathy that he had started to think that maybe part of her argument was right.

Not that he had admitted any of his doubts to her. That would have amounted to weakness. Instead, he had tried to make himself remember that in order to survive personally he had to fight to protect his own bank balance. No-one else would do that for him. Except maybe Richard who had started to call him son, who had begun to make him believe they were actually of the same flesh and blood. Frequently, he had started to feel that they were on their way to forming a strong relationship in which Helen was merely an irrelevancy.

He fiddled with the maps of Hensbarrow that his mentor had been studying. Annoyingly, his wayward nerves would not steady.

'There must be another strike brewing, though. Feelings are not only high, they're ugly, especially among those we've been toughest on, who have nothing else to lose. Their anger seems to have incited the others. We were meant to have broken them by now, not turned them into a baying mob.'

'All ruffians, there's no other word to describe them. They're hardly worth our worries, our time or our breath,' said Richard, sharply dismissing the escalating troubles. And that definitely includes Alex, James through sourly. I find it hard to believe we've grown so far apart. I thought that as my brother he'd be pleased for my success. The others are a little better, although Samuel doesn't seem to care about anything else but himself. Billy's different, and Nathan's elsewhere, thank God. Only Alex, in his stupidity, seems to see everything I do as betrayal.

'There was some mention of possible trouble tonight,' Richard said, as an aside, between large mouthfuls of roast lamb. It was impossibly late, but they were eating dinner. They had been delayed by a series of business meetings in Falmouth and hadn't arrived home until eleven o'clock that evening. However, Richard had still insisted that the cook provided them with his choice of food. Eva was nowhere to be seen.

James looked up sharply from his unwanted plateful of piled meat and steaming vegetables, not being in the least hungry.

'Was there? I hadn't heard anything special was afoot, I mean no greater disruption than usual.'

'Oh yes. It was to be in your area, or starting from there. They were marching from Par Moor down towards St Austell. It was rumoured they had a list of owners' homes. They supposedly wanted to come and try to reason with us, as if they know what reason is.'

James instantly dropped his knife, which cluttered dully onto his laden plate. It was so quiet the sound reverberated around the sumptuous, but nevertheless starkly chilling room. They were alone save for the maid, struggling to keep awake behind them, and Eva who James presumed was in bed somewhere in the house.

'Well why didn't you mention it before?' he snapped, weary senses immediately alert. 'Aren't you afraid they might come here? And if Alex is involved, which is highly likely, then my home will be a target too.'

Richard merely continued eating with obvious relish. It had been a full day and his appetite was alive and well.

'I'm sure it was all talk. That's all they seem to be full of at the moment. Words and wind. Neither the men, nor their actions, are of any consequence.'

Although his brittle sentiments were uttered with total conviction they didn't soothe James. In fact his worries intensified.

'Don't be so sure. When they're together and riled I wouldn't like to trust any of them. And remember Helen and the boy are at Tregrehan all alone. There are no servants there, not even neighbours to protect them.'

Something approaching guilt was stabbing at James. It was the first time that day they had mentioned Helen, despite her being the wife of one of them and the daughter of the other. Work had taken complete and utter precedence, that and the continuing extension of Courteney interests. Glynn had been ignored as well.

James had to admit he had never known Richard inquire of his grandson's happiness or development, only of his health. Richard didn't, it seemed, want a sickly grandson. Since Glynn's birth there had been no talk of how Helen was coping, or whether the baby was happy and content. All questions dealt with whether or not he was ailing.

James remembered Helen had once told him that her father never had any patience with illness. Anyone in less than one hundred percent health in the family only, from his point of view, succeeded in weakening the Courteney name.

James let his fork fall from his grip as well. 'All the same, though you seem to think no-one will be hurt, I ought to get home as quickly as possible. Just to check all is well, and stop myself thinking it might be otherwise.'

Richard considered the matter for a brief moment, while attacking his roast potatoes with vigour.

'All right, perhaps you'd better get back to Tregrehan. We don't want anything happening to that house of yours. It cost a pretty penny and I wouldn't like those oafs to be the ruin of it.'

The indifference shown to his own daughter and grandson shafted through James, sending him shivering in disbelief. Of a sudden he saw in Richard Courteney a reflection of himself, and experienced a gaping emptiness. His host, quite unaware of what he was thinking, swept the attendant sauces aside in dismissal, and pulled a pile of papers into the centre of the table.

'Before you go let's finalise a few matters. Tell me if you're happy enough to take these on, then I can put in offers as soon as it's feasible. If a strike does come from all this then I believe that will be the right time to make approaches.'

James rode home as quickly as his horse,

which had already covered the miles to Falmouth and back, would permit. As he went his anxiety increased. When he passed through St Austell, and took the main track towards St Blazey, evidence of the anger that had stampeded that way was unmistakable. There was an air of oppression, and he could smell smoke, see the remains of ricks burning. It was then that fear truly flooded over him. It was gone two o'clock in the morning.

A ridiculous time to be out still, he thought viciously. But then once Richard begins planning nothing is permitted to interrupt. I should have returned here four hours back. Panicking now, he spurred on the tired gelding, and the guilt that had been nagging at him since Richard had let slip rumours of the mob on the march, threatened to become overwhelming. Helen and Glynn were his responsibility, something he didn't like to be seen shirking in public. And, although he also didn't like admitting it, he too was worried about his property. He now saw the house as his, not an extension of the family he had married into. Surely he had done enough of Richard's dirty work to make it his possession?

The fields lay blackened in the dully washed moon's light, a few embers glowing here and there, but with the grass mainly raped and spent by fire. Then he noticed sparks high on the horizon in the direction of St Blazey Gate and Tregrehan, and tried to force the pace. Why the hell hadn't Richard said something earlier?

By that time he had begun to expect the worst, and when he reached his house, with his throat parched from the smoky atmosphere, and his heartbeat racing so fast he felt sick, it seemed that the worst had happened. For a second he believed he was going to bring up all the food he had unwillingly swallowed. He almost fell off his horse in his haste to check the destruction, then staggered towards an outhouse, still afire and crackling outrageously in its death throes. The shambles of the building that had been his home lay behind it.

'Helen,' he yelled, his voice strained and disjointed. 'Helen, where are you? Come out. It's all right, it's me. What the hell happened?'

In terror, in anger, in remorse, he stumbled to the front door, only to discover it didn't exist any more. Mouth agape, shoulders hunched rather than thrown back in his usual determined manner, he realised that each and every window had been shattered. Through smarting eyes he also numbly noticed charred piles of furniture, shreds of paper somersaulting in the air, and the remnants of at least three bonfires. All but three and a half walls and a drunken roof remained.

Helen appeared swiftly enough, emerging from the shambles, running to him, arms outstretched.

'I'm sorry . . I'm so sorry,' she cried, babbling the words, relieved he had come at last, that the burden didn't remain hers alone, but so afraid of his reaction. 'They've done so much, taken so much. Smashed all that was good.'

He pushed roughly past her.

'Have they destroyed everything? What about my papers, my study?'

'I saved a lot of your private papers before we ran. We had to leave, you see. I couldn't stay, especially not with Glynn here. Most of what I managed to save is intact.'

Her pert face was streaked with dirt, lending her even more of a ragamuffin look, while her clothes were ripped, and the trailing hem of her skirt burnt. She looked in danger of fainting at any second from shock and complete exhaustion. He took no notice.

He hasn't even asked if I'm hurt, or if Glynn's all right, she thought fiercely. His possessions, his pathetically petty papers come way before us.

Completely drained of any hope, or energy, she dashed back more tears, unseen in the night.

I must have cried enough this evening to fill the sea at Carlyon Bay, she thought. I refuse to weep any more.

In a bid to make him understand exactly what had happened in his absence, she tried to grab his arm.

'We're lucky they didn't completely burn the house as they did the barns. We should be grateful the drink they had downed before marching over here, meant they had done their worst before they reached us. I think that few knew where they were, or what they were doing.'

'Grateful . . .grateful for nothing you fool,' he exploded, turning on her, catching her by her thin wrists and shaking her in his anxiety.

'The bastards . . the bastards. Was my damned brother among them?'

His words prompted real anger within her, despite her overwhelming tiredness. Earlier in the night she had been too terrified to allow herself to experience such a reaction. But the fear had begun to dissipate now her son, and she herself, had apparently survived the worst the night had involved.

'If it hadn't been for your so-called 'damned'

brother Glynn and I might not be here now. Alex ran ahead to warn us, thinking you'd be here too, and when he found out that we were alone he rushed us away from all the danger. We were petrified, Glynn and I, before he arrived. We were just standing at the window, watching, seeing the lines of torches getting closer and closer. He, and those friends of his who also helped us, were like a gift from heaven.'

'While your blasted, inconsiderate husband was out pleasing himself with food, drink and yet more dealings.'

Sighing, she ran her sore, scratched fingers absent-mindedly through her hair, trying to tidy it, but not succeeding. The sickening smell of burning still seemed to be clinging to her, worming its way into her clothes, seeping into her skin.

'I wasn't saying that. I was only trying to make you see that Alex was not responsible in any way, for what happened. If anything he put his life in danger trying to stop them, to save us. His first thoughts were for Glynn and me.'

James was hardly bothering to listen. Instead he was listing in his mind all the cash, all the documents that had either been lying around his study, or in his desk.

How much had she managed to snatch before she ran for cover? Probably too little of what was important, he told himself with regret, and too much of what could be termed useless.

'It was he who incited them in the first place,' rasped. 'There's no excuse for him. He must have known there was no way to stop the hatred once it had started. I'd lay odds he came here for show, to mimic concern and

hide his real feelings. Is the boy asleep now?'
'Oh, you are a little concerned about Glynn then? Yes, yes he's asleep. I found some covers that weren't too badly affected by the fire, and he's in the one bed that managed to survive. Ours, or rather mine, was smashed to pieces. I hope he's having sweet dreams, but I doubt it very much. I just thank God he's too young at 14 months to have any idea of what was really happening.'

James walked from one wrecked room to another, through the smouldering materials and scraps, and smashed walls that now constituted his home, trying to cling onto a semblance of calm.

'You realise how much it will cost to replace the damage?' He turned on her. 'If only I'd been here. . '

'If you'd been with us, and you'd been graced with any sense, you'd have run even faster than we did,' she retorted.

'I'd never have bolted from such scum.'

'They'd have killed you if you hadn't. It was you they wanted, not us. You were the one who dismissed half of them from their jobs.'

In the absence of the men who had wrecked his home and his possessions he itched to strike out at the one person in front of him, the one person he knew was completely innocent. So in place of such unwarranted violence he forced himself to swivel around and, with his shining white hair illuminated by the shreds of moon and stars, walked deliberately into the remains of his study. There he found that his books had been ripped to pieces. All the documents that Helen had left behind in her flight had been torn or stamped upon. Earth and charred wood covered the expensive Chinese rugs he had chosen especially to enhance the room's decor. The pictures had gone from the walls, his pens had been deliberately broken and ink had been upturned and he guessed that that, too, was soaking into the rugs. As he looked around at the devastation he almost choked on his desire for revenge.

Helen's insistence that he could have done nothing to stop the rioters' desire to slash and burn, and the knowledge that the building's structure had mainly appeared to have survived to a certain extent, did not act as balm. To his mind the mess around him contributed to a declaration of absolute warfare.

'Where's Alex now, run like a scared rabbit rather than face me? he inquired sarcastically after storming back to face his wife.

She wanted to scream.

'Hardly. Why on earth should he be scared of you after being prepared to take on that demented crowd? They'd have attacked him for sure if they'd known he was trying to help your family. He stayed until the danger was well past, until he knew that Glynn and I were definitely safe, and then he went back to your family home to check on your mother. By then he had started to worry that she might have been alone, because he didn't know where Billy was.'

James sneered.

'She'll be all right. Why should they bother her?'

'She gave birth to you, didn't she?' Helen snapped.

Inside, she felt lost. Every muscle in her body ached. She was too empty to cry again, or feel deeper distress. All she wanted was sleep, even if it was snatched and lonely and her bed was a grimy floor. After her hell of an evening, and trying to deal with James's lack of concern, she had passed caring.

It was pitch dark and it was cold under a clear sky, and she kept checking on a still sleeping Glynn while she also watched James carry on with futile attempts at clearing some of the debris, knowing that whatever she tried to say or do her actions would be misconstrued. He was in a mood where he could not be cajoled, or even spoken to. Rage was warping him, as it had done the men who had stormed across the fields earlier.

However, she had misunderstood her husband to some extent. She had not taken into the account the shame he felt at not being there to protect her.

Am I as unconcerned about my wife and child as Richard was, or is, he quizzed himself while letting the fury hold sway on the surface. At that moment his respect for his father-in-law had not diminished.

Nevertheless, as he stood quickly breathing in the stench of ashes, he admitted that somehow that evening they had both been in the wrong. He shivered, and wondered with growing terror whether he was losing his way instead of finding it. The fear hurt.

111

Billy had detested his years spent in mining with every slice of his being. He was sure it shouldn't have been that way. The job should have gradually absorbed itself into him, naturally, over the years. His father and four brothers had taken on Bethany's mantle with no apparent worries, and it had always been accepted that he would follow them there which he did, of course, for there was no other option.

If he had tried to strike out for what he regarded as a more soul-enriching option, if he had admitted that a brush and canvas would have held a good deal more magic for him than a pick and shovel, the others would surely have turned on him with the same old ridicule. The ridicule his father had used on him so regularly, to such a destructive effect. His hatred of the life which had been forced upon him by the environment he had been born to had always been deep-rooted. It had been there from the day in childhood when he had started at Bethany helping to grade the ore. Depression had clamped down upon him even tighter when he had graduated to working underground. Instead of the dark he had craved the light, the free air, isolation. Since childhood he had seen so many sicken and die below the granite, so many brought back to the village after being crushed by rocks or broken to bits after falling to their death from ladders, that he wanted none of it. But, once he had stepped underground there seemed little chance of escaping his predestined future. It was accepted that the mine was to be his life, his perpetual straitjacket. And yet . . and yet, he had never allowed himself to believe in that totally. Even when he had been given a way out, when James offered him a position in the Bodmin works and he eventually agreed to 'turn clay', the determination to seek another road entirely remained within him. In the pits although there was no darkness to conquer, there was the turbulence of the industry he had joined, and two warring brothers, each anxious to pull him in a different direction.

Their rancour meant that he found himself unable to view what was happening around him in any clarity, caught in the midst of two intransigent sets of ideals.

As the troubles intensified, became uglier and flared out of what he saw as all sense of proportion, he tried to distance himself from both James and Alex. To his dismay, each seemed to place great emphasis on his loyalty. Deep down he sided with Alex, struggling for greater freedoms, but he didn't possess this brother's commitment to the cause. He didn't want to play his part in rioting, in hating, in living in torment. What he yearned for was peace and time to himself, to read, to sketch, to think, to let his mind widen and explore. At night, when rest refused to come, he lay awake considering the alternatives, working out the best way of finding the peace he so desired on his own terms. Should he follow Nathan to America, or try Mexico, South Africa, or Australia? As a Cornish miner, work would be simple to find, but that would still mean that, despite being away from Cornwall's confines, he would be existing mainly in darkness, knowing no other trade. Despite this, the instinct to run would not diminish. It increased as the fraternal battle he was unwillingly caught up in became bloodier. Both James and Alex were displaying growing impatience with him. Each was after his unreserved support, and was then full of scepticism when it was not given. In response he became even quieter, more secretive.

'You've got to make a decision sometime,' Alex had yelled. 'A firm one. One that means something.'

'I have made a decision, to cut myself off

from both of you, to forget your battles. Do you know, I've concluded that they don't belong to me.'
'That's playing the coward.'
'That's playing safe.'
James had been as scathing.
'What's the matter, are you running scared of Alex or something? I see you've put your name to this demand for back pay.'
'Of course I have. I'm not without some backbone. We're only asking for what we were promised.'
'Don't you know by now that I'll see you right whatever happens? Just as I would Alex if he would let me.'
Billy hadn't disguised his disgust.
'At the expense of all the others? No thank you. I don't ride roughshod over other people.'
'Fine words,' James had growled in response, his eyes as cold as his emotions. 'But you don't exactly live up to them. You lock yourself in your room while others go out and supposedly fight for their rights.'
'Fighting isn't my way.'
'No, we're much too much of a shrinking violet aren't we?'
So it had come to the point where they both thought him a coward. Were they right? He didn't know. As with life itself he found himself struggling through a limitless blanket of fog just trying to find partial answers.
Eventually, the alternatives came to possess him. At night the dread of the day ahead was so overwhelming he could not close his eyes without it welling up and enveloping him.
Alex was rarely at home any more as union business occupied all his spare hours. The cottage at Biscovey, once overflowing, was as

good as home only to his mother and himself. And the atmosphere between them both was strained.

Billy felt she resented him for being so unlike his father, so far from the image that had been set for the Rosevean brothers. Much as Nathan had once been resented. He knew he couldn't be as autocratic as his father, even if paid a king's ransom to become so.

During the lonely, early hours of one morning he stumbled into the kitchen to search for a bite to eat, anything to pass the hellish hours when he could not relax, even though sleep should be enveloping him. To his surprise his mother was there as well, sitting quite still, staring absently into the darkness, her face set in lines of unendurable sorrow. Thinking she hadn't seen him, he started to back away, but she called after him.

'Come back Billy, you must have wanted something.'

Her voice was surprisingly sharp. When she talked she usually sounded totally exhausted, her gnawing sadness seeping away all energy. Still anxious to leave, he kept edging away from her, thinking that there was no way that he could take an inquest.

'Not especially, I was hungry, that's all.'

'But you should be asleep.'

He allowed himself to hesitate. She sounded sympathetic, not accusing, more like the woman he remembered from when his father was alive.

'I'm afraid sleep's impossible. It's one of those nights.'

'One of many.'

'What do you mean?' he replied, swiftly.

'I hear you, you know,' answered Mary.

'Tossing, turning, coming down here, walking

your room.'

'I'm a light sleeper, that's all.'

'You never used to be, at least not quite so much.'

Were accusations now about to come? He turned back to the door, to return to bed. She stopped him again.

'Why don't you talk to me? It might help. It won't hurt, surely? Make the most of me while I've got the strength. I know I'm little use to you most of the time.'

'There's nothing to say. Nothing at all.'

Shaking her head in despair, she quickly stood up, leant forward, and took his hands in hers, as if he was a child still, then peered right into his face, although its contours were indistinct in the gloom.

I can't remember the last time I looked at him properly, she thought. While he was growing up my mind was wandering elsewhere, on problems that weren't really problems.

'I'm old,' she said, stroking the hands with the long fingers that resembled Nathan's so much. 'I look even older than I am, and I certainly feel older. I've given up on life early, and for that death's creeping up on me.'

'Mother please . . . '

'It's true, it's true. I've robbed myself of the need to feel life, happiness, inside me. It mustn't be the same for you.'

He shifted uncomfortably, trying to extricate himself from her grip, but did not succeed because she clung on.

'I'm sorry mother, I don't really understand what you're trying to tell me,' he whispered.

After a moment or two she did free him, then sat down again, and started to rock back and forth in the chair as if she, in turn, had become the child needing comfort. Her brain sought frantically for the right words.

'You may think I don't notice anything. You're wrong. I do open my eyes sometimes, take note of what's going on around me, rather than what's pounding away inside my brain.'

It was four o'clock, a dreadful hour, he thought, for attempted, but failed, stabs at profound conversations.

'I think I'll go up. I'll see you when morning's well and truly arrived.'

'You haven't been happy for a long while now have you?'

He considered how best to answer the weighted question, glad the dimness could obscure his expression.

'It depends, I think, on what you mean by unhappiness.'

'A lack of joy I suppose.'

'Joy's pretty hard to find.'

'I'm not talking about deep unhappiness. Not like Samuel who seems to have been born with a constant anger inside him. More of a general depression, mild maybe, but there all the same.'

'How can anyone say they've been happy most of their life? A few may be lucky enough to have been, but not many.'

'Maybe. The trouble is you're young. You should be able to find a way out. You shouldn't give in.'

How could he explain to this woman, a mother who had been distant from him for a long while now, the complexities of his life? Surely it would only lead to greater madness to listen to her any further. And she would be so different in the morning, when she had reverted to self-absorbed despair.

'Perhaps I might upset others by finding a

way out. Nothing is ever as easy as it appears.'

'You mean you would be likely to upset your family?'

'Maybe.'

She stopped rocking, and stood up once more. Sick light from a waning moon edged into the room and strained to illuminate her tiny, wasting figure as she moved beside him.

'Look Billy, please don't concern yourself with my feelings. My plans are almost non-existent. What I want should not affect your needs.'

She looked so ill, so shrivelled beside him, he wanted to be able literally to strip the years from her.

'But I do take note of you. I can't not. Nathan's thousands of miles away, and James and Alex are both so wrapped up in their own hatreds they're aware of no-one but themselves. You've got no-one left but me, surely you can see that? And you were so against Nathan going from here. We've never been a complete family since, not really.'

'I over-reacted with Nathan. He was right because he was wise enough to see it was his only chance. Now the money he sends is enough to feed me and keep this roof over my head. I've lived my life wrongly, Billy. I lived for your father, and by doing that I just became part of him. When he died, so did I really. Since then I've been a nothing, a no person.'

'Don't exaggerate.'

Shivering, she placed her arms around her waist, hugging herself.

'If I do, it's only slightly. Without him I do find it hard to . . . exist. The last thing I want is to tie you to me. It worries me to see you as you are. I don't think you could carry on this way for months, for years on end. You haven't the cussedness that I've got.'

'So what are you telling me, I mean actually saying?'

'I'm telling you to ignore them, to fly away as far as you want.'

'Even if my journey takes me thousands of miles away, over the Atlantic, to an area perhaps as far away as where Nathan is now living?'

'I told you to fly. You're young. Surely a few thousand miles shouldn't seem too far to you?'

'And you?'

'I'll stay here with my memories, and think now and then of the sons I once had. I'm different, I'm old, and afraid. In my position just a few feet of Cornish soil often seem hard to cover.'

Early summer 1877

1V

Alex stumbled blindly out of the fetid courtroom at Bodmin, nausea welling up inside him. It was market day. Stalls were trading on the large cobbled square right in front of the courthouse, overflowing with bright, cheap material, touting new inventions, quick-cure medicines, beauty tips for the ladies.

Animals that had been herded to town from a myriad of outlying moorland villages such as St Breward and St Tudy, were busy complaining vociferously in nearby pens. The pungent, earthy smell of cows and sheep and unwashed bodies, and the quickly escalating noise combined to make him feel worse. He had been seeking fresh air, then discovered none could be found, not until he could weave his way past the clamouring market and the dominant, brooding jail, and away from the town and onto the moor.

Although the riots and the burning hatred were a few weeks in the past, nothing had been resolved since. If anything, the festering distrust was running deeper, especially in the face of that day's trial, which had been brought as a result of the 'St Blazey disturbances'.

The physical damage caused in the madness of that night had been patched up, as much as was possible. But not everything could be. For the men another strike remained the sole answer to their tortuous campaign, while for those who had suffered mentally, terror remained. For Alex everything had suddenly adopted greater significance because he had sat in the courthouse and watched two of his colleagues being sentenced to three months apiece in a rotting prison cell for their so-called involvement in the night's violence and mayhem.

What tormented Alex more than anything was that he felt personally responsible for their plight. They were brothers from Lanlivery, Peter and Edwin Coombes, both in their late teens, and it had been he who had urged them to go along that night, assuring them that it would be a peaceful gathering. He had stressed that every clay worker with any hope for a decent future would be needed.

Although present amongst the initial gathering they hadn't gone on to participate in any of the rioting. It wasn't their way. Nevertheless, they had been caught by the authorities as they had turned for home, depressed by what they had seen happening, anxious to be far from the fires. Their peaceful natures meant that they were easier to apprehend than those giving rein to fury.

That morning, during a quick trial at which they had been unrepresented, they had been made to pay for the sins of others. One of the injustices which, to Alex, had seemed so obvious, was that the magistrates seemed to have been unable to separate truth from gossip, claim and rumour.

'Don't get yourself in such a lather,' said Joshua as Alex tried to explain such thoughts to him, outline how guilty he felt at the traumatic circumstances the brothers now found themselves in. 'You weren't to know how that night would end.'

Alex couldn't be reassured.

'The worst of it is that they weren't involved at all. They didn't do anything, besides walk with a few others. Those that smashed up everything that stood in their way, who were out to spill blood, were not clay workers but idiots out to cause mayhem. They weren't arrested though, were they? Oh no, of course not - the authorities just went for the softest targets.'

'You can't be held responsible for that, either. Try and reason more clearly. The trouble is you're taking more to heart than you used to. At one stage none of this sort of trouble would have bothered you quite so much.'

Alex, in no mood to be reasoned with, quickened his pace as he headed towards Lanivet and the open, gorse-flecked countryside. At that moment he hated Bodmin with all his soul. The stale, airless courtroom, the pitiless, monied magistrates, the blank, uncaring faces thronging the public gallery just for some fun and their morning's entertainment.

'I'm in this all too deep now for it not to bother me. There've been moments lately when I've felt like a mayfly struggling in a web.'

'What d'you mean?'

'Well, there's James on the other side. Not that I mind much about his bigoted opinions, but when it comes down to Glynn and Helen and what happened, or nearly happened, to them then I can't help being involved. And then there's the men. To say some have lost confidence in me would be a huge understatement. To most of them being a Rosevean and failing to light even a sheaf of hay, or threaten someone with injury during the protests, has made me very suspect.'

'You'll win through, you always have before. They've trusted you in the past, and they've always known you were a Rosevean.'

Alex shuddered, feeling suddenly small and insignificant as he made his way across the harsh, infertile surroundings. The capable, strong aura that had once personified him had evaporated. It seemed to him that, instead, he was floundering at the edge of a huge pit with no bottom.

'Maybe I've won the day on a few occasions in the past, but that's all gone. I tell you I've begun to feel hellish weak, like a dying rabbit waiting to be picked off by one of those darned buzzards circling up there.'

By then they had put two miles between themselves and the town, and were breathing fresh air again at last when she appeared. She seemed to tower above them both, her dark hair swinging below her waist, her eyes flashing in contempt, her sultry looks twisted in anger. Her appearance rooted Joshua to the spot. Alex initially only saw her as a blur, a blur he tried unthinkingly to side-step - but couldn't avoid.

With great deliberation she stopped him passing by, moving defiantly into his path, which forced him to glance up and take a real note of her. As he was in no mood for playing games, his instant scowl would have caused many to hurry onwards as quickly as humanly possible. But, undaunted, she stayed still, unflinchingly determined.

'Alex Rosevean,' she spat, 'brother of James?'

'Yes,' he answered curtly, though showing more interest in her than he had done a moment before. He had started to acknowledge that this was a woman you didn't merely side-step, whoever she was.

'I wanted to stop for a moment to thank you and your cursed brother for destroying my family.'

Alex, shaken enough by the day's events, was astounded by the accusation.

'Wh . . what?'

Sneering at him, she tossed back her hair, which blew in Medusa strands around her in the heightening weather. Her brow was wide and proud, her cheekbones high enough to cut her face into distinct planes, her manner imperious. Now he was taking real notice, she looked to him like a mythical goddess.

'I've no idea what you're talking about. I wish no harm to your family. I don't even know who you are.'

She remained standing in front of him with hands on hips, her right foot kicking at the ground in anger.

'Well you've been sitting watching my brothers being sent to jail for being stupid enough to be loyal to you and your wretched ideals. Can't you see any resemblance between me and those two poor devils who, only an hour or so ago, were hauled down from the dock and thrown into a cell?'

He couldn't. There was no resemblance between her and anyone he knew. She had unique features. Tanned skin that wasn't leathered and lined like most of the women who worked permanently outside, almond shaped eyes that were almost black, legs that hinted at being unbelievably long, curiously delicate, slim fingers, and a wide, wide mouth.

Joshua stood there, gaping at her still, while Alex tried to recollect some of his wits that the traumas and disappointments of the day had combined to dull.

'From what you have said I must suppose that you're somehow related to Edwin and Peter.'

'That's remarkably clever of you after what I've just explained. Yes, I definitely am related to them, I'm Jenifer Coombes, their sister.'

Alex continued to look blank, which didn't appease her.

'Don't you remember me being there that evening when you came around to our house? You came to persuade the boys to join your ridiculous union. And, to my everlasting regret, you had your way.'

Thinking back he couldn't recall her at all, although the visit to see the brothers was vivid in his mind. He thought that she should have made an impression because she certainly drew the eye, especially when she was quivering with emotion.

'No, I didn't expect you to,' she accused, 'you were too busy trying to make them see life from your point of view.'

'I was only explaining the truth, what I saw as the truth.'

She was unimpressed with that explanation, and let him know it.

'And tell me where did that get them? Robbed of a job, pitched into a stinking, bug-ridden jail, branded as troublemakers when they're the gentlest boys you could ever find.'

'I agree,' he said quietly. 'They should never have been arrested. They were turned into scapegoats.'

'If they hadn't listened to you that evening then no-one would have had the chance to turn them into anything.' Her shaking fury was beginning to give way completely to sarcasm. 'I see you're still in work, though. Your brother hasn't taken you off his list of workers despite your talk of freedom and unions. You haven't suffered like the others you've been leading by the nose, and by heavens how some of them have suffered.'

Alex tried to steady himself.

'He's kept me on because he wants everyone to look at me in the same way as you are. He wants my ideas to be seen as empty and worthless, can't you try to understand that?'

'I can't understand anything but the facts, and they all shame you, every single one of them. Why haven't you just walked out and joined the others?'

Alex was sweating by now, despite the south-westerly that was beginning to scythe through fern and heather. Stammering almost, he struggled to explain.

'M . . maybe I should have done so long ago. I thought I could help more by staying where I was, encouraging those who hadn't joined the union to do so, and demanding that those who had been sacked got their job back. I haven't accepted any money from James since this all started. But I see in hindsight that maybe I might have played it all wrongly.'

She said nothing in reply, and he found he was still gabbling on.

'Look if your family is short of money . . '

'Short of money,' she snorted. 'Oh no, not with my father unable to work and sicker than you could ever believe, and both my hard-working brothers in prison. How could we be hard up?'

She was playing havoc with his bruised conscience.

'There's a fund being set up by the National Union of Mineworkers and they might be able to help in a case like yours. And the men are bound to put some money in a kitty for you. If I can help too . . .'

There was nothing he could do, or say, to soften her.

'Come to you and your kind for money? You're the last person on earth I'd crawl to. Beg my way out of a situation that you put us into to start with? No, I didn't track you down to beg for help. I stopped you to let you know, in my own sweet way, what a marvellous job you've done in your powerful union position. Next time think of the ordinary person before you start speaking your wretched mind.'

'I was trying to help the ordinary person,' he said softly.

'Well you're doing a terrible job, worse than your stupid brother, and that's saying a good deal.'

At that she turned her back on him, and walked away, quickly, elegantly, the wind lifting her luxuriant hair once again and blowing it in a thunderous dark cloud around her. Alex watched transfixed as her figure, held as straight as she could manage, became progressively but somehow defiantly, smaller. After she disappeared into the distance he was left feeling so drained and weak he literally had to shake himself to generate reason once more.

'Thanks very much for your support, Josh,' he said eventually. 'You backed me up well there. Certainly helped me put over my point of view.'

Joshua tried a grin, failing in the attempt.

'I was robbed of speech. She certainly had a way of knocking the breath out of you. And her brothers are so quiet. I believe that she must have inherited all the family fire.'

After a while they, too, walked away, at a slower pace and in the footsteps of Jenifer, heading towards St Blazey. They were numbed, dazed, by what had taken place throughout the day.

'I'll have to see the parents,' Alex mumbled. 'I can't let it drop like this. If they do have money worries I must help. I have to.'

Joshua disagreed, and said so.

'Surely you can see that she didn't want your help? She made that plain enough. You're likely to be instantly, and forcibly, thrown out if you try to set foot inside her home.'

'But I've got to try. I might not be able to get through to her, maybe. Her mother and father, though, might be very different.'

'You may live in hope, but I'd let any hope die if I were you. That girl looks to me as if she could throw a fair punch or two. I for one, certainly wouldn't want to tangle any more with her.'

'Her brothers had just been led away into that sewer that passes as a prison. It was natural that she should be angry. She'll calm down.'
By the end of the day the union had declared another strike. The brothers' misfortune had proved the catalyst. All labour was withdrawn and the pits stood idle again, except for a few workers determined to carry on as normal because they needed a regular income for survival.

Many of those who had previously given into the owners, however, had found second strength, and come out.

V

When it was dusk James shuffled away from the moor, head down, any optimism or enthusiasm absent. It seemed to him that he had come full circle. He had no doubt Richard had heard the strike news and was already busy negotiating to buy more works as a result.

For himself there was no way he could summon enough strength to undertake further expansion of his faltering business. Enough troubles presented themselves as he tried to keep problems at bay. He didn't want more complications. What he already owned had come in too great a rush. He had to have time to learn from his mistakes, surely, before ploughing into more?

The trouble is there's no turning back, he thought, not now Richard thinks I want success as much as he does. The problem is I don't, and I'm only now beginning to realise it. But there's no quick answer, and I'll have to keep fighting the men, in the same way as all the other owners are. I've got to keep appearances up, try to show them that I'm as determined to win as I ever was.

The next day was wet, with rain driving inland in swathes, with absolute menace. First on James's agenda was a delayed visit to 'Trevarnioc'. Once there he found Richard concentrating on the future of two pits on Hensbarrow that were 'going begging'. The panic selling had already begun.

After studying the opportunities the pits offered the two men, both outwardly in complete control, later lolled in the palatial elegance of the St Austell mansion, talking of dynasties to come, though beneath the surface true desires for further power were only to be found in one heart.

Now, Richard insisted, was the time for James to make his mark. James, reclining amidst the opulent antiques, the glittering chandeliers, the silver and the gold, smiled absently and wondered as a side thought, for the umpteenth time, where Eva was. Was she still locked in the same unapproachable world where his own wife seemed to have placed herself? Once, he had envied the possessions that surrounded his in-laws. The first time he had stepped inside 'Trevarnioc', after Helen had tracked up to Biscovey with the invitation, he had been stunned by them. At that moment he wondered, though he would never have admitted it to the hulk of a man who was facing him, whether any of the material goods were worth the price.

Later they rode into town together, to the White Hart Hotel, scene of the previous meeting of owners. A re-run of the event had been planned, and this time the employers were after causing real pain. Before they had been furious, but their mood after the second strike call had become murderous. The first twenty minutes of the meeting were laced with calls for retribution and, as the hatred spewed out, becoming more manic by the second, James sunk into deeper depression. He deflected commiserations and questions about the ruined state of his house, unhappy at being pressed to repeat over, and over again, how terrible the past weeks had been, trying to put a wreck into some sort of order, striving to persuade Helen to go back home to her parents while renovation work took place, and facing her refusals. She had told him outright that if she left him there was a great possibility she might never return, and that for the sake of Glynn she didn't want to put the possibility to the test.

'We need to hire a band of soldiers in order to shoot the lot of them,' roared one after a scorching half an hour of rhetoric. 'That would solve all our problems at one stroke.'

By then James was really struggling.

'And leave us with no men to work the pits?' he retorted, breaking the silence that he had held hitherto. 'Very good, Henry, I can't imagine you doing all the hard labour for the wages you pay.'

His reaction had come automatically, without thinking, and although there was a slight titter after he finished he knew he had not played the game correctly. Richard's glare told him as much.

Immediately, he flushed with anger, at himself, sinking down lower into his chair, annoyed that he had said something that he might have really believed in, though should never have admitted to.

Have Alex and Helen succeeded in brainwashing me, he asked himself. Does part of me accept the men's case is right? I hope to God not. I must just shut up, and let the others speak their own rubbish. I can't betray myself any further, I don't damned well have an idea where it'll lead.'

'We must hold out against them,' urged Richard when he had powered to his feet. 'We can't move an inch. If we let this monster of a union survive and grow then there is no telling where we'll end up. They will ruin us.'

'Courteney's right, this must be nipped in the bud, stopped now, whatever the cost,' said one of the Bodmin contingent as smoke rose upwards, and then circulated in the room in familiar fashion.

'They can't hold out for long, surely?'

'Maybe not, but how long can we survive with our pits, our livelihoods put on hold? This is bound to break some of us, and the violence we've been threatened with doesn't help keep nerves on an even keel.'

Richard shrugged.

'So some of the weakest don't survive. I doubt if they would have stayed in the business much longer anyway.'

At that James felt shivers splinter through him. Not wanting to admit to the real reason for his reaction, he told himself his emotions were spiralling out of control because of the unseen days ahead, although a part of his brain was unable to block out the knowledge that it may have been due to the abhorrence of some of the company he was willingly keeping. The lack of concern for anyone but self was so marked at times.

We must be basically the same as the workers, he told himself as his colleagues ranted around him. We've got our own kind of union. We haven't got together, though out of mutual trust and ideals, more because we're too afraid to stand alone.

For a split second, against his will, he had seen those around him through Alex's eyes, then he blinked and the image vanished.

It was eventually decided that if the strike continued at any length every owner would urge the authorities to take action. Their preference was to have constables from across the Tamar drafted in. Many thought that officers from the local force might come to feel a sneaking sympathy for the men. They acknowledged that Cornish families were so close-knit, the communities so inter-related that in many cases they would be urging the upholders of the law to deal with their own kin.

Afterwards a few owners tried to engage James in conversation, failing in the attempt as he felt anything but talkative, deciding instead to slip out of the hotel mouthing muffled apologies. He should have stayed with Richard, he knew, and gone with him to visit one of the Hensbarrow pits that were on their shopping list. That was something he could not face, however. Undoubtedly, he was feeling more inclined to grab himself a stiff drink.

All his carefully acquired confidence and new class-structured attitudes were wilting. The humble miner was trying to break through when he should have been long buried. A quiet tete-a-tete with his mentor was out of the question in such circumstances.

Instead, he made his way to the Sun Inn, which stood in the shadows on the other side of the church. It was dark and genteelly decaying, a far cry from the luxury afforded by the White Hart. On the other hand, it was a bolt hole where he could merge with others in search of oblivion.

He was a modest drinker. Two brandies over lunch were enough for him normally. But on this occasion he started on doubles and didn't stop, welcoming with relief the resulting numbness and blurred thoughts and vision. They robbed him of the ability to self-analyse.

VI

Nathan adapted to the literary life with consummate ease. The newspaper desk took over from the adit and the ore with no inner turmoil on his part. And there was certainly enough happening in the town to keep his pen occupied.

The continuing trouble between the newcomers and the Apache Indians, the succession of fights and injuries and still, despite a clampdown and a gradual taming of the place, murders. More than enough to keep the pages full and the copy flowing.

Nonetheless, he remained closely involved with the running of local mines and those working within them, and as a result more than a quarter of the Clarion pages became devoted to mining activities.

Over time he discovered the town had only recently gained the name of Tombstone. It had happened after the first great silver strike had been made. A prospector, Ed Schieffelin, who found the lode, had been told that all he would find in the desolate Apache region would be tombstone.

But Nathan knew for sure there were more riches under the earth around Tombstone than so far had been developed.

His instincts were as sound as Ed

Schieffelin's had proved to be. Most newly formed companies were booming and the Cornishman-come-reporter became a familiar face around most of the mines, such as Grand Central, Contention, Tough Nut, Emerald and Lucky Lass, where he was instantly accepted. He was one of the brotherhood, knowing exactly what he was talking about, so he was deemed acceptable.

There were not only mining matters to deal with, though, or murders. Headline news was being made elsewhere on the day that he sauntered home from Seymour in Maricopa County where he had been interviewing Kernow-born James Hunt, who was a superintendent. The talk was that Tombstone was soon to come under the influence of the Earp brothers, Wyatt, Virgil and Morgan. They were expected to arrive within a couple of days and, if the rumour was correct, it was likely that the frontier town would never be quite the same again.

Nathan viewed the news with rising interest. Henry had given him an almost free rein at the Clarion in spite of his lack of journalistic experience, and he felt he could ask for no more than that. In past months he had found that the uncertain fires that had driven him for so long were dying, which meant he no longer had to rely on fury or despair to pull him through the days. There was a certain peace within him, allowing him to take some joy from basics such as a gentle sun on his bare shoulders and the distant sound of Wesleyan hymns sung on Sunday mornings, pleasures he would once have reviled without hesitation. Such shifts in his view of the world told him that he was on his way out of an abyss.

It was into this welcome peace that the shots rang.

He had reached Tombstone after travelling back there from Maricopa, but his mind remained fixed on where he had been that day, and on James Hunt and some interesting, rather unique, geological problems at the Seymour mine. Up until that moment he had felt no stirrings of impending terror. There was no anticipation of doom.

He was walking along to see Henry when, from the far end of the street appeared the familiar figure of Joe Trembeth. Shoulders hunched, shuffling gait, a hint of bow legs. Nathan thought he was hallucinating at first, that the worn, craggy features taking shape in front of him were just an apparition. Surely the man couldn't have strayed so far from Grass Valley, not while he was as ill as he was?

For a full 30 seconds he doubted his sanity, before accepting that what he was seeing was real. At that, he quickened his pace towards his former landlord. For once in his life he was unaccountably pleased to see someone he had grown to care for.

His lean face was beginning to break into a welcoming, ironic, grin when Joe drew out a gun, levelled it, and shot him.

Nathan felt no pain, more shock and utter amazement. Instantly, he fell to the ground before rolling over onto his back in the dust, and lying unmoving, disbelieving. Then, as if merely curious, he began to examine the oozing, sticky blood that was gradually seeping into his clothes from a gaping hole which he hazily reckoned must be near his stomach. With the pain still in abeyance, he struggled to stand again, failing because he

could hardly move at all. Vaguely, he could hear his breath sawing, before discovering that everything around him was fading into a blur and greying at the edges.
It also seemed that the many faces that seemed suddenly to have appeared on the street, were looking at him through the wrong end of a telescope. And then the pain did come, intense, unbearable pain, and he was certain he was going to black out entirely, and maybe never see the light of day again.
And all the while he couldn't quite avert his eyes from Joe, so his final image before he did sink into unconsciousness was that of his friend lifting the gun to his own temple, and firing.

V11

Alex, who was not used to doubting himself, found hesitancy had been creeping into his character by stealth since the campaign for fair working conditions, and what he saw as reasonable pay, became - to his mind - unyielding and desperate. Now that he was standing before Jenifer's home after visiting her brothers in jail, he knew doubts had overrun all else, meaning that there was no courage left within him.
He knocked quietly at the door. There was no reply, so with some effort he tried louder. As the door continued to stay shut he turned to go, in some relief. However, when he was half way down the damp, mossy path he heard it flung open with some force behind him.
It was dusk, and in the half light Jenifer was unable to see straightaway who was there. She was already distraught. Over the past hour or so she had been crying so much her throat

hurt, and her eyes had swollen uncomfortably. If it isn't the doctor, she thought, I'll go completely crazy.

'Did anyone knock?' she yelled. 'Someone's there, surely. Lizzie, is it you? Have you managed to get help?'

That was enough to tell Alex that he had stumbled into yet another situation where his appearance would never be appreciated. But against instincts to hang back in the shadows like an intruder, and ignore the pain that was evident in her voice, he moved back along the path, negotiating a number of overgrown bushes as he went.

'Don't get worried, it's only me, Alex Rosevean, certainly not someone out to rob, or hurt, you.'

His voice, a strange mixture of roughness and culture that was not usual among the locals, had told her instantly who it was.

'What the hell do you want here at this time?' she snapped, quickly wiping her eyes with the backs of her hands.

'I came to talk . . with you and your family. That was all. I've come from seeing your brothers. I thought I'd tell you how they were.'

She stepped towards him and, to his surprise, grabbed his left arm and dragged him back towards the door so harshly he almost fell. Before he could react he was in a tiny, square hall.

'I ought to tell you to disappear,' she rasped, 'but at this moment I really need you. Follow me.'

When his eyes had accustomed themselves to the dull, flickering, lights he could see she was trembling. That stunned him. Before she had been so tough, so composed, so apparently unbreakable.

'What . . ?' he ventured.

She broke in sharply before he could find any phrase he might consider appropriate in such an uncertain situation.

'I said follow me. It's my father. He's fallen, and neither I, nor my mother, can move him.'

The further he went into the cottage, the murkier the light became, although a few gas lamps were valiantly striving to inject some brightness. Groping his way behind her, they moved down a small, grubby corridor, and then turned into a L shaped, squat room with a rather pathetic open fire at the end of it. The room in which he now remembered sitting with her brothers and talking them into joining the union.

In front of the fire lay an unmoving bulk of a man, by the side of whom a second figure rocked on her knees, weeping uncontrollably. Mrs Coombes. Tall and equally bulky and, from what Alex could remember, liable to nervous tension at the best of times.

'It's all right, mother,' murmured Jenifer, masking a sob in her own voice as she ran over. 'Someone's here to help.'

'How long has he been like this?' shot Alex, urgency reaching him too as he crouched next to the seemingly unconscious man.

His throat constricted, suddenly going dry as parchment. Whatever he had walked into he had suddenly realised could never be solved in moments, if at all.

'About 15 minutes,' whispered Jenifer. 'He collapsed as he was walking across the room. We tried to catch him, to hold him, to stop him falling, but it was impossible. He's so heavy.'

'Has he moved since?'

Jenifer looked across at him quickly.
'No, he's been like this ever since. There is a pulse, though, I've felt it.'
'Why the hell haven't you sent for a doctor?'
'Lizzie next door went to fetch him. We've heard nothing more since she went, right after it happened. When your knock came at the door I thought it was her coming back at last.'
'Let me have a proper look at him before we decide what to do.'

Jenifer's father had fallen face down, which meant Alex could see none of his features. He didn't like to admit it, but instinct told him he didn't really need to see any further, having viewed enough of death while working at Bethany. There was a lack of an aura about those whose soul had just left their body, a complete absence of vitality, which he could sense then and had done so even from across the room.

Trying at the same time not to let Jenifer see how concerned he was, he squatted down away from the fire to let the flames, such as they were, lend him extra light. The man was heavy enough, he guessed, when conscious. At least eighteen stone. With shaking hands he felt for a pulse, to check whether one was detectable. Despite what Jenifer had said he could find no life there.

'Let's move him on his back before we go any further,' he said slowly.

Jenifer was beside him in a flash.
'Why . . why? What do you think?'
'One stage at a time.'

Together they mustered enough strength to roll him over as gently as possible so that his heavily jowled, bloated, face was visible.

Alex felt for the heartbeat this time. None.
'Out of the way,' he hissed, more harshly than

he meant.

Surely there was a chance?

Until then Jenifer's mother had been watching on, as if in a daze. As Alex set himself astride the body, and began to try to pump the heart with his fists, that changed. She launched herself towards him.

'Leave him alone. Leave him be. You'll kill him, you'll kill him.'

Screaming in despair, she went for Alex's back, her dirty, torn fingernails digging into his shoulders. For a split second he thought himself in a madhouse. Then Jenifer intervened and, with some difficulty, pulled her mother away.

'Don't be so stupid, you can't do that. He's trying to save father's life. He knows what he's doing.' 'He's killing him. Look at him, you can see he is.'

'What he's doing is trying to get his heart going again. You've got to let Mr Rosevean give him a chance,' Jenifer pleaded, the full horror of what was happening seeping through to her.

Had she made herself imagine the pulse? Shadows played across the walls, grotesque and chilling. Fear clutched at her.

Again and again Alex hit and massaged the man's chest, working until the sweat was running down his face and neck, despite having known from the start that it was a useless exercise. He had probably been dead before he hit the floor. But how could he give up the fight for life, be seen to give it up, when both mother and daughter were watching on with such abject dread in their eyes?

In the midst of it all he glanced over at Jenifer. She was overpowering no more, but instead was more like a terrified child crouching in a corner in terror of retribution. With a heart of his own that was full of dread, and sorrow, he kept on working on the body of the man he knew he could not save until the doctor eventually walked through the door and assumed authority. He went straight up to the patient, felt both pulse and heart, then re-checked.

'How long have you been trying to revive him?'

He turned around to face Alex, panting behind him following his exertions.

'Eight, ten minutes.'

'Well it was a waste of effort, I'm afraid. I would guess that he's been dead rather longer than that.'

'What?' Jenifer pushed in between them. 'Are you sure? You can't be right, you can't be. Alex has tried so hard to save him. He must have done something.'

Her mother's resulting cries ripped through the stale air, her emotions turning to fury as she threw herself towards Alex, who quickly managed to duck as she hurled herself at him once again.

'I told you he was killing him, I told you so. He was fine before he came.'

Alex whirled around, catching her from behind to still her, twisting his face away as she fought with him, trying to tear at eyes, and mouth, at anywhere where she could do damage.

'I did all I could. I tried to bring him back to life.'

'You can't blame him, Agnes,' the doctor broke in, also trying to restrain her. 'You know George's been ill for a long, long time.'

There was no convincing the grieving woman.

She would not cease her struggling and cursing until Jenifer and Alex hauled her upstairs where she was laid on a narrow, sloping bed and was given a sleeping draught. By then her hair was matted, the spittle was dripping from the side of her mouth, sweat had stained her clothes, and Alex was retching.

Faced with such trauma he had helped Jenifer settle her mother, not only because she was past being manageable, but also because he hadn't wanted to be left alone with the body. Gradually, he was beginning to wonder if he was dealing with any kind of reality. The whole evening had become so surreal he thought it could not be truth, only horrific fabrication.

'I'll stay with her until she finally calms,' said Jenifer, sitting on the bed, her complexion stripped of colour as she lent over and tried to keep the tossing, near demented woman between the few blankets.

'What other help do you need?' ventured Alex, unwilling to walk out, though equally desperate not to stay.

At least Jenifer hadn't collapsed. Her innate willpower was now pushing its way to the surface. The worst had happened and couldn't be altered, and now she was in charge again.

'What about your father, downstairs?'

'I'll see to that,' said the doctor, behind him, having followed them to check on Jenifer's mother. 'They're old patients of mine. Jenifer will have enough to contend with at the moment, with her mother, believe me. As for the boys, well they can't help from prison I suppose, although they should be told as soon as possible.'

'Perhaps I could do that . . '

'That's up to you, but there's nothing more you can do here,' interrupted Jenifer. 'You've done your best, now go, please go. We, mother and I, can suffer this together.'

Alex, who wanted to argue, found himself turning instantly to almost tumble down the narrow, dangerous stairs, back through the living room, eyes averted from the body this time, along the dingy hall to reach the cold night air. He couldn't bear to look at George Trevear any more. Despite there being no smell yet, the stench of decay seemed to be following him out of the house.

With guilt piercing him, he felt he would have to return there someday soon. However much he might want to, he couldn't ignore the repercussions of the situation he had walked so innocently into.

Not only will the boys have to be told, he thought, the family will also need some help with money now, whatever Jenifer might say about it.

The desperation which had been eating at him during the past days had intensified still further. Every day was beset with problems which seemed to be eating away at his confidence, and shredding his self-esteem. And the strike was only just beginning again.

V111

It was a night for torment. Samuel believed his own personal torture had been growing inside him, like an abscess, ever since he had discovered that Nathan was the source of the letters. From that moment all the trust he had placed in Lorna had fallen away to dust. There had been no real reconciliation between them. His seething jealousy had seen to that.

It was true that he had managed to keep his temper in check since she had threatened him with the shotgun, holding back words which would have finally annihilated the wreckage that was their marriage. Nevertheless, there was no liking or friendship left between them, despite that. Their always chilly relationship was best described as irreversibly lost.

In his fleeting, rational, moments he knew he was responsible for the situation. His actions had meant that any respect and affection she might have felt towards him had been beaten out of her. He had abused her too often to dream there could ever be a way back to the hesitant mutual alliance they had briefly shared. Unable to find a way back to any show of lightness of spirit, he had ensured that she had suffered with him, and as a result she had never been given any hope of enjoying the sweet life he had once promised.

Now she was possibly dying because of him. The evening was closing in fast, a breeze worrying the unseen cypress trees lining the pathway along which he had walked. Bats criss-crossed overhead, while something, maybe a young badger, scurried along ahead of him, frightened by his echoing footsteps. At that moment he was hurrying to work, obeying his own animal instincts, trying to shut his mind to what he had left behind in his home, the home he had built for her.

A few hours beforehand the anger that he had curbed for months on end had exploded from him like a mindless torrent. As his thoughts tried to deal with the violence he had unleashed upon the woman he had supposedly loved, he believed he had been driven to harm her by the devil himself.

Because of his actions, while he wound his

way southwards to the mine at Tregrehan she was lying broken and bleeding on the kitchen floor.

Shuddering, he dwelt on the memory of the injuries he had inflicted upon her, with such hatred and such relish. For the past hour he had been forcing himself to chase them away, thinking that if he allowed himself to revisit them in too great a detail he would go mad for certain.

She needs help, though. She must do the way I left her, covered in blood, unmoving. But I can't face her again, not yet. And it wouldn't have happened if she hadn't tormented me, the whore. If Jack Kitt hadn't paid her so much attention yesterday, and she hadn't been seen to enjoy it so much I'd never have hit her.

He was walking in a daze, his own forehead cut from the fight, his arm and right hand hurting too. The pain hardly permeated, though. He was past caring about her, or himself. The main reason he was going to work was because he had instinctively believed he would lose all reason if he didn't cling to routine.

Surely she would be better when he returned? He couldn't have laid into her as much as he imagined. Those thoughts of his were just part of an emotional overreaction to their argument.

The T junction between the lane that led to Biscovey and Par Moor came into sight before he hesitated, allowing himself to glance back, as if a glance would give him the right answers.

Maybe he should have told someone, asked a neighbour to look after her, though if he had done that they would have known the extent to which he had lost his sanity and had hurt her, and he didn't want the whole world privy to what happened within his own four walls. The walls he had built himself. It was his business.

Apart from that, hitting your wife wasn't that unusual. He knew damned well that most miners' wives suffered the same. They kept quiet about it. It was part of their rough, harsh lives. Something to be accepted.

At the mine no-one noticed his melancholic mood. They were used to his depressions, and his brooding. With his dark thoughts still oppressing him, he said nothing, spoke to no-one.

It was as he made his way down to his level that he realised he was not seeing the railway tracks, nor the adits or ladders but Lorna, one moment raging at him and threatening to shoot him, the next still and silent, crushed by his kicks and punches. He hated himself for losing control to such an extent, letting the poison seep through again, but she had definitely asked for it, hadn't she? Hadn't she?

The more he worked the more the darkness enclosed him, making him slip further and further into inner turmoil. He acknowledged no-one, and when they yelled warning shouts to him about the rock fall he listened to none of those either. He died instantly. One of the rocks smashed his skull to pulp, putting an end to the pain.

1X

When James awoke he had no idea where he was, no ready memory of the night before.

The bed was definitely not his, the sheets were stained, grubby and smelt of grime rather than fresh air, and the room was oppressive.

No white walls and early morning sunshine, more a dull combination of brown and green with cobwebs hanging in loops from the corners. Grimacing, he realised that his entire body ached, his head was blazing, as if on fire, and there was an unhealthy, stale taste in his mouth that made him feel sick. He was also naked. No hand-made pyjamas, or gown, wrapped comfortably around him.

Through barely opened eyes he could just about see the clothes he had worn the day before, that had been so neatly pressed when he had first stepped into them, strewn in various untidy heaps around the bed. Despite that, when he heard the heavy footsteps on the stairway he still half expected Helen to open the door and slip in with his breakfast neatly arranged on a tray, a hesitant, doubtful smile on her face, with Glynn sliding shyly in behind her.

Instead of his small family, which he took utterly for granted, a middle-aged woman appeared. Coarse black hair hung past her shoulders in clumps. A dirty, probably yellow, gown was slung around her. As she hadn't buttoned it properly he could see her sagging breasts, and unwanted glimpses of her belly. Her face verged on fading prettiness, though was spoiled beyond measure by dark, open pores and a slack mouth that could not quite hide a row of far from white or perfect teeth. She was a complete stranger.

Instantly, he recoiled from her, pulling the stained covers up around his chest. The image of the broad, blond Greek god was immediately tarnished. Rather than a deity he resembled a scruffy, naughty, child caught eating in bed when he should have been deep asleep.

'Who the hell are you?' he spluttered.

Adopting a knowing smile, she wheezed noisily before sitting down on the bed beside him with great familiarity.

'Can' t remember anything, can you my lover? Well I didn't really expect you to, the state you were in, and we didn't do much together did we? You ran out of steam too early. Now, if you could have held out a little longer we might have had some real fun.'

It can't be true, he told himself. This is like a well worn joke. Waking up in another woman's cramped and untidy room and remembering hardly anything of what led you there.

'What's the time?'

He croaked the words, as the rough blankets scratched skin he hadn't wanted to expose. How much had he revealed the night before?

'Six, I suppose, something like that. Maybe a little earlier. I always wake with the birds whatever's happened before. I don't like my gentlemen staying too long. If you don't mind me saying so, once morning comes I don't trust them and I like them to be gone.'

Time at least was with him. With luck, he might be able to make it home to Tregrehan before anything appeared amiss. The night and what had, or had not, happened could be quietly filed away. That was unless Glynn had also decided to wake early. Giving a quick prayer, he hoped against all he believed in, that his young son was still fast asleep.

'I suppose I'm still in St Austell,' he whispered, 'and I didn't stray too far from the inn?'

'The Sun's just five minutes walk away. They said they'd look after your horse there, for a price. Mean to run back to your wife now do you?'

'Yes,' he answered, more to himself. 'Run back to my loving wife.'

Then, although she was watching on, he forced himself to get up and pull on his crumpled clothes. There wasn't any time to play the injured party, especially after what he must have attempted to do only hours before. He had no energy. His legs felt like lead weights, his mind had frozen. But he had to move, whatever his body was telling him, he had to escape the bed, and the room.

It did not help that as he hobbled around, hands on hips, that she followed his every step, smirking at him as she did so, knowing exactly what panicked thoughts were chasing through his mind.

Failing awkwardly to escape in a hurry, he did his utmost to ignore her as he pulled on his shirt, followed by his trousers.

'Aren't you going to offer me anything for my services then?' she asked. 'There was a bed for the night and comfort offered you when you were lonely and without that loving wife of yours.'

'Take enough from my purse if you haven't already.'

'Now that's a bit harsh, I've taken nothing of yours, so far.'

Without embarrassment she moved straight to where the purse was, on top of a dresser riddled with woodworm, and smothered in dust.

'I don't know how much is in there,' he muttered. 'I could have spent it all on drink.

You may be out of luck.'
However much he tried to, he couldn't remember much about the Sun Inn at all, bar making his way there initially, although unwanted snatches of the meeting at the White Hart were coming back, combined with memories of the alcohol he had ordered but had not really wanted, except as a deadener. Hastily, she took the cash she wanted, afterwards unexpectedly bending forward to kiss him on his forehead, the front of her clothes gaping further as she did so. She smelt fetid, or maybe it was his fear that did so. All he knew was that he wanted to run. Dragging on his waistcoat, he lurched out of the room, almost tumbling down the twisting stairs in his haste to escape.

Such was his appearance he felt more vagrant than James Rosevean Esquire, pit owner. It was raining outside, an unrelenting, miserable form of rain that he almost welcomed, relieved that it might wake and wash him. Above all, he hoped that Helen would be fast asleep when he did return, that the events of the day before, and his own plethora of self-doubts could pass into obscurity without him ever having to dissect the full facts.

Thinking rationally, he realised he must have attracted some sort of attention amongst the clientele of The Sun. He could not fool himself that the truth would not filter back to Helen or Richard, or both, eventually, no matter that most of his colleagues had been too busy discussing their problems in the more select bar of the White Hart. Beset with such worries he then began shivering as the rain started to soak straight through to his skin, and longing for his home, despite it showing so many scars from the riots.

His concerns also refused to stray far from Helen. Would she even care if she did discover he had spent a night with someone else? Somehow, he doubted it.

I've forced her to become hardened to anything I do, he berated himself. Only my pride and my so-called reputation as a sober and moderate man would suffer if others did discover anything about my actions last night. That might annoy Richard. He puts too great a store by reputation, which is ironic when you consider his own bloody string of women. But then again maybe I'm putting too much emphasis on my own so-called importance. Surely the strike will overshadow anything I may or may not have done?

The sickness that had wormed its way into his stomach as soon as he had woken gradually ebbed away as he moved eastwards on his mount, and then made his way down muddy lanes to Tregrehan. By the time his shattered home was in sight all he felt was that the invidious, freezing cold that had enveloped him entirely.

He thanked God some sort of home did remain for him to return to. With Helen's help he had patched up the damage to the structure of the house as best as he could on a temporary basis. However, many of their possessions had yet to be replaced which meant it was almost bare inside. Any furniture there was in the rooms was makeshift, the carpet made of rag rugs. He was back to living as he had once done in the cottage at Biscovey.

Strangely, he had found within himself little incentive to push to renew everything automatically, as if he had lost basic interest in making his once prized property better than any others around. What it had once represented now seemed tainted to him. Gradually, he had come to believe that eventually the only alternative would be to move on to somewhere which held no disturbing history, somewhere untouched by any hatred shown towards him and his family. Initially, he had supposed Helen would start throwing out hints about the state of the building until he had agreed to buy new throughout, but he had to admit no such suggestions had been made as yet. She seemed equally subdued on the whole matter, as she now did with the whole of her life. Realising deep inside, that he was the cause of her lack of ebullience, of any joy, he was only glad his in-laws didn't call round at regular intervals to see how their daughter's personal life was faring.

During his ride from St Austell he had convinced himself that she would still be asleep when he returned. As he was on many fronts, he was wrong. She was up, a small, solitary figure curled up in the one chair which had remained untouched. Seeing her, he swore quietly, realising that she must have already heard him open the door, which meant that there was no point in trying to creep around.

'You must be dripping wet,' she said, not turning towards him, speaking in a tired, flat voice that squeezed the contrition from him. 'It's been pouring all night. The storm was pretty bad, the worst I can remember for years. Glynn hated the lightning. I tried my best to tell him it wouldn't hurt, but he wasn't convinced. The roof's been leaking too.'

James, who had slept through both thunder and lightning, nodded in agreement, not

trusting himself to speak straight away.
'You'd better get changed quickly into some dry clothes,' she carried on, keeping her tone as unemotional as she could make it.
'I hadn't expected to see you up, I must admit,' he ventured, standing awkwardly in the doorway to what passed as their dining room, very unsure of his ground.
After turning around to look at him properly, she pulled herself upwards, to stand, though after a moment or two she crumpled into the chair again. Only then did it occur to him that her clothes were wet too, that she was shivering as violently, or more so perhaps, than he.
Instantly concerned, he moved towards her then, baulking from holding her, stopping in front of her. He wasn't sure of her responses.
'You talk about me, but what about you? You're hardly dry. You haven't been out looking for me, or something stupid like that have you?'
Remorse again, biting hard.
'No . . no, or rather yes,' she answered, rubbing her damp, straggling hair with a cloth she clasped in her hand, then bending down to feel the bottom of her dirtied petticoats. 'I have been out, but not searching for you.'
'Then what, why?'
Forcing himself to think before he spoke again, he stared at her, wanting to order her into the mess that currently served as her bedroom to change, to put on layers of warm clothes before she invited illness, but stopping from doing so because he knew he had no right to order her to do anything. Past deeds of his meant that he had thrown away all rights over her.
Noticeably, she was gripping the sides of her

chair so hard he imagined she was trying to rip it apart. Feeling his questioning gaze upon her, she glanced up at him, her own eyes infinitely sad, red-rimmed pools in an alabaster face. So obvious was her distress that his mind was sent whirling. Had she already discovered he had spent the night with a woman whose name he had never asked?

'I don't know how to put this,' she whispered, 'but you need . . you have to know. I can't break it to your mother. I haven't the strength left, and I think that it's your place to, although maybe Alex . . '

'My dear, what the hell are you rambling on about?'

She looked at him quickly. Had he called her dear?

'It's Samuel. He's dead. He's been killed in an accident at Wheal Eliza. And Lorna . . well Lorna is badly injured. I think he beat her before he went on shift, harder probably than he meant. You know how vicious his temper is . . was. It must have been playing on his mind. They say he didn't listen to the warnings.'

James felt as if he was trapped in a nightmare. He had got a fever. He was imagining everything, beginning from early morning, waking up in a filthy bed.

Tottering towards her, then kneeling down beside the chair, he took her small, cold hand in his. Although it was their first physical contact for months, neither of them were in the state of mind to appreciate that.

'Was there any explosion then, or flooding? Was anybody else hurt? How did he die?'

Clutching his arm to try to help steady herself, she shook her hair, which did nothing to improve the style. It persisted in hanging straight, almost obscuring her eyes, making her look like a shy child, and heightening her vulnerability. His sluggish senses did note how clean she smelt, how naturally clear her skin was, while his brain struggled with the fact that his brother was dead.

'No, no-one was hurt apart from Samuel. It wasn't a huge accident, as they go. As I said, they believe that he would have escaped like the others, but when they yelled he didn't listen, wouldn't move, stayed there like a statue.'

He'd never move on anything unless he wanted to, James thought, instantly silently reprimanding himself. Never would he see his brother, for all his obvious faults, alive again, something which was near impossible to accept.

'What about Lorna then? You said she was injured. How do you know about her? Were you sent to tell her about Samuel? Couldn't they have done that themselves or at least waited for me?'

'It didn't happen quite like that,' she said quietly, as if in a trance.

Then she went on to explain how one of the neighbours had called on Lorna soon after Samuel left for work. The woman was sure something was wrong. She'd heard screams and terrified shouting. After deciding to investigate, she found Lorna beaten, and bleeding profusely. Despite trying to rouse her there and then, she had not succeeded.

'Then she panicked, thinking Lorna was dying,' Helen went on. 'She didn't know what to do, so she rushed here to ask me to help. I took Glynn with me, and we went right over. It all took some time, so by then Lorna was coming round, though she was in a terrible state. He must really have battered her. I wish I hadn't taken Glynn along. It was awful, awful.'

Her words came out in a monotone as she related the full horror of her night, the broken and weeping woman she had found, the rasping sobs and the profuse amount of blood. She had been through a huge range of emotions during the past hours. The factual was all that remained.

James, realising that she was only masking the depths of her distress, went to gather her into his arms, though still holding back at the last second. As he did he thought that the word awful summed up so much of what had happened to both of them in the past 24 hours. It's typical of the way fate's playing with me that I should be away again at the time I was really needed. All a re-run of those wretched riots.

'There was always so much hate boiling in Samuel,' he groaned, finally taking off his wet coat. 'His anger would come out of nowhere, knock you off your feet. Still I suppose he's paid the biggest price of all. But dead, I can't believe that. It seems impossible.'

Helen twisted her hands with their neat, clipped fingernails.

'I thought Lorna had paid the full price, too, when I saw the amount of blood there was around. Then, again, when I had cleaned her up it didn't seem as bad as I feared. There are bones broken, despite that, along with her spirit. I left her with friends. I've never seen them before. They seemed kind enough.'

'And medical help?'

'That soon came. The whole village was soon roused. You know how close it is when something bad's happened. They all want to be involved. I stayed until I knew she was as comfy as possible, then Glynn and I walked back. It was torrential by then. That's when both of us got really soaked.'

He was beginning to understand that she had been through as much, probably a great deal more, turmoil as he. The main, gaping, difference was her troubles hadn't been self-inflicted, as his had been.

'I've promised to go back today,' she went on.'I'm family in a way. The friends, good as they are, aren't.'

Such was the turmoil within him, that he was still trying completely to grasp the chain of events.

'How do you know about Samuel then?'

'The mine captain, Richard Williams, turned up here soon after the accident happened, because he hadn't wanted to tell Lorna outright - was too scared how she would react. That was just before Lorna's neighbour arrived and I heard about Lorna's own injuries. Mr Williams said he hadn't the nerve to go to see her on his own with such dire news, and we were the nearest relatives within easy reach.

'Samuel's body's been brought to the surface, it's in one of the old mine buildings. We'll have to collect it, arrange everything ourselves. Lorna's in no state, or wouldn't want to anyway, and as far as I know no-one else in your family's been told yet, though they've probably heard from someone. I couldn't face going over to your mother's cottage, so I'm afraid I've left that job to you.'

'I feel so sorry for you,' he said, meaning it, wanting to hug her and protect her from all the ills the world, as well as he himself, had to offer. Instead, he merely squeezed the top of her arm.

'Come on, let's get you changed, and into bed.'

She instantly flinched at his touch, the movement so marked he couldn't help but notice.

'What about Glynn, he'll be up soon?'

'I've got meetings this morning, but for once I'll cancel them. Don't worry about the boy.'

There was some sliver of relief in the fact that she hadn't asked for a reason for his night-time absence. He was starting to hope he might get by without one. In spite of that he believed he owed her some sort of explanation for why he had been away all night.

'I . . I'm sorry I wasn't here. Something untoward happened. It wasn't expected. It won't happen again.'

At that, she looked at him, weary-eyed, sick and discouraged by everything she had been forced to accept since her marriage.

'I know where you've been. I've already been told about your drinking exploits. Richard Williams kindly supplied details of what had apparently gone on in some inn in St Austell.'

Shock left him spluttering, searching frantically for relevant explanations. The words had seemed to hit him in the solar plexus.

There's no hiding the truth now, he thought, if ever I thought you could keep truths secret in this tight little world of ours.

Watching his reaction, she held up both her hands to try to calm him.

'Don't worry. It honestly doesn't bother me. We've led our lives separately for so long now, how can I suddenly start criticising?'

She always seemed to read him so well, which made him feel worse.

'Also, don't worry about my father's reaction to whatever happened,' she added. 'Restraint in the face of alcohol and other women was maybe the only drawback he ever found in you. Now he'll think you've gone ahead and proved your manhood, like he's done so often. I must admit he's always held his drink well, although with his affairs he seems to have used less tact. Perhaps he might accept you as a real mirror image after this.'

Her well rehearsed, matter-of-fact, totally unemotional attitude stunned him. It saddened as well, for it seemed to auger much less well for the future than tears and anger would have done. It was a future he now grasped, that he wanted to spend with her, and not entirely for the money, or the family connections.

X

Suzannah was sitting by Nathan's bedside when he awoke. It was midday. The sun, high in the sky, was pouring into his room, exposing every stain, every layer of dust. The dust and the grime, apart from the oh-so-familiar girl, were the first things he noticed. Unlike James, he could instantly remember, with great precision, what had happened before he had passed out. There was nothing whatsoever to give him the blessing of sweet forgetfulness. Visions of gun and bullet, of suicide, were dreadfully sharp and clear. Slowly, as if his body was totally divorced from his mind, he lifted a hand from underneath the heavy, uncomfortable covers which were imprisoning him. Pain rose up and hit him, in every part of his body. Each muscle hurt. His head throbbed unbearably, even more if he moved what seemed like a fraction of an inch.

As sense returned he slowly began to feel his torso for signs of injury, doing so with such difficulty he felt as if he was an immobile 90-year-old. His problems increased because he was bandaged so tightly around his chest and stomach that he felt as if he was trussed up like a fowl ready for the pot. It was almost impossible for him to feel his fingers, or any limb below his waist.

Someone had obviously carried out an expert job patching him up, trying to mend the injuries caused by his old friend.

Knowing that he must have been unconscious for quite a while, he fought to stay awake, finding it exhausting just trying to focus on his surroundings. He wondered if the bullet, or bullets, were still inside him.

What had really happened out there, when he had least expected it? Why Joe? Why a gun? Joe never touched guns. But he had done. He had appeared in the middle of Tombstone with one in his hands, and for some reason, for some deep, desperate reason he had expertly used it.

Nathan wrestled for reasons which would have explained the violence, the self-imposed death, discovering instead it was easier to edge back into the darkness. And that was what he did, despite battling, for a while, against giving way to forgetfulness.

For the next 24 hours he would wake to a mind full of unsolvable problems before thankfully dipping back into welcoming blackness.

When he did fully return to the world, with his eyes focussing without too much agony, he saw her properly. She was huddled uncomfortably in the chair which stood about ten yards from his bed, her long legs tucked underneath her. Her head hung downwards, her features obscured, and she seemed to be hugging herself, as if in need of comfort.

If he had thought of her at all since his arrival in Tombstone it had been for her brazen attitude to life, her frightening vitality.

Always she had worn bright, vivid colours. It was not so now. She was in a plain, pale grey dress. Her once luxuriant hair was scraped back from her face, pulled into a severe bun, while her hands looked as if they had been worked hard - because they were red raw.

After a minute or so he could see her thin arms were rising and falling rhythmically, and he could hear a faint ticking of breath which betrayed the fact that she was obviously dozing. The sight of her did little to ease his nerves, or the now accelerating pain.

If she's come here to tell me why her father killed himself, after trying to blast me to kingdom come, I don't want to hear it, he thought. If she wants an explanation from me then there's nothing I can give her.

Her supple young body had unnerved him before. Now her quietness, and the unknown reason for her being there, beside his bed, so far from her home, served the same purpose. She must know what happened, he told himself. But then again maybe no-one has had the courage to tell her, or even knows who she is. Maybe she's just reached here, and found me. For God's sake, how long have I been out of it?'

He lay deliberately still for ten minutes or so, studying her between barely opened eyes. Such was his confusion, his sense of weakness, that he didn't want to have to face her. He didn't have enough nerve.

However, it was obvious that, without prompting, she wasn't going to move, or wake for a while, so he eventually said, with as much force as his croaking voice would permit: 'Have they told you about your father?'

In his desire for understanding, he had concluded that it was better, perhaps, to get the worst over straight away.

At the sound of his voice, strained as it was, she came to with a start. Her face jerked upwards, and one of her hands flew to clutch at her long, creamy throat. His voice had shaken her. The doctor had assured her that he wouldn't wake properly for at least another 24 hours, and when he did he would be extremely weak. The advice, it immediately seemed to her, had not been correct, because Nathan had sounded much, much stronger than that.

'Oh, you scared me,' she stuttered. 'Dr Townsend was certain you wouldn't be conscious for a while yet. For an hour or so they thought you wouldn't survive at all. The bullet went through you.'

'How long have you been here? he asked, his breathing shallow and difficult. 'I would have thought it rather like minding a corpse.'

Immediately he winced, both in pain and at his own, thoughtless, choice of words.

Was somebody sitting elsewhere with the body of her father, or had he already been buried beneath unsanctified Tombstone soil? Were the worms already having their way?

To escape such harrowing thoughts he wanted to slip instantly into sleep again, so avoiding the hurt and fear that were circling him.

He needn't have worried about her reaction to his remark, however, for she seemed

unperturbed by it.
'There was nowhere else for me to go,' she said slowly. 'I ended up here, playing nurse, because it was what I wanted to do.'
Unable to think straight, he couldn't summon up any reply. Her gaze pierced him, boring straight through him as the bullet evidently had done.
Bur, studying her further, he felt that she looked as devoid of hope as he was. All vivacity had evaporated.
'I . .I'm confused,' he hesitated. 'Tell me, please. Do you know all about your father? Do you know why it happened?'
'I know what happened the day you were shot, yes. I was there.'
At her words, he struggled to sit up higher, in order to see her better. With a great deal of effort, and pain, he managed to raise himself about three inches. Definitely, she did not figure in his hazy recollection of the scene.
'You can't have been. What do you mean?'
At his words, she began to mumble, almost incoherently. He had to strain to hear so hard that he came near to fainting.
'I was . . I was there. I was running over to him, trying to stop him. I couldn't because he was so mad there was nothing I could do. We'd been together, talking, only a few minutes before he . . shot you, but he'd broken away from me, pushed me and sent me falling and I got left too far behind. May God forgive me, I couldn't stop him shooting you, couldn't stop him killing himself.'
Nathan tensed himself before asking the next, and for him, the most pressing question of all.
'But why did he do it? Hunt me down? Because that's what I'm sure he must have done.'

'Don't ask me that. I can't answer it, I just can't. Haven't you any idea?'
If she didn't know, what chance did he stand? He closed his eyes, seeking escape again from the world.

XI

It was two days later before they carried on with their awkward, stilted conversation. He remained imprisoned by sheets, while she was still by his bedside, as if on perpetual nursing duty.
'It was after you left. Whenever your name was mentioned he started to get angry, really angry. No-one could reason with him, and believe me I tried. Eventually he began to talk about finding you, making you pay.'
With a pounding head, he tried to find a position in the bed where his body, which was feeling so stiff, so very, very sore, could find some rest. It didn't help that his mind was, at the same time, so extremely muddled. Had he honestly imagined only a week or so before that his life was straightening out at last?
'I can't follow that. We had no disagreements while I lived with your family. You gave me more problems than your mother and father did, and as for your father he and I got on well together, or so I thought.'
'Well that's as might be. Whatever happened back then, when I know I was sometimes a nuisance to you, I'll cause you no problems now. That's over. Life's caught up with you and me both, wouldn't you say?'
Did that mean - was she admitting - that her young, seductive fires were quenched ahead of time? His head was beginning to spin. There remained a limit to the strain he could

take.

'Where's your mother then?', he asked, suddenly realising that she didn't seem to have accompanied her husband, or daughter. 'Back in Grass Valley still, all alone, unknowing?'

Suzannah, kneeling by the side of him, lifted a stray lock of her fair hair, twirled it around and around her fingers and then wove it absent-mindedly between them. He could hardly see the gesture. The sun was so bright it was dazzling his eyes which had grown accustomed to gloom over the past days.

'She died about four months ago.'

'I'm sorry, so sorry. That's perhaps another reason why you seem so alone, why he may have been so, so desperate.'

'Perhaps. He certainly did change after she died, became more isolated and insular. There is only me now.'

She looked at him quizzically as he lay back, fatigued, on the one, thin pillow, his face almost skeletal, his eyes lying deep in their dark sockets. It was obvious that he was too weak to take in much, too weak maybe to come through the ordeal as the Nathan he had once been.

'I'd thought, perhaps, I could stay here for a while,' she continued. 'You haven't a nurse, and you'll need one for a while yet. That's no small wound you've to recover from. Dear old misguided father did his work too well.'

Nathan deliberately moaned in negative response. He was awake enough to understand that he didn't want her that close. The shooting had changed nothing, only complicated everything. Surely she had not basically changed from the sultry young woman with the tantalising wiles and body that he admired, but hadn't had the energy to desire?'

'Look, this isn't the best place for a young woman to stay,' he whispered, meaning that he didn't want her there in any way, shape or form, but was also aware in the state he was in that there was little he could physically attempt at that very moment to get rid of her.

'I don't care what the conditions are like. This street will be fine for me. I don't know if you can take really anything in but I'd like you to believe that since we last met I've learnt to make the best of what I've been given, without trying to tempt others into providing me with it.'

'If you stay, and it will have to be for a short while only, you'll have to look after yourself,' he warned.

'I know that Nathan. I'm here to look after you.'

When she had disappeared from the room, to sort out some food for them both, he subsided into the pillows. What he wanted was the strength to follow her into the kitchen, to interrogate her, to find out the real reason for her father being in Tombstone, for he was absolutely sure she must have an idea why Joe had gone as far as hunting him down with a gun. The man had also blown his own brains out, for pity's sake.

With his muscles almost unable to move, he lay between the thin sheets, partially hallucinating, sweating, striving to unscramble the whole crazy mess. Joe had been solid, dependable, God-fearing. There seemed to have been no lunacy in the crevices of his mind.'

But then who was to judge sanity? Weren't there dregs of madness in the far reaches of everyone? Was he responsible for Joe's suicide?

The fears and questions tore at him, denying him real rest, even after the doctor arrived and administered a sleeping draught which was one and a half times one of normal strength.

CHAPTER SIX

Summer 1877

1

The worries had not faded weeks later, and were continuing to crowd in on him like a host of spectres. By then, though, his wasted body had shown some response to treatment and he had also resumed writing, although only in short bursts, when the continuing pain ebbed.

Instead of the desk at the Clarion he tried to prop himself up on his pillow and use a small, rickety table by his bed as a rest for his writing hand. He had enough time also to read the back papers published when he was unconscious and unable to focus on anything, and was able to derive wry amusement from the fact that Henry had made sure that he had been front page news on the day of the shooting.

Suzannah continued to show no signs of wanting to move on, but nevertheless had bothered him little. He had to admit that she had left him alone more than he had envisaged he would, while in small ways proving to be invaluable. Although he learnt to dress his chest wounds himself he found walking difficult and painful. It seemed only sensible to let her keep house and assist him when help was required, as long as that was her choice as well.

Despite trying to ignore her for the majority

of the time, he had taken in enough to appreciate that she had ensured that he had undergone the best recuperation period someone with his injuries could require. She had, as well, become a willing go-between between his stopgap bed-come-office, and the untidy, cramped newsroom of the Clarion. Within a month or so he was, to a great extent, back on his feet. It could only be termed a recovery in a physical sense, however, for intellectually he could not rid himself of the barrage of 'whys' that he had not been able to begin to answer regarding Joe's bid to murder him, and his eventual suicide.

Suzannah seemed to have forced herself to block out the whole tragedy in the same way as she was seemingly blanketing out life itself and replacing it with, what appeared to Nathan to be, a fey, semi-existence.

Eventually, he came to concede the only way to uncover any answers was to return to Grass Valley, to where he and Joe had once forged a friendship.

Someone there, he convinced himself, must have an idea of the reasons behind Joe's apparent breakdown.

He explained his logic to Suzannah one afternoon, when he had finished a feature article on the Earp brothers. It was a story he had researched in as much depth as a now partial invalid could. The brothers, Wyatt, James, Virgil, Morgan and Warren, were now said to be definitely all hoping to descend upon the area. Some were already in town, with their wives and children. Others were expected.

A number of them had already made enquiries about buying real estate and local businesses.

Morgan was said to be considering a job in the police department, while other gossip suggested that Wyatt, who was a faro dealer in the Long Branch Saloon in Dodge City, where he was also assistant marshal, would be on his way soon.

The story had been occupying him for days, but at that moment everything about the brothers had been obliterated, for him, by the complexities of his very own and personal mystery.

'Someone close to Joe in Grass Valley must know why your father tracked me down with so much hate in his heart', he insisted to Suzannah, his voice so intense she was forced to pay attention. 'All I can think is that he must have been obsessed with something I did, or didn't do. It stands to reason that he must have discussed it with a friend or someone he worked with. I've just got to find that person.'

As he spoke she was so close to him that her thick, burnished hair was merging with his dark curls.

'That's some task,' she whispered.

'Maybe, but it could equally be a simple enough one. I'm not exactly a stranger to Grass Valley and its people. I lived with them for some while. I've got enough background knowledge, I'm sure I've simply got to be strong enough to go back and ask.'

It seemed to him that she paled slightly at his words, the girl who now gave the impression that she had turned from the tigress she had been, to mouse.

'But you're not strong enough. You can't even manage to walk the length of Tough Nut Street unaided. You can't go back yet.'

'I'm not talking about leaving tomorrow,' he

retorted. 'And you can return with me when I do go. You've got to accept that you need to go back there sometime. From what you've told me your father just shut up the house with all your possessions in it, and left. It's all still there, waiting for you. This will be the best way for you to travel back. I'll be able to make sure you arrive safely.'

Although he had been trying to include her in his plans, to help her, she moved deliberately away from him as if he had insulted her.

'You've no need to worry about me, I'm not your responsibility.'

'That may be true, but despite all that happened, or because of it, I feel I owe something to Joe. I need to know why, I need to know what I did to upset, to anger. him, to such an extent.'

He didn't add that once he had fled to a different continent to escape the burden of obligation. Now, all of a sudden, he wanted to accept it.

'How long before you plan to leave?' she asked coldly, moving further away from him, much to his relief.

'Two months at least, which will be around November. I'm not pushing my recovery. I've decided to start respecting the fact that good health is a real bonus. I don't want to rush it, and make myself worse as a result.'

That evening he went out alone, the first time he had done so since he had been carried back to his bed with blood seeping from his chest, and he walked up to Joe's grave which lay bare of flowers or sentiment. It was merely a mound of baked earth with a crude cross leaning from it, at a drunken angle. The area around it was empty, barren, isolated and unloved and, what seemed worse, far from the mizzle and the wooded, secretive valleys of the man's homeland.

Standing there affected Nathan more than he had expected. It was a bludgeoning, sobering reminder of the unavoidable end of all life. As he picked up some of the earth from the grave and let it trickle through his fingers, he thought of the thousands of Cornishmen and women who lay beneath foreign soil in America, Mexico and South Africa, their very being slowly merging into the ground they had come to dig, to win jewels and metals from. And where would he lay at his end? So further fear was all he found at Joe's pauper's grave, a grave that had not been given the blessing of being sited in consecrated ground.

The growing, corrosive mystery of why also remained.

11

Edwin and Peter Coombes became martyrs during their fetid weeks of imprisonment. Most knew in their hearts that the two genial, slow-tempered men had not been among the troublemakers. They were honest enough youngsters who had suffered the obvious misfortune of being used by owners and magistrates who wanted an example set.

It was well-known that in the midst of the worst of the rioting the constables had been too scared to isolate the main offenders. They had eventually decided upon a line of least resistance which had led them to Peter and Edwin. The fact that their father had died while they were still suffering the deprivations of a jail cell had only added to the waves of sympathy and genuine feelings of concern.

After her father's burial Jenifer had discovered that Alex had at least spoken some truth to her during their two, strained, encounters. The financial threat to her family had lessened. Money had poured in. Miners she had never seen before called at her home in person to offer what they could afford, and envelopes fat with pennies and shillings had been pushed anonymously through the door. But when Alex called again in person she refused to take the cash he offered personally. With great relish she pushed the coins back at him.

Despite greeting him on the doorstep she would not move aside to let him through, and would not openly welcome him. Strangely, she found it difficult to analyse her deep-rooted antipathy to him. Certainly the anger she had harboured for him had diminished somewhat, but nevertheless instinct and some trepidation sent her shying away from the hollow-cheeked, emotionally-charged man confronting her, as if he presented constant danger.

'We've been given so much already,' she snapped, standing haughtily in front of him, regal once more. 'We're getting by. Please keep your money. I was told you're out of work yourself now. You finally found the sense to walk away from your brother and his job, so you're as badly off as we all are.'

Such was the sharp tone of her voice that he felt snubbed by her, and showed it, the muscles in his chin and around his mouth tensing quickly.

'You seem to have taken gratefully from everyone else who wants to help your family. Do you still resent me so much?'

Over the past week she had lost weight, which only enhanced the ferocity, and the wildness of the eye that he had often seen in a creature about to be snared.

'It's just that you owe us nothing. I . . I'm grateful for what you tried to do that night when father died. I should have thanked you before. There hasn't been time, so much else has had to be done.'

With defiance, he stood his ground in front of her, determined not to be cowed by her attitude. Her thanks had been delivered with ice in her voice.

'I wish I could have been more help, could have saved him. I felt dreadful when I left, as if I was running out at the worst moment.'

'That's ridiculous,' she laughed harshly. 'You did all you could. The doctor himself said so.'

While speaking she had moved back further inside the cottage, and was starting to shut the door on him, wanting him gone, and quickly. The family home lay in a hamlet between Lanlivery and Luxulyan which nestled in a hidden, shady valley. As a result, the vegetation that surrounded the plain building was so lush and damp and intrusive it was hard to distinguish ferns from stone. The surroundings made him feel as if he was standing at the mouth of a cave, a mouth that was being very firmly and deliberately closed on him.

'All right, you won't accept money or apologies from me,' he stammered, anxious to speak again before the door was completely shut, but I'm afraid I do have one more request.'

She stood tall and immobile in the dark shadows. If she hadn't slimmed so alarmingly, if he hadn't already witnessed her near breaking point, she would have appeared absolutely formidable.

'The boys are due to be released in four days,' he ploughed on. 'I thought you might be walking to Bodmin to meet them.'

'I believe I might,' she answered, with full sarcasm. 'What d'ye expect me to do, treat it like any other day, carry on as usual?'

'Of course not, I was only asking.'

Aggrieved at his own lack of confidence, he took a ragged breath. Where the devil had all his self-possession seeped away to? Breathing in deeply, he strove to gather the tattered dregs that remained.

'Anyway If you don't mind I'd like to go with you. I also want to be there when they come out.'

At that, her expression, which had been of pained indifference bordering on irritation, changed to one of apprehension.

'Why, because you blame yourself for what happened? Don't worry, my brothers have always thought Alex Rosevean was wonderful.'

'No, I don't want to go because, or entirely because, of that. I have to admit I do feel very involved, and I had hoped they might agree to head over to Roche before going home. A few of their friends want to welcome them there.'

Her emerging despair, and her annoyance with him, darkened further. Instantly he understood by her reaction, that his words had not been received kindly. Her eyes had narrowed, like a cat about to pounce on prey, the lines around her mouth had deepened, and her jaw tensed tightly. It also seemed to him that she had aged five years in one moment.

'What sort of welcome?' she demanded, almost hiding behind the nearly closed door now, her voice gritty. 'How big? Don't tell me, there'll be around 300 milling around like hungry, lost sheep and you want Peter and Edwin to stir them up again, start supporting that union of yours once more.'

'That's not so,' he said quickly, taking a step towards her, anxious to reassure. 'As I said, only friends will be there.'

'So you claim. But can I take your word? I don't think so.'

'You haven't completely answered me yet,' he persisted. 'Shall we walk to the jail together?'

He felt like a beggar.

'They say we're all free in this country, though almost everyone knows that's not really true. I can't stop you from going to Bodmin, or meeting my brothers. I have to admit that for some peculiar reason they think a lot of you. But I don't know if they'll go back to Roche before coming here to see mother. It seems pointless to me. For myself I very much hope that after they're let out they'll stay as far away from you as possible.'

Eventually, they did walk across the moors together, the strained atmosphere between them making it a long, muted journey. Lack of sleep was beginning to exhaust Alex completely, while she had been through so much that she was too dulled to want to trade petty conversation, especially with someone she had convinced herself she distrusted absolutely.

In truth, the process of grieving for her father was just hitting her, the real sense of loss having only recently begun to sink in - but that paled in comparison with what was happening to her mother. Her mind and bodily health were deteriorating so fast that Jenifer hardly knew where to turn. In spite of covering up the instability to a point she was unsure how much longer she could hold out, the main trouble being she couldn't talk, or reason, with her any more.

It wasn't depression that was eating into Agnes Coombes, as it had assailed Mary Rosevean for so many years. It was more telling than that. Jenifer could imagine the outcome, her mother ending her days in the town they were heading for. Not in the jail, but in the asylum which was a prison in itself. Strangely, the lull between Alex and herself wasn't quite as uneasy as she had anticipated. She fell quite easily into leggy step beside him, her willowy figure dominant again, her personality buried, with a great deal of effort, once more under mysterious layers. And on this occasion he could sense that there was no out and out hatred for him in her heart, although he had an idea that was because more pressing matters were preoccupying her. It was this calmer attitude of hers which helped keep his own emotions relatively even.

It was a penetratingly cold autumn day. Jenifer was well prepared for the weather, having put on heavy, warm clothing that masked, rather than added glamour, to her dramatic looks. She had only been concerned with cheating the elements. Even so, when he offered her his outer coat to hang over her shoulders she was tempted to accept because, despite her layers, the chill was beginning to permeate. Nevertheless, she refused the offer, as she had done his money. Her independence, her determination not to be in his debt again, remained fierce.

The jail dominated the outskirts of town, rising fortress-like from the cobbles, throwing a malevolent shadow over the hovels which clung around it. Slits and heavy, forbidding bars, stood for windows, a gibbet hung ominously outside as a warning to all the poor devils who had passed through the huge gates and into her stinking bowels. There was a sense of impregnability and darkness of spirit about it that caught in the throat, frayed the nerve ends.

The journey had taken longer than either Alex or Jenifer had bargained for, and when they arrived the boys had already been released, and were waiting, wild-eyed outside. They were dirty and unkempt. Their hair hung in louse-ridden knots, their skin was grey and pitted, and both were more than a stone lighter. But they were in strange high spirits for, although the jail killed the spirit of many who spent unwanted time there, the fact was that neither had ever been quite alone in the midst of the starkness and inhumanity they had faced over the past months. Their mental closeness had given them a spiritual buoyancy, their very knowledge of their innocence, and the injustice of their situation, helping them survive the terror and the ordeal.

When he saw them Alex stopped in his tracks. They were already surrounded by a surprisingly large number of friends and well-wishers who were adding some festivity to the depressing aura of the place. There were pit banners held aloft in defiance and they, and a handful of flags, festooned the prison yard with unexpected colour.

Alex was greeted warmly enough despite some of the animosity that had been extended towards him during past weeks, some of it from a number he had considered friends. However, many of those revelling in the

delight of the brothers' freedom had kept faith with him. They were not among those who had come to suspect greatly where the loyalties of James Rosevean's brother lay.
'Are you ready then Alex?' someone called, his voice carrying above all the hub-bub.
'There's talk of more than 200 of us gathering at Roche, have you heard the same boy?'
'Yes,' another yelled,' I've a fair mind this'll be a day to remember, and don't we damned well need it?'
The whole, mildly out of control situation stunned him. He was painfully aware how it must appear to Jenifer, knowing she would never accept that he hadn't anticipated such a huge reaction to the boys' freedom.
Although he was temporarily lost for words, she was not. She turned on him in the midst of the joyous crowd, her dark, liquid eyes with their violet lights unexpectedly piercing his soul.
'You knew this, didn't you, when I told you how afraid I was about what would happen? You told me I was being stupid. You swore there wouldn't be hundreds of them, but there will be, won't there? Did you want me here because it would make it seem all their family is behind them and your union, so that they would all think you've got my support? I suppose they've got no idea that we've been pushed to the front of your pathetic battle against all our wishes?'
Quickly, he tried to explain.
'I didn't think it would be like this. I just thought there might be a few others, I swear that I never expected anything like this.'
Peter, who was only yards away, noticed the disagreement and, knowing how intimidating his sister's temper could be, and anxious to

avoid any dispute on such a day, threw himself towards her and hugged her. It was an attempt at a diversion.

She didn't recoil from him despite his filthy condition, and his rank smell, instead clinging onto him in utter relief.

'Come on Jenny, don't look so sour faced. These are friends, they've helped you out, haven't they? All they want to do is walk home with us, and maybe take a little detour on the way. After all we've been through we don't intend to shrink away from here as if we are criminals.'

However deep her relief at seeing them again, she wasn't to be sweet talked.

'I've food at home, enough for a quiet family celebration tea, although celebration is perhaps not the best word after what's happened to father. Forget all this talk of more marches. They'll have you back inside that rotting hole within hours. Remember it's the magistrates who are the pit owners.

Peter was barely listening. The excitement created by being out in free, fresh air, and the size of the welcoming committee had taken over.

'I told you, we've not survived in that desperate place to slink away as if we were guilty in the first place.'

'We'll only be walking with friends, nothing else,' said Edwin, rushing to join in, smiling vacantly at the faces surrounding them. 'Do they look as if they want to do more than walk and talk?'

He was so full of the occasion he would, if pushed, have agreed to have done anything the masses wanted of him.

In reply she angrily pulled her scarf tighter around her head, and sighed very pointedly, although that was lost in the hectic noise whirling around them. Fine, long black tendrils of her hair escaped and swept across her face, curling into her mouth and eyes. The cold was worming and twisting its way even deeper into her muscles and sinews, and even the sight of her brothers, unhampered by chains, did not somehow help entirely.

If they had been on their own, if I could have greeted them on my own, it would have been so different, she thought bitterly.

She rounded on Alex, aware he was hanging back, trying to distance himself from the excitement surrounding him, and had not yet moved away into the throng.

'Your hundreds of friends may not seem to be in the burning mood at the moment, but give them a beer each at Roche and they soon will be.'

'Come on Jenifer,' he said slowly, encouraged to a small extent by the positive attitude of her brothers. 'That isn't what they intend, I promise you. This time I really do promise.'

'You may well say that now Mr high-and-mighty Rosevean,' she hissed, ready for a fight herself, 'but from all accounts this rabble takes precious little notice of you when their tempers are up. Their actions sent you running scared during the last spate of troubles.'

Peter intervened again. 'Don't get so worked up, Jenifer, please. I know all this is because of what happened to us, and because of father. We're mortal sorry about father. I don't think we've quite accepted he's gone yet. We should have been with you when it happened, and we'll make it up to you somehow. But as to who we walk with, we can make up our own minds about that. You're only our sister, and only 22 at that, not one of our parents.'

They've got no idea what's waiting for them when they get home, she panicked. Hardly cosy family warmth any more. More like a mad morgue, home of the living dead.
'Mother's waiting, and anxious,' she said, trying to prepare them to some extent. 'You must understand what all this, what father's death, has done to her.'
'She'll see us soon enough. This won't take long. We're just happy to be out of jail, and we want to show it, that's all.
They were in no mood for caution, or to understand any veiled warnings - their spirits were too high.
'But you can share your joy with all your family, at home, surely?' she persisted, aware that everyone else was beginning to gawp at her, knowing her views were unwanted, and deeply resenting the fact.
'But we want our feelings known. We want to show that you can still win even if you're pushed into jail unjustly,' pleaded Edwin. 'We're not beaten, and the pit owners have got to realise that.'
At his reaction, she whirled around to face Alex again. He was a target she certainly didn't mind upsetting.
'You see what I mean. They're after trouble already. You've certainly got two converts there. Congratulations.'

111

Despite protests she left on her own five minutes later, striding off in a temper to make her solitary way home. Her brothers showed little concern about her departure, feeling they had done their utmost to change her mind, not understanding why she was so opposed to them going to Roche.

Alex watched her disappear over the bleak horizon with some unease. The trouble was he understood perfectly what had driven her back to Lanlivery without them. He had to admit emotions were running higher than he had imagined they would, and because of that he now reluctantly believed that she could be right about the outcome of the day.

Anxiously, he looked around at the raucous melee. Both boys could, like she said, be locked away inside the jail again by this evening, he thought, along with a few others too.

How the hell would they face another spell behind bars, or would worse follow if they appeared before a judge again on the same charge for a second time? There wasn't much leniency in the system.

But also, he could understand the demonstration of feeling. The strike has been dragging on for weeks, he reminded himself. Families have reached starvation level in some cases, and there's little enthusiasm around. Children are crying for food, women are dressing babies in rags, and the prospect of the men going back to work and winning the right to speak for themselves is growing dimmer every day. When the chance for celebration comes along, it's natural that as many as possible grasp the opportunity.

There had been no talks with the owners, with the sides remaining as deeply entrenched as ever. Because of the tensions the plans had gone ahead to use police forces from outside the county, and as a result there had been a few bloody encounters which meant the men's determination had plunged to a low ebb. They had needed a rallying point, and the boys' release, plus the mere fact that they had managed to survive, had provided that.

There were still surprises to come. The reception at Roche itself surpassed everything that had been planned. The large, initially vociferous, group that had trekked across the moor from Bodmin had lost some of its verve by the time its members arrived at the village. The banners they carried were no longer unfurled, and instead were borne along dispiritedly. Even Pete was beginning to wish that he had walked straight home with Jenifer instead. All were very cold by then, shivering and in need of refreshment. The suggestion that about 200 could be waiting for them, once so readily accepted, had gradually faded and then ebbed away as they had walked, and they were prepared for disenchantment.

It took their breath away, therefore, to see, when they staggered into the centre of Roche, a mass of faces which were fifty, sixty even, deep in some places. After their lack of faith regarding the support that would be awaiting them, they stood rooted at the mass sight, unable to believe it. Was it a mirage?

In turn, when those waiting had spotted the arrivals from the jail they gave out a roar of welcome, and the large groups in the jostling ranks moved along the rutted road towards them, cheering and singing, the boom of their Cornish voices echoing in the crisp air. Suddenly, all the banners were held aloft again, and were being waved like long, tattered wisps of confetti which meant that, in spite of the hostile weather, there was an instant carnival atmosphere. Those who had journeyed with Peter and Edwin were overwhelmed by the sheer force of numbers. Within minutes the brothers, the champions of the day, were swept onto heaving, seething shoulders to be paraded through to the Roche Inn.

Alex found himself hanging back with Joshua, looking on from the outside again, unable to find quite the same bubbling, untroubled excitement, which was so evident around him, from within himself.

'Thank heavens that their sister isn't here. I don't think she'd be happy with this, even though no-one's causing trouble. They seem tame enough but I wonder if she would be convinced. And where are the police? Those foreigners they've foisted on us can't be far away.'

'Knowing the hatred that woman feels for you I think she'd probably accuse you of organising this whole occasion. I wouldn't be surprised if she thought you'd dragged each of these men here, individually.'

Everything came to a halt at the Inn where pints and pasties were much in evidence, although few could even see, let alone reach, the bar. And then the show moved onto Roche rock where it had been decided that a mass rally should be staged. Even more supporters were set to join in within the next hour.

The exhilaration was catching. When the speeches did finally begin a wave of optimism seemed to wash over all the attendees. Each speaker was applauded with fervour, almost adulation. Good spirits dominated, and because of that a tangible atmosphere of comradeship kept everyone standing in the icy open air for around two hours, chanting, singing and trying to portray strength in numbers.

Alex eventually began considering his return to Biscovey in a happier state of mind than he had been in for weeks. Relieved at the peaceful enough outcome of the evening he decided it was safe to leave Peter and Edwin at Roche, continuing to enjoy the limelight after their time spent in the murk and soul-destroying isolation of jail.

As he turned to journey south, though, he imagined Jenifer sitting, waiting, in the damp cottage for her brothers' return, trying to pacify her mother and assure her that nothing untoward would have happened this time. Initially, it was the only blight on his briefly re-emerging sense of determination.

As he neared the sea, and smelt the brine on the air, his head cleared and thoughts of her antipathy to the strike began to dominate further, which made the brief sense of light-headed well-being suffer even further. In the end, the fears that all the fight, the enthusiasm, had been for nothing, began to outweigh all else. The union of minds may have occurred during the day but he knew the men's actions were causing anguish and empty stomachs.

The push for a union was dividing families. It was bringing in constables from parts of the country that had never even heard of china clay, that were as alien to Cornwall as China itself. It was leading to unwarranted arrests and it had left men and youngsters injured. And the men had almost reached the end of their road in their efforts to fight for their rights.

There were few routes left for the emergent union to take. Apart from clinging onto self-respect, and holding out as long as fate would allow, there was precious little more that its supporters could do to ensure victory.

It took a couple of hours in his own company

to wreck the sense of camaraderie completely, but after the elation came numbing desolation.

1V

The 7000 ton steamship churned through the water, striving to ride a sea that was being whipped up to a fury, and smashing its hull from all sides. The pale half moon, and stars that strained in the night sky, barely illuminated the crashing black waves and the vessel's four masts and single funnel. Only the tortuous white wake shone brightly. Billy, watching the flecks of writhing foam disappear into the thick darkness, wished that he could lock himself in his cabin until they had found a way safely through the unavoidable, approaching, storm. There was to be no chance of that. Unfortunately, he was not a passenger, able to scuttle into his cabin whenever he wanted. He was part of the crew. He had joined the ship on impulse. It had seemed that one moment he had been in Biscovey, the next he had been journeying to Tilbury to join the next ship to sail from there for America. An hour out of dock he had wanted to be back on dry land. Now he was sailing past the coast of Cornwall the desire to be back home again, on dry land, was immense. In the midst of the heightening gale he cursed himself and his apparent inability to come to lasting decisions.

The few decisions I do stick to, he thought, turn out to be disasters. I've got more than a gut feeling that this is one of them. I'm no sailor, I don't even enjoy being at sea, what the hell has led me here?

Deep inside he knew the reason. He had been led there by a desire to escape. He only wished that he had thought more deeply about the sort of escape he would choose. Did he really want a new land, plus uncertainty, certainly loneliness?

In the end his family had let him go with no questions asked. None of them seemed to care one jot about the fact that he was leaving. Not one of them had appeared to say farewell as they had done once, when Nathan had left Cornwall and they had all gathered at the railway station. But then, he reasoned, those days were over completely. Samuel was dead, Alex and James were embroiled in their own battles, and their mother had given her blessing many weeks before he finally went. Only hours after arriving at Tilbury dock, and glimpsing his first sight of the Thames, he had signed on as crew. The ship, the Tamarind, had left port the following morning, before he could properly absorb what he had done. Uncertainty had settled into his mind as soon as the weather worsened, bringing with it, for him, an unaccountable fear that nearly incapacitated him.

The Tamarind was a modern trans-Atlantic liner for both passengers and cattle. She had a maximum speed of 14 knots, was fitted with eight watertight bulkheads, boasted a music room, smoking room, and elegantly decorated stateroom, and carried 53 passengers and 96 crew besides himself, as well as seven cattlemen and general cargo which included beer, antimony, church ornaments and seed. Unbeknown to him when he had signed on, she had been beset by trouble from before her launch the previous year. A strike had put back her completion date which meant she had then been rushed through to avoid losing money on a late delivery. As a result, she leaked so badly during her inaugural crossing to America she had to go into dry dock in New York for repairs before returning to England.

With darkness encasing him, almost as it had done in the mine, Billy stood on deck, grasping the rail and staring out to where he knew the Cornish coast lay. As he thought of the unseen days stretching ahead of him the pent-up worries and frustrations that had been bottled up inside him since his youth tugged at his mind, to such a degree that at one moment he was afraid that he might actually jump into the water, end it all, cheat the pain. Terror was etched into his face, alongside anger that he should be so lacking in courage. The spray that was pounding the straining sides of the ship had already soaked him through, freezing him so much that his hands were beginning to show signs of starting to swell. The physical pain was registering, alongside the inner despair, when another of the crew members came and stood beside him. He was older, small and bearded, walking upright despite the heaving seas, and obviously more at one with the elements confronting them.

Billy, with his gangling features that were totally bereft of Rosevean muscle, looked unbelievably frail in the teeth of the treacherous weather, as if he would achieve his wish and be whipped overboard with just one extra-ferocious offshore gust. He was standing with his bony shoulders hunched, his head drooping. His silhouette shouted defeat.

'Are you all right, son? You look as if you've just won yourself a pot of gold, and then had it stolen from you.'

'Not quite,' snapped Billy, resenting the

intrusion into his thoughts. 'I've never as much as sniffed a fortune, I've left the quest for pots of money to greedier members of my family.'

'Just worried about what the weather's throwing at us then? If you are, I don't blame you. I feel a mite scared myself.'

Billy was slightly amazed by the confession. The man was, unlike him, an experienced sailor which meant that he had expected sarcasm from him, not sympathy.

'What d'you mean by that?'

'What I'm saying. It's only a feeling, I suppose. She isn't the luckiest ship I've sailed on. Those leaks don't give you much confidence. I should have turned my back on her after that last crossing. I was lazy, couldn't find the energy, but that's how I've been all my life, a drifter, and not a doer.'

Billy shuddered into his dripping clothes. He had wanted encouragement instead of doom. His grip on the handrail tightened.

She's a luxurious ship, he told himself. Four boilers, a triple-expansion engine capable of 5500 horsepower. Why then do I feel as if I'm on a raft?

'Where are we now, exactly?'

'If you ask me, not where we should be.'

The shuddering turned to definite alarm.

'You don't think we're on the right course?'

'I'm sure the captain would probably swear we are, but to my way of thinking we're too near land, hugging the coast too tight. Perhaps he's afraid we'll have to run for cover when the gale gets worse. I can't follow that. You shouldn't play games with this bit of coastline, it's swallowed too many lives as you should well know. I was told you're a Cornishman, aren't you?'

Five minutes passed and still Billy did not, could not, move. He was trying to press the raging doubts into his subconscious. One moment he had been welcoming death, the next he was terrified that it might come. In a bid to stave off panic, he told himself that nothing abnormal was happening. The passengers were sitting down for dinner, the children were being put to bed, cattle were being fed in their holds, and most of the crew were out of sight, carrying on business as normal. Apart from the towering waves, nothing whatsoever was amiss.

However, when the warning came, heard above the screaming air, instinct immediately told him what it was. His automatic reaction was to want to run, even though he knew there was nowhere to go. Now, perhaps, was the time to jump into the sea, the only place for escape, but his legs were rooted to the deck. He was crew, and as such told himself he had to stay and help, however tragic the outcome might be.

Pouring, bucketing rain continued, and it was in the middle of the worst of the torrential downpour that an ominous grating sound was heard, instantly revealing itself as metal touching rock. It was this that caused the panic. Suddenly, the bucking deck was awash with people, passengers rushing from their dinner tables as soon as the reek of fear spread.

All were desperate to reach the top deck, to find fresh air, and for many the next moments were lost in a rabid blur. Fights almost broke out over the lifeboats, children were hauled over shoulders in screaming darkness, and the Tamarind literally started shuddering. Then her lights went out - and the blackness was total.

Billy found he was crying, which made him feel nauseated by his own weakness. Someone yelled at him because he was seen as among those in charge. They were wanting help, wanting to know why the lights had gone. All he could do was mumble that he couldn't answer that question, for he didn't know the engines had been flooded, which meant the generators were no longer working.

Faces continued to push past him, disbelief at the chaos around them written across their blurred features. Distressingly, he found himself caught up in the mass of charging, sodden bodies, a cacophony of distress, and a crowd of arms and legs.

Desperation, and blind dread, left him retching until he was actually sick, although such was the confusion that no-one noticed him spewing up, not even those who were almost on top of him at the time. His ears were ringing, his stomach churning beyond credibility. All he did want at that moment was to disappear, to have the terror taken away. Then he realised that, in the midst of it all, someone else was yelling just at him.

'Give us a bloody hand. Get moving. We've got to free some lifeboats, else only a handful of these poor devils will get through this alive.'

It was the man who had been speaking to him only fifteen minutes before, a quarter of an hour which seemed like three decades.

'I can't, I can't do anything.'

'Do you want the children to die? We've got to do something. The boats are tangled in the ropes.'

The old man grasped Billy by the shoulder and dragged him over to the side of the vessel.

With the rain pummelling his face the youngest Rosevean could hardly distinguish any shapes as he was dragged to the side of the ship, then pushed into one of the lifeboats and forced to use his hands to feel for the ropes which were preventing it from dropping freely.

'Was that a warning shot just now?' he yelled, at the top of his voice, stumbling and falling at the same time, because a number of the passengers were trying to scramble over him into the boat.

'Course it was. We're meant to be three miles off the coast, but there's no way we are. That'll be a warning from the coastguard. We haven't reached Falmouth yet and the Manacles are somewhere round here. It's that thought that's chilling my blood, together with the rising water.'

As if catching the mood of swirling fright the cattle could be heard above the screams of people and the wind, stamping and calling louder. The herdsmen were trying to quieten them, with little result.

'Are we going to go down? Billy wheezed, still fighting with the ropes, and ducking flailing limbs at the same time.

'We've altered course, that's something. Didn't you feel her? Perhaps we won't need the boats after all.'

That last thought allowed some relief to begin flooding into Billy's body. His legs started to regain a bit of strength, while his blue, cold fingers which were fiddling desperately with the ropes started working with more certainty. And then there was another grating sound, this being one that rent the air with a finality that could not be disputed. The screeching stopped for a second, a deathly hush falling in its place. Then the water was pouring in from all sides, and the deck listing to such an angle that it would never right itself again, together convincing all on board that there were only mere minutes left until she disappeared beneath the waves.

She had been driven right onto the Minstrel Rock, at the heart of the Manacles.

Billy was pushed out of the way as more hands tore at the lifeboat. He watched on horrified as cattle stampeded out of their pens and charged both into the sea and into the crowds of distraught passengers.

Thinking that death was fast approaching, he closed his eyes and jumped, wanting the water to swallow him, wanting an end to it all. He didn't want to be afraid any more.

Spring 1878

V

Suzannah had changed out of all recognition. Nathan fully accepted that fact after she had lived in the same house as him for over three months. He had suffered a relapse following the evening when he had pulled himself along to Joe's grave. That had overtaxed his strength, proving to him that he had been idiotic to think he was fit before the healing process had had time to finish.

His wounds had re-opened and he had even started bleeding internally. With him bed-bound Suzannah's presence had become undeniably necessary once more. But during the extra weeks of necessary inactivity, he began to despise his weakness to such an extent that he wondered whether it was worth battling for fitness again. Would recovery ever come? The doctor had gone as far as warning him that if he did too much too quickly again he could inflict permanent damage that would serve only to shorten his life.

During his weeks of enforced inactivity he realised that the girl who had been achingly lovely had not only obviously aged, she had also become drab, downcast and characterless. As he lay there, staring at her while she tackled the cooking and the mundane, menial tasks that she now seemed to revel in, it seemed incredible to him that she had once almost succeeded in seducing him.

Now, she hardly spoke above a whisper, as if her opinions were of no worth. She never looked in a mirror to re-arrange hair, or inspect her looks. Never now would she dream of painting her face, he thought, and it seemed to him that if any man called to see him she would shy away from them as if they reeked of evil.

Although the change in her was so evident to him, he thought he'd no right to ask her questions as to why she had changed to such a degree, as since her arrival at Tombstone she had never attempted to pry into his life. Not as she had once wanted to do on every possible occasion.

Part of him had suspected that once he had accepted her into his routine, and she had realised he was as good as at her mercy, all that would begin to change. That her previously wayward, strong personality would come to the fore and she would take over both himself and his life, basic as it was.

Undoubtedly, such suspicions were wrong. There was no threat to the masculine isolation of his home. It was as if he was living side by side with someone who had no views, opinions, or even personal needs of her own. When she nursed him she only touched him if entirely necessary. The hands never strayed as they would have done back in the days of Grass Valley, when Joe was still alive. Her eyes also never gave a hint of any depth of longing. It seemed that the old Suzannah had died, and another, unknown being, had stepped into the empty shell of her body.

Her father's death continued to plague him, dogging his thoughts as the crossing had done during his first few years in America. As Lorna, or rather the memory of her, still did. Night after night he awoke sweating and soundlessly screaming, seeing only Joe shooting himself, reading the blind hate written across his face that he was to blast away by his own hand.

Self-reproach remained, for surely he must have been culpable of something to provoke such violence, and keeping Suzannah with him, providing her with a safe four walls, was to him some form of atonement. But he had not buried the idea of travelling back to Grass Valley to discover the reason why Joe had sought him out again, to try to kill him. He just had to wait until he was definitely recovered, definitely fully back to health.

Even though Nathan had come to accept Suzannah as the meek and mild creature she had supposedly metamorphosed into, Henry felt very differently about her. She both intrigued and worried him. Despite knowing it was none of his business, and being well aware that any journalistic interest in Joe's suicide had long since passed, he could not help but feel entangled in the case. In almost paternal fashion, he wanted to protect Nathan from further hurt, and was also convinced that there were good reasons why Suzannah was so far from forthcoming about her father. Very rarely did she mention either his suicide, or her mother, or her previous life, in any detail whatsoever. It was as if she had wiped it all from her memory, something which was, to him, unfathomable.

He arrived one evening to collect the copy that Nathan had been writing on the increasing demise of the Cornish tin industry. At the sight of him Suzannah scuttled away, as if any contact with him would contaminate her. Undeniably, she always seemed uneasy in his company, which added to Henry's belief that she could sense his doubts about her.

'I see she's still here,' he began as soon as she had softly shut the door behind her and left Nathan's room. 'I thought by now she'd have moved back to whence she came from. Life with you as an invalid must be about as exciting as watching dust fly around in scrubland.'

Nathan shifted his position in the bed and sighed audibly. Suzannah had become an enigma he preferred not to think about any more.

'She's nowhere else to go.'

'She's got a home in Grass Valley,' his editor answered curtly, fixing himself a small drink and pulling up a rickety chair from which he first removed a haphazard pile of mining volumes.

'You know I want her to get back there as soon as possible,' stressed Nathan, trying to placate him, and thinking simultaneously that Henry himself was also a bit of an enigma. When was he ever open about his past?

He added: 'And there are other reasons why I

want to go back there myself, not just to ensure she is out of my life for good.'

'I'd wager a lot of money you'll never get her to set foot outside this town again. That girl, woman, whatever she is, is going to cling on like blazes to this little nest she's made for herself here. This is where she feels safe. There is something she definitely does not want you to face. She must know more about what drove her father to try to kill you than she's ever let on. It's plainly obvious that she must know some, or all, of the answers.'

They were re-visiting a tired, old argument. 'You know very well that I think the same way as you do. At the moment, though, if I mention Joe's name she doesn't speak to me for days on end. She swears she doesn't know, or understand, anything. Each time I venture to mention her father she maintains the same story, that he must have had a brainstorm, that she did her best to stop him, that he had been behaving wildly for weeks.'

'You no more believe any of that than I do,' replied Henry, almost falling off the unsteady chair and, to his dismay, knocking over some of his brandy.

All right, maybe I don't swallow it, or at least all of it. On the other hand, do I really want to know the answers? Would knowing why achieve anything? Would it instead be like opening Pandora's box?'

They eventually wearied themselves with the conversation, progressing after a while from Suzannah and the mysteries she presented, to more mundane matters.

Between them they had been compiling some background information on the Earps, who were buying up more of the town as each day went by. The brothers had spent most of their childhood in Illinois and Iowa, later moving with their parents to San Bernardino in California. Wyatt, who was yet to arrive, but who was said to be intrigued by the growing number of discoveries of silver, was currently in the Black Hills of Dakota after gold. By all accounts he had already been a stagecoach driver and a buffalo hunter, as well as a Wells Fargo agent.

Henry was secretly looking forward to Wyatt's arrival in Tombstone, if it ever did happen the way his brothers were promising. By all accounts he would provide plenty of copy.

V1

The strike was over. The union had been strangled at birth. The defiance and the boiling tempers, and the quest for justice, had run their course. It had been ended by a joint need, that of the men for money, for food, for the basic necessities, and that of the owners to put their pits back to work before bankruptcy crept up and destroyed their businesses.

For the clay workers there was the matter of having to bury immediate hopes of forming a joint force. Nevertheless, they gleaned minute satisfaction from the fact that those who had been sacked for joining the premature 'baby union' were reinstated. That meant that when they returned together there was at least among some of them the burning belief that the owners could not deny them their aims for long. The idea of combined strength had merely been set aside for future resurrection. When Alex and James next met at the Bodmin pits they had reverted to the roles of boss and worker, Alex having been re-hired along with all others. Antagonism simmered, though never past sparring. Both fires had been quenched a good deal during the previous weeks.

Alex opened the latest bout of such sparring as they stood side by side, faces towards the wind, surrounded by vast banks of white, as well as by shadows, chimneys and clouds of flying white dust which grimed every pore, and by ravens hovering on slip-streams above. 'I hear you've been expanding while we've been starving,' he said, glancing upwards at his older brother who was taller by a good four inches. 'Latest reports insist that you and your father-in-law grasped the opportunity to snap up four more pits, at rock bottom prices, all near Hensbarrow.'

James hesitated before answering, wishing only to be left alone. At that moment he hadn't the vigour to tackle conversations with Alex. And it seemed strange to him that his reputation as a businessman appeared to have been growing by the day, at the same rate as his spirits had been diminishing.

'You heard right, but it wasn't entirely my idea.'

'You were merely the yes man.'

'Maybe.'

'Well whatever lay behind it you're apparently well on your way to becoming a very important man in these parts, exactly what you always wanted to be,' stressed Alex sharply, though not with enough venom to display traces of true irony. 'You must be fast entering the big league. The Stocker and Martin families better protect their interests. You're obviously after becoming the grandest clay company owner in Kernow.'

The paltry sun was lighting on James, on his

wide shoulders and fair hair, though the shining mane of hair wasn't as distinctive any more, and despite Alex's words the image of the all-conquering hero seemed to have faded slightly.

'Hardly, I've enough worries at the moment without trying to quadruple them. You and your kind have no idea what a strain these last months have been for owners.' Quickly, he added: 'They've been bad for you, I know. We've suffered as well, though, remember that.'

The resentment rose to the surface then. With little encouragement Alex could have flattened him.

'Mental strain maybe James, but I'm certain you didn't have to worry yourself senseless about whether or not there would be enough food on the table for the next meal, or if your children have had enough to eat. Or even if you'll be locked up by magistrates, the same way Peter and Edwin were. I don't think you have any idea what worries are.'

'Don't exaggerate, don't throw in my face the one in a thousand case,' snapped James quickly, wanting to obliterate such thoughts.

'Exaggerating am I? You come down from your fancy new beliefs and return to your roots for a few days, go back to the cottages where they manage to scrape a living if they're lucky, though really never get any further, and you'll quickly rediscover what I mean.'

At that James walked away. There was enough on his conscience without burdening himself with more. In fact, he couldn't bear any more. Since Richard had taken on extra work as part of the business expansion that Alex had referred to, and then passed it onto his 'company partner', James had found his life utterly dominated by meetings, paperwork, bills and demands.

They preoccupied his thoughts, especially when he was away from his home, which still had not been anywhere near properly repaired. And, when he had tried to point out how fast the work was accumulating and threatening to drown him, Richard had merely stared at him in annoyed amazement. Such absorption was all that he had ever wanted from his own life. 'You sleep at Tregrehan, sometimes,' he had stressed with a sly emphasis, as the story of James's night at the Sun Inn was now public knowledge. 'Isn't that enough? I find that the more absent I am from my home, despite all its admitted attractions, the better I am.'

James had answered softly: 'I don't quite see things in the same light as you evidently do.'

'You could have fooled me. Your attitude over the last years seems to have mirrored mine exactly. I wasn't being fooled was I?'

'No . . no, you weren't wrong,' James admitted, his confidence sagging as he realised how far he was slipping away from being the person he had tried to mould himself into. Over the past months he was beginning to accept that he no longer had a tight grip on what to Richard were realities, on issues that he had stupidly and recklessly assumed he had totally mastered.

That evening, he and Helen were due to dine out. They had been invited to the home of a family from whom Richard and James were buying one of the four pits, and for once his wife had been included in the invitation. A few weeks before, when the strike had still been on and the future had remained so uncertain, he would have refused to go. But, with some of the problems apparently easing he considered he could, maybe, stand some socialising.

It shook him to realise that it would be the first time he had taken Helen out to dine for almost a year. It seemed that, without knowing it, he had deliberately adopted the habit of going everywhere on his own. It was, after all, the way Richard worked, on the surmise that the less his wife, or anyone else, knew what he was doing the better. In the initial heady year of pit ownership James had assumed it was the best way to handle business meetings of any kind.

At that moment in time, and during many moments afterwards, he hadn't wanted to listen to Helen's views on the rights and wrongs of a deal, or even any trivial reflection of hers.

Although he had come to alter such ideas slightly, he believed Helen had reached a stage where she preferred to be uninvolved. Undoubtedly, she didn't hide the fact she felt little empathy with the company he kept, and she frequently reminded him that she had endured enough of what she termed as false owner class pomp when living at 'Trevarnioc'.

This, though, was to be a meal with a family, not with a clutch of money-orientated men, and he felt it was a different occasion than most. Alex and Richard had combined to delay him, and he arrived home an hour after he promised, giving himself only 30 minutes before they had to depart for their dinner date at Porthpean, and hoping that the ride by pony and trap would not take too long.

By then his mind was barely working, still half caught up in a replay of the exchange he had had with his brother. Helen was already ready, dressed in a plain but alluring powder blue outfit, her hair which she usually wore straight and loose, curled for once and swept up on top of her head.

The style should have made her look more fashionable. Instead, he felt that it served to make her seem younger and more sensitive. When he finally arrived she made no mention of the time. In fact, she hardly acknowledged him at all, and he went upstairs to change, in a subdued mood. The house was still in the process of being virtually rebuilt. There may have remained little outward trace of the fire. On the inside, however, it was different, as they still hadn't bothered to refurbish past the basics. That took more effort than either was prepared to give, and as a result the warm, homely atmosphere that Helen had originally created had fled. By most standards the house was grand, but it was now purely plain, damaged in very many places, and functional at best in others.

When James returned downstairs she was sitting in one of the chairs that Alex had given them from the family cottage at Biscovey, and was reading. There was no sound of childish laughter. Glynn, who had started to grow tall and gawky during the previous months, had gone to stay the night with a neighbour. James, suddenly feeling awkward in front of her, sat down opposite his young wife and studied her awhile, even though it was time to leave.

'Why don't you wear the necklace I bought you last week?' he asked, trying to crack the polite ice that was always noticeable between them. 'That and one of the bracelets. I bought them especially so that they would match.'

'I'm all right, I'm fine without them,' she insisted, glancing at the marble clock on the mantelshelf and reluctantly putting her book aside.

'No .. no, come on. They cost me a great deal and I'd like to see you wearing them. I do believe they would go well with the colour of your dress, and set off that hairstyle of yours.' Determined to make sure that she at least tried on the jewellery, he took her hand and dragged her upstairs and into her bedroom, which happened to be the smallest of the rooms in the house. Glynn generally slept in the room opposite, with James having set up a bed for himself downstairs in his study.

He opened the top drawer of her newly-bought dressing table where he knew all her jewellery was now kept. Not locked in a safe as he had so often urged her to do. It had amazed him that, during the riots, when their bedrooms had been overrun by those intent on destruction, the most valuable of her items had been overlooked, or missed in the dark. The furniture had been smashed to firewood, but the jewellery had been discovered afterwards, right at the back of a surviving drawer in the rubble.

He sorted through the items, all of which lay unopened and still in their boxes. His assumption was that they had stayed untouched because he hadn't taken her anywhere grand enough to warrant her wearing them.

Smiling, he took a newly acquired diamond and pearl necklace out of its wrapping and draped it around her neck. Then he pinned a white gold brooch with pearls set in it onto her dress, making a show of positioning it properly. At that her youthful look vanished.

The gems added worldliness to her.
'What do you think?' he asked, standing behind her, making her stare at her reflection and, for once, sparing a few moments to take pride in her appearance. 'You really do look lovely tonight. Now tell me what you see in that mirror. You've changed so much since I pulled you out of the waves. I must admit most of the time I fail to grasp just how much you have grown up.'
But when she turned around to look at him, he was surprised by the bleak expression on her face.
'Do you honestly want to know what I see?'
'Of course.'
'Well, I don't see myself at all, I see my mother.'
That shook him.
'Surely not? I've never seen any comparisons between you two, or you and your father for that matter. In fact I've often wondered if you have any of their respective traits at all.'
Gently, but decisively, she took off both necklace and brooch, placing them back into their flimsy wrappings and then their boxes. When she clicked the catches on the boxes shut the noise sounded sharp and direct, like an unspoken challenge.
'When I was living at home, every month or so my father would buy my mother jewellery, as far back I suppose as I can remember. Of course, he didn't buy out of love, but because he hadn't been home for weeks on end. And if that wasn't the reason it was because an important function was coming up, and he wanted others to see his wife luxuriously dressed.
She was, is, you understand I'm sure, the living example of his so-called generosity.

Eventually he gave her so much she could have opened a shop herself, if she had wanted to, and I can see her now, standing for hours in front of a mirror like this, preening herself, admiring her wealth. It was all she had left you see, all she still has, and it is all so pathetically meaningless.'

'Hardly meaningless,' he protested, feeling that just at the moment when he had thought he was moving closer to her she was, in truth, slipping away from him again. 'She must be worth a fortune by now.'

Helen slammed the drawer shut.

'Wealth, power, that's all you and my blasted father can think of. What good has it ever done her? Diamonds, emeralds, rubies, they don't offer any real warmth. She's got trinkets, nothing else. No loving husband, no-one to care for her with any feeling, to make her laugh, to give her a healthy sense of reality. Well if you think I'm so easily bought, and you believe you can persuade me to put that junk before real living, I'm afraid you're in a dream world. I want none of it.'

Never before had she spoken to him so passionately, not under all the provocation he had given her, not even when she had known he had slept with another woman. And now . . when he had only tried to be concerned, to take notice. . .

'My stars, they were presents, that's all. I'll sell them if you want, if that will set your mind at rest.'

Carefully, she re-opened the drawer, took out the stacks of boxes, and handed them to him, one by one.

'That's a good idea, though only if you're going to use the money wisely. It might help some of those who actually went without food during the strike, and I can assure you many did. A few of them, I believe, your friends from years back.'

Exasperated, he threw the jewellery on the bed.

'Well, as these trinkets undoubtedly haven't made you happy, what will? You only have to let me know. Unfortunately, I can't read minds, so I wouldn't be able to make a near enough guess.'

'That's it. You don't know what gives me pleasure, do you, or what pleases Glynn for that matter, because you've never bothered to find out. You don't know what I'm interested in, what I do with all the hours when you're not here.' She picked up her coat from the back of the chair, throwing it around her shoulders, then put on her gloves. 'Well, I suppose it's a bit late for me to worry about that now. I've accepted the way we've gone and I've learnt not to ask for more. I do want you to realise, however, that I object to the way you try to buy me, so save your money and don't bother with any more false gestures. Now come on, or we'll be late and they might retaliate by placing an extra £3,000 on the price of the pit. Then what on earth would my father say?'

That literally staggered him. They usually chatted indifferently, touching on matters that didn't have one iota of importance attached to them, skirting around anything that they might feel deeply about. Now that she had laid her true emotions bare, it pained him to discover that he could be hurt by knowing how great the gulf was between them.

Summer 1878

V11

When they reached Sara Pendray's house, perched precariously on the cliffs above Porthpean beach, James's mood was sour. It was not improved by the fact that the pretentious hostess, daughter of a Mevagissey fisherman and now wife to a man who had clawed his way to respectability through more foul means than fair, was decked in gems that did little bar enhance the wrinkles on her neck and her ageing, scrawny wrists.

Beside her Helen shone, mainly because she was bereft of jewellery and let her own personality burst through.

Also, within the space of a few minutes, James knew instinctively that he had made a mistake in bringing his wife. It was not going to be the cosy little family gathering Richard had outlined.

He found the Pendrays liked to exude the wealth which they, like him, had once only aspired to. They had an overdressed and over-polite butler who answered the door with much affectation, and a flurry of maids who had ensured the table was laid with silver and glistening cut glass. As the Roseveans were slightly late they sat down to the silver and glass, and to the meal, almost straight away.

When they were seated the talk also began immediately, even though it was stilted and brittle, mostly aimed at the impudence shown by the workers during the recent strike.

As he listened to their cutting tones, and raucous condemnations, James couldn't block out the words that Alex had spoken with such derision: 'Go back to your roots'.

He almost found himself repeating them to Sara Pendray in much the same fashion as he had unexpectedly given voice to inner feelings at the owners' meeting. That, and the very artificiality of the occasion, unnerved him still further.

In Alex's eyes, and probably in Helen's as well, he thought, I'm classed in the same bracket as these blinkered idiots. I'm even more powerful than this family because of Richard's backing, and isn't that what I've been striving for since I first set foot in 'Trevarnioc'? Isn't it what I've been making sacrifices for?

The Pendrays' two sons, both in their mid-twenties, were also at the table. Each was being groomed for the family's banking hierarchy and in turn had been cutting their teeth on financial matters. As they progressed through the meal's varied courses neither of them tried to hide the fact that they were unexpectedly taken with Helen, so rarely seen outside Tregrehan. It was almost as if they were vying for her attention.

James stopped trying to separate salmon flesh from bones for a moment, during his third course, and shot a disguised glance at his wife. Despite her mature choice of dress and the poise she had adopted for the occasion she still seemed to him more like the young girl who had run along sands and skipped over rocks than the mother of a young child and the wife of a supposed man of business.

But he was to discover in the next thirty minutes, or so, that when she was forced into a corner she could become more than a good conversationalist. After a tricky start, when she froze in front of her hosts, he noticed her make a sterling effort to relax in their company.

For herself, Helen knew within moments that

despite the high class veneer the Pendrays were no-one to be afraid of. Once she had gained confidence in herself she did not draw back from stating her own views on the subjects they mentioned, both local and national, even though that was not always the accepted move in such masculine company. Quietly, but determinedly, she made it obvious she was as much for the clay workers as they were against them.

All the while she was very much aware that the main explanation for why they were sitting back and taking in what she was saying, rather than talking her down, was because she was the daughter of Richard Courteney. For once she didn't let that factor worry her.

First of all they had dwelt on matters which had occurred over the last couple of years, among them the Russo-Turkish war in which Disraeli had supported Turkey, and the Prime Minister's success in persuading parliament to grant Queen Victoria the title of Empress of India.

The struggles between the Liberal party, led by Gladstone, and the Conservatives, which were all continuing apace, were highlighted as well as the knowledge that the relationship between the Queen and Gladstone was much more stormy than sunny.

With the year 1878, topics of the moment were, as well, the work Samuel Plimsoll was undertaking, aimed at preventing ship owners sending unseaworthy or overloaded ships to sea, and the objections from factory owners which were being put forward to the proposed Workshops Act. Under this act all workshops and factories employing more than 50 people were to be inspected regularly by government inspectors rather than by local authorities, as had happened previously.

Local matters debated included the possibility of the slurry from the china clay pits being piped to the dries on the quaysides at Par, Charlestown and Pentewan. All believed that this would mean that the need to use the railways would become out of date.

The Pendrays talked animatedly of how the old methods of air-drying at the pits had largely been overtaken by coal-fired kilns, or dries, how beam engines had laid waterwheels to waste and how the new mineral lines which were being constructed would eventually see the end of the use of horse and cart as well.

Helen's spirits seemed to heighten throughout the evening, as much through the good wine as anything else, and as her cheeks flushed and her usually downcast eyes sparkled, and provoked, James discovered that each of the sons appeared to be taken enough to begin openly flirting with her.

Alarmingly, as he sat and watched them prime her with questions about the strike and appear more than interested in her replies, and as he saw each reach out at the least opportunity to touch her hand or her hair, something that felt remarkably like jealousy began to snake into his heart. At the table she was seated opposite him, and he deliberately turned to Elaine Pendray, the daughter, on his right and tried to engage her in conversation, rather than continuing to watch Helen. It was not easy. True to her family tradition, she preferred to talk endlessly of company matters in which he had come to realise, very slowly, that his interest was fast evaporating.

The flirting continued, as he saw it, after the over-blown, exhausting meal was finally finished. While he continued to be embroiled in petty, technical details about his take-over of the Pendrays' pit his wife remained at the far end of the L shaped room, with its subtle pastel and peach colours, its array of mirrors cleverly arranged to make it look more spacious than it was in reality, and its elegant furniture.

Once more, he struggled to ignore her, then found he could not. Whenever he turned towards her she seemed relaxed and radiant, laughing completely naturally with the two young men she had not seen until three hours earlier. In fact, she was secretly revelling in the attention, the more so when she felt her husband's eyes upon her.

Why not make the most of it, she thought. It's only harmless fun. I'll probably never run into the Pendrays again, and I've been starved of masculine attention throughout my life, first with father and then his damned alter ego over there. I deserve a little attention, surely?

James knew she did, too, and because of that let it all pass without a word, and said nothing to her about the manner in which each had kept up with their company as they let their horse pick her way home in the dark to Tregrehan. His spirit was uneasy, though. The jealousy remained, and appeared to be growing within him, like an amorphous being. It finally told him what he had refused to admit to himself since the morning when he had awoken in a grubby, unknown bed which belonged to a stranger. He had finally fallen in love with his wife.

The trouble was that en route he had alienated her so much he feared she no longer cared for him.

V111

Nathan looked across the dour room at Suzannah, head bent over a calico dress which she was laboriously mending, although it had been stitched and re-stitched so often he wondered if it could stand the strains of being repaired again. It was one of the dresses she wore persistently.
Gone were the clinging red velvet and the provocative satin she used to prance through the streets in. Gradually, he had come to realise that she deliberately refused to spend money on herself any more, which amazed him, because ordering clothes had been a passion. He only had to close his eyes and he could envisage her, and her mother, in Grass Valley striving to outdo each other with tales of the latest fashions from at home and abroad.
After his months of sapping, hated illness and injury he was feeling real strength flooding back. It was an overwhelming relief to be almost healthy again; to be able to fend for himself once more; to regain independence; to walk for miles on his own; to be able to think in the open air and experience a warmth burning on his bare shoulders and glowing on his skin.
Over the long weeks of inactivity he had grown to hate his quarters, despise their stale smell and near complete lack of natural light. Obviously, his tan had faded through the months of inactivity, his muscles had wasted, and his sinews were like jelly, but he knew normality was within his grasp again.
Nevertheless, hints of re-emergent peace were marred by the fact that Lorna hadn't contacted him for a long, long while. Through her letters

she had told him about Samuel's death, and he had thought that she would, as a result, find it easier to pour out her feelings to him, even though it had to be through the medium of pen and paper. He had even harboured a distant hope that she might consider travelling out to America to be with him. That hadn't occurred. Since the shooting there hadn't been one line. When the knock came he had been contemplating going to sleep early. Having walked about seven miles that afternoon, the exertion was beginning to tell, reminding him for the umpteenth occasion that he had to take recovery very slowly. Without speaking, Suzannah put her work down in a neat pile and opened the door. Nathan knew better now than to argue with her about her exceptionally meek desire to play servant, accepting that if that was what she wanted then so be it, for the present at least.
The visitor was Henry who barged his way in and pushed her roughly aside before rolling into the tiny, main room all too obviously drunk. It wasn't just his manner that betrayed him. He absolutely reeked of cheap whisky. Suzannah had shrunk away from him, but somehow managed to say: 'Nathan's just about to go to sleep. He's tired.'
In answer Henry unsteadily pulled off his huge, heavy jacket and attempted to throw it at her.
'When the master of this shack of a home tells me himself that he's off to bed and wants me gone then I'll leave. When I hear it from you, a nothing, a nobody, then I'll ignore it totally.'
Once she would have stood up for herself with all the fury of a wounded lioness. This time she reacted merely by staring at Nathan, her eyes pleading with him, as if expecting

him to defend her. Instead, he said absolutely nothing, although he was quietly cursing them both. All he wanted was rest and isolation, certainly not melodramatics.

'Come on in Henry,' he said at last, with a distinct lack of enthusiasm, 'but control that temper of yours. It doesn't show very often, but once someone's riled you then you're a difficult man to deal with.'

Henry merely grunted in reply, so Nathan continued: 'Where have you been for the last five days then? I trust you haven't been drinking for all of them. I don't think I've ever seen you in such a state, although I suppose there's a first time for everything. You also could rival me as I was back when I was in the mountains by the look of your clothes.'

Henry perched himself by the table, covered in papers and books as always. Nathan glowered at him until he realised that not only were the man's eyes sunken and rimmed with red, they were also infinitely sad. The usual sardonic humour was totally absent. This was a stranger. As a result, he decided it was for the best to stop talking and keep quiet instead, and after a minute or two his boss spoke in a gravely, disjointed voice.

'I can't really remember how much I've had, but then you see disappointment, misery, always has driven me to the bottle. Stupid isn't it - at my great age I should be used to it now, and be able to beat both the bottle and all that desperation.'

'Being able to handle dejection is a tall order for anyone. But are you talking about anything specific, or is this only a usual dissatisfaction with life?'

'Dissatisfaction with you, I'm afraid, dear

boy. Unfortunately, with you specifically, I'm afraid.'

That stunned and confused him. Nathan lent forward, his lean, wasted features showing more interest than they had for several weeks. 'Why, is it something I've written? It can't be something I've gone out and done, I've been cooped in here for weeks upon wretched weeks.'

Henry took obvious note of Suzannah, hovering like a wayward spirit in the background, worry showing even through the scanty twilight in the features that could never be truly plain, no matter how much she might try to disguise, or even disfigure, them.'

Nathan followed his gaze.

'Whatever it is, leave Suzannah alone. There really is no reason to feel so antagonistic towards her.'

His words fell on a closed mind.

'When are you both off to Grass Valley then Nathan? Your recovery's gone well in the past three weeks. I can see a real vast improvement in you.'

'I'm planning to leave reasonably soon. I have to say, though, that one thing I've learnt in the past months is that there's no rush. Grass Valley isn't going to disintegrate overnight. It'll be there, waiting for me, with all the answers I want, whenever I feel strong enough again to go.'

'Soon, you bastard. Never you mean.'

The tension in the room heightened. Suzannah could feel herself breaking out in an instant rash with the stress of it. The perspiration also stood out sharply on her brow. What did she feel most, fear or anger, for this stupid, wizened wreck of a man who had made such a ridiculous, illogical attachment to Nathan?

Nathan himself was in some confusion about what was happening. Was it some form of accusation for unknown misdeeds, or confrontation about something that he was supposedly planning?

'I meant exactly what I said,' he protested, imagining that whatever the impetus behind Henry's arrival that evening, he was about to be put under a sustained attack for some unquantified reason. 'I'll go as soon as I'm fit enough. You know very well that it won't be a gentle stroll down to Crinnis Beach, near where I used to live in Cornwall, will it? Everything's a trek in this enormous country, even though the train will take me some of the way.'

'For the respect of what friendship we have, or did have, don't lie to me, don't take me for a fool, any more,' Henry yelled. 'I know now that there's no point at all in you returning there.'

'Pray let me in on the secret then,' said Nathan icily, furiously wondering whether the drink was talking, or whether Henry really did have an idea what he was rambling on about. 'I don't know any reason why I shouldn't.'

'Because you already, absolutely, know why Joe tried to kill you.'

Suzannah intervened then, literally throwing herself between them so that she tripped and tumbled onto Nathan. As she was shaking violently this made it harder for her to try to steady herself.

'Please leave him alone, Mr Sears,' she screamed. 'Can't you see he should be resting, not listening to all of this?'

All thoughts of rest had now utterly vanished for Nathan who was on his feet, still unable to grasp what was happening.

'Don't get so upset trying to protect me Suzannah, this argument has nothing to do with you. Save your breath. I want to know exactly what Henry's getting at.'

'But he's drunk, he doesn't know what he's saying.'

Nathan continued staring directly at Henry, whose desperately sad, rheumy eyes seemed to be blazing with almost manic zeal.

'Maybe, though it might help him. He seems to be desperate to accuse me of something. Let him talk.'

His reply was not quite what Henry had been anticipating, but by that stage he was past caring. Betrayal hurt him. It had happened many times before, and destroyed his faith too often before.

'I'm a journalist, remember,' he spat. 'I was in the game long before you blundered along. I don't play at it for the sake of producing pages of beautiful words. I write stories. I don't ignore puzzles, instead I try to solve them.'

'Now you're talking in riddles,' Nathan retorted bitingly, 'and it's too late in the day for you to expect me to start unravelling them.'

Henry, who was not as senseless with drink as had first appeared, leant forward so that he was only inches from Nathan's face.

'Don't you think that stealing a man's savings and making his daughter pregnant before running like hell is a good enough reason for attempting murder? Does that make the riddle simpler for you to understand?'

No-one spoke for a long, tortuous, moment but a small mewing sound escaped from Suzannah's drained lips.

Eventually Nathan breathed: 'What . . what

have you been throwing down your throat,
Henry. You're talking complete nonsense.'
Then Suzannah, knowing she would have to
move or faint, grabbed Henry's arm, clutching
on to it with a searing intensity.

'Go, please, before you make him relapse.
Can't you see the state he's in? He doesn't
understand any of these, these malicious
tales.'

'Tales are they? So this old Irishman I've
been speaking to, who knows all there is
about Grass Valley and the Cornish who've
lived there these past five years was wrong
was he? He imagined that you, my gorgeous
little virgin, or so you would try to have us all
believe, was pregnant. That you give birth to a
little boy.'

'Stop it, stop it now, you idiot.'

Tears hung in dramatic droplets on
Suzannah's luxuriant eyelashes, refusing to
fall, only distorting the honey-coloured eyes.
She refused to give him the satisfaction of her
complete breakdown.

By this stage Nathan was very aware that
none of what was happening was due to an
inebriated game. Tension gripped him like a
vice. The trouble was he still wasn't quite sure
why, although he grasped, with great clarity,
that Henry's accusations had hit home with
Suzannah.

'Don't upset yourself. There's no need. What
he says is untrue, so it can't hurt you that
much,' he said, hoping to ease both her and
the developing situation. All he wanted was
for the unbearable tension to ease. As he
hadn't really taken in any of Henry's claims,
deep unease hadn't yet entered his soul.

'You don't understand. He wants to destroy
us, both of us.'

Seeing by his response that Nathan might prove to be a saviour she hadn't bargained on, Suzannah grabbed him round the waist, wanting his physical reassurance. Carefully, he disengaged himself.

'Just go into the other room. Don't take what he's saying to heart. We are both aware that he knows nothing about you. I'm sure I can sort this out.'

'But he can hurt me, believe me. You have to understand.'

Nathan, who remained totally bemused, then turned his full, undiluted, attention on Henry who was watching on with an expression of utter contempt on his aquiline features.

'Where did you meet this Irishman then, in your befuddled, alcoholic dreams? Or have you travelled to Grass Valley and back in these last five days. Fly like the birds did you?'

'No. I could have made most of the journey by train remember, though, as you just pointed out. However, there was no need for me to go anywhere. I met him purely by accident, right here. Amazingly, he was drinking alongside me in the saloon, and passed out across my bar stool, which rather endeared him to me. When he came back to consciousness we got to talking. They were ramblings at first, maybe, but in my befuddled brain some things started to make sense. He knew your Joe, and you and your fame because of that pump you two apparently managed to design, very, very well.'

'He probably met Joe once. How can you believe whatever nonsense he told you about? These towns are full of drifters prepared to tell you whatever you want to hear. They'll say anything for another shot of whisky.'

'He knew exactly why Joe wanted to kill you, that's what he knew. How on earth did you expect to keep it quiet for so long? It was hardly a secret in Grass Valley now was it?'
At that Nathan bellowed at him, giving full rein to the frustration which had been building up inside him during the months he had been caged in his lodgings.
'Well it's a secret that's damned well been kept from me. Stop talking rubbish, and just tell me. Tell me.'
'Why? You very well know my dear, upstanding boy what that man confided in me. You must know. You ran out on Joe, and you left her very much with child.' He nodded towards Suzannah. 'And before you left their home, the home you had been given refuge in, you calmly stole all his money. But then, for someone who was once accused of murder, that is nothing, I suppose.'
All Nathan's precious, new-found strength was slipping away from him, being steamrolled by a stream of lies.
'You think I did that and never mentioned a word, after all the trust there's been between us, and that there was also between Joe and I? You think I did that? And you've always known that I was once accused of murder, very wrongly I have to stress. I told you. I explained everything when you hired me.'
Henry scowled at the surroundings in contempt.
'The way you two have been holed up here recently, I would say yes to all allegations. You've listened to nothing and no-one since she came.'
'Well let's get one fact straight. There's no way Suzannah could have had my child. It's physically impossible. If she did have my

baby then it's definitely worth a front page lead because it must have been the Second Coming.'

Suzannah felt both pairs of eyes burn into her, and she realised there was no escape. How could she have ever believed that there could be? This was the price then for greed and the selfish, Godforsaken blindness of youth? Closing her own eyes, so that she didn't have to look into their eyes, she spoke quickly, thinking that perhaps the faster the words were out the less impact they would create.

'My father was always foolish when it came to me. He believed everything I said. I think that I lied to him ever since I can remember, and he always swallowed every little story. If I had told him that the sea had turned red he would have taken it for truth and assumed himself colour-blind.'

Nathan was reeling. His headache, which had been a perpetual part of life until a fortnight before, was roaring back in force. There was a deep, sucking, ache in his chest.

'So you told him I'd made you pregnant. Why?'

'Why? she groaned, trying to control her acute distress. 'Because I warned you as much didn't I? Because I wanted revenge. You walked out on me and the spoilt little minx that I was, I wouldn't allow that, so I slept with the next man who made a move towards me. I had this stupid idea that if you somehow found out I was pregnant you'd come back. The trouble was that when the baby was born I didn't want him. You can't imagine how I felt when I realised that he looked so much like the stupid oaf I'd been with. I hate to admit it, but at that time I was even relieved when he died. Jaundice the doctor said. I've paid for that since, though. Not a night has gone by that I haven't dreamt of that baby.'

'The money,' prompted Nathan, advancing on her, quelling the bile rising within him. 'What about the money, where does that come in?'

Slowly, she shrugged her slim shoulders, as if now indifferent. From her point of view the worst had been told.

'Mother died soon after and he didn't know what was happening. I took it. It was doing nothing, just lying in a dumb box under his bed. I decided he would never have spent it on anything worthwhile.'

'And you blamed it all, everything, on me?' Nathan was trembling alarmingly, not sure if it was from shock or anger, or perhaps a dire combination of them both. With a mind in turmoil, he tried to relax knotted muscles, failing instantly.

'It was a way out, or so it seemed at the time. Like everything else I rushed into it. I didn't stop to think of what might happen as a result. God forgive me, I thought only of myself.'

'Why let him come after me, why let the lie go on for so long? You must have had some sort of idea what was going to happen when he did find me?'

At that Nathan swept away some of the stack of papers from the table, with a vicious swipe of his elbow. It was an alternative to slapping her across the face. They fell to the floor with a thud, and some half-hearted flapping, dislodging a good amount of dust. He wanted to rip them, and everything else, to shreds. For a second the old fury was well and truly upon him.

Henry merely watched on, dumbfounded, as the confessions he had triggered continued to tumble out.

'I suppose I didn't believe, wouldn't let myself believe, that he was going to go through with anything awful.' Suzannah pulled compulsively at her hair that had been savagely shorn of its tantalising curls. 'I didn't think he had the nerve. I thought they were empty threats, and besides I wanted to see you again. I tagged on behind. I guessed I had nothing to lose and everything to find, and I convinced myself his anger would slowly fizzle out, like his life that was by then ebbing out of him. His lungs were really bad at the end. Some days he could hardly get up. How wrong can you be?'

'Then what about all this caring and this nursing you've been letting consume you?' asked Nathan, cuttingly. 'What was the ultimate plan, what were you going to do eventually? Poison me, or suffocate me in my sleep and disappear with my money, what there is of it?'

She wanted to crawl away craven, like the lowest being ever created, but wouldn't let herself fold. I began this, she thought. I've got to live with it.

'I'd convinced myself I wanted you. It all came to an end when father killed himself. I'm not the same person any more. I'm a shell pretending to live. I killed my baby, I killed father, I almost killed you. It's too much to bear, and I can only deal with it all by being someone else, someone who's got no wants, and no past.'

'The damage you caused. How have you managed to cope with that, stay here with me, and keep silent about it?'

The tears fell then. They coursed in rivulets down her face, choked noisily in her throat, and totally blinded her.

'I know exactly what I did, so much so that five, six times a day, every day, I've thought of suicide myself. Life's so cheap around here anyway, and that might be my only way out.'

1X

Billy kept to his cabin, despite a heaving stomach that craved fresh air. The thought of stepping on deck scared him witless.
Memories of the 'Tamarind', of clinging in a cold, careless sea to the keel of an upturned lifeboat while bodies with fish-like eyes and expressions of puzzlement washed around him, were still too traumatic.
It had been three months since the storm, and the wreck which he had been the only crew member to survive. About 90 days since the men of the Porthoustock lifeboat had hauled him to safety. A total of 106 had died, and only the week before the headless corpse of 'Tamarind's' captain had been washed ashore in Caenarfon Bay, still wearing his uniform jacket.
Billy had craved amnesia, wanting to forget everything about the night, about the hours clinging onto life in the water. Instead, he found himself remembering every single detail. How the lifeboatmen had righted the small vessel he had automatically clung to like a limpet. How they had found, to his additional horror, two poor women and a dead child beneath it.
One of the women had been trapped by her leg, and part of the boat had had to be cut away to free her, the men working in unbelievably atrocious conditions. They thought she had been there with the dead child for over an hour. All of the local lifeboats,

from Falmouth, the Lizard, Cadgwith and Coverack, as well as Porthoustock, had put to sea. Over the next few weeks most of the bodies they had rescued had been buried in St Keverne churchyard, but some had been embalmed and shipped back to their American homeland.

An enquiry was to be held, ahead of which he had already given a lengthy statement, although he felt sure no-one would ever know the true facts behind why the ship had been on the wrong course. With every other crew member, and the captain, dead there was little way of establishing the absolute truth.

During the resulting inquiry he had told the investigators as much as he could, being painfully aware at the same time of the ineptitude of his answers. Basically, he was no seaman and, he told himself, he had been as much use as the youngest and most inexperienced of the passengers. The only information that might have been of benefit to the inquiry was what he had been told while in conversation with the other crew member. Reports in the newspapers had talked of grudges against the company, Atlantic Transport Line, and had mentioned a theory that the helmsman had steered a wrong course, despite being given the correct instructions. It was all hearsay. No-one, it appeared, knew anything approaching facts or the truth.

The salvage had already begun. Two vessels had been moored over the wreck, and divers were bringing up ingots of tin, antimony and lead. Reporters, anxious to keep the story in the newspapers, had gone on also to relay the news that the 'Tamarind' had been insured by Lloyds and other companies for a total of

£112,000.

Billy found it impossible to understand why fate had allowed him to survive. It seemed a ridiculous joke to him that all the other crew, who had been so much more experienced, had met their ultimate fate instead.

What the hell have I to offer the world, I've no talent, no abilities, he thought as the ship he was now reluctantly on had lurched and sent him skidding across his cabin. In fact I've no faith, no real hopes, nothing. There's probably only never-ending emptiness ahead, however far this ship takes me.

Deep in his heart he knew he hadn't wanted to board another liner, especially this one that seemed to be hugging the coastline in much the same way as the other had, that smelt the same as the 'Tamarind', that was bursting with the bright, expectant faces of other passengers off to strike out for a different life in a different county.

Instinctively, he had recoiled from the idea of going back to the ocean, but when he considered the alternatives he had realised that there was nothing to be gained by returning to Biscovey. The problems that had been haunting him throughout his life would be lying there in wait for him again, unsolved. A once hazy intention, that had become more definite over the past few months, was to head for Tombstone, to find Nathan. Billy's insecurities were never far from the surface, which meant that he wanted someone there, in the background, to guide him, a person to lean on when the problems multiplied and became much too much for him to bear individually. His memories of Nathan were of someone who was strong and dependable, despite the drinking and the despair of his last years in the village. Such glances of the past had come to colour his dreams for the future, and he was placing all sanity on the assumption that, with Nathan's help, he could at least create an existence for himself that went deeper than mere survival. Hadn't hundreds of thousands managed it before him?

From the outset he had decided that mining would be out. Instead, he would try to find some form of alternative work. The idea of spending the rest of his days crouched in twisting tunnels now brought on his own kind of blackness. With such fears uppermost in his mind, he didn't realise how close to his eldest brother he had finally become.

X

To his confusion and dismay James began to be directly torn between business and the continuing viability of his companies, and the wish to lead a normal, settled home life. For the first time since his marriage business didn't seem to triumph on every single occasion. On Glynn's second birthday he was absolutely determined to be with his wife and rapidly growing son.

Now he was seeing life from a subtly different angle, he was beginning to fear that if he didn't make the effort soon to communicate with Glynn on some level the boy would become totally alienated from him. He had come to be painfully aware that the youngster looked upon him with apprehension rather than natural love.

On the day in question, he rose early and rode over to 'Trevarnioc' straight away, for what he expected to be a quick meeting. However, he was to find that Richard tried to detain him with what seemed like a barrage of insignificant, petty details, as if sensing the gradual change in his partner's values, and being determined to keep him tied down as a result.

'I had hoped you'd come with me to visit the site of one of our proposed new railways,' he told James brusquely as the younger man attempted slowly to back towards the imposing front door with its grand array of shining locks and chains. 'It's all arranged, and has been for days. It's not an occasion when we should let anyone down.'

'You didn't warn me, I had no idea. You can't just assume that I'll be available every time you feel like arranging something. Surely politeness dictates that you should ask me first?'

Despite the unexpected flare of rebellion Richard was undaunted.

'I said that I wanted to see you early. You should realise by now that that means we'll be busy all day.'

James knew exactly where he wanted to take him. On the wild part of Bodmin Moor near to Liskeard, at Minions, close to ancient granite sites such as the Cheesewring and King Doniert's stone. There had been talk of extending the Liskeard to Looe line, which had been built to take copper from the South and North Caradon mines and granite from the Cheesewring and nearby quarries, to Looe for shipping. The added line would snake around the eastern side of windswept Caradon Hill, the highest point for many miles, from which it was possible to see, on a clear day, across to the fringes of Dartmoor.

A further extension, to Launceston, had also been mooted, with perhaps a passenger service between Launceston and Looe. Richard, he knew very well, had acquired a vast shareholding in both the South and West Caradon mines.

They were in the immense, tiled hall of the Courteney mansion with its marble frieze around the walls and the Courtney arms depicting two griffins and a lion carved into the stonework at appropriate moments. Every word they spoke echoed around them, intensifying its meaning. Having edged his way to such a short distance from the exit James decided he wasn't going to stray back into the depths of the house, where all good intentions would be lost. His rebelliousness would fade if escape was not so near.

'Well, I'm here early as instructed, and we've gone through three hefty sets of figures. I've done my duty to you, now it's time to do the same for the rest of my family. I can't make any further meetings today. It's Glynn's birthday, I promised to at least see him.'

'He won't miss you,' said Richard curtly. 'He never has before.'

Melancholy bubbled up inside James. He was up against the unyielding ice-covered wall which Helen had tried to break through throughout her childhood, but had never managed to breach.

'With respect, I don't think you know anything about my son. You haven't set eyes on him for at least 12 or more months.'

James's waning enthusiasm for the family's burgeoning enterprises had been evident to Richard since the beginning of the last strike. He hadn't been overtly critical at the time, because he had put down the slight change of attitude to a passing phase, as if James was a child. Patience, however, was not one of his virtues. He was quickly reassessing his son-in-law, and was discovering what he believed were a good many flaws in his armour of ambition.

'There will be chances enough to waste on your wife and child when you've established yourself,' he fumed. 'Before that, though, you must put yourself . . '

'Entirely at your mercy?'

'Not quite.'

James sought for some clear way of explaining his ambivalent feelings.

'Look, as far as I see it you want me to become a replica of yourself. In fact both my brother Alex, and Helen for that matter, believe that you have already achieved that. And maybe they are right. I did for a while. I have to admit that I enjoy business and the notion of power. I like the challenge and the confidence that that gives me. However, in carrying out that business I don't intend to drift as far away from the closest members of my family as you have from yours.'

None of that touched Richard, who remained unimpressed, convinced that whatever James said he must eventually return to his senses. He told himself that the worries of the strike had drained the younger man, both mentally and physically.

I have no doubt that all this stupidity is down to one certain person, he thought. My daughter. It seems obvious that she's been plaguing him about the lack of hours spent with her, that she's playing at being a selfish madam again. That's nothing to worry about. It's easily overcome.

'I have to point out that I'm as close to both Helen and my wife as I've ever wanted to be,' he countered.

'Good for you,' James retorted, 'but at the moment I surely can't say as much for myself. In the post of husband and father I've hardly notched up any achievements so far.'

'You can't be expected to share much of your life with Helen. She has no head for business, no desire to become involved in business, and probably will not allow herself to understand the size and importance of your commitments.'

'She's got a more astute brain than you've ever given her credit for, though need she have a good head for business? I can't see why she should.'

'She's my flesh and blood. Mine. She should have inherited a passion for it. More's the pity she wasn't a son, and time has proved she isn't a solid enough substitute for one.'

With that James totally grasped all that Helen had suffered since the moment of her birth, the second her sex had been announced to her waiting father. The complete lack of sympathy appalled him, as it should have done years before.

And have I taken the same path, he thought. I see now, that my attitude on the evening we dined at the Pendrays told me as much. I've given her money and security but nothing else. No warmth or support at all. Worst of all I was never denied in the same way. My mother and father, despite their rule of iron and sometimes odd, cold attitudes, at least when father was alive, did in their own ways, care.

'You've survived well enough on your own, without a son,' he said in a sharper tone than he had used with his mentor before.

Richard, oblivious to the concern snaking into his son-in-law's thoughts, lightened his expression visibly.

'Yes, I made myself carry on, see a point to it all. And now, as a kind of reward I have you, more than worthy in your past words and deeds to be called son, and I have Glynn. The line, fortunately, will continue there. I can at least thank Helen for that, although it would be nice if the boy could adopt the Courteney name sometime in the future.'

What he said both surprised and appalled James.

'Glynn does mean something to you then?' Richard seemed to shrink in on himself at that, shrivel and age before James's sight. The powerhouse that he was, the dominance that was so entirely masculine, disappeared is if it had been literally switched off.

'I try to banish them, but thoughts of death are unfortunately close these days. So many of my colleagues, a good deal of them starting off in business at the same time as me, have gone to their graves recently. When I was young, like most I suppose, I believed myself immortal.

'The dreams that I had then were mammoth, the energy that I had was immense. Now I have been finally forced to accept that it is not forever, that the riches and the company kingdom I've amassed will one day slip from my grasp. The realisation that I can bequeath them to someone of my own blood does bring with it a modicum of comfort. I only hope young Glynn, when he is old enough, will rise to such a task.'

James studied both the man by his side, and the grand entrance of the plush, yet basically characterless house, as if he was seeing them both afresh, and he realised that his father-in-law would be left with nothing at the end of his span on earth bar wealth. No warm memories, funny stories, love. What he had achieved was limited to the material and therefore, in commonsense as well as Biblical terms, totally meaningless.

And is Glynn's sole future to inherit this man's power and acquisitive blight that have together blocked him from seeing the world in an understanding or even realistic way, he questioned.

He felt desolate, not only for himself, so deeply entangled in Richard's web, but also for his own small son, the child of Rosevean as well as Courteney blood, who probably had come to see him more as a tyrant than as father.

Helen was surprised when he returned early, and couldn't help showing it. She noted his earnest, almost pleading expression, as much as she did the rather unwieldy parcel, covered in brown paper, that he was carrying in his arms. There was still a tremor in her heart every time she saw him, although dull tremor was now all it was. The shattering, palpitating emotions that had assailed her in her initial desire for him had dried up. When she had first been told that he had slept with another woman she had experienced only minor betrayal. The shock of Samuel's death and the sheer exhaustion of that night had chilled her enough to push gossip about her husband and his illicit night spent away from her into the background.

Later, though, the knowledge of his adultery did begin to tear into her, and eventually, in the middle of yet another lonely, sleepless night, she had reasoned that her need for James's love would have to change, be smothered and snuffed out. In that moment she was determined that never again would he be able to inflict so much agony upon her, especially when she had done nothing to deserve so much pain.

In the end she had decided that it would be best for them to continue sleeping in separate rooms. If it suited him, it would stay fine for her, take away the awfulness of lying next to him, wanting him, while he merely turned his back on her.

All the idealism she had fostered when she had married him had dissipated. Only sadness remained, and a lingering regret that it had slipped away so quickly and with, on his part at least, so little mourning.

But for Glynn's sake, she told herself, politeness and a veneer of love must remain, so when he came back hours earlier than she had gauged from 'Trevarnioc' she said: 'I hadn't expected you to remember that it was Glynn's birthday. And you were up so early this morning I couldn't call out and remind you in case I woke Glynn.' She added lightly, indifferently: 'I thought I heard you moving around as early as early as five o'clock.'

Hesitantly, he sat down in his usual, easy chair, placing the parcel carefully in front of him. He remembered how her tender, heart-shaped face had radiated delight when she had once seen him, how his unexpected appearance at the door would bring lights of pure happiness to her eyes.

Now she hardly reacts at all, he admitted as he idly twisted the string that was wrapped around the present. Added to that when she speaks to me it's in a matter-of-fact tone as if she is carrying on a mundane conversation about the price of bread in Elias Varcoe's shop.

'I have remembered, though, and it's a beautiful spring day out there. What are we going to do with it, surely not waste it?'

As I have wasted so many others, he added to himself.

'Are you actually suggesting that we spend the day together as a family, and with such a flimsy excuse as a birthday?' she enquired, not bothering to hide or even mute her sarcasm.

He thought it wisest to ignore it.

'That's the general idea, yes. I thought we could go out for the remainder of the day. I've told your father as much and, as I said, it's glorious.'

Determined to keep the atmosphere between them light and easy, because it was their son's big day, she decided to play along with him, and see where his plans would take them.

They agreed on a picnic and climbed into their pony and trap together for the second time in a number of weeks. After discussion, they headed north, across country to Respryn, on the banks of the young, clear, fast-flowing River Fowey, and near to the grounds of Lanhydrock House, the impressive home of the Robartes family of bankers, once the more lowly Roberts family of Bodmin, but now much more influential in the world.

It was a journey of about seven miles, which almost took them very near the lowering jail in which Peter and Edwin had served their three months.

Helen, once she had made up her mind to go, determined to exact the most from such an unexpected opportunity. Afraid that the sun might disappear she hurriedly packed some chicken joints that had fortunately already been cooked for dinner, and some fruit and cakes and cheese and ham.

Glynn reluctantly left at home his father's gift of a carved wooden railway engine complete with coaches, and they set off in a companionable enough silence as the amiable pony trotted her way through the sweet-smelling, and flower strewn lanes of Lanlivery and Sweetshouse, with their high banks and their ruts that had deepened in the winter, and then dried hard in the recent hotter weather.

As they went Glynn clung on fast to his mother's hand, quizzically glancing up at his broad, vital father every now and then. He couldn't remember when he had last been out with both parents, and even to his innocent brain the fact that they were together seemed to hold a great deal of significance.

The shyness that he felt towards James extended to them all. Helen spent most of the journey, not studying the wildlife as she would usually have done, but wondering what could have possessed her husband to walk out on a meeting arranged by her father, and compound that decision by deciding he would rather be out with his son.

Visits to 'Trevarnioc', especially of late, since the purchase of the new pits, had been day-long affairs. It was all so out of character. Had he argued with her father? Had some negotiations fallen apart so drastically that he wanted escape from them?

Was he taking them out as a ploy because he wanted something from her in return? More freedom perhaps, if there was more freedom for her to give him, a promise from her that she would look the other way because he was on the verge of starting a regular affair, or breaking into more ventures of which she would disapprove? If none of those were the case perhaps instead he had finally decided that enough was enough, and wanted to leave her.

Despite her fears to the contrary the sun burned even brighter as morning slipped into a glorious afternoon. When they arrived at Respryn and the trap clattered over the ancient stone bridge that spanned the river, the warm rays were streaming down benevolently. They were playing on the ripples of the water in which the salmon swam, and dappling through the huge trees that had grown in the parkland around Lanhydrock for centuries, back as far as the Civil War when Richard Grenville and his Royalist troops had swept in and dislodged the Parliamentarian owner and his family to claim the house for King and country.

The atmosphere, heavy with the scents of the oncoming summer, made Helen drowsy with near contentment. She spread out the cloth she had packed on the lush grass and laid out the food while her husband and son took a slow, quiet stroll together, following the river northwards towards its source.

Glynn managed to toddle reasonably well over the tufts of coarse grass that grew near the riverbank, but occasionally took a tumble from which he had to be rescued. After the pair had disappeared from her sight, into the heat haze and the stunted trees which hugged the river and sent gnarled roots shooting in all directions, she stretched out, allowing herself to enjoy the mellowness of it all.

The smell of the fresh grass and young honeysuckle and May blossom, the playful rippling of the water and the far-off drone of hurrying bees made her feel slightly wayward, as absorbed in life as she had been when she had joyously clambered across the rocks at Charlestown.

On the other side of the water slumbered the aristocratic house, standing stately and serene, with Richard 'Skellum' Grenville long since gone and the Robartes in residence many years since. She thought idly of the myriad of landed and titled gentry that her husband and her father rubbed shoulders with constantly. Most of them had mining to thank for the wealth their families had accumulated, although those who called Lanhydrock their home owned their position instead to the world of finance.

Lord de Dunstanville of the Basset family had controlled the famous Dolcoath mine, while Lord Falmouth owned a number of mines in the parishes of Chacewater and Gwennap. Many of the families had been involved in developing ports and railways. Portreath had come into being due to the Bassets, Newquay and Par thanks to the Treffrys of Place House at Fowey. While she lay estimating just how far her father's empire would stretch by the time immortality caught up with him the delicious freedom of the outing finally seeped into Glynn. He forgot all about wanting to go back to his mother, and shelter behind her, and began to relish being with his father, exploring this new part of the world.

Delighting in the freedom he ran around like a wound-up toy, chasing the butterflies flitting over the rolling meadows or turning his attention to the multi-coloured dragonflies, the first to emerge that year, hovering near the river, and generally making a bee line for anything that moved.

James let him go, at the same time keeping a

tolerant eye on him as they eventually turned and headed back for something to eat. When they reached Helen again Glynn settled enough to devour his food, while his parents sat tongue-tied in the warmth, still shy together, and worked their way through the spread in a silence that almost approached the companionable.

'Funny how even plain fare always tastes that much nicer when eaten like this, in the open,' she said, keeping the subject unemotional, not wanting to upset the tenor of the day.

'You're so right. I'd completely forgotten. I can't remember the last time I chose to do something like this.'

'Or enjoy yourself?' she prompted, not being able to help herself.

He was on his knees, sorting through the basket for another slab of cheese and he stared down at her then through fair eyelashes, so intensely that she was forced to drop her own gaze.

'Maybe that too,' he answered, wanting to tread carefully with her, afraid of saying something that would make her shrink still further from him. 'Are you enjoying yourself at the moment?' he asked tentatively.

Before replying, she fiddled nervously with the cuffs of her dress, as if she was a child pulling at anything she could lay her hands on because her parents had asked her a difficult question.

'I have to admit I am. I'd thought we would have yet another uneventful day at home, by this time probably trying to amuse a boy who might just be aware that this should be a special day.'

'I aimed for surprise.'

'Rest assured you succeeded.'

Gently, he touched her hand, disappointed to find there was no smile, no warm impish grin in response. She held herself in check instead, her slim body curved away from him, and he grieved silently and reminded himself that she should not be blamed for any coolness between them. It was his fault, absolutely.
They both jumped instantaneously when they heard a splash, both guessing the worst. Together they rushed to the bank. Glynn, chasing one butterfly too many, had fallen in and was bobbing helplessly in the middle of the river, his plump little arms flailing, the shock on his face obvious.
'For God's sake do something,' Helen cried, throwing off her shoes, and ready to jump herself. James grabbed her around the waist. 'Don't worry, I'll go. The river's fast-flowing here I know, but it's not particularly deep.'
He didn't bother removing anything, wading in straight away and fighting the current as he went. By the time he reached Glynn, who was by then struggling so much he was fast exhausting himself, he was waist deep. At that point, realising that the currents were in full spate, James shot out a strong arm and grasped his son by his shirt collar. Glynn then clung to him as if he would never let go, his desperate grip hindering James slightly and making it heavy going for him as he fought his way back to the bank, and Helen, against the rushing white water.
As they approached she sank on her knees and helped haul her son to safety, clutching him to her as soon as he was free of the water. James climbed up afterwards, and lay beside them both, breathing heavily, his clothes completely sodden, his shoes clogged with mud. Glynn started to shiver violently, mainly

due to delayed shock, and Helen fought off an immobility that had gripped her momentarily. Seeing him trembling so, she ran over to snatch up the tablecloth that they had put food on. Partly eaten chicken legs and slices of ham went flying as she wrapped her son in it and tried to rub him dry.

James, streaming rivulets himself, went to help her. Both of them were shuddering with an anxiety that made their movements uncoordinated and jerky, though once they realised that Glynn was basically unhurt and quite chatty despite his ducking they allowed themselves to relax slightly. In truth, his fright had fled as soon as James had reached him, feeling suddenly safe in his arms, and he now seemed to be slowly regarding it all as a great joke.

'Do you want to go home after all that?' ventured James to Helen when most of Glynn's clothes had been taken off, wrung out, and left to dry on the branches of a tree, while he ran around in a spare shirt and little else.

James had stripped to his bare chest, but had decided that it was best his trousers dried as he wore them. He had put on no fat despite the numerous dinners that Richard had forced him to attend, and Helen could not stop her eyes straying to his body.

Without the expensive clothes, the gold rings and cufflinks, and the tough attitude that he regularly wore for business meetings and negotiations he was once again the honest, hard-working, muscular miner who had burst his way into her teenage life and heart. Or he appeared to be.

Beset by such thoughts, she strove to lighten her voice, and avert her eyes in case they revealed too much.

'No, no he seems rather unaffected by it. Funny, I always think him timid, and sometimes he definitely is, so much so it worries me. You wouldn't think so right now, though.'

All three, for differing reasons, were determined that the accident shouldn't dampen the outing, and after the initial shock it didn't. What it did do was bring down the barriers between Glynn and his father. The boy hardly left his side after both had successfully dried. By the time it came to leave Respryn they were rolling on the ground together, making a stab at Cornish wrestling, with James very aware that he had to be careful of squashing two-year-old limbs. Helen lay back and watched them, delighted that they were so blatantly enjoying themselves, even though it seemed so incongruous to her. She refused to accept that it could last.

I haven't seen James in such a carefree mood since before we were married, she mused, still happy in a sun which had lost only a little of its midday heat. I mustn't be fooled by it, though. He's quite a good actor when the situation demands. I must remember that my father is able to destroy anyone's ability for simple, unalloyed pleasure if he puts a mind to it.

On the way back they spoke little but made the best of the occasion, with Glynn noticeably sitting between his parents, rather than leaning away from James, as he had done on the way. It was a situation James himself happily noted, despite realising at the same time that Helen had become more withdrawn on the journey back. The restraint between them had as good as disappeared while they were by the river - now it was back in force, or so it seemed.

'Is anything the matter, you've gone very quiet on me?' he said gruffly.

'Nothing, nothing, I was only thinking about Glynn and the river.'

'Don't upset yourself about that, not now. He's fine, look at him, look at that wide grin.'

'No, you misunderstand, it's not that,' she answered quickly, alarmed to find that she was bordering on tears. 'The danger was soon over, thanks to you. It's only that the whole afternoon brought back memories of you pulling me from the sea. First wife, then son.'

He was, at last, back on her wavelength.

'It seems so long ago I suppose, but it isn't, is it?'

'The trouble is so much has happened,' she whispered. 'So much has happened since then that shouldn't have. It hurts.'

He swallowed, and tried to steady his mind. She had started to speak to him from the heart, and surely that was a breakthrough?

'You're right, so much has changed. But nothing is irreversible. Can't we go back to the beginning, to what we first hoped for?'

'That's why I was crying. I, too, was wishing for the impossible.'

X1

Alex was devastated when his mother died. Her death had not been unexpected. She had been ailing from the day she was widowed, never spurring herself on to recover, content to eat little and waste away in melancholy. Alex, like the rest of the village, had been anticipating it.

He had imagined that he would grieve deeply but quietly, relieved that she had been released from her constant despair. But, unexpectedly, the loss rushed upon him like an avalanche, knocking him backwards, burying him in sorrow. Initially, he couldn't understand why his reaction should be such. Then, in between the bouts of black depression and cold anger, he did see the reasons. Self-pity was at work. His mother had been the last one who had cared.

With her gone, he admitted, there is no-one left who gives a fig what I do. Samuel's in the grave, Nathan and Billy have fled to find peace of their own, and James, James and I seem fated to sit on different sides of the fence.

For Alex the strike had been personally disastrous, draining him of all self-confidence. Little remained bar a husk, a parody of his former self and old dreams, though he kept the reality well hidden. The mask he had learned to assume for the outside world somehow, however, remained strong and impregnable.

Admittedly, James did seem to have thawed towards him somewhat since the end of the union troubles, and they had not quarrelled with any real passion since then.

Nevertheless, that small saving grace did not break Alex's sense of isolation. Helen and James did help him arrange the details of the funeral, however, and he stood side by side with them at the graveside as his mother's coffin was lowered down next to that of his father.

Finally reunited, he thought, though he wasn't quite sure whether that would be what his father, always such an independent character, would have wanted.

Afterwards the mourners returned to the Tregrehan house brought by Richard Courteney when Helen became a bride. It was edging back to its pristine condition from before the destruction of the riots, though that could perhaps never be completely achieved again. Alex walked back with a surprisingly large group of people. The numbers at the service had amazed him. Initially, he hadn't accepted the significance of her death, but she was one of the old guard whose family had lived in Biscovey, and been part of its fabric, for centuries.

They had subconsciously gone, many of them, out of a respect for an age that was changing, as much as for the woman who had died. In the past few years they had started to see that the mining industry was reaching the end of its prosperity for good, the fishing industry was also suffering, and an influx of foreigners from across the Tamar, starting to travel to Cornwall by rail, was marking the start of another time, an era, perhaps, in which many could see all things they regarded as truly Cornish gradually being eroded away.

Alex returned with his brother and Helen because that was expected of him. However. he marked his time and then, after a short while, slipped away from the post-funeral gathering and wandered back towards Biscovey village, not wanting to be embroiled in tales of the woman who now lay still in St Mary's churchyard.

He had silently detested what he saw as the hypocrisy of the event. Sisters who hadn't called to see her for years, weeping, relatives who had never helped while she had sat enwrapped in her soul-destroying sadness, cursing ill-fate.

As it was he didn't go back home but turned back on himself and, without really knowing where he was heading, he made for the Britannia where Nathan's brush with murder had taken place.

After beginning with pints of ale from the local St Austell brewery, he then quickly progressed to whatever harder drink caught his eye. He knew when he had passed his limit and also knew, in his muddled way, that when the limit had been reached the moment had arrived when he ought to stagger back to his empty bed, welcome sleep and let the torment subside. On that evening, though, he ignored all such warnings, studiously ordering refill after refill until he reached the stage when cares muted and died.

The fight started before he knew what had happened. Quietly, rather than overtly, he had been becoming less and less sober throughout the evening, while surrounded by many who had not shown such outward restraint. A group from St Blaise had been generally insulting anyone within earshot for an hour or so, and eventually two other customers took exception. Threats of combat became actuality when one of their drinks was taken from the table in front of them and deliberately tipped over the grimy, straw scattered floor.

The violence erupted so suddenly that Alex had no chance of reaching the door to evade trouble, even if he had been able to move quickly enough rather than merely stumbling. But, as the furore broke out around him, he realised that this was what he had been waiting for for days - a chance to let the anger escape. Without any thought for his safety he pushed his way into the snarling throng with impatience, desperate to be part of it all.

At first, he ignored the punches that instantly rammed into his body, absorbing them with little trouble or extreme injury, and in the first surge of exhilaration gave as good as he received. It didn't matter to him that the drink had blurred his vision from the outset, though panic did start stabbing at his senses when everything around him began to occur in slow, jarring, motion. The timing that had earned him some fame in wrestling circles had deserted him. Within about ten minutes he found he couldn't coordinate his muscles to attack properly, and he also couldn't defend himself. He could identify with no-one, and there was no-one to help him.

As it developed in ferocity the fight became one big free-for-all that took up nearly all of the bar, much of it stocked with drink run in from Brittany, and there was no way to dodge the flurry of fists when the time for retreat was reached.

This was what Nathan had once excelled in. Is he somewhere now, getting beaten up in the self-same way? Alex thought as someone powered yet another fist deep into his stomach.

By then he knew that he was being badly hurt, although numbness was keeping pain at bay and he was too unsteady to change a situation in which he was completely outnumbered. He was at the mercy of equally drunken, though more battle-hardened, strangers.

Eventually, his legs went from under him, and he fell headfirst to the floor. Once there he could not clamber upwards again because feet had started to slam into every part of his body. Vaguely, he heard a voice cry from a blood-rimmed far distance: 'Lay off, or you'll kill him.'

'Come on, that's enough. You've done enough damage.'

That didn't stop it. The kicks went on and on until unconsciousness mercifully began to claim him. Then, through puffy, barely opened eyes he saw a couple of figures push their way through the shadows, and realised the shouting had begun to die down. Finally, the blows stopped long enough for the blood to course slowly down from his temples.

More hands appeared, and he whimpered and shrunk from them, but they were kinder and altogether more gentle, and he allowed himself to be borne upwards by them.

Someone said: 'For all our sakes, and his, get him out of here.'

'Don't worry, he'll be all right with us, though this should have been stopped ages ago. Don't you lot ever learn?'

'He needs a doctor, that's what he wants.'

'And his head examined. He didn't start anything, but he joined in quick enough, as if his life depended on it.'

'You know his mother was buried today, old Rosevean's widow.'

'That'll explain some of it then.'

'The way he was knocking the brandy back he almost joined her.'

Before he passed out Alex just about gathered that his saviours were Jenifer's brothers. There was no way he could speak to them, however, because his mouth was so swollen and the overall pain had quickly become so intense he could hardly think. Vaguely, he wondered what they were going to do with him. Without doubt, he didn't want to be taken back to Tregrehan and James and Helen

- or be in the Biscovey cottage all alone. Through the pain, and bruises, he went to try to say something, whether it was to be intelligible or not, but then all went blank. Jenifer was there when he awoke, standing by his bed, arms folded in stern admonishment, her eyes boring into him, dressed in the dullest brown imaginable but magnificent all the same.

He was always uneasy when she was near, worse on this occasion as the unease was mixed with acute embarrassment. Instantly, he knew he wanted to be away from her.

With this uppermost among the confused thoughts peppering his brain, he struggled to sit up, finding it extremely difficult to do so because he felt as if he had been pegged down. He couldn't move more than a few inches. The only alternative was to lie still and pray she was not in a mocking mood.

'This is the last thing I'd have wanted,' he tried to explain through lips that were twice their normal size.

She glared down at him.

'You mean you'd have rather ended up kicked to death on the filthy floor of that stupid inn?'

'No.'

'You mean you don't like finding me here, caring for you, watching the strong become the weak?'

Without any conviction, he attempted to laugh off his pain and distress, soon finding there was no way of winning that battle either.

'I can't think of anyone better to wake to. What I meant was I'm sorry to cause you so much trouble. Heaven knows why I've ended up here.'

Her mane of hair was hanging loose. She seemed even slimmer than the last time they had met, and with her height her whiplash features made her look gaunt, but not enough to diminish her wild magnetism.

'Sorry you should be. You've disrupted us greatly, most of all the poor little mare who had to carry you back here. She's in the stable now recovering from carrying your drunken weight all the way from that stinking inn. And as for me, I really don't know why I'm waiting on you like this. After what happened at Bodmin I'd decided to ignore you completely the next time we met.'

As always seemed to happen, she unnerved him so. Even if his head had been clear, and he had been free of injuries, he knew he wouldn't have known how to deal with any of her comments.

'It wasn't my doing. Bodmin, I mean.'

Grimacing at him, she didn't condescend to lift the sarcastic tone of her voice, or alter the deliberately masked expression on her face with his wide eyebrows and soft, unmarked skin.

'I understand that now, or at least a little of it. I have to say, though, that you riled me so much at the time I wasn't able to see matters straight.'

Again he struggled to sit up and throw off the blanket that had been placed over him, but discovered, to his horror, that when he did move, to any perceptible degree, his headache increased a hundredfold.

'I can't stay. I can't hold you up any longer. What hour is it? Can I make it home by daylight?'

'You're going nowhere, at least for another twelve hours. You'd faint on the way. The doctor warned us that you might be more badly injured than first appeared. According to Peter and Edwin you were kicked quite badly. Anyway, the doctor's returning tomorrow.'

'I might be stronger than any of you think,' Alex groaned, continuing to make futile efforts to sit right up.

'If you ask me you're much frailer than you think, in many ways. Not only in that fight. The boys tell me . . '

'Tell you what?'

Cursing under her breath, she moved to the door, aware that maybe her tongue had been working independently from her mind. She had just washed her black hair, which shimmered as she walked, reminding him of light glinting on the wing of a raven.

'Never mind. Just, perhaps, that some of that fire of yours, that tends to get others into trouble, has gone of late, or maybe been dulled by events.'

After she had gone, he lay back and failed to banish either her words or the terrible loneliness and indecision that remained within him.

She's so right, he thought bitterly. All that stupid self-importance, and belief, has been blown to kingdom come.

Giving up all ideas of moving out of the bed for at least a few hours, he asked himself if it had all been carried inside solely by the enthusiastic certainties of youth. Now, when he was suddenly aware of responsibilities and not mere ideals, and saw himself going through a coming of age, was it all just disintegrating?

It was apparently late afternoon. The boys were absent, and he presumed them to be working, if indeed they had managed to find themselves work anywhere since their return home. It was something he had meant to check out, and had never got around to. It seemed that he was alone with Jenifer, and he could hear her moving around near the cloam oven, built into the large fireplace.

He imagined her piling furze around the fireplace, ready for a good blaze when the situation demanded, or setting to work on a broth or stew which would be cooked in the iron pot hanging over the oven. Compared with James's house this was another world. The interior was damp and drab, the windows tiny, the ceilings and walls un-plastered and the furniture crude.

Through village gossip he knew that their mother had eventually moved in with a tolerant friend, as she had not been able to find it within herself to welcome her sons back into their home. She blamed them, not specifically for their father's death, more for the general dearth of money for survival. Feeling pathetic and useless, Alex lay still under the sheets and listened to Jenifer carrying out every-day, mundane enough tasks, preparing vegetables and making heavy cake from dark barley flour and currants. In his present state he found the sounds strangely comforting, even though there was a sadness that he would not hear them in his family home again. There was no woman left. In fact, he reminded himself, he was the only Rosevean left in Biscovey.

After dozing, and then coming round and lying thinking for another hour or so, he was determined to make a serious attempt to make his way homewards. Being so dependent on a woman, especially this one, appalled him. Sheer will power, laced with a fear of showing utter weakness, allowed him to haul himself from the wooden framed bed and pull the bloodied and torn clothes, which had been left in a pile in the corner, over his aching body.

Jenifer certainly did not expect him when he appeared downstairs and had to stifle a scream when he peered hesitantly around the door, literally clinging to the door handle to keep himself upright. When she realised who it was she immediately scowled.

He thought how her features altered so when sullenness set in. All was darkness. Yet when she smiled . . .

'I was going to bring you something to eat. And those clothes are dreadful. I mean to wash them. What are you doing?'

'I can't stay. It was my stupid fault that I got dragged into the fight. It's not as if anyone else is to blame. I was too far gone to help myself.'

'Oh yes, they were right to beat you senseless were they?'

Instinctively, he lifted his shoulders as if to say the situation was beyond him, then suffered for the movement. Staring at each other, each feeling awkward, they said nothing for a while.

Eventually, uneasy with the strained quietness she blurted out: 'Tell the truth, you smelt food didn't you? It was your stomach that got you out of bed.'

'No . . to be honest I don't think my stomach could take much food. What I do think would be best is that I should leave now and let you concentrate on what you really want to do. The fresh air will bring me round.'

'You really are anxious to go aren't you?'

His mind told him to agree with her, but at the same time he knew he had to sit down quickly as his legs were refusing to bear his weight any more.

'You know that I'm grateful for everything, but it may be something to do with misplaced pride. If you're worried about what the doctor said, I swear I'll call on him myself later.'

'Your pride has a lot to answer for, hasn't it' she said tartly, stirring the boiling broth, though being so distracted she almost splashed herself in the process.

He nearly said that she was a fine one to talk of pride, standing before him like an age-old priestess, but quelled the words.

Instead he said: 'I prefer it that way.'

'Give me the other reasons as well. You don't like the nurse, or the memories this place holds for you, such as my father slumped dead in front of the fire. That's all too hard to bear, isn't it, because you couldn't save him, like you couldn't save that union of yours?'

'It's nothing to do with the nurse, or any memories. I want to lick my wounds on my own, that's all. I don't want to pull you or your family into my problems. I did that once before and you could have killed me for it.'

At that he could have sworn tears glistened in her eyes. Once again, she had shown both strength and vulnerability in the space of seconds. Watching on, he gaped, and then aware of what he was doing, pulled himself to his feet again and unsteadily started to walk towards her. As he advanced she shrunk back at first, then slowly drew herself up to her full height and turned away. By the time she turned back her eyes were dry.

'As I said before it's nothing but pride,' she insisted. 'Thinking you can do it all on your own when sometimes it's impossible.'

She was stopped from saying more by her

brothers bursting in on them, back from working on building a friend's new home, which had earned them a pittance, dirty and hungry and still full of energy despite the hours of hard labour. There was only an age gap of about two and three years between them and their injured guest, but in the face of their enthusiasm Alex felt defeated, careworn and old.

The boys remained local heroes, and were still living on the euphoria that had carried them along since leaving jail, and it showed in their ebullience, their grasp of the moment.

'Alex wants to return home already,' said Jenifer crisply, fully in control again. 'He won't believe me when I say that he needs at least another day's rest. As you are the two saviours who stepped in to save him in the first place why don't you have a sensible word with him?'

She had allies. By combined effort the brothers managed to bully Alex into staying until the following morning. In face of their arguments he gave in with little defiance, acknowledging deep inside himself that it was not just his own lack of energy, but more dealing with Jenifer's strange attitude, that had drained the determination from him. Strangely, she made no comment about his change of mind. Mainly it was because a sudden need within her, to have him stay longer had sparked private confusion. In a bid to make sense of it she told herself she had only asked her brothers to force it on him because she could recognise another soul in distress, even if it was this particular Rosevean.

CHAPTER SEVEN

The beginning of 1879

1

When Suzannah slipped away from Nathan's lodgings in Tough Nut Street he felt a dozen ropes which had mentally bound him since Joe's death falling away from him his body and soul.
Not only did he now understand the circumstances that had led up to his old friend trying to kill him, and then succeeding in taking his own life, he could also just about manage to comprehend the fact that no guilt could be attached to himself personally. Nevertheless, try as he might, he could not

recapture any of the ease that had seeped into his life in the months before the shooting.

The writing still came, with a difference. This time he had to work hard for it. It would not flow unbidden, without effort. And even when he returned to work with Henry in the office, the hectic pace of full-time employment, and the constraint that somehow remained between the two of them, did little to help. It didn't worry him that Suzannah had not left Tombstone. She had found her own lodgings in town, and had organised a job for herself in the shack that passed as a food store.

He found it simple to ignore her, simpler still because she went out of her way to avoid him. Her obsession with Nathan was over. The admissions about her father's suicide had finally laid her former self to rest, as if they had served as a purge.

Nathan discovered the nights were his worst time, and they became harder to bear as time went on. The dreams that came were continuously of childhood and, with alarming clarity, of Lorna. In the mornings he would awake exhausted, rather than refreshed by sleep, and angry that despite all his attempts to sever past ties they were still there, determined to chafe at his mind. He wanted them exorcised, then found that was an impossible hope, for during the following evening the dreams would unceasingly return. The catalyst was the letter telling him of his mother's funeral. As it had done with Alex, news of her death shattered any sense of well-being. What hurt most was knowing that he had done little, if anything, to help her through the widowhood she had feared, and endured. He could not shrug that thought aside.

For weeks after receiving the news from Lorna he kept to himself completely, only going out to the Clarion office, seldom speaking, ignoring Henry. As if in atonement he hardly ate at all while taking more exercise than usual, forcing himself to walk for solitary miles and, as in the days he had spent in the mountains, deliberately hardening up muscles and honing reflexes. It was as if he was preparing for a final fight, or flight, for life. The Spartan routine lasted for three months, by which time he had come to realise that he had to return to Biscovey. Whether or not he was to remain there once back - that was a different matter. But his heart told him he had to make the trip home to Cornwall if he was ever to achieve real purpose again. The healing had to finish finally where the hurt had first begun.

One complication was that he was painfully aware that Billy was on his way across to America and so, out of a loyalty which he had believed was long dead, he stayed on until his youngest brother's arrival. There was no-one else to pave the way for the boy, and he saw it as a duty to help, a duty that not long before he would probably have shirked. There was also the fact that out of all his brothers it had been Billy who had written to him on a regular basis.

Duty, however, could not disguise the fact that once he had made the decision to leave it unnerved him to stay tied to an existence he now wanted to discard.

Ties, ties and ties again, he thought, with partial resentment. He reasoned, eventually, that perhaps when he had finally cut himself free he could stay free, but that did not quell his annoyance at self-imposed restrictions.

11

Billy finally reached Tombstone by the beginning of 1879. He had endured a long, hard journey and arrived at the noisy, seedy, simmering frontier town penniless and in ill health. Gradually, he had worked his way across cattle ranching country, scratching together enough money to survive, staying far from the mining towns and the majority of the Cornish.

En route he found that cowboys dominated Wyoming, Montana and the Dakotas as they did New Mexico, Colorado, Arizona and Texas where they had first emerged, adapted from the Mexican and Spanish vaquero. Out of a need to survive, he learnt their simple, but basically harsh, way of existence, swapping kaolin and tin mining expertise for work that required knowledge on how to protect longhorns - the crossbred, heavy beef cattle that were descended from those brought over by the Spanish in the seventeenth century.

Over campfire discussions he was told of the cattle kings and barons of the country, such as John Chisum of New Mexico who owned 100,000 head of cattle, and Richard King who was king of 600,000 acres with 100,000 cattle and 10,000 horses.

While battling on to Tombstone, taking the train where he could, he ran into Granville Stuart of Montana who had acquired notoriety because of his predilection for lynching cattle rustlers, and he took himself off for a week or so to Yellowstone where Jim Bridge had been the first person to see the area's hot springs and gushing geysers.

There he explored the stumps of redwood

forests petrified beneath volcanic ash and slept out in the open in a land carpeted with petrified grass, with petrified animals and birds, and where fish swimming from cold water unfortunately ventured into the hot springs, only to be boiled alive.

Later, he travelled where the pony express ran from St Joseph on the Missouri to San Francisco, and through the wild and lawless population of Montana and South Dakota where there had been a gold strike in the Black Hills in 1874. Staying for a very short while in Deadwood, he learnt that it had spectacularly risen from nothing since the strike, and was linked with Martha Burke, or Calamity Jane, the US Cavalry scout and pony express rider.

Never one to delight in robust health, by the time he reached Grass Valley he had lost weight alarmingly and had also been suffering from influenza and was feverish - in reality past caring what happened to him. With the little money he still had he found a room near one of the four breweries, holing himself up there for five days, praying for the illness to clear and leave him strong enough to continue.

Grass Valley was enjoying a resurgent boom time following a depression during the early 1870s. New mines had opened up, there were 16 sawmills, 17 quartz mills and a burgeoning social and domestic life which took in a Haydn and Handel society, a brass band founded by John Thomas from Porthtowan, drill sharpening contests, eight hotels, six lawyers, 32 saloons, five cobblers, four bakers, eight doctors, two undertakers and three dentists performing extractions by electricity, and with anaesthetic only if it was requested.

His arrival coincided with the annual wrestling tournament which took place in a ring of 60 square feet, made of boards and covered by a light canvas which gave the appearance of a tent. It admitted plenty of air, while excluding strong sunlight, and on the first day he was able to leave his poky room he sat in one of the 800 seats for spectators and watched the bouts.

The wrestlers fought in bare feet, clothed from the waist down in light pantaloons and thin drawers. Above the waist, in true Cornish style, they donned a loose jacket of strong canvas, fastened in the front with cords. Memories of home crowded in on him, in fact he felt he was back in Cornwall, and they brought with them an added desire to plough on and find Nathan.

He had intended to stay longer in Grass Valley, to recover properly, but forced himself to leave the next day. He had spoken to only a couple of people since his arrival. Fortunately, they did not know he was another Rosevean, otherwise the tale of Joe Trembeth and his brother would have been outlined to him in every gory detail. It was like any Cornish village, gossip abounded and intensified.

Nathan didn't recognise him when he reached Tombstone. Billy had hardly shaved since setting foot in America, so had acquired a straggling brown beard that aged him by about ten years or even more. Illness had left him emaciated, and his filthy clothes hung off a skeletal frame.

The two brothers were strangers. They had never been close in Biscovey, the years between them proving too great to bridge properly.

And now the gap will stay, Nathan admitted to himself with regret. He doesn't know it yet but I'll soon be quitting on him again. But then again, maybe in spirit he's been miles apart from every one of us since birth.

For a week or so he didn't mention his plans, mainly due to cowardice, although he tried to convince himself it was because of compassion. As Billy was staying with him in his lodgings, Nathan decided to watch his brother settle of sorts before gathering enough strength to try to explain to him that he wouldn't be around for much longer - in fact that he was fleeing again - this time back to the land he once only wanted to escape from. After his arrival, Billy as good as slept for three whole days, only waking to eat or drink. The last few hundred miles had drained him totally. Arizona had also had an influence on him, being a land apart. With no-one to guide him, he had briefly wandered into Monument Valley with its red, white, purple and vermillion rocks, and its apparent rooms of stones and crystals. Once he was there he had felt trapped by the columns and turrets of rocks which had been shaped over centuries by the wind. Although he could have headed from there to the Grand Canyon which, he had heard, wound for about 280 miles along the Colorado river cutting a river over a mile deep and up to 14 miles wide, it was a prospect he resisted.

He found out, though, that Arizona, which also boasted a painted desert with thousands of great logs brilliant with jasper and agate, was struggling to achieve statehood.

Its first white settlement had been established in 1692 by Jesuit missionaries at Geuvavi, although it was the ancient home of the Navajo Indians. Despite fighting long and hard for their independence, they had signed a treaty after being starved into submission and lived, by the time Billy arrived, on their reservation where they had become shepherds, weavers and silversmiths.

The Indian problem had reached a conclusion, but Nathan feared slightly for his brother's future in the town he had just arrived in - for he was very aware that trouble, even greater than usual for the restless, violent area he had adopted for a while, was brewing.

The Earps were still in Tombstone, and looked like staying with Wyatt, hired as a shotgun messenger by the Wells Fargo company, on his way to join his brothers there. Over the past months tension had been growing between their faction and the Clanton-McLaury gang, and most sensed that the dispute, although currently low-level, would not end with a gentle shaking of hands. Nathan had hinted as much in one of his articles, although he had drawn back from describing Wyatt as a cardsharp and suspected stage robber, for the man seemed unable to view himself in his true light. Despite his reputation he appeared anxious to promote himself as law-abiding, although he had befriended known gunmen like Doc Holliday and Bat Masterson.

While it was Virgil who took on the post as town marshal, with Morgan entrenched in the police department, he accepted a job as a guard at the Oriental saloon where he acquired the gambling concession. This was after his plans to set up a stage line had failed because two were already established in Tombstone.

Once Billy had shown teetering steps towards some sort of recovery, however weak, Nathan tried to drop hints about his departure. It was an unsuccessful move because his brother was too absorbed in the confusion and bustle of his new surroundings to take in what was being said. As a result, when Nathan resorted to telling him, very starkly, what was on his mind, Billy was stunned. His initial reaction was one of utter dejection.

'I can't believe you mean to go back. You were part of the reason I came over here. All the setbacks I went through to get across the Atlantic, the ship, the cattle, the walking, the walking that went on and on and on, the crowded unhealthy trains. All for nothing. To find someone who doesn't want to know me.'

Nathan winced. It seemed as if he was dealing with an angry, frightened little boy. He kept telling himself that Billy was no boy - he had reached adulthood a long time before, and was now well into his twenties.

'You're saying that in the heat of the moment, because what I've told you is so unexpected. Of course I want to know you. We're of the same blood, the same roots. You've got to accept, though, that we all have our own roads to follow, and at the moment mine is turning back on itself. Let's face it, our lives have never run parallel, and I doubt if they ever will. Whatever happens you'll survive well enough without me. I never was the best of companions. I never offered you much help while you were growing up.'

Billy changed tack. He couldn't imagine himself living in such wild, lawless territory alone.

'Bad companion or not, don't you think it would be best if I went back to Cornwall with you?'

'For what reason, apart from the fear of staying here? If you think long enough you'll realise you've been on your own since you were born. But having said that you'll run into enough Cornishmen here. You'll never feel isolated, I promise, not unless you want to.'

Nathan hadn't expected his arguments to influence Billy, so the next morning he tried alternative persuasion. After stalling some opposition from the new arrival, he guided his brother along the town's tattered, although thriving main street, and stopped outside the hardware shop.

It was nothing to look at, having been cobbled together in days, for everything in Tombstone had been built to be purely functional and little else. The man who had run it had been shot in the back during a saloon brawl over unpaid debts some weeks before, and Nathan had stepped in and bought it, seeing it as something to bargain with when Billy arrived, for he had known very well that his youngest brother had been determined not to return to mining. The shop at least was above ground.

'Why are we just standing here?' Billy ventured.

'We're standing looking at the hardware store, actually my hardware, or rather your, hardware store. I've bought it for you, as I thought that you'd prefer to serve the mines rather than work in them.'

After throwing such unexpected information Billy's way, he carefully studied his brother's strained and pallid face, now bereft of beard.

'I haven't misjudged have I? You didn't come here for the elusive gold and silver? I really don't think so. Like me I think you've come here to find yourself.'

Above them, the sun was burning down like a blowtorch. In spite of its intensity Billy was shivering. Noticing his reaction, and putting it down to a mild form of shock, Nathan touched him lightly across his back, knowing as he did so that the shoulder blades were too visible.

'I have to admit I'm not sure this place is for you,' he went on. 'If you're still the artist, if father didn't beat all that natural talent out of you, then Tombstone and Arizona are far too harsh for you.'

Billy ignored him. Nathan had touched a raw nerve. He now only sketched fleetingly. The compulsion remained, despite the fact that he, himself, had come to regard it as an unhealthy obsession. In the years since his father's death he had still not yet been able to confront his own deepest, hidden emotions. Unlike Nathan, he hadn't used the longest nights to come to terms with past, present and future.

'You think I'm capable of running a store? I certainly believe I haven't any talent for that.'

'You can but try,' encouraged Nathan, accepting that this last-moment scheme probably was all wrong for Billy. Though what else was there for him until he found enough courage to give freedom to his true self? While in Tombstone he had to earn money. America was not benevolent to destitutes.

During the next few days there were moments when Billy seriously considered aiming for New York on his own, joining the cattle drives as he had done on occasion on his way. He had not been easily accepted - there was no way he was a natural cowboy, but he could ride well, and for that reason the others begrudgingly had allowed him to enter their ranks.

Those experiences, however, had taught him the drawbacks. The life was dangerous and dirty, with the rewards a pittance. The ordinary cow hand usually earned only thirty to forty dollars a month, and the time on the trail was full of agonising boredom.

Apart from the need to overcome the tedium there were rattlesnakes, hostile Indians and cattle thieves to cope with. He had looked the part in his boots, leather chaps to protect his legs when he rode in thorny bushy surroundings, his Stetson hat, the bandana around his neck which served as a mask against the dust on the trail, and the tourniquet he carried in case of an emergency.

Nevertheless. he had been unlike the others. An outcast, really, as he felt he had been since childhood.

After taking two days of thought he finally agreed to at least attempt to run the store for a while. If nothing else, it would give him a niche of sorts. Henry, uncomfortable still with the wrong assumptions he had made about Nathan, was trying to rebuild bridges of friendship between himself and his erstwhile employee by offering to keep a weathered eye on Billy, even though after meeting him for just a short conversation he didn't believe the newcomer had the necessary nerve to survive in Tombstone for long.

Nathan arranged for his rented room, basic as it was, to be transferred to his brother's name as well, and then convinced himself that Billy had no right to ask for more from him. Surely he had been handed a stability that very few new immigrants would have access to?

When it came to his last day in Tombstone, he left with regrets. America with its vastness, its staggering variety, had been good to him, had renewed and toughened him in mind and spirit, and most importantly had placed a pen in his hand and an ability to write words people wanted to read, instead of the tools he had grown used to since his early days at Wheal Bethany.

Billy had brought him up-to-date with all the latest news. This meant he was now aware of the chasms between not only Alex and James, but also James and Helen. He knew as well that Lorna lived alone, ran a dressmaking business that had an increasing number of customers, looked older than her years, and brooded on the destruction of her life.

111

Winter was holding the country in its vice when Billy watched him leave. For his part it took a great deal of restraint not to prevent himself running after him. But he was stopped by the knowledge that if he returned to Cornwall nothing would have changed for him, and change was what he needed. Now he had become slightly settled, and could see that the store at least would give him some level of regular income, he was able to realise, with some clarity, that once back he would only want to turn on his heel again to go in search of the unknown.

At least here, he thought, everyone seems to be starting out again. I must stand a chance. Nathan went on to reach San Francisco, named Yerba Buena by the Spanish after a wild plant which grew in the area. It was renamed after the Mission San Francisco de Assis, and since its rise as a result of the gold rush its crowded buildings had burned down

many, many times.
Nothing could serve to halt its growth, though, and by the time Nathan's ship left the land-locked bay connected with the ocean by the Golden Gate channel, it had become the most important harbour on the Pacific coast.

1V

Dissension between James and his father-in-law had been increasing slowly and inevitably since the innumerable strains and stresses brought about by the previous year's strike. However, even he had been unaware of the extent it had reached. The point of no return came one morning after Richard had casually signed their way into three more pits without even consulting him, one at Gothers where an air dry had been built some years before to catch the mica from the clay.
James was aware of the drying process in detail, knowing that after it was washed the liquid clay would be pumped from a settling tip into pans which were lined with sand that had been made level and firm. The clay would solidify in the pans when the weather was warm and dry, and shrinking and cracking would allow it to be removed in pieces from which any adhering sand would be scraped. The dried mica-clay would then be stored ready for orders after being transported to waiting sheds by horse and cart, with a donkey in the pulling chains.
The pits they had bought were worthwhile, shrewd, purchases, but James was finding it impossible to cope with the sheer scale of the new responsibilities which had been heaped upon him since just before the strike.
Some day, he thought, he would be unable to

cope at all because he would be totally overwhelmed. There was too much to grasp, too much minutiae to deal with, and understand.

The main change was that, unlike the first years of his marriage, he was beginning to try to juggle a reasonable private life alongside the public and the business ones.

And his efforts made as husband and father had not gone entirely unrewarded. Despite fears to the contrary, he had found, to his relief, that the barriers between himself and Helen were showing some signs of weakening, and he had also discovered, slightly to his amazement, that not only did he like her company but he valued it highly. Above all else, the lively intelligence that she showed when he gave her time had gone to prove how short-sighted he had been about her qualities in the past.

It did not mean that the difficulties between them had even been partially conquered. All was still perilous. There may have been some progress made, but he knew she didn't trust him entirely any more, for very good reason - and he accepted it was going to take patience and endurance to edge back to the way they had been initially. Even then their relationship had had faults aplenty, the main one being that he had married her for her family connections, and for no other reason.

And Glynn, with his young and quickly forgiving heart? What he had won with him during the past months could be as easily lost. Even if his wife and child hadn't existed, he was now convinced that he still wouldn't have wanted to burden himself with a greater workload. His ambition was exhausting itself. It had flowered out of a passion to beat a fear that poverty might be waiting for him around the corner.

The desires he had held for wealth were the same of those which dominated a vast majority of hopefuls who had been in the same position as he, but his monetary wishes fell far short of Richard Courteney's megalomania. Now, when he had flirted for a long time with the opportunities they could offer, he had come to see that in spite of such temptations and rewards, he didn't want to be swallowed by them. They had proved to be too dangerous a mistress.

His undisguised reluctance to buy his way into further pit expansion was eventually seen as treachery by Richard.

'You complain about ridiculous, paltry burdens. Anyone listening to you would think you're running a huge worldwide industry. For the last few months I've heard nothing constructive from you, only pathetic stories about the number of meetings I've asked you to go to and lists of petty problems, problems that we all have and which should be dealt with quickly and efficiently with no cause for complaint. Deal with the pressure, revel in it, then you'll rediscover all that old drive. We've got a long way to go yet.'

They were in the heart of china clay country, to the north of St Austell. Mist was hovering around them, and the view from there, down to the clay dries around Par, and to Par Docks with its tall stack that was a landmark for all around, was obscured. Mountains of rubble from working or abandoned pits raked the damp sky, and the pockmarks on the earth from the numerous ventures were filled with water, azure in some places, turquoise in others, although on such a day they were

mostly drab. It was a strange country, more like the moon than the earth, and as James looked around he found it very difficult to accept that he co-owned a good deal of it.
On a fine, bright, day, the whiteness of the landscape was so blinding that those working there, about 35 to each pit, would frequently have to shade their eyes. White smoke and steam from an array of chimneys, and steam from the trains chugging in the distance, would rise in swirls to meet scudding clouds. The steam engines themselves were often lovingly looked after, the drivers keeping them clean and polished and ensuring that, when not needed, they were taken back to their engine houses rather than being left in the open air to gather grime.
The trouble was none of it excited James any more. From within himself he could not find the self-importance for his way of life that the drivers did for their petted engines with their brass that shone.
Slowly, he said with as much certainty as possible: 'If I'm honest with you I'd have to say I think I've gone as far as I want to.'
At that moment he was determined to stand his ground, although one problem was that he felt that he did owe Richard some loyalty. Throughout their partnership his father-in-law had done what he, in his blinkered way, thought to be best, James told himself. He opened doors of wealth and privilege to me, and for him that is all that matters in life. Richard, totally unaware of such thoughts, remained dismissive.
'I don't want to hear any such talk. We've got our hands on an industry that has an assured future, that can only get bigger. We're not just making mud pies. By the end of the century I

want our family to have its hands so tightly round its neck that no-one will ever be able to prise them away from it.'

Such hopes were very familiar. James had heard them voiced on many occasions, and always with the same emotive emphasis.

'What about the Stockers, the Higmans and the Martins, and the other giants of the clay world? Do you expect them simply to fall by the wayside for you?' he inquired, with some irony.

Richard's certainty could never be dented.

'All right, we may have to share the riches with some, but only a few. In time, believe me, all of the smaller, inefficiently run firms will have disappeared. If we can exert control over most of the railways, and have shares in the main ports, then we have to end up on top.'

'And what will be the cost to the family you're so anxious will benefit from this empire?'

James wrapped his cloak tighter around himself, as the mist thickened. By his side the much older man had not seemed to notice the increasing cold, one reason being his annoyance at the way the conversation was taking unwanted diversions from the most important matters in hand.

'I don't quite follow what you're trying to say.'

'You must be able to. I can't believe that you're that blind. Look how those in your family, small as it is, have already suffered because of your indifference to them, and your need for more and more power.'

The words were out, and they stood and confronted each other, the chimneys belching in the background, real bitterness building between them as Richard grasped that he was dealing with full scale rebellion.

'I totally resent that,' he snapped.

James, having put himself on a set path, carried on. He had reached a point of decision, arrived at the mythical crossroads - and being fully aware of what was happening was about to select a track he had never imagined he would walk. What worried him most, however buoyed he suddenly felt, was that he had no idea where it would take him.

'You may resent it, but the facts are clear to me. You may never admit to it but because of your misjudged aims your wife has been so neglected by you, so starved of affection, that she's become old and bigoted before her time. I would say there's a great deal of suffering involved there, even if neither Eva herself, nor you, will ever admit it.'

Richard had drawn himself up to his full, intimidating height. Anger was turning him puce, making his breathing come heavy and fast and filling his jowls. James wished fervently that he had a strong drink in his hand, though on the surface continued in a cool, unwavering tone.

'And it doesn't stop with your wife. Helen's full of insecurities, some of which I have to admit I've added to by my own boorish behaviour. Mainly, though, they're there because she's been made to feel a failure since birth. That's down to your refusal to reassure her that, despite being a daughter, she was just as loved as if she had been a son.'

If Richard had had a whip in his hand he would have used it instantly. His adopted 'son', to whom he had dedicated years of his precious time and energy, was turning into an enemy, and that was not within the rules.

'I've never blamed her for being of the wrong sex. Never, not once, in so many words. You're talking utter, ill-informed nonsense. What tripe has she happily been feeding you?'

'Am I talking nonsense? Think back. You certainly haven't shown much interest in her since we married. Not once have you asked me if she is well, or happy. Not once have you visited our home just to see her. And then there's me. You didn;t let her marry me because you thought I'd make her happy. You knew all too well I wasn't in love with her.'

He hesitated at that, then went on with the rest.

'No, I seemed to you to be a younger image of yourself. You thought you saw in me a ruthlessness, however raw, however innocent. I was someone you could mould. So you used her to get at me. I must admit I was there for the taking, but nevertheless that was how it worked.'

'Well, if you think that was the case it seems my usually good common sense damned well misdirected me that time.'

'I'm afraid it did,' James softly acknowledged. 'I know I was quite, or should I say definitely, content to go along with it all, for a long time. But I'm finally coming to what senses I have left.'

'Losing them more like, I think. What the hell's prompted all this rubbish you're coming up with today? You must know by now I'm not someone to cross lightly. I'd think hard before you say any more.'

'And then there's Glynn,' continued James relentlessly now, carrying on in the same determined vein.

After all the tussles with Alex he had finally learnt the art of self control, at least on the surface.

'Yes, I was going to remind you of Glynn. If you're so intent on throwing everything I've given you away then I warn you that Glynn will inherit it all instead, and I'll do my very best to make him understand why I don't consider his parents worthy enough to be given a penny.'

'If that's meant to frighten me then you've judged me wrongly once again. I don't want you money, and nor does Helen, and neither do I want my son to have any of it. I don't want him to have such a burden as a legacy.'

'Now you're behaving like a hysterical woman.'

James stood looking over at the white peaks of Hensbarrow, now so shrouded in fog they could hardly be distinguished. He could make out no other signs of life around, despite themselves, although not far away he knew activity in the pits was at its height. It was as if the mist had enveloped them in their own small, sad, world from which there would be no easy escape.

'This isn't hysteria. I'm speaking seriously about the way I view events. I'm grateful for the help you gave me, I always will be. Despite that, though, I've reached the stage when I know that I'm being used. I'm now certain that if I don't halt this mad rush that I've got caught up in I can see myself losing my family for want of riches I don't really need.'

'You understand that if I withdraw my support for you, insist on selling all the assets we jointly hold, you'll only be left with your original pit. Some money, not enough for you to buy that house at Trenarren I've been told you've got your eye on, or send Glynn away to that school you've chosen for him.'

'I'm very, very aware of all that,' James said slowly.

'Then you know who to blame then when you've dug that financial grave of yours. You've just robbed yourself, and that family of yours, of a future.'

Use of the word future brought a halt to the exchange. James had run out of bravery. What would his future be? He bowed his head. What the hell had he done? He had spoken at last from the heart. The trouble was he felt his intellect had remained dormant throughout the exchange.

V

Helen grasped that something was wrong as soon as he arrived home. On the way from his sharp, bitter, exchange with Richard, he had contemplated stopping off at an inn to find oblivion in a haze of brandy, but had been prevented from doing that by vivid memories of what had happened the last time he had sought to solve his problems in that manner. He wanted no repetition of the Sun Inn episode. That would destroy his life completely. It had nearly disintegrated as it was, and the argument with Helen's father might have caused the final rift.

Above all, though, he didn't want his own idiocy to be the sole root cause.

Instead, he had travelled straight from the moor, and the dampness had seeped right into him. His clothes were streaked white with clay dust, his face was drained of colour, his eyes sunken, his skin clammy. Apart from that, he was even shaking. Usually he and Helen said little when he first arrived home, as conversation between them continued to remain stilted. On this occasion, though, she started at the sight of him and rushed up to him to take off his heavy coat. Her nerves had leapt in dread. Something must be terribly wrong.

'What is it? What's happened?'

'Is it so obvious that something has?'

'Well, yes. Look in the mirror and you'll know the answer to that. You're trembling. Do you need a drink to steady yourself?' Those were the first words that came into her head. They were indifferent enough, she thought. They didn't give too much away.

'Yes, perhaps a stiff brandy would help.' Hesitantly, he lowered himself into one of the chairs, stretched out his long legs towards the fire, and then looked anywhere but into her anxious eyes. Surely the best way to tackle a problem, he thought, was to plough ahead and face it as soon as possible.

'You don't particularly mind if you don't get to move to that house at Trenarren do you?'

The house he referred to had swallowed up almost all of the past nine months or so, since the outing to Respryn. It had been put up for sale some while after their picnic and he had shown immediate interest as soon as he had been told it was on the market, and at a reasonable enough price.

Set outside of St Austell, off the road between the town and the village of Pentewan, it stood in a prime, though rather remote position, overlooking the entire bay. It was nowhere near as magnificent as 'Trevarnioc' had once been before the riot, but it had style and boasted a swathe of land that rambled idly down to an enclosed stony cove with a smart pier. It also had six bedrooms, stables and a dairy, and in all respects was a million miles from Biscovey.

During the past months he had imagined Helen wandering through its rooms, and down to the beach, with a finally accepted contentment, and Glynn running happily across the tidy lawns. It was a symbol of the class that he had been aspiring to ever since entering the world of clay, and he saw it as fit for a family he loved.

Mention of house negotiations led to the concern dropping immediately from Helen's expression. Of an instant her nerves had settled.

'Is that all this drama is about, the fact that the sale on that mausoleum has fallen through?'

She said more in that sentence than she had done during the long hours when she had trailed behind him through the countless rooms of the house, listening to him describing how he would decorate every inch to whatever style they wished, how he would change the garden so that it fitted a classical ideal, how he would alter the angle of the driveway to make it more impressive, and even brush up the external brickwork.

At her reaction he winced. Without hesitation he had been quite prepared to spend to his limit on the place, merely for his pretensions. Not once had he grasped the fact that she had regarded it as a mausoleum.

How would she have survived if he had installed her there, in a home she abhorred, and then abandoned her within four hated walls while he sped away to meeting after meeting? Had he ever stopped to consider her feelings while he was rambling on about his plans, or listen to what she had tried to say? He should have known. She hated

'Trevarnioc' too.
'Yes, the sale has fallen through,' he said as levelly as he could, putting his quickly finished glass down. His stomach was churning. 'I've also had an argument with your father.'
She looked more interested.
'What kind of argument?'
She knelt down beside him, and started to pull off his wet boots, footwear that was proving stubbornness itself to remove. Looking down, he noticed how her hair with its light streaks was turning blonde at the tips, how it smelt of honeysuckle. She was quietly beautiful, and she was wholesome, and she was a good mother, and he had tried to change her.
'A major one, I'm afraid. For once I let my tongue run away with me, as I've done so many times with Alex. I annoyed him more than I ever thought could be possible. To be honest I deliberately infuriated him, and the result is that he's now likely to sell off all of our joint assets.
'If he does go ahead and officially break our partnership, I'll or rather we'll, be left with one Bodmin pit, a sprinkling of money, and very little else.'
While he had been speaking she had become very still, the colour draining from her face at speed, until it was as pasty as his.
'Why did you argue?' she whispered.
Bleakly, he looked down at her.
She seems shocked, he thought miserably. Have I misjudged the situation entirely? Despite everything she's said is she really deeply attached to her father? I don't know whether I've got the energy to go into reasons. I believe that I hardly understand them myself.

'He wanted me to take on more responsibilities. There was talk of even more railways, companies and pits. I called a halt to it, that's all. I couldn't take it anymore.'
Watching her every move, he sank further back into his chair. At his words she didn't edge any nearer to him, which was what he wanted. Despite still kneeling, she had straightened her back, and let her arms hang lifeless by her sides. The pale lemon dress she was wearing was spread around her on the floor, contrasting with the green rug in front of the fire.
'This rift, is it likely to last?'
'I b'lieve that if I went back to him tonight, grovelling for forgiveness, he'd thaw. If I don't it will be permanent.'
Then she leant towards him, allowing him to notice that her eyes were moist. It felt to him that it was exceptionally important - for both of them - that he should make sure that she was fully aware of the implications which were most definitely linked to the path he had chosen to take.
'You really do understand what differences it will make to us don't you? After the amount of regular money we've been used to, and allowed ourselves, for living from day to day, we're going to find it a strain to keep going. That is until we learn to adapt, to follow a much more frugal existence.'
Silently, she started to cry, her slight frame heaving under her clean cotton dress, and he could have wept as well. It had been mostly for her that he had broken with Richard, to try to prove that he did now see her father for what he was. What would be the consequences if that was the wrong move? Surely she was crying because her father was,

once more, turning on her? And he, her husband, had instigated the new chasm between them.

'I'm sorry,' sighed, his voice breaking.

He stroked the top of her arm, desperately wanting to hold her but at the same time being unsure of how she would react.

'What for?' she sobbed.

'You're crying. I had no idea such a disagreement would hurt you so much. I'll make it right. I'll ride over to 'Trevarnioc' right now and apologise, try to convince him that I was tired and out of sorts earlier on, and scared of the future, anything to make him forgive me.'

At his words she breathed in deeply, trying to steady herself. She had forgotten that he had never been close enough to her to be able to read her mind.

'These tears are from relief, you silly fool,' she gulped. 'I never thought that you would find the guts or the foresight. If you dare go round there and apologise it really would be the end for us.'

CHAPTER EIGHT

1

1880

It was dark and frousty in the shop. Admittedly there was none of the frightening blackness of the mines, but the place was murky, cramped and still unnerving. Until he began running the business Billy hadn't realised how much he hated being closed in by any walls, be they above ground or below. The abhorrence, therefore, wasn't confined to the twisting levels that forbade standing and carried the perpetual and very real chance of rock falls. The panic even rose within him when he was in his own shop, with daylight straining through the windows, carrying out the most mundane of tasks.

He could take an hour of stocking shelves, of serving quite a reasonable stream of customers, or putting on a welcome, servile smile for the cowboy who had just reached town and still had a wallet full of money, and the newcomer wanting to buy the best tools, and even for the dangerous drifter with a Winchester rifle in hand.

A two hour stint could border on the unbearable but he could continue forcing himself to count his luck. To do that, he would tell himself that without Nathan's many contacts, or his money, he wouldn't have decent lodgings, or a business of his own. Probably, he would be underground, hacking out the earth, or would be on the trail again, or propping up an unwashed bar and blowing the last of his savings on a disastrous game of poker.

After a couple of hours, however, the restlessness would steal over him completely and he would stare out of the small window, at the stinking, dusty main street, at the O K Corral in the distance, at the melee of humanity and their rushing hopes and fears, and he would want freedom. For a while he would make himself stay behind the counter, serving with a forced smile, repeating the day's gossip to each customer who seemed to want to stay and chat, talking of the latest strike and the feuds that were building in town.

Gossip was not hard to come by. It was said that Wyatt Earp had his eye on stepping into the shoes of John Behan and becoming county sheriff. It was a move that many anticipated would be violently opposed by brothers Ike and Billy Clanton and Tom and Frank McLaury, who had carved a local niche for themselves as highly successful cattle rustlers. Despite Billy's good intentions and genuine interest in relaying such news to his next customer he would feel the sweat start stealing over him, and the nausea growing. But, he frequently told himself, at least the bouts of sickness weren't as bad as they had been in Wheal Bethany.

Nothing, he thought, could be as gut wrenchingly bad as that, but the meagre reassurance went no way towards solving his basic unhappiness.

On some days he thought he could cope, he could overcome most of the problems that seemed only to be in his mind, and make the business a thriving and lasting one.

Trying to be positive, he figured that he had to make it last while he had the chance, while the wealth and hope remained in the town. Local large scale production of silver was undoubtedly increasing, and there had been a rising number of gold strikes as well.

The Earps, with Doc Holliday in tow, had arrived at the right time, it was a boom town. It was during the bad days that he was sure he wouldn't make it, the defeatism bringing shame with it. Shame that he was so ineffectual, that he was nowhere near to being the commanding, able man that his father had tried time and time again to mould him into. He had to admit that, once again thanks to Nathan, he had been accepted, even by the more boisterous elements in town. And in some ways he could almost have been at home still as there were so many Rowes, Hendrys and Cragos around, so much evidence of dry Cornish wit.

Apart from that, he thought he had enough common sense to make it work, and being a miner was well aware of the job served by all the items he was stocking. Nevertheless, the imprisoning effect of the place managed to erase every advantage.

When the black mood crept over him he discovered that sanity was only to be found when he ventured out into the fantastic open, ancient territory that Arizona had on display, exploring the land that could offer green cattle country one minute, and seemingly arid desert the next. There, in almost cathedral-like isolation, he started to sketch again.

Peace came when he gave his mind permission to wander, put pencil to paper and create. After a couple of hours of such activity he could guarantee to himself that he would always feel calmer, cleaner, refreshed and awash with the conviction that he had achieved something important and substantial, not petty, and fleeting, and with very little point.

The sketches remained his secret obsession. As he had done in Cornwall, ever since his father had derided his efforts so mercilessly, he hid them. Quietly, as if he had been breaking some secret code by forming them, he put them under his bed, safely out of sight - although in truth only Henry had ever been inside his lodgings since he had moved in there.

Even he, himself, rarely looked at them again. The completion of them was therapy enough with the snatched respites spent alone by the Gila River, which had marked the main overland trail to California during the gold rush more than 30 years before, becoming addictive. The main point to him was that his

spirit needed them. Without them life threatened to become unbearable again.
In the end the shop inevitably suffered from his absences. He would shut it, convincing himself that he would only spend lunchtime away from the counter, and he would never return, at least until night had fallen. Occasionally, he didn't bother to open at all, taking himself off to Cochise country where the chief of the Chiricahua Apaches had kept the US Army at bay for ten years. The shop was broken into twice in his absence, with money taken, and items spirited away, though even that served as no warning to him.
As promised, Henry had been trying to keep a paternal eye on him, and it reached the stage where he felt he had to speak out in his usual blunt, practical fashion. Before doing so, he held back for a couple of days, trying to formulate the right approach to the problem, because he anticipated a welter of difficulties. It had been simple facing up to Nathan with forthright talking, even if his straightforward facts had been wrong, as he had discovered when he had accused him of so many ill-judged sins. The task was not so easy with Billy, who appeared a truly evasive character. His shyness had crippled him for so long it appeared that it was almost impossible for him to overcome it, and all criticism, whoever it came from, seemed to Henry to stem from previous parental criticism.
'The enthusiasm for hardware has waned a little hasn't it?' said Henry as an opening shot when he finally ran his prey to ground.
Billy was at work, despite one glance at his expression showing he was far from happy about it. The sun was streaming in, capturing in its rays the motes floating in the warm air,

promising a balmy day ahead with excellent light.

Billy regarded Henry as a meddling old man, beset by a wracking cough and apparently losing weight by the day, someone who, just because he had helped Nathan, seemed to be able to reserve the right to interfere in his life. He was immediately on the defensive, although he had to steel himself to stay his ground.

'Why do you say that?'

Constantly he told himself that he didn't want to become too involved with Henry, or anyone for that matter. Above all, he did not hold the same respect for the editor of the Clarion that Nathan seemed to have held. Henry, who had started to walk with something of a stoop, and whose weathered skin was so dry wrinkles were forming within the wrinkles, cast a disenchanted eye over the ill-stocked shelves.

'I suppose you realise you've hardly been here at all this week, that people have been turning up to buy items and just found the door shut on them?'

Billy bristled at the interference.

'I wouldn't say that at all. I've been here, behind the counter, every morning, except maybe on Tuesday.'

'And then left soon after.'

'I would say many hours after. Why, have you been spying on me? A very pointless exercise if you have.'

There was an uncomfortable old horsehair chair by the side of the counter. Henry, feeling rather breathless, gingerly sat down on it. Usually it creaked in protest at the weight of its occupant, though Henry had lost so many pounds that it made not a sound. Billy glared at him, his thin lips pursed, sunlight showing up the bristles of the beard he was starting to grow again.

Henry acknowledged that he had a battle on if he wanted to keep to the assurances he had given Nathan. To his surprise he was discovering it was a battle that he relished, in the same way as he had derived satisfaction from showing Nathan that he had as much talent for writing as for mining.

'Look, I'm not criticising, although it might seem that way. Nathan gave you this place outright. It's yours. Basically it's nothing to do with me. I'm merely pointing out to you that you won't make it pay its way like this. You must understand that you can achieve so much in this land if you work hard, but work is the word.

'You have to put mind, determination and soul into it, and with so much happening here at the moment, with the silver and gold being found as it is, it should be a simpler task than in those places where the riches are long gone.'

'And I'm not working I suppose?' said Billy petulantly, annoyed at himself.

He knew he was sounding, and acting, like a sulky child.

'You know very well you're not.'

'Well, maybe I'm not one of the crowd. Maybe I don't fit into your supposedly ideal way of living. Maybe I don't want the same sort of success as everyone else, all I want from life is to exist and go my own way.'

Henry sighed heavily, coughed huskily, and stared at the youngster through watery, rheumy eyes. Nathan had said he was an innocent. He wasn't far wrong, though he had a fair amount of his brother's stubbornness and determined idealism.

'Please listen to what I'm trying, very tactfully, to tell you. Surely you can see that without money, without position, you'll end up drifting, achieving nothing? You'll be at the mercy of others, can't you see that? And then you'll end up going their way, certainly not your own.'

A customer came in at that moment, an Irishman with a shock of jet black hair and an accent so thick that Billy could hardly understand it, and for a while they had to break off from their conversation.

Once he recognised the Cornish accent it was noticeable that the man from Dublin became very cool with Billy. There was an enmity between the two races. The Cornish, who were an industrial elite and had no political ambitions, always voted Republican to keep out the Roman Catholic interests of their Irish rivals - who had taken to politics in the same fashion as the Cousin Jacks had burrowed below the crust of the earth.

Nevertheless, a purchase was made, and once the Irishman had left, it was Billy who spoke first.

'So are you saying that I have to live in a manner that I hate just to ensure that I'm one of those up on top of the pile, even if at the end of the day I'm a sadder, lonelier person than any drifter?'

Why do I always feel that I'm the odd one out, he asked himself at the same time. Why can I never escape the belief that I've tackled my whole life in the wrong way, that whatever I say to explain myself I always sound inadequate?

As Henry was the current antagonist he shifted the blame to him.

'You can't see things in the same way that I can,' he went on irritably. 'I hardly know you. I can't discuss my hopes, my dreams with you.'

'Or with anybody it seems. Nathan said you had always been a stranger to him. That you held yourself in check, that you were difficult to reach.'

Billy shivered despite the heat, disguising the action by wiping his dusty hands down the navy apron he was wearing. It was much too long for his small frame, and he knew he looked vaguely idiotic in it.

'The great Nathan. Well he was never exactly a wide, open book, but I suppose he'd have made this place succeed with very little effort on his part.'

'He would have worked exceptionally hard here if he had to, even if he wasn't too enthusiastic about it.'

'But you're being very unfair. You can't compare us. He and I are so different. We're after such opposing things.'

Henry smiled his tired, ironic smile, thinking back over the past two years. The Clarion hadn't been the same since Nathan had left. It had lost much of its vigour, and a good deal of its expertise. He had been a very sound newspaperman, even if he had been new to the trade.

Certainly, he would have been a great help that week when news of the death of Billy the Kid had begun to filter in. It was rumoured that his former friend, Pat Garrett, had tracked him down to the home of a friend in Fort Sumner, New Mexico, and had surprised and shot him dead in a darkened room. Nathan had written the story earlier that year when the Kid had killed two deputies and escaped from jail after being sentenced to hang.

'You two aren't so very far apart for brothers. Nathan lived as basically as you do. I can honestly say he definitely was no lover of wealth or power. He only wanted to be in a position from which he could command his own life.'

'Well, don't we all?'

'You soon won't be able to command your own life if you carry on in the same fashion.'

Once the old man had finally ambled away Billy tried to overcome his irritation and consider what had been said. He didn't want to lose the shop, mainly because he couldn't afford to let it slip. It did give him the chance to spend some time enjoying the quiet passions that drove him. Grudgingly, he accepted that he would have to carry on with the stock-buying, the apron-wearing, the regular hours behind the counter in order to make the profits reasonable.

Hard as it might seem, he would have to discipline himself more.

Such decisions did not cheer him. Salvation, apart from in the moments snatched for himself, was still to him an infinity away.

11

James looked down at the curled, sleeping figure of his wife illuminated by moonlight, at the rich brown hair curling slightly behind her ears and around her forehead, at the pert nose and the full, generous lips, and he admitted deep within his heart that he had been a blind idiot. That night they had slept together for the first time in over a year, made love until they were exhausted and their limbs were spent and their minds tumbling with the

wonder of it all.
Smiling to himself, he thought of the desire they had shared, the newness of it, as if they had never been together before. And he honestly felt that they hadn't before, not on that sweet, desperate, gasping level.
He had kissed her all over, dwelling in the softest of places. Holding her hard against him, he had wanted to envelope her, body and soul, had stroked her and had eventually slipped into her knowing that he loved her with complete intensity and needed her above all others. And how she had loved him. No-one had ever aroused him so much before, or wanted him with so much obvious passion. Until the last few days he had never truly looked at her. He hadn't noticed the freckles across the bridge of her nose, her high cheekbones, her lovely back and kind, gentle eyes, not even during the very first night of their married life, not even when she had walked naked in front of him in the years when they had initially slept together.
She was not prim, or modest about her body, giving so willingly of herself that it had humbled him.
I've taken it all for granted, he thought, never bothered to take pleasure in watching her, loving her. He gazed at her lithe, taught waist, her small, delicate nipples, her lean thighs.
My God, I've taken her with indifference in the past, even roughness, stupidly believing I was favouring her just by using her. Now I know how completely crass I was, how much time I've wasted. And I so nearly threw it away. Until now I don't think I've known what real love or caring is. I've never given myself the chance to find out.
While she continued to sleep he lay in the

still, velvet silence of the night, breathing contentedly as she snuggled into the crook of his arm, struggling with the teeming thoughts and ideas that were peppering his brain. In many ways he was walking into new territory. He didn't want to return to the self-absorption or the pretence of his previous existence, though he was sure that from that moment he was going to find day in, day out, financial survival hard to tackle.

With his father-in-law's help, and experience and contacts, entering the local business world had been relatively easy. Now he was on his own things would be very different.

It frightened him because he had extra responsibilities. Helen and Glynn had always been there, but now they meant more to him than anything else the world could offer and he wanted the best for them. It had not been so before. If he had striven to hand them the best, it had all been for pretence and show. For no other reason than that.

Helen stirred and murmured, and he tried to stop moving so as not to disturb her further. It was too late. Her eyelids fluttered open and within minutes she was sitting up next to him.

'What's the matter?' she asked groggily, turning so that her eyes were level with his. 'Can't you sleep?'

Bending down to her, he brushed his lips across hers. Then he ran her hair through his fingers, before cradling her in his arms.

'I was sound asleep until a noise came from outside, loud enough to wake me straight away. Perhaps our resident fox was out and about, worrying Ben's chickens.'

'Well try to drift off again. It must only be about four.'

He tightened his grasp of her and thought how

warm she was against him, how pliant and yielding.

'It seems unbelievably strange to be lying next to you again.'

'Is that a hidden complaint?' she asked, grinning at him. 'Are you being subtle and really telling me that I'm taking up all the room. Now you've had your wicked way with me all you want is for me to creep back to my room and let you stretch out in your bed.'

'You do that and you'll be in trouble. No, I've come to the conclusion that I adore the heat of you, delight in having your body next to mine.'

'They were always here for you.'

She grinned again, and in the light of the full moon he could see the elfin look return to her features.

'I know . . . I know. Your husband is a difficult, blind fool.'

'And a marvellous lover.'

He kissed her forehead and squeezed her waist, remembering what immense pleasure, even grandeur there had been.

'You're not worried about my father still are you?' she asked quietly. 'I mean about us being able to manage with very little money?'

His reaction was to shake his head, then hesitate. He had reached the stage where he had to start being honest with her, and with himself.

'Yes, I suppose I am a little. I did rely on him a great deal. I'm not much of a brain on my own, I'm the simple miner from Biscovey I always was. And I'm scared of letting you and Glynn down.'

'You wouldn't have said that six months ago.'

'I lived in a dream world six months ago.'

'I've got great faith in you, husband.

Although you didn't believe it I always have done.'

'Thank goodness someone has.'

She lay against him for a while, listening to his heart beating in his broad chest, wondering whether to broach an idea that had only just come to her, that she hadn't had time enough to assimilate properly.

Then she said: 'I'd go and see Alex if I were you.'

'What, to patch up one of my other quarrels? I suppose so. You always did like him didn't you? I might as well try to heal all the breaches caused by my high and mighty attitude. In fact, thinking about it, he'd probably have made you a better mate than I've done so far. I don't think he would have hurt you like I have.'

She ignored the last few sentences.

'What I'm thinking of is approaching him to ask him to become your partner in business. He has a good brain, he knows the industry, and he has contacts with the men who work within it.'

At first he wanted to dismiss what she had said outright, though he managed to stop himself. A tiny scrap of his newly emergent self saw some sense in it.

'Maybe, maybe I will give it some thought, if that's what you want. If you truly think that such a partnership might work without too much misunderstanding between both Alex and I.'

With a myriad of thoughts besetting him, he pulled her close to him, then kissed slowly, tenderly, clinging on to her in need, wanting to feel her soft young lips on his forever. She gave a small mewing sound and rubbed herself against him, and suddenly all he could

hear was the blood pounding inside him and her urgent groaning as he touched her breasts. All he could feel was her flesh burning into him and her soul opening for him.
Joy, much wanted, elusive, joy, came again.

111

While James was scaling emotional heights Alex continued to flounder in dark valleys of despair. His unwanted sojourn with Jenifer and her brothers had healed him physically. It had also left him in as frayed a mental state as he had been after his mother's funeral.
He had finally let Peter and Edwin, together with the doctor, persuade him to stay at Lanlivery for two further days before he returned home. His thoughts were that 48 hours might be time enough for him to deal with the tensions that definitely remained between Jenifer and himself. There was within him a belief that it could be long enough for him to demonstrate his appreciation to her for her nursing and care - without his presence becoming a tie and a nuisance to her.
Unfortunately, it hadn't worked out that way. Soon after the brothers had been released from Bodmin Jail he had been told that Jenifer had been seen out with Thomas Patten, a worker on the Cornwall Minerals Railway that had been formed within the past ten years and incorporated all the lines built by Treffry, a wealthy, forward-looking, Cornish landowner who had lived at Place House, Fowey.
Alex knew Patten well enough. He was good-looking in his way with deep-set eyes with an unnerving stare, amazingly perfect teeth, fine

bone structure, and an easy strength that had built him into some sort of folk hero and, Alex believed, a character who was a bully at heart. Indeed, those who crossed Thomas soon discovered that fact. Some had been beaten to pulp.

Alex had briefly considered how a girl with intelligence and insight could fall under the spell of such a potentially brutal oaf, and assumed that whatever there was between them would soon fade. She would see the light.

He hadn't thought of the association between them since waking up battered and bruised in her house, so he was amazed when he hobbled downstairs on his last evening there to find Patten sitting by the fire, dominating the room, with Jenifer perched awkwardly on his large lap.

Alex had quickly backed away, instantly startled and embarrassed that he had interrupted them.

I'm sorry,' he had stuttered, lamely, desperate not to create a scene.

Although he might not like seeing her with the man, he decided it was none of his business who she asked into her own home. 'I didn't realise you were here Thomas. I didn't hear anyone arrive.'

Patten, 6'5" tall, twice as broad as James, undulating with muscle and scared of nothing that the world could throw at him, made it known that he was far from delighted to see Alex Rosevean.

'What the hell is he doing here?' he had yelled, turning on Jenifer, his thick neck throbbing red with anger, pushing her away from him with such force that she fell off his lap, almost tumbling to the floor.

With inborn grace she managed to regain her balance, though could not stop herself feeling foolish and somehow cheapened in front of Alex.

'I told you he was here, I explained,' she said, her eyes pleading with him to understand and accept.

'You told me he was here for just one night, and only because your stupid brothers brought him back. He should have been well gone by now.'

'He needed the rest. It doesn't hurt anyone that he's here, surely?'

Backing away from both of them, she kept glancing between the two men, one leaning weakly in the doorway, ashen-faced, still bandaged but with his ever present defiance still evident, as if he was challenging the entire universe, the other quivering with brute force.

'She's right, I'm here because the boys asked me. No other reason,' weighed in Alex, knowing he had to try hard to defuse the situation that he was partly responsible for.

'Just get the hell out of here,' Patten growled, the fury erupting from him as he advanced on Alex. 'She's mine, and I don't want her involved with a mindless lunatic like you.'

Alex was ready to swallow that. He was in her home, and out of respect for Jenifer and her family he would have suffered a barrage of insults. During the past years he had taken so much baiting he was an expert at turning the other cheek when necessity called for such action - and so was quite prepared to walk away like a lamb.

Indeed, he was almost through the door when Patten turned his anger upon Jenifer, a move that instantly left Alex rooted to the floor, unable to leave her.

'Do you want everyone to think you're a whore?' Patten shouted, roughly catching hold of her, pulling one of her arms up behind her back until she had to bite her lip to stop herself crying out in protest.

'Of course not. There's no reason, no reason at all. Why are you saying that?'

'Having him here, night in, night out. Sleeping under the same roof. Doesn't that say something about you?'

'Edwin and Peter, they were here too. I wasn't on my own with him. It was they who brought him back here.' She struggled free, shooting Alex a venomous glare as she did so. 'We're barely even friends, let alone anything more. He didn't want to stay here, he really didn't. He doesn't enjoy being near me.'

Alex wanted to protest, but the dam had burst and Thomas was ready for more insults. Words rarely pacified him once his temper was up.

'You won't let me get within three feet of you, even after six months or more, and yet you let this soft-headed oaf paw you . . '

'Stop it,' Jenifer cried, hating Thomas, hating Alex, hating the whole tangled mess she was in. 'You're not talking sense.'

Alex felt he couldn't ignore what was happening in front of him any more. Knowing he couldn't leave her at such a moment, he stepped back into the room, slamming the crookedly hung door behind him. In front of him was a hard wooden settle, a bench that had been kicked askew by Patten, and a couple of stools, all throwing shadows in the strained light of some homemade rush-lights. There were no rugs, curtains, or cushions.

'Leave her alone you brainless idiot. She's

telling you the truth. I mean nothing to her.'
But his refusal to bow out of the argument goaded Thomas's limited patience beyond endurance. Grunting in fury, he launched himself across the room at the other man, and for the second time in four days Alex found himself fighting for his life.

The difference was that this time there was no drink to deaden and to blur. He saw and felt everything in detail, the absolute, almost manic hatred in the other man's face, the flying splinters of wood as they crashed around the room like a pair of raging bulls, the blood that oozed from his arm as it was ripped with a shard from a smashed plate. And he could also hear, above the groaning and the cursing, Jenifer screaming and then begging for them to stop.

Desperate for the pummelling to ease, he did try to do so but there was no halting his opponent who was using every ounce of muscle and fat to destroy.

In a brief moment of respite, he considered collapsing, playing dead, being stopped from doing so because he was afraid for Jenifer's safety if Patten won the day. He thought the man was capable of anything in that irrational mood.

Alex's strength had been stretched by the previous fight, and he had weakened within minutes, offering only token resistance. Patten had the upper hand, much as the others in the Britannia had had absolute advantage once they had punched him into near submission. In one lithe movement Patten bludgeoned him across his back with his arm, then kicked him under the chin as Alex went crashing to the floor by the fire, in the same place, in the same position, he thought, as Jenifer's father

had been in when he had died.
That knowledge stunned him more than Patten's violence.
It's a warning, he panicked, I'm not meant to survive this.
It was as if he was back on the floor of the inn, rolling from side to side to dodge the kicks, and Patten with his heavy work boots on, and his mad intensity, was quite capable of damaging him so much he would never be able to stand again.
It was only by chance that his shattered hand brushed against a large piece of driftwood that had been thrown askance near the fire. He clasped his fingers around it tightly and, knowing he had to take the slightest of opportunities, pulled himself up as far as he could before powering it across Patten's skull as he came in for the kill.
Patten looked upwards for a second after he was hit, dazed, unbelieving, and then he slumped downwards. There was a noticeable shudder as he hit the ground, and then a strained and traumatic hush fell over the room with its overturned furniture and litter of broken crockery.
Alex clutched the mantelshelf for support. Gripping onto it, he watched through eyes that would not focus properly as Jenifer threw herself on the floor, searching urgently for Thomas's pulse. Her face was pale and blotchy, her eyes wild with terror.
She glared up at him, her wet eyes visible to him through his own sweat and tears, and hissed: 'Get out, you moron. Get out of here.'
'But . . ' he muttered, wanting to help clear up, pay for the damage, pay for her kindness of the previous days, though finding that his brain wasn't able to select the right words

speedily enough.
Slowly, as if in a daze that would never leave her, she picked herself up then and stood before him, shaking so much that her teeth chattered.
'Get out before I call for help. I don't want you here any more. I don't want to have to see you. Go.'

1V

He hadn't recovered from the fight, from Jenifer's hatred, when James called at the cottage, at his old home. Alex hadn't bothered to bandage himself or even bathe his wounds. On returning to familiar surroundings, he had fallen into what had been his mother's favourite chair and had just sat there, inert, staring blankly ahead. Still in the stupor, he answered the door, then automatically sank back into the chair again before really noting who it was. One more nail in the coffin.
'Oh, it's you. Finally come to get rid of me for good have you? Come to rob me of a job? Although you let me rejoin the firm again, really I'm just a mere worker again rather than one of your pawns you can use to break the union, so you can take my job away on the quiet and no-one will know or care. Well go on. I certainly haven't the wish to fight you this time.'
He spoke in a disjointed voice that was broken and unbelievably tired. James didn't move, but just hovered in front of his brother, as if stunned. He was unsettled enough about his reason for the visit. The state of Alex

served to bemuse him even further. Wishing that Helen had come with him, as she would have known what to do in such an unexpected situation, he wondered whether he ought to mention the dried blood on his brother's skin and clothing.

Eventually, he presumed that Alex already knew how haunted, how dishevelled he looked, and said nothing. Knowing that he was on a mission of peace, he wanted to tread carefully, and was desperately afraid of provoking when he should be mending bridges.

'Why should I refuse to let you work for me now, when I didn't before, when you quitting your job was entirely your own decision?'

'I may have been taken back on the payroll, but I've been away from work for four days without explanation,' Alex answered flatly. 'Tomorrow will be the fifth. Isn't that taking advantage of the plain fact that my boss is of my own flesh and blood, something you warned me I should never consider doing?'

James took in the untidy, ill-kempt cottage that had once been so full of people, that had been a home of day to day worries and confrontations and loves, but which was now bereft of all but a sick and injured man, and perhaps his parents' 'ghosts'.

'I wouldn't have known you hadn't turned up,' he answered. 'I've hardly been at work myself this week.'

That provoked a grim smile from Alex, accompanied by a lift of a black and blood-stained eyebrow.

'That's a marvel. What's been detaining you then? You're usually so absolutely dedicated. More married to your very extensive business enterprises than to poor Helen.'

That gave James the chance to come straight to the heart of his visit to Biscovey, a part of the world he continued to avoid if at all possible. Slowly, he edged a little way towards Alex, though not so near as to alarm him.

'That may have been so once. It certainly isn't any more. You see, like you I haven't been quite myself during the last couple of days. My world has been changing at some rate. As of a short while ago my fortunes changed. Currently, in truth I haven't any business enterprises left, Alex, only the pit I started off with.'

'What?'

That brought Alex to his feet. His head immediately swirled, and he found his lips had swollen so much that speech was difficult. But what James had said had made him genuinely interested, although he wished his head didn't feel as if it had been cleaved in two.

James hesitated a second.

Is Helen right? he taunted himself. Should I lay myself open to someone who's been more enemy than kin to me in the last few years? To hell with it, she's been right on so many more issues than I have been since we married, so why not on this one?

The decision made, he told his story in great factual depth, thinking that the clearer the explanation the easier it might be for even he, himself, to see everything in perspective.

At the finish, when the crystal clear meaning of his brother's tale had filtered into his brain, Alex could do no more than sit back in the chair, rocking up and down as if in need of comfort and guidance. It was all too much for one day, when the simplest tasks seemed impossible to him.

'Say something then. Don't sit as if you've gone soft in the head,' snapped James who had expected anger or sarcasm or bitter laughter from his almost estranged brother, anything but stunned acceptance.

'I'm only trying to understand exactly what you've told me. It's difficult to grasp. Compared to mine your world appeared so certain, your future so plain. I can't believe that you, you of all people, found the courage to throw it all away.'

What had Helen said - 'I didn't think you had the guts'. Did they both see him as so morally weak?'

'Believe me, I found it,' he said evenly. 'It was a long struggle, but I've got back to some sort of reality, the sort I had when I lived here, I swear I have.'

'And you want me as a partner? Why on earth choose me?' Alex persisted. 'I can't quite see that part. There's no way I can step into Richard Courteney's shoes, that must be obvious. We're so far apart in ways and thinking. In fact I hate the man. And besides that, I've got very little money I can invest with you.'

James started urgently pacing, much as Richard usually had done, up and down his sumptuous study at 'Trevarnioc' when he was trying to rationalise problems. For some unaccountable reason he discovered that he was nervous.

'I have to admit the idea of going into partnership with you was Helen's rather than mine. She always has had a soft spot for you. I even stupidly thought at one time . . but never mind, she convinced me of your qualities. You know the men and they respect you. You've got a good, clear, sound brain, and I can trust you.'

A good, sound brain, Alex thought. How wrong you can be.

'You still haven't mentioned one important fact, although I just touched on it,' he said out loud, wincing with the effort of holding a vital conversation when his lips felt as if they had doubled in size.

'What might that be?'

'What I've already spoken of - my lack of money. I've only pennies. I won't be of any help to you financially. All my savings went towards keeping people afloat when the strike was threatening to leave them with absolutely nothing.'

James had carried wild hopes that his brother might have had some very healthy savings, though in his heart of hearts he had known that he was whistling in the wind, chasing the impossible.

'I don't expect cash from you. I've a bit of money in hand, and I might be able to attract a little more from elsewhere. The trouble is I don't want to carry the burden of being an owner all myself. I also don't want to concentrate on profits and ignore everything else, like I have been doing. I've been there and it's not worth the sweat or the mental agony.'

Although he sounded so honest about it all. Alex could, however, still envisage drawbacks by the score.

'You may have changed a lot, but I haven't. I tell you that if I do accept a partnership with you it will definitely be the men and not the profits that will come first. What you're basically telling me is that you want me there to share all the troubles and problems. It's not very inviting.'

'It's honest, though, and you've been urging me to be bluntly honest since heaven knows when. And remember you'll share the successes too. Don't you think that together we won't have any? You're so damned self-confident I b'lieve you could carry anything off.'

'Oh how are the mighty fallen,' whispered Alex to himself.

James didn't quite catch what he said.

'Sorry?'

'Oh nothing, nothing of much consequence. It just seems to me that you and I have come tumbling down a few personal mountains in the past weeks. We've been going up different ones, I'll grant you, but it now appears that we've both made a hash of everything.'

'I still don't really follow. My mind isn't that sharp at the minute. I'm muddled, unsure. Are you trying to say that life for you isn't too good? I have to say Helen would be horrified if she could see that state you're in now. What on earth has happened to you?'

'I went to help a woman who didn't want help, or protection.' Alex summoned a wry grin. 'The result hasn't done that self-confidence of mine that you talked about much good.'

'Well maybe we could do a bit of rebuilding together.'

'Maybe. Give me time to think about it will you?'

James stood to go.

'If that's what you want. And time off work as well. Don't come back until all the scars are healed.'

'I wouldn't tell me that, brother. That might mean never.'

V

When the gentle knock came on the door Lorna, deep in a stack of sewing, assumed it was Mrs Varcoe coming to collect the winter dress she had ordered. She tossed her now long auburn hair back from her face and called: 'Come in', without being diverted from putting the finishing touches to the silk blouse that was in progress.

It wasn't until a few seconds after she heard the door open, when Mrs Varcoe's loud, raucous voice failed to ring out in greeting, that she thought something was amiss and lifted her head. And then she sat as if struck numb.

It was Nathan. Thinner, browner, older, less hungry-looking, though still very much Nathan.

'My God, it's you,' was all she could manage before being flooded with the acute desire to hide.

However much he had altered she knew that she had changed to a much greater extent.

She had moved to Polruan two months before, to a former fisherman's property overlooking Fowey Harbour. It was from there that she was running her small, dress-making business, having been accepted among the locals as a rather drab spinster from across the river, one who liked to keep herself to herself, but who had inordinate skill as a seamstress.

This view had been perpetuated by the fact that she rarely ventured out, or bothered much about her own appearance. Looks had ceased to mean anything to her. She rarely ate well, which meant that she was now so thin she was bordering on the skeletal. And although her

hair remained auburn the colour had dulled, its richness seeping away with the years.
Her clothes, unlike the flattering outfits she made for others, were ill-fitting, and overall she had aged as much mentally as physically, which showed. The life she had had with Samuel, and its outcome, mixed with the disappointments she had endured, had brought about a general malaise, only broken by her determination to at least carve an independent living for herself. All the hardships were reflected in the defeat that was evident in her sad, tired eyes.
'You didn't know I was back?' he asked softly, edging nearer to her, moving slowly as if he was afraid she would bolt any second.
At that moment he was doing, in reality, what he had done a thousand times in dreams, almost a decade since leaving Cornish shores. She didn't run, staying statue-like as he moved close enough to her for a touch, a kiss.
'No . . no, I didn't,' she stammered, noting that her hands were perspiring and inner panic was increasing.
Shaking as if her body and mind would never be still again, she put down the blouse she was holding before her perspiration stained it.
'I've seen James and Alex. I'm sure half of Biscovey must know I'm back. I've been told, though, that you've cut most of your ties there.'
His voice had deepened, become throatier, the accent slightly less Cornish.
'I keep to myself these days,' she answered tersely as the breath began to return to her lungs. 'And I'd have no call to speak to your brothers, or bother contacting them. I've cut all ties with the Roseveans.'
Polruan was once the principal port in the

harbour, though its sister across the water, Fowey, had long since overtaken it in importance.

It had gradually come to be more of a fishing village, with a couple of reasonably busy boat-building yards, one based on the Coal Wharf on the river frontage. It had a sprinkling of second class villas that hugged the hillside at the mouth of the river, and a number of homes standing quite regally within their own green grounds.

A passenger ferry plied across the river to Fowey at regular intervals throughout the day, and Nathan watched it leave the tiny granite jetty, creating a tiny wake as it negotiated its way through the barques and barquentines to Whitehouse Slip at Fowey. Everything seemed so small, like a toy town, to him after the broad, exposed spaces of America.

'So Billy wasn't exaggerating. You have turned yourself into a recluse.'

He sounded as if he was criticising her. He wasn't. Really the words were used to cover the horror of finding her disillusioned and middle-aged in a seemingly cheerless, dingy room. Always, he had remembered her with a halo of sunlight around silken hair, and with wide, generous lips always ready to break into a radiant smile at the first sight of him.

Still stunned by his arrival, she pushed the blouse to the far side of her work table, determinedly staying sitting at the same time, and not asking him to sit with her. She didn't want him to relax in her territory. He had no right to.

'I'm living the best way that suits me. You have a nerve walking back into my life after all you've done to me, and throwing down your opinions as if I would think they really matter.'

Hearing her bitterness, he hauled his gaze away from the river, a view that could never upset him, and studied her.

Realising that he had tackled their first meeting for many years in the wrong manner, he sighed: 'Yes, yes, you're right, but I wasn't being critical.'

Steeling himself for further recriminations, he prayed that her hostility wouldn't be great enough to drive him back to Biscovey straight away. To some extent he had known that his visit would not be overly welcome to her, which meant that an amiable confrontation had never been expected.

At the same time she was regaining some of her equilibrium, and was equally sure she didn't want him realising how much his old betrayals had crushed her. In fact, she'd cut her tongue out before she did that.

In response to such thoughts she straightened her back, rubbed her hands on a nearby piece of spare cloth, pulled back the blouse towards her, and resumed work, although the stitching she was attempting was so poor she knew she would have to unpick it once he had gone.

'I've been back in Cornwall about a week now,' he said, seeing from her set expression that she had suspended emotions. The lines around her pursed mouth were deep, her skin sallow.

'Oh, a whole seven days. Do you intend on staying on this occasion, or are all those troubles of yours still urging you on, pushing you to keep running?'

Studiously, he ignored her sarcasm, and that and his contained manner irked her further, fuelling her resentment.

'I made myself some money in America.'

'Good for you, though please don't by starting to throw it around in here. I don't want your money, or pity. I pay my own way. Do tell me though, have you still got this fortune, or have you poured it away at some bar somewhere?'

'No,' he countered, itching to rip both needle, cotton and material from her hands, wanting to shake her until she smiled her glorious smile, until the weariness fell from her. 'I've used quite a lot of it to buy a house in Looe, on the banks of the river there, and a local newspaper.'

That staggered her so much that her fingers stilled.

'A newspaper. What on earth are you going to do with that?'

'Ensure it makes a profit for the first time in over three years.'

But you're a miner, Nathan. In every muscle you've got, you're a miner. You told me in your letters that you'd written a few articles, though I had no idea you'd ever consider owning a newspaper.'

Needing to do something, he stood up and went to look over her shoulder at the material she was working on. He would have got even closer, but was prevented from doing so by the way she openly cowered from him. They had both misjudged each other. Although she had told him of her change of direction he had never been able to imagine her as a dressmaker by trade.

'I was a miner. I arrived in Tombstone, and then I became a writer, of sorts. In this venture, though, I do intend to join the two. I'll deal with local news, and also concentrate on stories about some of those who've gone abroad - to Australia, South Africa, Mexico and America - in fact anywhere where there are mines and Cornish miners. Enough have struck out in the last thirty years to form a whole nation living on foreign soil.'

Finally, she threw her needlework down in disgust. It was no use even trying to make headway, she was ruining it and the material was not cheap.

'Well, what has all this got to do with me? Have you come here to boast, or to get my approval for this newspaper idea of yours? I'm nothing in your life, you're nothing in mine. What you do is irrelevant to me.'

He had rehearsed his speech for days, months, years.

'I know I was a bad influence on your life. I hurt you, so I understand why you're so angry. The thing is, though, it was better that I left. In fact back then there was no alternative for me. The trouble was it didn't stop me wanting you, as I thought it would do. Those letters, sent to you and received from you, meant a good, a great deal to me.'

At his words she hung her head. Her hair fell forward and she flipped it back, just wanting him to go.

She's so vulnerable, Nathan thought sadly, and stopped himself talking any more of the past. He had an idea how much pain she felt.

'Anyway, I couldn't come back to this part of Cornwall, to my home, without seeing you, someone who was so much a part of my old life. I did think that perhaps you'd like to see this new house of mine and maybe the newspaper office. I'd like another opinion on both. I bought them within days, on impulse, and now I'm starting to doubt my decisions.'

With a great deal of effort she turned to face him and take in the affluence that had become part of him, the good clothes, the gold watch, the assurance where once there had been doubts and drama. The alarming vitality which remained was channelled instead of being unleashed without direction.

'Go with you to Looe so you can flaunt your success and good fortune? I don't think so.' Hearing the censure in her tone, he frowned, running his fingers through his hair as he always had done when upset.

'That wasn't the reason. I haven't come back to flaunt. Look Lorna, coming to look at one house and a newspaper building that is very far from being grand, would not destroy you. I do want another opinion.'

The insensitive, arrogant halfwit, she thought. Doesn't he have any notion of what he has put me through?

'Oh, but it would upset Nathan. You can't turn me back to the person I used to be. You've moved further away from me than you ever had before Joel Harman died that night. You can't ever again be the man I loved, just as I can never be that girl you chose to run from. All I ask is that you leave me now, and don't judge me. That's not much to ask, surely?'

Chastened, he rose to go, although he was not going to quit her life that simply. In that respect he remained undefeated.

'I've promised to see James and Helen today. There's much I've got to catch up on with them. They seem very close now, thank goodness. From the few words that Billy, and you, had written to me I thought them a mismatch.'

'Yes,' she admitted, thinking that he was deliberately changing the subject, 'there were some difficult years for them.'

'I'm coming back, though. There's a horse

waiting for me on the other side of the river, and it won't take me long to ride to the Crown at Luxulyan, lunch with them, and then ride back again. I'll return here by late afternoon, and hopefully by then you'll have changed your mind about Looe. It'll only be for a couple of hours, and it can't harm.'

She knew exactly who it was when the knock came at 4.30pm. Having watched the ferry dock at the quay, and with her cottage only three minutes walk away, she had been able to follow his figure as he disembarked, until he headed up the steep main street, where he would eventually turn right.

Before that her eyes had followed every move of the ferry as it had inched its way towards Polruan through the sailing ships and the larger china clay vessels, anchored up in the middle of the estuary. The water at the mouth of the river was relatively smooth that day, but there was some swell and every now and then the ferry would dip into the waves and almost be lost from view.

There were moments when all she wanted to do was stare out of her window and watch the world go by, a world that she now felt desperately detached from. Further up from her home, nearer the entrance of the river, was an old blockhouse, now decayed, from which a chain used to be extended across the harbour to St Catherine's Castle on the Fowey side. Its aim had been to protect the ancient town of Foye from pirates.

Would that there was something that could protect me and my heart from Nathan, she thought with rancour.

As if she had no control over her movements, she opened the door to him, standing at the same time in front of him, blocking the entrance. She had considered changing her dowdy clothes, in the end deciding not to give him the satisfaction of doing so. Part of her hadn't really expected him to return. The old Nathan wouldn't have bothered to be so persistent, except maybe at the outset of their affair.

She did not have to spell out her answer. He intuitively knew it by the way she stood there, her lips pressed tightly together, her arms folded. There was no welcome in her features, no sunshine. He could have sworn that for a split second he saw Samuel standing behind her, with exactly the same defiant expression. And if some of his ill-humour had been passed on to her during their marriage it's not her fault, he chided himself. I'm the one who idly ripped her confidence in herself to shreds.

Lorna spoke first.

'I haven't altered my decision, nor will I. You're wasting your energies even bothering with me.'

Her front door opened right onto the street that wound up alongside the river to the blockhouse. As a result, he was standing in full public view, which made it impossible for him to try to relax himself, or her.

'Do you expect to spend the rest of your days then sitting in that poky room, bent over scraps of cloth, with a scowl on your face and short words for anyone who dares to intrude?'

'Only when you're the intruder. Everyone else is invited,' she snapped.

The day had drained him. The reunions, the business dealings, the explanations, the desire to put past wrongs right, had required enormous effort. That lunchtime he had tried to be professional and practical with James, when his brother had approached him for a

loan, although such intentions had failed miserably. In the end, he had given the money with no conditions attached, as if, he thought, trying to buy himself back into favour.
'I see, all too well,' he answered, stifling his annoyance and dismay. Determined not to capitulate completely, he produced a piece of card from his pocket, plunging it into her hand. She recoiled from his touch as if he was about to infect her.
'Here are the addresses of my new home, and of the newspaper office. Have them both. If you're ever curious enough about what I'm up to come and see me. We . . I . . really do need to talk properly to each other, and I do have this idea that you could be a positive influence on me.'
As she was standing so near to him, literally only inches away, he wished fervently that he could have held her, if only for a fleeting moment.
'I won't intrude on you any more. I can see my presence is upsetting you. But if I don't see you again, for a while at least, look after yourself Lorna better than you've obviously been doing. You owe it to yourself.'
He turned, and as soon as he had done so she slammed the door shut with such force that she thought she might have damaged it. Then she leant against it for an age, unable to move, staying there until her muscles began to ache with the tension inside her. Quivering, she made her way back to her work, using the back of her hand as she went to wipe away the very unwanted, dropping tears.
She told herself they had sprung from rage, but that had burned out a long time before. What was left, what was always left, was the all-enveloping loss.

V1

Alex eventually moved in with James, Helen and Glynn at Tregrehan, and the old cottage at Biscovey stood empty and uncared for. The two brothers had been tentative with each other, rather like unsure lovers, at the start of their new and unexpected, alliance, though gradually they learned to accept that each had changed and they had become too weary to prolong any more fraternal feuding.
Helen had offered Alex what had been the room where James had slept alone, and he barely hesitated in accepting a way out of his solitary existence.
It was a temporary measure, he agreed, thinking at the same time that being with them would give him a sane, comfortable base from which to reassess both himself, and his aspirations.
If he was honest with himself he was surprised how well the new partnership was working. Initially, he had expected intense disagreements, even fights, as their past record was fraught with conflict. Instead, he discovered that his brother had mellowed to an extraordinary degree, the more so since Helen had fallen pregnant again. And he, well he had mellowed too, though not through the love of a good woman, more because of a number of chastening experiences.
When the Rosevean partnership had first been announced he had had to endure a great deal of sniping from those who saw him as an ex-rebel selling out for money and status. Some

of this had been quietened when improvements were put into effect at their pit. Sick pay was initiated, safer conditions were enforced and insurance schemes became a reality.

J and A Rosevean, although nowhere near being the richest company around, did begin gaining the reputation of being one of the best employers.

With the help of Nathan they had scraped together enough cash for another enterprise with reasonable promise. They bought into a granite quarry at Luxulyan which had been opened in the mid 1860s by the enterprising William Polkinghorne.

The deal was struck after Alex had inspected the quarry, later persuading James that it was right to buy.

Contracts had already been lined up with the government for the quarry to supply between 150,000 and 200,000 tons of dressed granite. The beauty was that the stone was so easy to transport to the port at Par. A railway existed linking the china clay districts of Roche and St Austell, as well as all the Luxulyan granite quarries, with the docks.

The steam engines had to negotiate a steep incline, but a portion of the River Par, which sprang to life in the parish of Roche, had been carried over the Luxulyan valley by a vast viaduct for the purpose of working the machinery needed for overcoming this hazard. The viaduct/aqueduct, built by Joseph Thomas Treffry, crossed the lush valley on ten arches each of 40' span. It was supported by piers 28' by ten and a half feet at the base and was 650' long and 98' high.

James didn't want to own the world any more. Although their income wasn't spectacular, for with the improvements they had enforced the outgoings had increased, it was enough for him. The question was, how long would it be enough? He didn't expect Richard to take his defection lightly, without retaliation, and in past days there had been signs that this was well and truly the case.

Mr Courteney had begun to use his influence among the gentry, the land-owners, the businessmen and the backers who had once been anxious to deal with James. Now many of them were refusing to reply to any of his correspondence, or consider his requests. Deals had begun to fall through at the last moment for no apparent reason bar perversity, and those major families who controlled vital railways and ports had started to demand higher rental charges from the Roseveans than from anyone else. It meant that the already tighter profit was being pared down to the bone.

As the anti-Rosevean campaign began to bite, over the summer months of 1880, Alex and James became more concerned than each would, for a while, admit to the other. They tried to shrug their worries off, assuring themselves that matters would ease as soon as Richard's spite had run its course. The strategy failed to work. In the end the strength of the opposition could not be denied.

'Richard told me once he had the ability to close down any smaller company he wished,' muttered James one evening when they were sitting around the table after their evening meal, and were dissecting their ever-mounting troubles. 'Now we're one of those companies, and I for one feel like a fly about to be swatted. I tell you I know for a certainty he can make all his threats come good. I've seen

him at work, and he is absolutely ruthless.'
He was hunched forward, resting his chin on one upturned palm, with his other hand tightly holding Helen around her waist, though he was staring at the floor, rather than at his wife, because he knew if he faced her full on she would be able to read the depth of his concern in his expression. Part of him was grateful for the new-found domestic contentment, while the other part was beset by regrets.

'He won't shut us down without a fight from both of us,' chipped in Alex decisively. 'J and A Rosevean is about all I have left in the world, so I'll keep going to the bitter end. I'll take him down with me if I have to.'

'Haven't you two had enough battles?' weighed in Helen, who had had a lifetime of watching her father plotting the destruction of others and, in her eyes, achieving very little as a result. 'Remember that he is like an old dog fox who's out-thought most people for years. You must plan this sensibly if you want a hope of coming out the best in the long run.'

James, not wanting her worried in any way, eventually leant towards her and kissed her lightly, forcing himself to assure her: 'This time right is on our side. Don't fret. I'll take him extremely seriously.'

'We both will,' agreed Alex. 'If what you say is true he must have made quite a number of enemies over the years. Perhaps we can link up with some of them. And what about Nathan? He might be able to help now he's a respected newspaper owner. He's surprised me you know, since he returned home. He definitely is someone to have on your side, and he's got a personal interest in all this too. We're using some of his money, remember.'

The camaraderie that was now part of their

relationship was evident, but it was to come under some strain a few weeks later. By then they were under immense pressure. Their rents at Par and Charlestown docks had been pushed up so high that they had gone into debt to afford them, and they were also finding it difficult to book space on the railways that took, very importantly for them, the china clay and the granite to the ports.

James, on the brink of misery the day before, believed he had stumbled across an answer to their woes, if the money required for it was available from Nathan.

He had been offered a stake in the proposed further development of another port in St Austell Bay, that of Pentewan, which lay betweenTrenarren and Mevagissey within a large, sandy bay. Pentewan had had a dock for many years, though it had silted slightly, causing business to decline quite rapidly. The idea was to clear the harbour entrance again and build it up into a true rival to Par.

Sir Christopher Hawkins had been responsible for the beginnings of the harbour in 1829, and the four mile long railway that was linked to it. The wagons full of china clay had travelled for many years, by gravity, from a depot off West Hill at St Austell, and came to rest on a level along the line. Horses pulled them the remainder of their journey to the waiting ships.

The recurrent silting of the harbour was due to the clay waste brought down the river, and the lower end of the railway line was often flooded. However, locomotives had been introduced about ten years before, and although there was no official passenger service, passengers still used the line, worked by the engine which had been aptly named

'Pentewan'.

This railway was to be improved even further, with proposals for the poor harbour facilities to be vastly updated.

On paper the scheme looked faultless to James, as if it had been waiting for them, primed to solve their problems. The company which had been especially formed to push the plans through did not include Richard, or any of his cronies.

Above all, the business would have complete control over its own port and railway. This meant that neither he, nor Alex, would have to worry anymore about the attitude of other owners, as they would be truly independent, spared having to spend every hour of seemingly every day begging for some sort of reasonable rental, or decent space for their trucks.

With these benefits uppermost in his mind, he had as good as promised his co-operation, and the necessary funding, before he consulted with Alex. He had concluded that while his brother might be the true expert in clay, he was the business driver of the partnership.

However, as soon as Alex heard the full details of the Pentewan scheme he was full of doubts, which he didn't keep to himself. Everything about the plans unsettled him. J and A Rosevean had no great wealth of funds to play with, and it was obvious to him that one foolhardy move would send them to destruction.

'You're mad to even consider it,' he said bluntly, despite trying not to seem too condemning.

He didn't want to antagonise too much. He wanted to state his point, while simultaneously holding back from causing a split between them, as that would cause nothing but harm - and play straight into Richard Courteney's hands.

James couldn't but help defend his point of view immediately, as his tatters of remaining dignity could easily be eradicated.

'What prompts you to say that? You haven't even looked at the papers I've brought home with me. They tell you the whole story, and they're very convincing. I took myself off to Fowey this afternoon, sat on my own in Readymoney Cove and thought of nothing else but this plan. It's wholly sound.'

'I know Pentewan very well,' Alex persisted. 'It's silting badly, and has been for decades. It's a problem that won't go away. It'll only get worse.'

'That's the whole idea of the proposal, to counteract the silting once and for all. The port's been very successful in the past. It can easily be viable again. Remember that, apart from china clay and china stone, outgoing traffic from there in the not long-ago past has also taken in iron ore and tin, and in-going freights have been of coal, limestone and sand.'

'Are you listening to me? What they hope to do is impossible. In this case the sea will have its way whatever men attempt. Those involved in this company you're talking about have got their heads in the clouds, or they've been duped too.'

In response James flung the papers down in front of him, displaying bluntly that he was not persuaded by his brother's argument. Alex picked them up, though did not study them. He decided to change his attack.

'All right. Let's turn this entire argument around. Who are the other men involved?

Where is all the money coming from?'
'I was approached by an Amos Baker and Dennis Arnold from Plymstock, just over the Tamar.'
'I've never heard of them,' Alex insisted, keeping his voice down to some extent because he had an idea that Helen was in the adjoining room.
If she was, he told himself, she must have heard them. That worried him, because he didn't like to quarrel in his brother's house, with her so close, not when they had opened their doors to him, and let him live there. But, in this matter, there was no alternative but to put forward his views.
'Well you wouldn't have, would you? When was the last time you attended a meeting of pit owners? You don't mix in their sort of company. The details are very clear and succinct. Flick through those documents, you'll see how ill-founded your fears are. It's a marvellous idea, or at least that's how I see it.'
'I agree to a certain extent. If it worked it would solve everything for us. The trouble is, James, there's no way it will work.'
'Read the papers, for all our sakes, please read the papers.'
Accepting that he had to make an effort, Alex set aside all objections and retired to the table with the bundle. It took him a full hour to assess every scrap of information, but had really absorbed all that he needed to know after five minutes.
When he had finished James's annoyance hadn't abated. Alex was determined to stick to his ground, however, for there was too much at stake for him to give way.
'Why, and when did they approach you?' he

enquired softly.

'They made contact about seven weeks back, but didn't explain everything then. I had vaguely heard of them before. They told me that they understand the difficulties companies like ours face, and realise we're under pressure. They thought I was reliable. I have some reputation left. Past history wasn't all created by Helen's father.'

Alex stretched, held back his quick retort, and walked to the window. It was a damp autumn day, with the Cornish mizzle enveloping the tiny village of Tregrehan. He couldn't envisage it clearing for another three or four hours and by then it would be night. Once the drizzle arrived it seemed to want to cling to the south coast of the county for hours, even days on end.

'Are you sure you weren't particularly recommended?'

James couldn't contain his impatience.

'Ye gods Alex, come to the point. What are you driving at? By your attitude you either haven't read those papers thoroughly, or you're determined not to change your mind whatever facts are put before you. Which is it?'

Alex rubbed his right hand, hard and calloused, over his forehead, searching for the best way to say what was in his mind. Then he turned away from the grey late afternoon to face the room, and his fraternal partner, who he really did not want to upset further.

'It's an ideal scheme from one respect James. It's a marvellous plan if someone's aiming to entice away all our, or should I say, your, money from us, and then pour it into a useless drain.'

'Do you think I'm a total fool?' James

breathed, as Alex's reasoning became slowly and painfully clear.

Was he really that naive? It pained him that he wasn't sure of the answer to that question.

'Of course you're no idiot. You've been placed in such a position that you have to consider every opportunity that comes your way in case it holds within it a chance for our long-term survival. With that in mind, it does seem to be a beneficial scheme, on the surface. Nevertheless, you must believe me when I say Pentewan will continue to silt.

'Nothing will prevent that. Money might help it this year, but next year those sand banks will build up again, with a vengeance. It would be a bottomless pit for any further funds we might find from Nathan, or elsewhere. It would absorb every penny and in the end show no reward whatsoever. It's a trap.'

James struggled to salvage some self-respect.

'Look, you may think I've been duped, but if I can prove that Baker and Arnold are genuine will you at least re-consider the plan?'

Alex hesitated, not wishing to give such a rash promise, though accepting he had to meet his brother half way, and be seen to be doing it, for the sake of continuing harmony.

'Well, all I can say is that you must dig deep, and not be sidetracked. They won't have made an obvious deal with Courteney, though I'm certain he must be involved somewhere along the line, he must be. My intuition has proved me wrong many, many times, I admit that, but in this case I'm sure it's right.'

James remained stung by the way the conversation had gone, by how simply his optimism had been sunk.

'Oh, I'll dig very deep because I'm equally

sure of my judgement, and of the honesty of those two men.'

He woke before dawn, only to discover that Alex was already up, dressed, and about to leave the house for Bodmin. Despite the passing of night the tension that had built between them the previous evening was still there, and would not completely evaporate. They could not relax in each other's company. Anxious to be away, to prove how right he had been, James left without a word. Alex had wanted to ask him where he was going, deciding in the end it was tactful not to pose too many questions.

Instead, he asked Helen when she appeared moments after he heard James ride away. She was in the process of bending down to straighten Glynn's clothing and place a warm jacket around him, and as she did so Alex noticed how quickly her waist was thickening.

'I'm not exactly sure where he's gone,' she said gently. 'He tossed and turned all night. He couldn't settle, and try as I could I couldn't reach him. You really upset him yesterday.'

'I'm sorry. That's the farthest apart we've been since our . . our reconciliation. It wasn't intentional. Perhaps I shouldn't have moved in with you, perhaps this partnership is a huge mistake. It shouldn't be though. I've no dispute with him any more, in fact I've come to respect him.'

Helen smiled.

'Despite all that when you're sure you're right you don't hesitate to press it home do you, don't draw back from going in for the kill? You say what you think in a very definite manner, but I suppose that's because you're a true Rosevean. The trouble was you didn't give him any comfort.'

'I tried to soften my words, I really did. You must understand that now isn't the time for us to be caught out. We've got to be alert and decisive or else your father's going to smash us. We're fighting a battle that's almost impossible to win, as I'm sure you already know.'

She gave Glynn a kiss, checked again that he was dressed properly, and then let him toddle off to play outside, within sight of her. Then she straightened herself. Her stomach felt heavy. It was not a good morning for her. She hadn't been sick when carrying Glynn. Perhaps this is a girl, she told herself.

'You are positive my father's behind this approach aren't you. It's one of his little ploys isn't it?'

'Don't you think so?'

'I'm exactly the same as you. I wouldn't be at all surprised by anything my father said, or did.'

Helen was alone when James returned that evening, and although he tried to appear as if all was well and instantly grabbed Glynn, taking him off to have a romp in their dining room, she knew something had worried him. The stoop of the shoulders and the refusal to meet her gaze told her that the day had not been good.

After Glynn was put to bed she went to place her arms around James's neck. She wanted some affection, even if he didn't. The old instincts returned, and he automatically rejected her concerned embrace, twisting away from her with such vehemence that she was almost sent flying. Seeing her falter, he caught her quickly and desperately pulled her to him, putting a hand behind her head and burying her face into his neck, letting it stay there so he could take in the reassuring feel, and smell, of her.

'I'm sorry darling, so sorry,' he choked as he gave way to dejection. 'You're pregnant as well. I should be cosseting you, not hurling you across the room. What the hell have you ever done to the world to be landed with me?'

Relieved that all was at least well between them again she wriggled free, took his hand, and led him through to their bedroom where she sat him down on the edge of the bed and took his boots off. Then she sat beside him, stroking his forehead.

'Now please tell me, my love, what the matter is.'

'I'm stupid, that's what the trouble is. So sure of myself and yet I have to say, so pathetically dense.'

'And why have you come to that very wrong conclusion? Where did you take yourself off to this morning?'

'I rode to St Austell, left the horse there and then took the train to Plymouth. There I asked around, and turned up some unpleasant truths.'

She saw it all, although if she was honest she had guessed what had happened as soon as he arrived home.

'And Alex was right, about my father, and about Pentewan?'

'Yes, yes, Alex was right. Baker and Arnold did approach me on your father's instructions. The scheme is genuine enough, and so are the documents they gave me. A consortium is trying to improve the port, but those that were trying to entice me into it are in Richard's pay.

'It's obvious, with hindsight, that the whole

thing's a huge gamble. I doubt if they will succeed in keeping it clear of sandbanks. It would be a thankless, expensive task trying to keep that harbour open.

'I went to look at Pentewan on my own when I came home - not with them as I did before. When I was there a few days ago, with them, they blinkered me, telling me the wonders of what was going to happen. I talked to different people this afternoon, those who work there already and have no advantage in lying to me.'

'So my father's absolutely determined to bankrupt us?'

'Do you know what galls me most? The fact that Richard understands how brainless I am, how likely I was to grasp any chance, however derisory it might be, of escaping those blood-sucking dues we're being forced to pay. He played me as if I had no intellect, and how right he was. It seemed such a marvellous solution, at least to my few senses.'

Helen tightened her arms around him protectively.

'Well he was wrong, wasn't he?

'What do you mean? I was quite prepared to go along with it all. I welcomed his bait with open arms.'

'But you were wise enough to take Alex on as a partner, and to listen to him and consider what he was saying. That wouldn't have happened once, you would have ploughed ahead regardless.'

After a while he lifted his head, kissed her with longing for a full minute or so, and managed a weak smile.

'Yes, I suppose you can say all that. Thank God for a perceptive brother, and a remarkable wife.'

'Thank God for your new humility, you mean.'

V11

The tussle with Richard Courteney and his hangers-on was to preoccupy Alex for months. It was the only subject on his mind bar one. He also wanted to see Jenifer again, to apologise for the brawl in her house and make her understand that he would never knowingly hurt her.

It was fear of her hostility to him that kept him at bay. After the confrontation in her home, he had sent her money for necessary repairs as he was sure that at least two of her chairs had been broken during the fight, as well as a stack of crockery.

The money had been sent via Peter and Edwin, though not before he had quizzed them about their sister.

Was she happy? How was Thomas treating her? They had failed to see what all his concern was about. They had assured him that Jenifer was 'brave', and eventually he perceived that as long as she kept house for them, fetching their meals on time, cleaning up after them, she would always be 'brave'. It seemed, to him, that they were oblivious to any of her in-depth feelings. She was their older sister who had stepped into their mother's place in the way of natural succession rather than being a woman with her own needs and desires.

After debating for weeks whether or not to visit her they unexpectedly came face to face with each other in the heart of St Austell, outside the White Hart. At the time she was heading towards Fore Street, walking quickly with her head held high, her figure erect despite the fact that she was carrying two quite full bags, inducing second glances with her peculiarly purposeful but innately smooth movements, like a cat on the prowl.

Jenifer saw him at the same moment as he noticed her, but she would not acknowledge him, merely quickening her pace still further. However, now the chance was there he was anxious to grab it. At least in St Austell, with horses thundering past, or pawing the ground outside the inn, and shoppers thronging the paths, they were on neutral territory.

Intent on seizing the opportunity, he ran straight up behind her, calling her name out loud so that she could not ignore him without creating a minor scene.

'Jenifer, I've been wanting to see you,' he insisted, stopping in front of her. 'Don't walk on, you can't be in that much of a hurry, and there's so much I want to say. I need to thank you for looking after me, and want to apologise for the way it finished. I had hoped to check that all's well with you.'

Her hair was loose and reached her waist in jet black strands, her cheeks were flushed and for once her clothes were bright with challenge.

'I am well, thank you, and I appreciate your concern, but whatever you want I'm afraid I haven't got time to waste. I'm really in a hurry, so if you'd step aside like the gentleman I'm sure you are now and then . . '

She was flustered. Although it didn't show too much it betrayed itself in her jerking hands and her extra sharp speech.

He's changed again since we last met, she thought. He's more assured, in control again. I wish he didn't unsettle me quite so much. It angers me.

Alex didn't move.

'I so regret the last time we met, how it ended with me and Thomas.' He stood in front of her with his feet slightly apart, his arms outstretched, within inches of clasping her. 'You've got to understand, he was insulting you. I lost my head. I could take whatever he said until he turned on you.'

'It's all right. It's in the past and forgotten,' she said tartly, trying to dismiss both the subject, which distressed her, and Alex.

'Not by Patten, I'm sure. He's not the type to forgive, or forget.'

'I wouldn't know. I haven't seen him since.'

'Well that's no bad miss,' he said instinctively, pleased at the news and not bothering to hide his reaction.

As a result she turned on him, not heeding now the fact that they were in full view of shoppers, farmers rushing to market and a steady stream of guests going in and out of the inn.

'And just what would you know about it all? Nothing. You never do know anything, not really. Nothing of any use. He might have been offering me a way out. Perhaps he meant more to me than you could ever hope to guess.'

Looking around, he knew that he didn't want to argue on the street. Both of them probably knew half the people pushing past them, and he suddenly felt very exposed. Her change of mood had unnerved him as well. Certainly, he hadn't anticipated breaking through her supposedly ice cool barrier so easily.

'Hush now, please. Look, have you already finished everything that you came into town

for?'
'What if I have?'
'I'll take you home. It's a long way to walk with those bags, and there's rain in the offing. Glance over there and you'll see the clouds gathering Mevagissey way. I've a pony and trap, they're over there by the Market House.'
'I'd much prefer to walk,' she snapped. 'I don't want to be a trial. And there is always the train.'
Why did he always see himself in her?
'Isn't that exactly what I said to you before you persuaded me to stay on in your home when I was hurt?' he murmured, taking hold of her bags with no intention of being stopped.
The weight of them surprised him. Surely she'd never even make it to St Blazey carrying them herself, he thought. It's miles away. What if she has to do this every week? As he was in no mood to accept a refusal he eventually carried both bags in his right hand, although it strained him, and took one of her arms with his left hand, literally propelling her across the street and through the churchyard towards the Sun Inn and the massive granite Market House, opened in 1844 and roofed in Delabole slates. In spite of his determination she did not go with him gracefully.
'You needn't be so brutal. Leave me be. You seem to have enough trouble with my shopping, without tackling me as well.'
'And you needn't always be so . . wretchedly obstinate.'
The pony and trap was where he had said it would be, tethered outside the steps to the huge building with its vaulted ceiling and massive pillars, and its galleries and enormous

roof trusses. Once there he went to help her into the trap, with little success as she pushed him away and climbed in unaided.

They journeyed along the main road eastwards towards St Blazey which lay at the foot of the track to Luxulyan Valley, a strained and embarrassed reticence between them. Now that she was so close to him, and could not storm off in her usual imperious way, he found himself tongue-tied. Her whole body language showed that she was seething with annoyance and fury, that her quiet, reflective hike into town had been turned into an ordeal.

They bowled past Holmbush, then the turning to Tregrehan on the left and the Britannia Inn on the right, before the Welsh mountain pony pulled them up the hill through St Blazey Gate, by the turning for Biscovey, and then trotted downwards into St Blazey itself. There Alex turned off the road onto the forecourt of the Packhorse Inn, which stood right in the centre.

The clouds had been left behind them. A grey mass could still be seen though, looking menacing over St Austell way, but where they now were the sky was only porcelain blue. With jangling nerves, Jenifer suddenly turned towards Alex and grasped his shirt as the pony came to a halt.

'What are we doing here, why have we stopped?'

'I'm letting Bracken have some water. She always likes to stop here at the horse trough. It's quite a natural thing to do. In fact that's why it's here.'

'I'll get down then, and have a rest on the wall over there by the path. I don't like perching up here like the lady I'm not.'

In spite of being aware of the truth, that she wanted to be as far from him as she could, he refused to let that bother him. As she got down from the trap he watched her closely, drawn to the trim waist that swayed so rhythmically, and the tumbling hair, and in that moment his life took on a set, forward pattern again.

In a minute of clarity, he knew once again who he was and where he was heading. He also knew how to get there.

When he had tended to Bracken he sauntered over to Jenifer, sitting on the wall, staring down at the cluttered street with an absent gaze. St Blazey was lively enough in its own right, especially in the evenings with the shops traditionally staying open late there on specific nights.

If she was honest she had no need to traipse so far to buy the staples that her family needed. The long walk to St Austell had been taken to occupy her mind, to ensure she wasn't at home on her own for too many hours, where she was apt to mope.

'We're ready to go again, but I thought we could make one more stop before I finally see you right home.'

'Oh yes?'

'I thought we could take a stroll through the Luxulyan Valley, not a long walk, just for a minute or two. It's one of the quietest places I know in which to talk, that's if you avoid the granite quarries.'

'Maybe I don't want to walk, or talk, with you, have you considered that? It's only just bearable having to sit beside you in the trap,' she retorted, flushing.

'I'm listening to no objections today, and the reins are in my hands.'

Eventually, she gave way, though in bad humour. Once they had resumed their journey he left the road that would have taken them to her home, and detoured along one of the tracks that criss-crossed the substantial, beautiful woods that were so resplendent with bluebells and rhododendrons in the spring. The vegetation was thick and lush, shading them from the weather. He was sure he could hear thunder in the distance, but where they were the ferns and bushes grew so luxuriantly they could hardly see clouds. It was green, and serene.

Trying to counteract doubts about what he was planning, he guided Bracken towards a hidden lake where he often came fishing, especially when he needed to be alone, to think, as had happened more in the last few years than ever before. When he stopped the trap, she didn't want to leave what she had come to regard as some sort of sanctuary, but he gave her little option, and with a face that resembled the thunder rumbling to the west, she alighted.

'Believe me,' he said as they set off beside the softly lapping water, you're best without Patten. He's brutish, and he's a loser as well as a womaniser. As far as I know he always has been and you'd be misguided if you thought he'd change now. I think it would be an impossibility.'

Within about a quarter of a mile he halted beside one of the great granite boulders that littered the area around Luxulyan, sat on his haunches and pulled her down beside him. After then throwing his coat on the grass he gestured for her to use it to sit on, and she perched primly on it, a scowl etched into her startling features.

With some ease she tucked her long legs underneath her, making him notice again how supple she was. But she pointedly turned her back on him, and stared across at the other side of the valley.

'Well, whatever you may say about him, perhaps losers ought to stick together,' she answered harshly.

'Good heavens, you may bracket me in that category, but please don't place yourself in the same class as him. You don't do you?'

'And by what right do you judge either me or him?' she rebuked him harshly, turning round once more to look at him with as much haughtiness as she could muster.

'I know you. I know him. I judge on sound evidence.'

Standing up suddenly, he threw a round pebble down into the river running at the base of the aqueduct, the resulting splash echoing around them. Behind them rose a hillside from which an enormous block of Cornish porphyry, weighing seventy tons, had been taken to form a sarcophagus of intense deep grey mottled with black, pink, and pale buff, and streaked with white, for the burial of the Duke of Wellington.

Alex remembered how his mother told him she had gone up there to see the tomb of Luxulyanite before it was removed to St Paul's Cathedral, and he wondered what she would have thought of the path he had decided his life should take. At least she would have been pleased by his partnership with James, though perhaps not by the financial stresses they were both now suffering.

'You know nothing of me, nothing of how I feel inside,' whispered Jenifer eventually.

'I'm a widow. Is that something you knew?'
He froze.
'No-one told me that. You didn't tell me, neither did your brothers.'
'Why should I let you know everything about my past? Everyone seems to have forgotten, anyway. I was so young when I married, just sixteen, and he died three weeks later.
'It was the usual story of a mine accident. He was in a skip that ran out of rails underground. There were nine of them, one a boy aged 12. They ran into some beams and were decapitated. Pathetic isn't it? There I was a bride one week and a widow almost the next, and after that I was never young again. I had my chances but I lost them all when Johnny died. I have no money, no prospects. Thomas was at least serious about marrying me.'
'You don't mean you were honestly thinking about marrying him?'
'I would have done so if he had asked, and he would have asked if you hadn't interfered, of that I'm sure.'
'He'd have made your life a misery.'
'I would at least have had a life. All I know at the moment is cooking and cleaning for the boys, looking after them, being a general dogsbody, getting older by the second. And what will I be when they marry, which probably won't be long now? Middle-aged and in the way. That's all my future holds.'
Although still slightly stunned by what she had told him, he wanted literally to shake some sense into her, but kept his hands still with a great amount of effort.
'My stars, think of the number of unattached men around here. You're not telling me that there aren't any, apart from that fool Patten,

who have found you attractive enough to . . '
'To roll me on a beach somewhere and have a good time with me for an hour or so . .? Oh there are many of those, and a great deal of them are already married. But there's no-one who would go as far as the altar. There are many other comely women, too, who are available, and the majority of them are either younger than me, come from wealthier families, or aren't used goods.'

'I find it impossible to understand you. Where's that accursed dignity of yours, or is it all pretence? A good pretence, but a charade all the same.'

By then he had found he was sweating in what seemed to be balmy air, while perversely the storm was definitely developing in the distance. He estimated that in another twenty minutes the stream below them, and the lake, would be lashed with rain, but he wanted more time with her.

Up until that point he had said nothing of what was inside him. He now knew that above everything, he wanted her. To roll on a beach, in the long grass, or on a soft, comfortable bed, oh yes, but also for always. Deep within himself he was aware that he could not imagine himself with any other woman beside him, bar this particular one. The sight of her made his senses swim.

Desire gripped him so hard he could not understand how she had not guessed his need for her, or how he had not known of his love for her from the very first moment they had met. She was so beautiful, sitting beside him with her head tipped back slightly so that the growing breeze ruffled her long hair. How he needed her.

His pulses sped so fast he thought he would

keel over in front of her. He wanted to possess her there and then, amongst a carpet of leaves and ferns with the water rushing in front of them, later to swirl into the marsh behind them.

'All right,' he said, shaking as he put thoughts into words. 'What if I asked you to marry me? What if I offered you a future? What would you say then?'

Just wanting to persuade her of his utter conviction, he clutched at her skirt, then let her go as she started to resist him.

'I'm serious. I'm asking you to marry me.'

Once on her feet she strode away from him, back towards the waiting pony, trying to ignore him as he sprinted after her, determined not to lose her.

'Aren't you listening to me? he yelled. 'I mean everything I've said.'

'And what if I said 'yes' Alex, what would you do then? Can't you see that you'd be tied to me for the rest of your life, when really you don't love, or want me? I'm not certain you even like me.'

'I'll turn your own words back on you. You don't know how I feel Jenifer, because I didn't, not until a really short while ago. If you did you definitely wouldn't question the wanting, the love, the needing that is all inside of me.'

She was shaking now. She had shut herself away from deep emotions, deliberately armouring herself against anything that sprung from the heart, and indifference to anyone other than her family had moulded her into the isolated character she had become. Thinking back, she couldn't even recollect if she had ever loved her husband, because she had shut out that memory too.

'You're drunk again. Either that or you've decided that you can't fight, or reason, with me, so you've decided to tease me instead,' she jeered.

When he reached her, he shot an arm around her slender waist and swiftly tugged her to him.

Surprisingly, she offered no resistance. In fact, just when she really wanted to duel with him the most, the tears were paradoxically beginning to come. He saw, and loved her the more.

'You know that I've had nothing to drink. You're mixing me up with Bracken over there, she's the only one who supped at the Packhorse,' he breathed, his lips only inches from hers. 'If you're so desperate to escape a future on your own, then accept me. Give me a chance.'

'You'll regret it instantly,' she muttered, trying not to look into his eyes, despite feeling drawn to them.

'I'm going to take that as a yes,' he grinned, of a sudden more light-headed than he had been in an age. 'There will be no regrets, on either side, I swear. In this case I have second sight.'

As she started to protest once more, the gathering storm swept upon them, with heavy clouds sailing over their heads from behind the great swathes of trees, and obscuring most of their view of the Valley, the resulting large drops of rain splashing round them and giving a foretaste of the heavy soaking that was to come.

He made a dash for the trap, pulling her behind him, and as they went her reply was whipped away, and lost.

October 1881

VIII

Suzannah couldn't help being drawn to Billy. The main reason being that he was, on the surface, totally unlike Nathan, and was also remote from the great majority of the rough, uncultured inhabitants of Tombstone to whom money, indulgence and battle was the all. Basically he was a loner, like she had become, like - she had to admit - Nathan had been. The difference was that while his brother had traits similar to an Arizona cactus, able to grow strong and independent in a desert, able to sustain any conditions, his youngest brother was more of an unusual hot house flower, likely to wilt at the slightest change in temperature.
It didn't take long for her to discover that he was shy and secretive in a town that had few secrets, one that was steeling itself for trouble because the dispute between the Earps and the Clanton-McLaury men was reaching breaking point.
Billy's hardware shop was only yards from where Suzannah worked, and she took to calling in on him on her way home every day. The new, restrained Suzannah still had the upper hand, even though she kept the tigress she had once threatened to be well at bay. The frantic nightmares she had of her father continued to drain her, and while they persisted she could not forget for one waking moment the bloodshed she had been responsible for.
It was the evenings she hated, which was one reason why, after Billy had been in Tombstone for around ten months, she offered

to cook for him. Idly, he accepted, not having the inclination to argue. It was the beginning of a routine. Once more she became a regular visitor to the lodgings in Tough Nut Street, knowing that if she was not there she would be home in her squat, bare room, brooding and alone. And she was sure he would have done the same in his.

While she was there, though, they barely communicated with each other, each being grateful enough for shared company in a world that scared both of them. Rarely did she think of Nathan, having tried hard to eradicate that part of her past. There had been no resurrection of the untamed, sensual girl who had lured the eldest brother between the sheets.

Her hair was cropped, she kept her gaze downcast most of the time so as not to attract attention, and when once she could have had her pick of men she tempted only rare bursts of interest from Tombstone's masculine element.

Billy was walking her home after she had called on the afternoon of 26 October 1881, to check that he wanted her to cook a meal for him that evening, their path due to take them past the O K Corral, when he sprang a question on her that she had never anticipated.

'Would you move in with me. Stay there permanently?'

It was blustery. She paused only slightly as she put up her hand to stop her hat flying away towards the dusty horizon.

'I can't take that seriously, Billy.'

'That's the story of my entire life. No-one ever listens to me properly, or takes me seriously,' he countered. 'You stayed in the same house with Nathan didn't you, and that

was all right. I'm not asking you to become my lover, or my wife. All I want is a companion . . and . . '
'And?'
'And I need someone to help me with the store, someone who's proved that they can be capable, and who knows enough about me without me having to explain myself to them all the time. I'm no good with strangers, trying to establish common ground with them just exhausts me. I'm well aware we hardly know each other, but there is that tie through Nathan, who. I'm sure, talked about me to you now and then, in the same way as he often wrote about you.'
She winced at that. What tales had Nathan told about her? Probably not the entire truth. Billy was growing a beard again, which was so thin and wispy it made him look faintly ridiculous. His chest and shoulders had never quite filled out, there was a shyness about his expression that bordered on panic, and even his voice betrayed his inborn diffidence, as it had never deepened to the same extent as his brothers. She saw him as a boy trying against all odds to be a man. And he was in a town that revelled in destroying such innocents. Trying to consider in depth what he had asked of her, she took off her hat and paused a moment. They were on Fremont Street, one of the main thoroughfares, that was usually alive with sound. Suddenly, she realised that the atmosphere surrounding them seemed different. It was hushed, but not in a restful way, more as if the elements themselves were in waiting, holding their breath as if in anticipation.
There were few other people around when there should have been crowds. It niggled at

her.

'Are you sure you're in a position to trust me? Surely Henry, or Nathan, has filled you in on my many defects. Surely you've been told that . . . that I'm not the most reliable of women, that my own father killed himself because of my lies and your brother nearly died too. I'm only here still because I've nowhere else to go. I'm a piece of this country's flotsam, and it's nobody's fault but my own. Would you really want to trust your livelihood to me?'

'I'm not interested in what's happened in the past, to other people. I only know I can't trust myself to keep the business afloat.'

'You must try. Without that shop you'd be as aimless as me. And besides, if I moved in with you you realise how people would talk. No-one would believe that all we have between us is a shared loneliness. Believe me, Henry's left me well aware of the dangers I present to you.

'Since your arrival he hasn't stopped lecturing me about you, telling me to stay away. I suppose it's partly to annoy him that I keep going to see you as it is.'

Billy nodded, remembering how Henry had also lectured him about the hazards of getting close to Suzannah. On many an occasion he had dissected her character in such great depth and, Billy thought, with such a great deal of relish, that his warnings had rebounded. They had left him believing that Suzannah surely couldn't be so calculating. They also didn't take into account that in Billy's mind he needed Suzannah. To him she spelt deliverance from a routine he despised.

'Poor Henry. He's seen too much in his lifetime, that's his trouble. He can sniff a lie from an impressive distance,' she reasoned, 'and perhaps lies are all he can notice now. Add to that the fact that I think he came to look upon Nathan as the son he never had, and so was amazingly protective of him. Nevertheless, if I were you I'd listen to his advice about me, and heed it.'

'You're not convincing me. No-one out here is exactly shining white are they? We're all searching or running from old injuries or mistakes.'

Smiling, she didn't disagree. She didn't believe she could, because what he had said had summed up the cauldron that Tombstone was.

'We are, I presume, talking about a business arrangement that has nothing to do with you and I getting together in other ways?'

'Of course.'

'You don't want more of me then? You're not after comfort in the middle of the night?'

In reaction, he shuddered, as if the thought was appalling, although it was more out of awkwardness at the idea that any woman would be blind and misguided enough to want him in that way.

'I'm trying to free myself of complications, not make them worse. I won't restrict you. You can have as many men friends as you like, it won't bother me.'

He blinked his eyes, trying to clear the little voice at the back of his mind that was simultaneously telling him it would hurt, that for a reason he couldn't fathom he would be jealous.

'There'll be no male company, I promise you. I don't want complications either. But I won't agree unless my wage equals the one I get now.'

'As long as the shop ticks over you'll have high enough wages. I want only enough profit to keep the business running, and us in food.' Suzannah turned to him to check again that it wouldn't be a decision he would regret as soon as he woke next morning, and as she did so saw a movement out of the corner of her eye which made her come to an instant halt. In that moment she had seen what appeared to be a group of men moving across her line of vision, with one bearing a gun level with his shoulder, as if he had prey within his sights. Looking again, she saw the resolve in Wyatt Earp's eyes, and bit down on her lip to stop a scream escaping which would draw attention to them.

'For God's sake get down Billy,' she hissed, pushing him hard in the small of his back so that together they went tumbling to the ground. Moments later a shot clipped the air with such ferocity she literally clutched her racing heart. She'd seen too many killings, she wanted to see no other bodies lying prone in the dust with their lifeblood seeping away, as her father's had done.

'Who is it?' Billy whispered coarsely, grasping her sleeve, lifting his head slightly from the dry and dusty earth to try to see what was happening without bringing attention to them.

'I'm not raising my head to look in case it gets blown away, but there are three of the Earps and Doc Holliday, I'm sure. There've been rumours about them and Ike Clanton and his brother for days, don't you ever listen to what people are saying?'

'Not often.'

'Well, apparently Virgil's deputised all his brothers and Doc Holliday.'

She was set to impart more information, stopped from doing so by an explosion of bullets that ripped into the air with a sickening finality that told her that there could be bodies galore littering the street within minutes.

In all, the shootings lasted 30 seconds. To them it seemed like three hours. At one stage two people rushed past them. They could hear the spurs on their boots as they dashed by, their breath rasping, curses pouring from their mouths. But neither Billy nor Suzannah wanted to see who it was. Both were by then certain that they were destined to die because they were in the wrong place at the wrong time.

It was with some amazement that, a full ten minutes after the last bullet rang out, they were able to stumble to their feet untouched. Gingerly, they brushed the dirt from their clothes, then slowly, together with crowds of others who had also taken cover, made their way over to the back of the O K Corral, where most of the violence seemed to have occurred. There, pools of blood had mixed with earth in the way Suzannah had envisaged, and three men lay dead, their corpses riddled and leaking and grotesquely exposed to everyone's gaze. In the space of those explosive 30 seconds Billy Clanton and Tom and Frank McLaury had been killed. Virgil and Morgan Earp had been badly wounded, Virgil in the leg and Morgan in the shoulder, but Wyatt was left unscathed.

Suzannah sank to her knees in front of the carnage, as by now it was reminding her so acutely of her father's attack on Nathan she thought she was going to keel over. Henry had arrived, though he was taking no notice of her. Instead he was too busy helping Sheriff

John Behan head off those who were by now arriving in strength.
Billy, the namesake of one of those lying dead at his feet, was rooted to the spot, stunned by what he had been witness to. It was seeing the terror on his face that eventually brought Henry rushing over to them.
'It's all right, Billy. It's over now, the showdown's over. The Sheriff tried his best to stop them, but they just pushed past. There's little you can do when they're so intent.'
And don't I know it, thought Suzannah.
Billy, unable to look away from the trio of dead men, was attempting to explain what they had witnessed.
'Suzannah and I were in Fremont Street. I had no idea, not at all. If she hadn't pushed me to the ground . . .'
'But she did, thank God. You were lucky, boy, spared for a purpose ay? Fortunately no-one was hurt but those involved in the feud.'
'Whatever, it's murder. That's all there is to it.'
'Murder's a way of life here, didn't you know that?'
'But it shouldn't be, not anywhere.'
With the spilt blood still so fresh he wanted to throw up. Although not wanting to keep staring at the bodies, so fresh, so distorted by brutality, he was drawn to them as if they were macabre magnets.
'We lay as if we were dead ourselves, because we thought we would be any moment. Two people at least stayed around to watch, they rushed past us as if they were being chased by the devil himself.'
'They were in a way. They must have been Ike Clanton and Claibourne, his friend. They apparently ran away during it all, when they

realised they were being ambushed. You're lucky they never shot you in the back as they went.'

'Lucky? I don't think I've ever been that.'

'Well, what really happened? What was the reason behind all this?' Suzannah said sharply. 'Does anyone know yet? You've got to write about it Henry, you've no Nathan here to hand the job to.'

'Do you want to interview Wyatt for me and find out?' Henry laughed dryly, thinking that perhaps Suzannah would be a match for any of the Earp brothers. 'Some are telling me the Earps opened fire with no good reason, others say they were only lawmen defending themselves. All that's sure is John Behan's already talking about arresting Wyatt and Doc Holliday on murder warrants.'

As soon as Suzannah had regained some composure she dragged Billy away from the Corral, where he had remained standing, as if mesmerised, as well as traumatised, by what had happened.

They walked back together to her lodgings, both in a daze, each feeling physically ill. Any fears either may have harboured about Bill's invitation to her about moving in with him now seemed insignificant. They didn't mention them again.

The next day Suzannah carried her meagre belongings back into the home she had once shared with Nathan, feeling as she did so that although this could be the chance of a new, brighter beginning, it was probably just another lap on a self-inflicted, weary, downhill journey.

Some months after returning to Cornwall and meeting up with his remaining family again, and loaning James and Alex enough money to see them through a few more weeks of their business problems, Nathan was embroiled in discussions in his editorial office at the Looe and Polperro Echo.

It was not a grand office, built in rather a tight space between the local branch of the Liskeard and district bank, and the Mechanics' Institute, but it was functional, and central, and served its purpose. One of the staff had brought in the latest batch of letters from exiles in Australia, which had led to Nathan being surrounded by mail, considering what best bits of information to use in the following edition of the weekly paper, which was published on a Friday.

Although relatively new to the business he was already making his mark at the editor's desk. Sales were up and so was advertising, which pleased him immensely for it was rising advertising that was going to keep the Echo financially sound.

Within his first few weeks there he had discovered that his decision to include columns packed with news of those who had emigrated was an inspired one. Not only had it impressed those living in Looe and its surrounding villages, but circulation had extended to elsewhere in the district, where previously the paper had made no inroads, as the main weekly there was The Cornish Times, based in Liskeard and with a large readership across South East Cornwall itself, to Saltash and the Tamar in the east, and Lostwithiel in the west.

That week he had concentrated on the news that Captain Francis Cotes, who had previously worked in Caradon's mines, had been appointed Colonial Government Mining Engineer to the diamond fields in West South Africa, a post worth about £3600 per year with expenses paid. Mention had also been made of a fatal accident at the Pachuca silver mines in Mexico in which two men from Talland had died. One, who was married, had only left Cornwall eight months before, and the other was the son of the parish clerk of West Looe, who already had four other members of his family buried in Mexican graves.

The lead story, however, had been given over to the suspension of payment of the Bank of California. Two brothers, who had lived in Looe for the past six months, had arrived the previous year from America and had placed their £36,000 savings which had been made over a 13 year period, into the bank. Since hearing of its collapse one of them had disappeared, and there were fears for the sanity of the second.

Nathan was well aware that the suspension would also affect, and perhaps ruin, a great number of other families in the county. There were many dependent upon remittances from California through the bank. Nevertheless, he was in a buoyant mood. James and Alex had been to see him that morning and, although they were continuing to struggle to keep their company in the black, he was pleased that they were prepared to seek his opinion, and to be honest with him about their worries. His staff were also proving to be capable and efficient. After the take-over of editorship and ownership he had put his faith in them by letting them keep their jobs, and they were paying him back with dividends.

He had inherited three journalists, who were all busy working around him at their respective desks, six printers, one member of the advertising department, and a youngster who manned the front desk with unnerving professionalism, and who always seemed undaunted by the fact that he was constantly beset by people wishing to place adverts, discover when a certain event was going to take place, or see the editor on a matter of supposedly great seriousness.

Nathan also seemed to be constantly besieged by locals who had a 'marvellous' story for him, although usually most of these were ultimately formed from pure imagination. In the general hub-bub it was difficult to concentrate on any one thing at a time, though the latest emigration figures were in front of him, and he was finding them interesting reading.

For one moment he did glimpse a thin, angular figure hovering in the doorway, but as in all newspaper offices there were always strangers wandering through, and he took little notice. He had a willing workforce, so presumed that someone else would deal with the woman at the door.

It wasn't until she had disappeared, and he had subconsciously noted her footsteps as she made her way out of the small corridor which led to the front office, that he realised who had been hovering there, briefly watching him.

Dropping the sheaf of figures he held, not caring in what order they fell to the untidy floor, he hurried after her. When he reached the street and the outside world she was already out of sight. Horses packed the road, and the residents of both East and West Looe seemed to be out in force.

The town was in a noisy, lively mood, the tide was high which meant the Looe river, which divided the two settlements, was flowing almost at the top of the reinforced banks. As the fish market had been doing a good trade, the pungent smell of mackerel and sardines was lacing the air in strength. There was no sign of Lorna whatsoever.

Pausing for a moment, he reasoned that if she was running back home she would head for the station. He was so annoyed with himself for allowing her to flee.

I only had to look up properly for a second, he thought, and I would have known her instantly. Instead all I spared her was a quick glance, that took in, and absorbed, absolutely nothing.

Wanting only to find her, he charged on towards the station, across the bridge, panting with the effort, pushing whoever he came across out of the way with no apology, cursing himself for being so preoccupied with his work that he had shut her out once again.

I must have gone the wrong way, he fumed. I'd have found her by now. And then he did catch a glimpse of her, hurrying herself, head bent, face down to the ground. He accelerated his pace until he was behind her, as she turned left from the bridge towards the station, which linked Looe with Liskeard, and the main line running between Penzance and London. Once he had completely reached her, he grabbed her by the elbow, which made her instantly whirl around, startled. On seeing who it was she jumped away from him, her eyes widening in an already drawn face.

'Stop Lorna. Why didn't you stay? You didn't even come into the office, let anyone tell me you had arrived.'

'I . . I didn't think you'd seen me. I really should never have gone to see you in the first place.'

After finally reaching her, he wasn't going to let her slip away. With a more gentle touch, he drew her away from the crowds, and down to the river bank so that they could hear each other speak above the clattering of wheels and hooves, and the gossiping of shoppers.

'But you did come. You put yourself out to find me. Why run when you had finally tracked me down?'

He'll never know how much I put myself out, she thought fiercely. He would never understand what I have put myself through these last few days.

She didn't answer him, so he tried again, gently but firmly.

'Why did you go? Come on, Lorna, tell me.'

'You were working. There were other people around you. You were obviously busy. I shouldn't have intruded.'

'I was only sorting through some letters, and looking at something that had come in the post. What did you expect me to be doing, sitting there like a stuffed animal, not talking, not thinking, not working at all?'

'I told you, there were so many people rushing around, I would have been in the way,' she repeated dully.

Stilling the first words in retaliation that came to him, because he wanted to yell at her, prod her, swear at her, anything to see a sliver of true emotion from her, he sought composure. How could he let her know that he wanted her to come alive, that he longed to rekindle her old brilliance?

Instead, not trusting himself to say any words

without deep thought, he merely squeezed her unresponsive hands with his own.

Eventually, after assessing what best to say, he murmured: 'You're being too sensitive. Didn't I ask you to come? And now you're here and I've caught up with you, I'm not letting you go that easily again. Let's return to the office. I'll clear up the few remaining jobs I have, which won't take long I promise, and then I'll take you for something to eat.'

Her resistance over she walked meekly back with him. Again, he thought it best to say very little, especially when he noticed that her expression kept glazing over, as if she was in a trance. What he did do was keep holding her arm in as protective a manner as he could, striving to reassure.

After a while, though, he could bear the silence between them no more, and started babbling instead.

'It's lucky you didn't arrive yesterday. It was publication day, being a Thursday. All hell was let loose. There was an explosion in a fuse works, and four people died. One girl escaped burning by jumping out of a window, but she was badly injured. It was a terrible sight, not forgotten in just a day or so, or even in years I would think. We worked like maniacs to get the story in because it happened just as the paper was going to bed.'

She did not reply but he carried on telling her about how the other people who were affected by the explosion had walked back to where they lived despite being badly injured themselves, how an inquest was being arranged.

Still seeking to destroy any tension between them, he went on to mention a feature on the still declining tin industry, a coming by-election - everything and nothing. Although there was so much he had to say to her that was personal, that was worth saying, he knew he had to wait until the perfect setting and until she was in the right frame of mind.

They re-emerged from the office an hour later. It was early afternoon and he decided to take her to a small tea shop that was situated at Hannafore, with views across the bay to Looe Island. It was quiet there, and friendly, with a proprietor who was anxious to please, for she knew that Nathan was the new owner and editor of the Echo. Lorna had insisted she didn't want to go anywhere grand. A pot of tea and the smallest amount of cake was enough for her to stomach.

In truth, she was still feeling queasy from the enormous effort it had taken actually to venture away from Polruan to face him. Too much to eat would have affected her badly churning insides completely, especially as rich foods had not featured in her diet for years, if ever at all. He had given way unwillingly, wanted to fete her more, alarmed by her insecurities.

They sat on opposite sides of the table, not touching, watching the fishing boats as they sailed close to the island that was inhabited only by the coastguards and which was owned by the Trelawnys. It was said that on its summit a chapel had once stood, dedicated to St George, and that before man arrived the choughs were known to have built their nests in its rabbit holes.

Still finding it hard to sit next to her without many words between them, he started to talk of America and of the differing perspectives the country had given him. It was a neutral subject that he hoped wouldn't upset her

further, which he could dwell upon for a long time if he had to - for she obviously had decided to offer little to the conversation.
As he surreptitiously assessed her, he realised that her face remained as drawn and worriedly lined as when he had so unexpectedly called upon her. She continued to give the appearance of being middle aged, though he thought there was a glimpse of a bloom showing where there had not been when he had first visited her in Polruan. Also, he convinced himself that her figure was not as hunched as she sat there, and that her clothes were marginally more flattering than those she had been wearing before.
I wonder if she realises that she was one of the main reasons for my return, he mused. Would it scare her too much if I told her?
But on the whole she sat like a lifeless, worn doll as he continued gabbling about the wild men and the woodsmen he had met in the backwoods of America, mentioning Billy the Kid and Army scouts such as Tom Horn, as well as the dry, dilapidated frontier towns he had travelled through and the leafy splendour that he had seen in the fall. Finally, when he thought his monologue might become too much for her and he suggested that she return with him to his new home, she merely nodded, as if she was too weary to disagree.
As they went to leave he let an arm stray around her waist, and bent down to run his lips over the top of her head, but instantaneously discovered that this was too sensual for her. At the touch of his lips she cringed as if he was a leper, the movement so marked that he was glad there was no-one else close to them, in case they believed he was trying to molest her.

His house, though not a huge residence because his savings had mostly been taken by the purchase of the Echo and through his family investments, hugged the sea wall at Millendreath, around the bay from Looe, the village's name being especially apt as it meant 'mill on the sands'.

When the seas were heavy the beach often revealed trunks of trees and peat, remnants of a past that had been all but washed away. Nathan showed her around the acre of garden that stretched upwards, towards the cliffs, and then she obediently followed as he took her through the two bedrooms and reception rooms. They were extremely sparsely furnished, and he aimed to keep it that way. He had no love of fuss or frills, in writing or in life. There were few homes in the small parish and he had wanted the house on sight. Already he accepted that it was unlikely he would want to move again.

The Indian summer was prolonging itself, to everyone's amazement. Winter was around the corner, but the temperatures kept trying to fool everyone that it was mid June. After the mini tour, he left her in the garden, sitting underneath one tree in a small copse of cherry trees, and went to pour them both a further pot of tea.

On his return he found that she had moved and was standing, staring at the sea, her silhouette match-thin and solitary. In the few minutes it had taken him to make refreshments it seemed to him, by her body language and the tight expression on her face, that she had withdrawn into herself even more. Silently cursing, he asked himself if he would ever manage to reach her again.

'They say once there was a valley between

Looe and Rame Head,' he told her as he set the tray with the tea and cups down. 'It's claimed that on a clear day, on the bottom of the sea and about a league out from shore you can see a giant slab of timber lying on its side, just as healthy as if it was growing on dry land still. You can also find timbers after there has been a bad storm, although they're rotting. All that is meant to confirm the valley theory, and the fact that Cornish lands once stretched far out to where there is now only water.'

She only gave a weak nod of acknowledgement to his story and, hating the continuing constraint between them, he ploughed on.

'I often stand here myself when I've a spare hour or more in the day. Funnily enough, the view seems to put my world into proportion for me. All this beauty is free, and that fact shouldn't be overlooked. It's more important than money or glory. That's something I learnt in those years of self-imposed exile. Being some place like this, where you can be at peace with yourself, is a necessary part of being able to cope. The mountains showed me that. Maybe it's not the usual lesson that America gives her immigrants, but it was mine.'

'I doubt very much if I could begin to find peace, even here,' she whispered. 'Lovely as it is, I think it's all too late.'

Such words dismayed him, but he didn't let himself react to them, but just moved forward a step or two towards her, and then stayed there with her, watching the wading birds searching amongst the small piles of seaweed at the shoreline, and staring towards the horizon in the direction of the Eddystone rocks where Smeaton's lighthouse had been

built to replace two that had been destroyed, the first by a storm, the second by fire.
To him she seemed to be in a state of perpetual bewilderment, as if she wasn't quite sure where she was, or why.
And then suddenly, without warning, she spoke again of Samuel, much like she had when he had visited her at Polruan. It unnerved him so much that he had to take a few deep gulps of salt air to steady himself.
'I was so relieved when he was killed,' she said. 'He was dead and I was happy. In fact there was a time, once, when I nearly killed him myself, and I can't forgive myself for any of that. I could have helped him, I'm sure, but I didn't. I only hurt him more. He was such a sad and lonely person.'
Nathan saw, in flashback, his brother, her dead husband, fighting mad on St Austell railway station, throwing himself into battle with him as the train steamed relentlessly in.
'You can't blame yourself for the way he was, Lorna. It was his natural disposition. Samuel wallowed in that sadness and loneliness.'
Lorna didn't hear, or choose to listen.
'He was happy at first. I could have made it last. If I hadn't riled him so much we would have had a child too. I would have been a mother.'
'Only a miracle worker could have made him consistently happy. Happiness was something Samuel would never trust.'
And neither would I trust happiness and laughter when I should have grabbed at both, he thought. When we were young, and you were so sweet and willing.
She shivered, though not from an autumn day that continued to be degrees higher than it should have been. Unsure how to reassure her,

when she seemed so tormented, he moved even closer to her.

'So all this anxiety that you seem to be carrying around with you. Where does it stem from, guilt?'

Instantly, she shook her head in denial, then stopped.

Why had she talked so freely? What right did he have to pry into her thoughts? She had travelled to Looe to beg him to leave her alone, to accept that neither of them could journey back through the years. To insist that she had changed beyond all hope, and would not revert. But if she said all that he would only argue - and arguments weakened her so.

'I don't know what it is, perhaps regret, although there really is no need for your question. I am what I have become. I fought for a while to stay young, and I lost. What Samuel's death has taught me is that there is no point in bothering. We're all going to go to our graves anyway, in the end.'

'I can't deny that, no-one can, though doesn't such a grim way of looking at the world stop you making the most of what's on offer while we are still living and breathing, and among those we know and love?'

'That's how it is. There are some things you cannot alter. Surely America taught you that as well Nathan?'

Five minutes later she asked if he would take her back to the station at Looe, and despite his pleas for her to stay, or let him take her back to Polruan himself, she won the day. Against his wishes, he reasoned that he couldn't hold her by force, especially as he had probably scared her enough as it was. His own rejuvenation seemed to have made her listlessness all the more tragic.

Begrudgingly, he did as he was asked and accompanied her to the station, waiting for the train with her although standing a good few feet away, careful of how she would react again if he invaded personal space, especially in public. Fearing the worst, he wondered if the day had achieved anything.

Will she come again? he asked himself. Dare I invite her a second time?

'Thank you for making the effort,' he said, rather formally, as the engine came into view, rattling along the tracks that followed the Looe river from Sandplace. 'Please come again, please Lorna. It was good for both of us. Or shall I see you in Polruan? I've got to visit James next week.'

'Why bother? I'm a lost cause. I'm no company for you, I'm not the person I used to be, you know that all too well now.'

In a flash she grasped both his hands in hers, knowing she had to make him understand. Up until then she had not said any of her rehearsed speech.

'I loved you for a while. You and I know that, so I can't deny it. Also understand, though, that all that could have been is now just a dream.'

'Don't be so sure,' he said urgently, catching a new depth in her eyes, in the inflection of her voice.

It was the first time she had spoken of the passion they had held for each other. Seconds afterwards the train arrived in a blanket of steam and soot, and she broke away from him, rushing towards a waiting carriage, lost without effort in the crowd of other passengers waiting to board for the return trip to Liskeard.

He was never to see her again.

Fifteen minutes later a truck laden with china clay became detached and hurtled down the line with no warning given. It gathered speed rapidly before smashing into the Great Western train, killing the driver instantly. Lorna's carriage leapt off the rails and crashed down a bank at such speed that the unprepared passengers were given a scant chance of survival. Lorna, crushed in the wreckage, died as rescuers vainly struggled to free her.

CHAPTER NINE

1882

1

Jenifer halted at intervals as she walked down to the front of Lanlivery church with its tower, which stood like a beacon, on view for miles around. Every sound associated with every movement she made echoed along the pews, and up into the roof, because the grand building was nearly empty. All family, and all friends, were absent besides her brothers.
On her part no other guests had been invited, because she had not expected the ceremony to go ahead. Even then she was still wondering, at this late stage, when the vicar was within just ten yards of her, if it would do so.
True, she had gone with Alex to talk the wedding over with the minister, and she had lengthened one of her dresses for the day, added a few strips of white lace to it, and improved the bodice. All that had been done, however, in a form of stupor, as if she had been drawn along by unbeatable forces she could not control.
Apart from the meeting with Rev Applegarth she had barely seen Alex since the day he had taken her back to Luxulyan. On a couple of

occasions he had called to see her briefly, the last time a week previously, though they had never been alone. In the intervening period between his proposal and her unexpected acceptance, he had not kissed her, or held her. Instead, he had sat by the fire, leaning forward so that their knees touched to an imperceptible degree, and had spoken of his plans for their joint future, while her brothers hovered nearby.

He told her that he had been cleaning the cottage at Biscovey for them to move into, scrubbing it free of the past, making it fit for the woman he loved. And she had laughed mirthlessly at all that he had said, not arguing with his illusions, though tempted to try to tear them to ribbons because she treated all his words as totally unreal.

As he heard her approaching towards the front pews Alex could not stop himself turning to watch her edge closer to him, walking down the aisle with its fine black and white wagon roof above, with richly carved timbers featuring seven angels. Jenifer's cream and white dress hugged her figure perfectly, accentuating every hollow and curve. It also contrasted with her dark features, lending her a radiance that he was sure he had never seen in another woman.

At that moment he recognised her carefully disguised terror. Knowing she was frightened, his firm belief that, despite her cool exterior, she was a wayward girl in need of strong love, was enhanced. Edwin was beside him, suited of sorts and appearing to have aged about ten years because of it. Peter was at Jenifer's arm to give her away and behind, lost in the empty rows of pews, sat James, Helen and Nathan. They were the sole witnesses. She had not even mentioned her marriage to her mother, being extra cautious about her reaction. Instead, she had left her mother's sole friend to break the news to her, if she thought fit. Jenifer, standing not far from the slate tablet showing a portrait of locally-born Jane Kendall as she had appeared in 1643, with a low-necked frock and necklace, went through her responses automatically. She was looking at the tablet, rather than the ring, when it was placed on her long, thin finger, as it represented so much that she could not comprehend.

After the short service was over, and they had signed the register, Alex pulled her gently to him to kiss her. At his touch she turned her face away, not wanting to feel his lips on hers. Instead, she wanted to exit the church, very fast, and very alone.

I haven't had much joy in my life, she thought, but at least I've usually been able to control much of what has happened to me. Now I really believe that that's changed completely.

But she did concede to herself that, for the past years, the wishes of her mother, and her brothers, had had an increasing effect on what she did. Most of her concerns stemmed, therefore, from the fact that she was so unsure where she stood with Alex because he continued to be too much of an unknown quantity. With her family she was very aware where she fitted into their lives.

With such thoughts tumbling around her mind, she stared over towards James and his wife, and Nathan.

All the Roseveans like to take the lead, she thought. Alex is certainly one of them. Surely he won't let me have my own way, make my own decisions, and mistakes. He has little patience with ideas that don't coincide with his, and I've willingly tied myself to him. What a stupid, easily led fool I am.

Helen had prepared a cold buffet, and the small group returned, negotiating the lanes in pony and trap, to Tregrehan afterwards. They sat down together in the largest of the reception rooms, which still showed slight signs of the destruction wrought upon it, grateful that the wine and good food would keep them occupied and lessen the need to speak about the event they had witnessed. The bride and groom showed none of the usual ebullience which followed the willing swapping of marital vows, and it took a great deal of effort to include them in any conversation. Not one of them, bar Alex, thought the marriage would last, in all but name, for more than a year.

Nathan was in no mood to talk whatever path the marriage ceremony had taken. The past weeks had been traumatic for him. Lorna had been buried only a fortnight before, and he blamed himself not only for her death, but for ruining her life in its entirety. He had hardly slept since news of the accident had broken, and he and two others from the Echo had rushed along the railway track to join the rescue teams.

Although he hadn't endured the trauma of seeing her body, he had been witness to the carnage: the obscenely twisted carriages; the splinters of wood and metal; the wide splashes of blood; the cries of the passengers who had managed to survive; the sight of many of those who had also met their deaths in the crash. It all meant that he absorbed exactly what terrors and pain she had suffered.

And if she had not gone to Looe to see me, if I had not pleaded with her to keep in contact, he thought, she would be still alive. She would not have strayed from Polruan, and laid herself open to such a sickening twist of fate. There had only been a handful at her funeral, just as there had been at the wedding. While she was being buried, in the graveyard at St Mary's, St Blazey Gate, he had stood watching in controlled distress, wishing so fervently that his life could have been taken instead of hers that for one dark, subconscious moment he had opened his eyes and imagined he saw nothing in his future but putrefaction and decay. Lack of sleep had led to his mind playing tricks, and deceiving him, as it had continued to do so ever since.

He struggled to keep awake during the wedding breakfast, to keep some sort of normal expression on his face as the muted celebrations went on around him. The others accepted it, as they were painfully aware that he was in no state to add anything relevant to the proceedings.

James kept a close eye on Helen, now six months pregnant and looking at least eight, but she showed no signs of tiring, nor did Glynn who had come out of his shell so much that he was now, aged five, a child reborn. His assurance was sky-high, so much so that Helen discovered she had to reproach him several times a day, hating to quell such enthusiasm, realising at the same time she was in danger of skimping on the discipline.

In the past she had worried because he was too good, too restrained. Now such concerns were forgotten. Glynn was busy entertaining his Uncle Alex, and devouring a great deal of the spread at the same time, when James slipped out of the room after his wife, who was anxious to check that all was well in the kitchen.

'Despite everything it seems to be going reasonably well,' he murmured to her. 'I had this dreadful premonition that one or other would refuse to go on with it at the last moment.'

'Well nothing went amiss. They're man and wife, just like you and I. And we were an unlikely couple too, weren't we?' she teased.

'You mean the uncouth miner and the rich man's daughter?'

'Something like that.'

'Well I hope Alex appreciates the woman he's found for himself more than I did mine in the beginning.' He kissed the back of her neck, immediately wanting her completely to himself. 'I nearly threw it all away.'

Needing his closeness, she caught hold of his hand and lay it across her swollen stomach for comfort.

'I'm worried about Nathan. Lorna's death has hit him really hard. He's come today, but he's not here in spirit. I don't think he's allowed himself to rest or eat properly since it happened.'

'He'll survive. He must. And he's got to understand that he wasn't in any way responsible for her death, that the crash was nothing to do with him. He definitely didn't set that rogue truck in motion.'

'We all know that. It doesn't alter the fact that he's putting himself through hell. First of all he thinks that if he hadn't left her and emigrated it wouldn't have happened. Then he tells himself that if he hadn't returned she would still be safe. He's crucifying himself, and actually being to see the aftermath of it all didn't help one bit.'

She gasped a little as the baby kicked hard, and he kissed her again, this time for long seconds.

'I'm sure he's learnt by now that you must never give up, completely give way, because the funny thing is with life that when you think you're beaten you can be given the most glorious chance of winning.'

At his words she beamed at him, realising he was talking from the heart.

'But does he know that, my darling? Will he give up now, all because of a lost dream?'

'I can't answer that. I know I'm his brother, but look at all the years that have gone missing, with me here and him over the other side of the ocean. I have to say, though, that he does seem to me to be someone who's mastered himself. He'll come to terms with it, although perhaps not straight away. It sounds selfish, but we do need him ourselves at the moment. Without his backing your father would have squeezed us dry by now.'

After the buffet Alex and Jenifer were to ride back to Biscovey. Instead, he unexpectedly turned the pony towards Crinnis and then guided her through Carlyon Bay, past Appletree mine, down through Charlestown and along the coast to Duporth, the 'black cove'. He pulled Bracken to a halt by a cluster of houses on the cliff, above the kidney shaped beach.

'What in the saints' names are we doing here?' she demanded, secretly relieved about the giant detour, as she hadn't been looking forward to going back to the cottage alone with him.

What a stupid state of affairs, she thought, when he's my husband. That's how I feel, though. I wish I knew exactly what he expects from me. Probably something I can never give.

'I thought we'd go for a walk,' he said softly. 'Like we did in Luxulyan Valley. I know we might not have the right clothes on, but I was able to talk to you then, say all those things that were rushing through my mind. I thought I'd try the same tactics again, clear away some of the doubts we might have about each other before we start our lives at Biscovey.'

'But it's nearly night time,' she objected. 'I'm in my finery, such as it is, and we'll hardly be able to see where we're walking. Shouldn't we have done this before we said our vows, when it was lighter?'

'The moon'll be full tonight, and that sky's clear. You'll be able to see where you're walking.'

'You're mad.'

'Maybe, maybe not.'

The unreality persisted as he took her arm and she let him guide her down from the trap, past the cottages and into the lane that dropped down to the sea. He put her wrap around her and then, self-consciously, placed the arm he was holding through his.

Trees met above them, blocking out the sky for a while, and the growing duskiness, and the leaves that littered the ground, made it rather treacherous walking. As they went he concentrated on making sure she didn't fall, forgetting her innate sense of balance, while she tried to ignore his attentions, but didn't quite succeed in doing so. It was so strange to be fussed over.

He had been partially right. Once they passed the dense trees it was nowhere near pitch dark. On the beach the evening light spun a pale golden glow on the waves as they rolled relentlessly to shore. It picked out the long fringes of the cliffs at Black Head and the row of trees silhouetted along the back of the headland, as well as the ships waiting in the bay for their berth at the dockside.

Jenifer began to feel light-headed in the fresh, tangy air. The wine had been partly responsible for that and she found that she did have to lean into him slightly as they wandered along the shoreline, dodging the wavelets. When they reached the far end of the beach he stopped, tentatively pulling her to him.

Gently, as if in slow motion he pressed her close against his chest, and although her brain told her to resist her body wouldn't do so. If anything, it gravitated towards him in mysterious, unwanted fashion.

Then his mouth found hers, uncertainly at first, caressing her lips like butterfly wings. He paused a moment to check that he wasn't distressing her, and then kissed with more ardour, moulding himself into her curves, making her respond with power and need.

His hands took over, slipping inside her dress, travelling over her bare, silky skin. A moan of enjoyment escaped her lips and spasms shook her. Shocked, she forced herself to draw away from him and began to gather her flapping clothes around her.

'What's possessed you?' she snapped.
'You're behaving like an animal.'

He answered by running his fingers down her long, sensual back once again.

'I'm making love to you. You're my wife. Rev Applegarth said so.'

'Maybe, but you're not having me here, not with all to see.'

Knowing he was walking a tightrope with her emotions, he jerked her wrap off of her in one quick movement, searching for the buttons on her dress. When they were undone he eased the material down off her shoulders, half expecting her to lash out at him as he did so.

'No-one's going to see us, my pretty one. You yourself told me the dark would be complete.'

'But it's not half as black as I thought it would be, and what we're doing, or intending to do, is improper.'

'What a boring word that is,' he sighed, kissing her again, this time very slowly, and at the same time gently drawing her down onto the wrap, which he had thrown onto the sand. 'Do you know,' he continued, as he lay over her, and smoothed her hair away from her rigid face, 'that eight weeks or so ago, when we were in Luxulyan Valley, I wanted to do this to you then. I wanted you among those leaves and mosses and wild flowers. I wanted to tear the clothes from you there and then, and have you thrashing beneath me, crying for me to love you.'

He terrified her. No-one had ever spoken to her that way before. The most her husband had ever achieved in their short while together had been to slump on top of her in a tired parody of love, after returning home exhausted from work. The act, to her, had nearly always ended in failure. The attempt had always left her lying awake for hours on end feeling dirty and used.

'You shouldn't speak of such things.'

Her limbs were by then sending out signals she could not understand, and were subjecting her to the most bitter sweet longings, which confused her so.

'Why? Why shouldn't I tell you how I felt,

how I feel. I love you.'

'How can you love me, we've been fighting ever since we first met?'

'That's surely a thousand times better than indifference?'

And then his mouth and hands were on her again, and her other clothes were falling from her, as if of their own account. Her skin was exposed to the air, to him, and she was naked on the sand with the waves slipping and sighing around her. Alex was running his tongue over her nipples, and her mind was exploding.

Within minutes restraint and frustration were gone and it was he who was on his back, and she who was riding him, glorying in her body and his, and every part of their union. She looked down and read the passion and delight alternating on his intense features. It excited her even more to know that her expression was a mirror image. She wanted him deeper, she wanted to cling on for always, and then her entire self shattered and she was screaming uncontrollably.

In those seconds she wanted the beauty of it to last for eternity and didn't want to ever let him go.

11

Suzannah soon proved to Billy that she had a business brain that was as sharp as any man's, perhaps even sharper than most. With little obvious effort she made the shop pay twice as much as before. Custom improved vastly despite the price rises she insisted upon, and the whole enterprise was slapped into efficiency.

From the start she had warned him that she

would run it as she wished, without interference, and he had been happy enough to give her all the slack that she wanted. All he asked for in return was just enough money from the profits to survive, to give him his own release from a life he found constricting. Custom had increased, to a certain extent, because Tombstone had become full to bursting point. The shooting at the O K Corral had attracted scores of wanderers, wanting from the town what others were evidently fighting over.

Controversy continued over the reasons behind the shoot-out. What was evident was that Doc Holliday and Wyatt Earp had been arrested on murder warrants. A preliminary court hearing was due to be held in town to determine the case, with Judge Spicer presiding. It was noted by many that Doc, a gambler and a gunfighter and a qualified dentist, had already notched up more than ten killings, which had given him notoriety even before the latest deaths.

Suzannah, who gained some fame from being able to recount to customers - at first hand - what had happened at the O K Corral as she had been a witness to events, relished the upturn in trade while Billy luxuriated in the hours alone.

Both of them had made few real friends. Suzannah never mixed with people outside work hours, although she knew most of the townsfolk and the majority of the gossip because of her situation behind the counter. In her heart she believed that the fewer people she really knew the fewer she would be able to hurt or betray. Billy figured the opposite. The fewer he really knew the fewer would be able to hurt him.

Despite the lack of space in the lodgings they, like she had done with Nathan, managed to live separate lives under the same roof. There were no disagreements because they rarely spoke. They respected each other's privacy and kept their own lives cocooned away from themselves, as well as others.

Running the shop had restored some of Suzannah's impetus for living. The voluptuous beauty remained under wraps, though there were still a good many wives who watched her through envious eyes. Henry continued to distrust her, refusing to see any change, or hope for redemption, in her morals. He maintained that the true, deceitful, wilful woman would rise from the self-flagellated ashes.

Indeed, once he realised how much Billy had come to depend upon her, he decided that it was his duty to persuade him that he had to send her packing, whether she had a head for business or not. Ahead of a confrontation with the younger man, he anticipated that Billy would reject such views, but that did not prevent him trying to alter his perception of her.

'She's basically dishonest,' he explained one evening after bringing around to Billy a letter he had received earlier that day from Nathan. Suzannah was still in the shop. Having finally had enough of the chaotic shelving, she was carrying out major refurbishments on her own.

'No more, no less, and you've placed her in sole charge of that store.'

'She runs the shop, that's all. I'm definitely not her keeper, nor she mine. What I feel for her is gratitude.'

'She tried to destroy Nathan, she'll ruin you.'

'I doubt it. I've got so little to ruin.'
Nathan's letter had unsettled Henry. In writing it the Cornishman had tried not to dwell on Lorna's death, but in reality all that had registered was his corrosive distress and sorrow. At the end he had enquired about Billy, and trusted that Henry was continuing to play godfather to him.
Henry wished, though, especially faced with the conundrum of Suzannah, that he had not had such responsibility placed upon him. Work now tired him, breath was harder to come by than usual, and memories, forgotten for decades, had been crowding in on him. Apart from that he was very much aware that Billy did not want him to play godfather to him.
The trouble was he had promised Nathan he would do so, and to him Nathan was as good as the only flesh and blood he had.
'What I really want to know is how you waste your days. Why do you bother employing her? What work does she do that you cannot do yourself?'
Billy, who was now sporting an embryonic moustache to match the beard, patted him on the back, accepting that the old man was engaged in carrying out some sort of duty for his brother.
'Oh Henry, there are all the reasons in the world, believe me. Don't I seem more content? I don't long for home, like Nathan feared I would. I've accepted that I'll be in this country of yours for a couple of years at least, and much of that is due to the worries Suzannah's taken away from me.'
He would say no more. If Henry was curious as to what he did with his spare hours then it was up to him to sniff out the truth. After all,

wasn't it true that he was the reporter, the sleuth?

The paintings he had completed remained hidden away, placed on canvas only to bring him inner peace. He never considered showing them to anyone else. The dread of ridicule was too ingrained. His reasons for gratitude to Suzannah were evident, to him, in many ways. Since taking over the reins at the shop she had never confronted him on any issues the way Henry had done, or grilled him about his secretive existence.

Due to the bargain they had made between them, she had the business to do with as she wished, and that was a decision she seemed to want to cling to.

Nevertheless, as the year 1882 slipped into spring, even Suzannah found that she could not ignore a nagging mystery that was so close to home. There was no way she wanted to hurt Billy, who had been generous to her in his naive way - a way which reminded her of an insecure, trusting younger brother.

But, in spite of that, he had become an enigma that she wanted to explore further, and she told herself that discovering more about him would only be for his own good. Surely she, more than anyone, knew how America could offer too many unhealthy diversions, and chances for self-destruction? All she wanted was to be sure that he was treading a safe path.

He was so embroiled in his needs, so anxious to be away into the barren, magnificent country around Tombstone where he could lose himself in his imagination, that he never noticed her following him. She shut the store for two consecutive days, sat and watched him work, saw him covering the canvasses with quick, compulsive strokes, and came to understand. On the third morning she crept back to the lodgings and searched his room until she had unearthed his hidden cache of sketches and paintings. Smothering the conscience that had dictated her life since her father's death, she decided on immediate action in case she began to renege on an idea formulating in her mind - and she took a watercolour of a worn, exhausted miner from his 'store'.

Despite appreciating the quality of it straight away, she studied it further that evening, when she was aware he was asleep and would not bother her. The man's gaunt, yet undaunted face stared bleakly out at her, revealing so much about himself and the unrelenting, rugged land that he had strayed into that it little mattered that no direct words were conveyed.

The following day she laid her own pride aside and went to see Henry, armed with her evidence. He was staggered when he opened the door of the litter-strewn Clarion office to see her standing, very sure of herself, outside. The meekness had gone. She was waiting for him with ramrod straight back, zeal in her eyes, and cheeks which were aflame. The sparkle had returned.

'I've come to see you,' she purred.

For the confrontation she had dressed demurely, not wanting to antagonise, but she hadn't bargained for a resurgence of her hidden spirit as she set about her task. It had come bubbling upwards from deep within her, without any encouragement.

Henry himself had endured a bad, sleepless night, and had planned a couple of hours in which he could concentrate on his report on the latest twist in the Earp brothers saga. Recently, Judge Spicer had discharged the defendants at the preliminary hearing, absolving them of blame for the deaths, and saying they had been 'fully justified in committing these homicides' - and that it was a necessary act done in the discharge of official duty.

The violence hadn't stopped, however. Only that week Morgan had been killed by unknown assassins, and Wyatt, his brother Warren and some of their friends had tracked down and murdered at least two of the suspects. Wyatt was now facing these further murder charges, and was on the run, some said for Colorado, or maybe even California. The news, therefore, was rich on the ground, but since Nathan had left Henry had been unable to tackle the Clarion with the same enthusiasm. With energies running low he certainly didn't want to have to spar with Suzannah that morning.

Of late, he had been thinking that maybe it was time to sell up, and take life much easier. Or would that be accepting defeat?

'Well I've no intention of seeing you, my dear,' he snapped at her as soon as she opened her mouth, putting a hand up to shut the door in her face. Ahead of her visit she had guessed what his reaction would very likely be, so had already jammed it with her body.

'It's about Billy. Please listen to me. I've come for your advice.'

On her way to the editorial office she had told herself that she must not be riled whatever kind of reception she was given.

Henry has good reason to see me as a meddlesome thorn in his side, she told herself. I have been one, and worse besides.

She persisted in trying to get through to him, thinking that perhaps intriguing him might be one way.

'He may not be a lost cause much longer.'

'Why . . . are you leaving?' came the answer, heavy with sarcasm.

Trying to stay calm, she took a deep, audible breath.

'If you would just set aside your intense dislike of me for one moment I might be able to explain why I'm here. For a start let me in. I can't talk to you properly half squashed in the door.'

With reluctance, he allowed her to enter, though at the same time pointedly did not offer her a seat.

'I can only spare two minutes. I can't grant you any more than that or there won't be a paper this week.'

'As you please. Two minutes will be enough,' she said, striving to appear quite unruffled. While he watched on with increasing suspicion in his ageing, watering eyes she delved into the large bag she had brought with her. Taking out the watercolour with some care, she pushed it roughly into his hands. Taken aback by what she was doing, he gave it a swift, uninterested glance.

'Very pretty. Do you want me to buy it or something?'

'Open that bitter, closed mind of yours a little, and look at it properly,' she pleaded. 'I want you to take it to an expert for me. I want a worthwhile opinion.'

'For goodness sake, I'm not your lackey. Get out of here.'

'It's not my picture, it's Billy's,' she carried on.

'Stolen it, have you?'

'Maybe, but I shall return it, have no fear. What you must understand is that he didn't buy it. He painted it. It belongs to Billy because he painted it, and there are many others stacked away where it came from. Can't you see how good it is?'

Henry shifted on his feet. Despite himself he was curious.

'You're an art expert now, as well as a liar and a schemer are you?'

'Look at it, Henry. We may have had differences, and all of them due to me, but I still regard you as someone who's retained a little bit of intelligence in the midst of this crazy world we're living in. Look at the painting properly, please.'

Begrudgingly, he obeyed her, thinking that it did look eye-catching, even professional, but knowing that he was far from being a decent art critic.

'Is this part of the answer to our mystery then? Is this what consumes him all his days?'

Realising that she had managed to appeal to his curiosity, she gave a smile that was completely natural, that was not given through hidden intentions.

'It is. I followed him twice last week, and watched him for hours. Maybe it was the wrong thing to do, but the suspense was annoying me so much, I had to know what he was up to.'

'It seems you're a detective as well, and a successful one. This is all well and good, but you haven't explained why you've come to me.'

'Yes I have. You're the man with the contacts. I know you can help, and there is no-one else I can turn to. I've kept too much to myself lately. I'm on nodding acquaintance with almost everyone in Tombstone, and at the same time friendly with no-one bar Billy. What is certain is that he needs the encouragement of someone he would respect, who can give him confidence. I believe that's all been battered out of him at some stage in his life.'

Henry carefully lay the painting down amongst the page proofs which were scattered around him.

'All right, say we contact someone behind his back, wouldn't we be deceiving him even further than you've already done? It's up to him what he does with his own work. Can't you see that he stores them away in secret because he wants to keep them to himself?'

'He's pushed them all under his bed, and if you let him he'll leave them there to rot. He must be unable, or unwilling, to see their potential worth. I think they embarrass him.'

'And how would you know that? It takes someone to bother about someone else's feelings to work something like that out.'

'I put myself out now and then,' she said soothingly. 'I've tried to alter. I'm not the same person who caused my father's suicide. She'd never have bothered with Billy in the first place. There are a hundred men in this town she would have turned her attention to before him - and I want to make it quite plain that my feelings for him are nothing like those I once had for Nathan. He's like a younger brother to me, I would say. Much as, I suspect, you see Nathan as a son to you.'

Henry, for the first time ever, began to listen to her, rather than seizing with tension every second he was in her company.

'All right. Supposing I do contact an expert and he gives an unfavourable opinion. What do we do then? Aren't we in danger of harming Billy's confidence still further by interfering?'

'If we're told the painting is of no worth then we tell Billy nothing. I'll just slip it back underneath his bed when he's not around. That way he doesn't get hurt.'

Henry continued to hesitate.

'I'll leave the picture here,' she insisted. 'Let me know what the reply is as soon as you've heard. Use your contacts, not for my sake because I won't gain anything, but for Billy's.'

Even then he refused to be entirely convinced, not wishing to be won over by Suzannah quite so quickly.

'What if I decide instead to tell him what you've done? He won't look at this lightly, and for you the shop may well go. He probably wouldn't want you there any more. There would be no more trading on his easy-going nature.'

'Do you really think that would help him? He might be angry with me, he might throw me out in the same way as Nathan did, but in the end he would be as miserable as me. By running the store as I do I give him space to breathe, to allow himself to be able to indulge in the one activity that gives him some purpose in life. I think he's lost without a brush in his hand, he probably always has been. It's a bit tragic he's had to come halfway across the world to find that out.'

'Aren't you exaggerating a bit? This is probably a phase he's passing through. He'll want to be a musician next, or a writer. He's young and he's lost and he's merely trying to find some direction.'

'Which you can help give to him,' she

whispered fiercely. 'Billy has talent. To me that is undeniable. Left to himself he will just squander it. And he's no child, jumping from one favourite toy to the next. He's a grown man.'

'And you see yourself as his saviour do you? You who have no talent at all but that for destroying others, your own family members and the man you professed to love included.'

His words had no power to touch her. She had said it all to herself almost every night since her father had shot himself.

'I thought I was asking you to be his saviour, although admittedly he already has a spiritual saviour, someone who might yet punish me for the deeds I have done. No, I want you to be of practical, earthly guidance to him.'

Henry stretched out his long, wasted legs, and rubbed his arthritic knees with his veined, gnarled hands. Glancing at the clock, he realised that he had given her much longer than two minutes.

'Remember, it is for Billy, and in a way for Nathan, not for me,' she countered, certain that she was making headway. 'You might not get anywhere. His work may be completely bereft of talent to experts, but then again it might not be. If your contact thinks highly of the pictures I'll break the news to Billy if you want. If the reaction is only mediocre then we both stay silent. He'll never know we had this little talk. Believe me, I don't want to taunt him. At the moment he's the only person in this world giving me stability, although it's very likely he doesn't realise it.'

111

The voices erupted from inside the house, the

shouts heard by James as he turned into the driveway of his Tregrehan home. Without wanting to be, he was reminded sharply of another evening when similar shouts had drifted across meadowlands to him from the Britannia. On that occasion, more than a decade before, he had ignored them. This time he knew exactly whose voices they were, and he was not going to walk onwards, smiling. He was in a strange mood - exhausted, uncertain, but mildly jubilant. The struggle to keep J and A Rosevean afloat was far from over. On the best of days it was full of doubts, and tiring in the extreme. Pressure remained on the railway companies to charge the company out of existence. Also, he had had to deal with rumours that his bank was due to withdraw his credit, and although the idle talk was false it had created its own set of problems which had come between himself and those who had willingly believed what he termed tittle-tattle.

In the past weeks he had hardly stopped congratulating himself that, at the insistence of Alex, he had switched all their funds to the Mount Charles Bank which had no ties with Richard. It was about the only financial institution in the district where the name Courteney held no sway.

As well as that, against all his new-found beliefs, and against the principles that Alex had adhered to for as long as he could remember, they had had to introduce wage cuts at the pits. There had, however, been no calls for strike action in retribution. The men had backed them, knowing exactly what was going on. The campaign against the firm was common knowledge.

Their demonstration of faith had affected

James greatly, and talking to the employees that afternoon had given him a needed lift. Where once they had shunned him at best, they now apparently wanted to trust him. He found that at last he was returning to his roots, and on the way was discovering that, despite everything, they remained strong and sound. But he had needed the boost that the men had given him - as he had started to wonder if it was all worthwhile.

Had Nathan and then Billy chosen the right way after all? Reading Nathan's paper made him grasp the number, and depth, of opportunities across the seas. Why the hell remain in Cornwall when the tide was so determined to run against him? But then there were Helen, and Glynn, and the new baby, now due any day. Surely he could not expect them to trail around the world after him? And it would be impossible to leave them. No, he accepted he had no option other than standing his ground and hoping.

By the time he reached the front door his temper was bubbling to the surface. He could hear that Richard was there and in full spate, his own anger reverberating in the air. James now only had to hear him pontificating, and he was ready for the kill.

His old mentor had put both himself and Helen through too much for the reaction to be otherwise.

James had been intending to stay in Plymouth that evening. There had been a meeting of pit owners called because of anxieties about the sick pay scheme he and Alex had introduced, and he presumed Richard was aware of that, and had perhaps called expecting his daughter and grandson to be there alone.

The meeting had been called because of fears

that with one firm prepared to adopt such a scheme others would be forced to, and the owners of J and A Rosevean had been asked to put their point of view to the gathering, to explain why they had taken such a dramatic step.

For a fleeting moment he considered the possibility that Richard had even arranged the meeting, to give himself a free evening in which he could confront Helen who, for all her disguised fire, was much more vulnerable on her own than with her husband alongside her, at least with the husband he had now become.

What scared him most was that it was only a week until the birth, and she had not been well for a couple of days. With worries rising, he rushed to the hall, heading straight for the main reception room.

'He's my grandson and I demand to see him,' Richard was yelling.

'He's asleep, I've told you. I'm not going to wake him.'

'I haven't seen him for months. Surely ten minutes wouldn't hurt?'

'It's no-one's fault but your own that you haven't seen him for so long. You've avoided him like the plague up until now.'

'You ungrateful little . . '

James was in the room in an instant, having already heard enough to know that his father-in-law was losing all sense of proportion. He found Richard holding Helen by her wrists, pulling her across towards the downstairs bedrooms, where Glynn slept, shaking her as she tried to resist.

James snapped. His temper already at boiling point, he threw himself at the big man, twisting his free arm up behind his back as soon as he was on him, little caring if he pulled it out of its socket as he dragged him further away from his daughter. Although Richard was taller and broader, that was of no influence. No-one would have overpowered James in the mood he was in.

'Leave her alone, you bully. Can't you see that she's almost about to give you, God help you, a second grandchild? If you cause her to have that baby before its due I'll take great pleasure in breaking every bone in your wretched, scheming, ageing body.'

'Glynn's my grandson. He's mine as well as yours,' retorted Richard between clenched teeth, kicking out like a cornered dog.

James sent him flying across the room, away from him, and for the first time it occurred to him that his father-in-law was slightly mad. The thought frightened him. Because it suddenly petrified him to imagine what Richard could attempt via insanity.

Struggling with such insights, he decided he had to get the man out of his home, though not until he had tried to calm the situation. He was faced by someone who was already trying to destroy him but if he gave way completely to the rage that was gripping him inside he would lose command of the situation. There were reasons why he had to be more logical. There was a great deal he needed to discuss with a more rational Richard Courteney.

Facing his father-in-law, as the older man also sought to regain some composure, and authority, he tried to decrease the tension, which was whipping around them, to a slightly lower degree.

'What do you want? What are you really here for? I was going to call on you tomorrow. We have to talk. I've been given some interesting news today, from the men in my pits and from my solicitor, and I have to say it needs mulling over with you.'

'He came about a legacy for Glynn,' muttered Helen, trying to fight the nausea welling up within her. Having retreated to a far corner of the room, she had moved back over to James and was clutching onto him for dear life, so grateful that he was there.

If only he, or someone like him, had been near me throughout my childhood, she told herself.

'I've told you before, we don't want Glynn to have any of your money,' insisted James, standing between his wife and Richard, and taking off his gloves slowly, with as great a show of normality as he could muster.

All the time he was wishing he could just sink into the nearest chair, sleep, and then wake to Helen's company.

'We want no talk of legacies from you. They do not, and will not, affect our lives - ever.'

It was seldom anyone spoke to Richard with such disdain, and the attitude therefore incensed him even more.

'You and my useless daughter have nothing to do with this matter. It's between the boy and me,' Richard replied, his voice laced with threat.

'The boy has a name. In case you've forgotten, it's Glynn,' answered James, mirroring the same attitude. 'You've seen him so infrequently I'm sure you'd probably not recognise him if he was standing within yards of you.

'The trouble is he knows you. He's scared stiff of you. Apart from that, both Helen and I know damned well that you're only interested in our son because he's your sole male descendant. There's no love, no caring, there never has been. You've nearly destroyed Helen with your egomania and you almost succeeded in turning me into a humourless, heartless copy of yourself. I'd hang myself from the scaffolding outside Bodmin jail before you were handed the chance to do the same with Glynn.'

'What tripe,' spluttered Richard, his complexion reddening by the second. 'I'll finish you for good before my life is over, James Rosevean, I swear I will.'

'You've already tried to tear my world apart, without success. Thanks to Nathan and a wise bank I'm still here, and our firm is still trading, and I intend everything to stay that way. I'll tell you something that's true - you were doing a better destruction job on me when we were in partnership, and I thought I was thriving.'

'You've seen nothing at all. I'll break that petty company of yours, and see you begging me for charity. A small amount of persuasion and I'm sure I could start enticing the majority of your workers to look elsewhere for work, perhaps that'll be my next tactic.'

'That they won't do, thanks to a brother who's much more foresight than you've ever had, they're firmly on our side.'

Richard was gone before anything further could be said. As he slammed the door behind him, leaving the remnants of his fury to reverberate around the room, Helen started sobbing. A small flow of tears at first, that then increased until she was in full flow, and couldn't stop herself.

James caught her, and she clung to him, sobbing harder than she could remember doing for years. More than during the worst days of her marriage, and the loneliest nights of her empty years at 'Trevarnioc'.

Seeing her in such a state made him equally distraught.

'Please don't Helen, you're scaring me. Please stop, it's not good for you in your condition, if at all.'

'It's all right . . it's all right. Let me cry. I've got to get this out of my system. These last months, last years, have been so worrying, and carrying the baby has been too. Perhaps it's been too much for me, trying to keep calm all the time right up until now. You've tried not to upset me but I've seen how desperate you and Alex have been, and I haven't been able to do anything positive to help you. That's the worst part of all this. Having my own father to blame, and not being able to do anything, not one thing, about it.'

Wanting to wipe all her cares away, he tipped up her tear-streaked face, and kissed her as gently as he could. She lay against him like a child, making him want to protect her from everything that life, at its worst, could ever throw at her.

'What I said about the men is true. They will stand by us, as will the bank, and Nathan. Thank the Lord he returned at the right time. Without his money, given without conditions, the firm would now be non-existent. And the encouraging thing is we still are existing. I think Richard is so unstable at present that some people are beginning to look at him with less awe than they have in the past.'

'You mean some people are just starting to wake up and realise that he isn't a gift from God to Cornish bosses?'

'Much like I did, I suppose, although perhaps they weren't duped as badly in the first place.'

The pains hit Helen from nowhere. One

moment she was enjoying the warmth of James's arms around her as she strove to recover from the unwanted encounter with her father, the next all thoughts of vendettas were wiped away by the knowledge that her waters were breaking, and that the baby was going to arrive in much quicker time than Glynn had. In fact Clare Mary Rosevean entered the world a bare fifty minutes after the first pain struck.
The midwife arrived with minutes to spare, to supervise the simple birth that had within it the power to dry all tears of despair.

1V

By the time the baby took her first breath Richard was taking his last as an able-bodied man. He had ridden home quivering with fury, and a deep desire for retribution, spurring his prize stallion on harder and harder, despite the fact that his groom had raised suspicions that morning that the horse might be showing signs of going lame. As he went, he was oblivious to everything else but the heightened need to crush James and his company beyond redemption.
Overcome with a deep-seated wish to destroy all who opposed him, he urged his stallion to canter along the muddy paths and over the fields while he himself paid little attention to their route, allowing instinct to carry him along. His mind was, instead, focused solely on ways of applying even greater constraints on J and A Rosevean, on influencing more people who could assist him, of moving in on the Mount Charles Bank and on the bank account that he wanted to wipe away.
The first pain was dull enough for him to try

to push it aside, presuming that it was due to the coldness that had started to seep into his body. Temperatures had dropped dramatically since the early afternoon, mainly because of a crystal clear sky with not a cloud in sight to act as a blanket for any remaining warmth. The late evening held within it a chill warning that although real winter was past it might be returning on a whim.

I'll not let a wretched, pathetic miner's boy defeat me, damn his bloody soul, he seethed, seeing not the stars nor the Cornish hedges or passing horsemen, but only James's drained face when he finally had to accept that there was nothing left to fight for.

Because of that he didn't even notice how his heart was accelerating and his pulses were being pushed out of control.

The final pain was to hit him like a hammer, bringing sanity to his senses. It stopped him revelling in his hatred, and filled him with panic. In his last frenetic moment before falling he realised what was happening, and knew that for once there was nothing he could do to prevent what was the inevitable. No form of blackmail or threats could stop the heart attack hitting.

The attack did not kill him. Nor did the fall from the now limping horse, a tumble that served to paralyse him from the neck downwards and leave him unable to summon help as he lay helpless, watching the growing night enclose the fields around.

A search party, formed after the stallion returned home alone, lame and sweating, found him lying frozen and filthy in a muddy ditch only half a mile from his mansion - his monument to wealth and power, and eventually doomed to be his prison.

It took ten of them to carry him back there, on a makeshift stretcher, and lay him on the floor of his study while the doctor was summoned. Few thought he would live beyond dusk. But a shell of the man did.

V

There were many more witnesses to the christening of Clare Mary Rosevean than there had been to the wedding of Alex and Jenifer Rosevean, despite the setting this time being smaller. Now they felt that Tregrehan was truly their home, and would hopefully remain that way for a long while, James and Helen decided that they would ask if the ceremony might take place in nearby Tregrehan Methodist Church, a venue James was well aware would have been frowned upon by his father.
Eva was noticeably absent from the guests. Richard's accident had not brought mother and daughter closer, even though it had served to give Eva a much freer life. She had used her husband's money to hire a nurse for him, and was happily spending the rest on herself. Richard was in no mental or physical condition to have any inkling of what was happening.
The money, in fact, created higher barriers between Eva and her daughter and grandchildren. Now she had, thanks to an easily flattered and bribed solicitor, access to all the funds she required, she wanted to distance herself still further from family members who might be seen to have any entitlement to some of it.
She was in the middle of contemplating selling all the companies and shares Richard

had an interest in, and putting 'Trevarnioc' on the market. Her intention was to move to Truro and establish herself with the fashionable elite there, such as the Lemon family of Carclew.

Richard, she was sure, could eventually be moved to some institution where he could be cared for by those who had some medical knowledge. Such freedoms enabled her to feel it was now her turn to shine in the world, and indulge herself to a much deserved excess.

There was no atmosphere of disbelief during the christening as there had been when Alex and Jenifer had married. This was a celebration, made even more poignant to James because it reminded him very sharply that he had not even bothered to turn up at the church for the whole service when his son had been baptized, having been called away elsewhere at the last moment.

Apart from the Roseveans a good deal of the populations of Biscovey, Tregrehan, and St Blazey Gate crammed into the small church. Before his partnership with Alex, James had held himself positively aloof from the villagers, but since they had joined forces, and brought in so many improvements for their employees, there had been a perceptive change. He had been forgiven for deviating away from their lives, and had been accepted, as Helen had been way back to the initial days of their marriage, despite her monied background.

Clare behaved herself beautifully throughout the service, in the contented way that was to become a feature of her nature. This was one of many positive contributions to an occasion which passed in a relaxed, light-hearted way and was enjoyed by all who attended, bar perhaps Nathan whose mind, like most days, was still unable to concentrate on minute by minute proceedings.

He spent the hour constantly glancing around, half expecting to see Lorna creeping in at the back and trying not to attract any attention. Occasionally, he still forgot that he would never see her again. She had been part of his thoughts for so long, even when he had been living thousands of miles distant from the land in which they had both been born.

If grieving could bring her back, he thought, then she would be beside me now, but grief won't bring about miracles, it's only there to be endured. She's at a greater distance from me than those thousands of miles, and this time I can't write to her, or plan to rejoin her. I can only whisper her name in the dead of night, and pray she hears.

What he wanted, what he needed, was to find understanding, to know if he could ever find love again. That, however, made his sadness unbearable, because in his soul he felt all such hopes were just that - hopes.

He left the church before anyone else, wandering off along the track leading back to the main St Austell to St Blazey road, initially picking his way through granite graves, with their Celtic crosses, in his quest for solitude. What he didn't want to do was to stay around and dampen the real happiness of the afternoon. But when he looked up Helen was there beside him.

Someone else had held the baby for her for a while. She was on her own. Since the birth she had put on weight slightly, and it served to make her more feminine. Contentment, like that which was to be a characteristic of her daughter, was also evident in her expression, softening her features. Her skin was fresh, unlined and unworried, her gaze concerned, and honest.

'I'm sorry Helen,' he said. 'I'm not being the best of guests. I'm afraid I wanted to be on my own for a while, I'm not that full of small talk today.'

Feeling he ought to explain more to her, he sat down on the wall dividing the track from the small hillocky meadow where the local youngsters played, and opposite the tiny local shop. She went and sat next to him, oblivious to the fact that her cream skirt would be muddied and grass stained.

'You don't still blame yourself for Lorna's death do you? James seems to think that you can't rid yourself of feeling responsible for the way she died, and the way she lived.'

His hair needed a cut. The curls had become completely unruly, the slight wind that was blowing pushing them right across his face. Due to that, he appeared slightly wild, but was really less wild than he had ever been.

'Let's say I've got so many regrets I don't know where to start.'

Hearing the sadness in his voice, she wanted to hug him, and then she thought - why not? Instinctively, she put her arms around him, and such was her concerned warmth that he leant closer to her.

'And what would have happened if you hadn't have gone abroad to America?' she asked.

'What would have happened to you here?'

'Goodness knows. I was pretty crazy at that stage of my life.'

'Precisely. You might have married her, though I'm pretty sure that wouldn't have been enough to quieten you back then. You needed a greater challenge. I believe that, like

James, you were not only trying to distance yourself from the memory of your father, you were also after proving something to him as well.'

Away, in the distance, they could see that all the guests were pouring out of the chapel. James was holding Glynn's hand, and Jenifer, absolutely radiant by the side of Alex, was now holding Clare. The three adults were in deep conversation. Helen hadn't been missed because James had known precisely where she was going.

Seeing the mass exodus, she pulled Nathan off the wall, and tugged him towards a side gate leading into a nearby lane that was to wind round to Bodelva.

'Let's take a small walk, the rest can look after themselves for a while.'

'But you're the star of the party.'

'No I'm not, Clare is, and my husband can cope very well on his own. He's proved that to himself in the past months.'

Meekly, he followed behind her. It was cool underneath the trees, and Helen shivered, though she was determined to snatch at least ten minutes with him. Ragged robin was beginning to show in the hedgerows, and the first few house martins of the year were visibly skimming the meadows, celebrating their feat of being the vanguard of the thousands to appear in the coming weeks. There was no-one else around.

'She chose to marry Samuel of her own free will,' Helen continued. 'That was what crippled her most. The marriage to him. I went to see her once, when I was in turmoil. I didn't have the insight then to know that she was having to bear much more than me.'

'She never would have tied herself to him if

I'd stayed put. Then again, if I hadn't rushed her when I did come back, if I hadn't tried to force her to go to Looe to see me, I'm sure we'd eventually have found each other again. Maybe, I could have made her believe that Samuel, and all those terrible things that happened with him, had never existed.'
'Don't you see, dear Nathan, that that is not true, because the old Lorna didn't exist any more? Regaining any true happiness was not possible for her. Too much had happened. Losing her child added years to her.'
'I made the most of America. After all that was thrown at me there I won through. I could have done the same with Lorna.'
'Lorna wasn't a country to conquer. She was human and much frailer than we all thought. Believe me Nathan, unless you had the ability to take her back in time and completely change the outcome of the years she spent with Samuel you could never have helped her.'
'Unfortunately, I'll never fully accept that.'
'Well then, try and live with it and don't allow any of your misplaced guilt to obscure whatever happiness there is in the future for you. We all care for you. Believe me, without your money and backing we'd all be in a sad and sorry mess, and that goes for Billy over in America too.'
He kissed her full on the lips, but in a fraternal fashion.
'James is a fortunate man. I'm very glad he's not too frightened to admit it to himself any more.'
Irrationally, tears sprang to her eyes, and she hastily blinked them away, not wanting Nathan to see them.
'And now you're back with us, are you going

to settle down?' she asked, too brightly. 'You've the newspaper, which is proving really successful, and more friends and admirers around you than you realise.'
'Settle down? I can't guarantee that, or say I definitely won't go back to America in the coming years. It's likely I'll stay, though. Despite everything I rather like my home at Millendreath, and I have to say that here, with James and Alex and you, and with wet Cornish weather and westerly winds in the place of the boiling sun as I've known it in Arizona, here is home.'

VI

The paintings and sketches adorning the walls in the small San Franciscan gallery made the casual visitors stand longer than they usually did at such exhibitions. One glance was not enough. The scenes and portraits evoked so much more than words would ever have done. The weather-beaten faces, some full of ill-disguised pain, others betraying complete desperation, the panoramic views of Nevada desert, of Californian orange groves, of abandoned tin mines, also held a majestic beauty that was indefinable.
Suzannah was much in evidence among the crowds, mingling with as many as possible, playing hostess to perfection, although it was sapping her more than she had ever imagined it would. It had taken a long, hard struggle convincing Billy that he should not be scared of allowing his world view to hang before critical eyes.
At first Henry had been proved right. It had split their fragile alliance. Billy had thrown Suzannah out of the lodgings, banned her

from the store, threatened to sell up and move on. But, eventually, an unlikely knight had come to her aid in the form of Henry himself, who had used the right amount of coercion.
'For pity's sake,' he had raged, 'stop running right now. Accept that you might be throwing away the only good opportunity that life might ever offer you. Give your dreams a chance to become reality. Forget who said what about your artistic talent in the past. This offer from the gallery owner is for now, and it's been made because your work deserves recognition. There's no shame in what you've achieved on those canvasses Billy. You've no reason to hide them.'
However, while Suzannah forced a wide smile on her face during the exhibition, and made herself mix with the guests, the artist himself hung back, an unknown, shy figure, expecting the reaction on this initial day of the exhibition, to be the same as his father's had been towards his work. He could hear him mocking him still.
'What trash. Who are you trying to fool? What a complete and utter waste of energy and materials.'
That voice from the past dominated him. He could not concentrate on anything else. The voices surrounding him were merely a hub-bub, while the faces blurred together and, to him, were also irrelevant.
All day he had felt as if he had hauled himself up in front of the universe for an inspection of character, and that all he would receive at the end of the trial would be wounding criticism. There had not been a moment when he, himself, had been able to focus on his paintings. Hung in this white-walled room they seemed as alien to him as everything else

going on around him.

About midday, after two hours of mingling, Suzannah sidled up to him, placing a weary and concerned arm around his hunched shoulders. Her hair had grown almost to her own shoulders and, despite a touch of grey, was nearly as healthily glossy as in former days in Grass Valley. Outwardly, she was a phoenix beginning to rise from her own particular ashes, but inwardly she would never return to the sweet cruelty of her youth.

'Why are you looking so dispirited? There's nothing to worry about, haven't you noticed the reactions?'

'This is a farce. They don't know anything about art. They'll walk out of that door and forget I ever existed. I would bet that not one of them cares about what those sketches are trying to say.'

'How stupid can you be? Everyone I've spoken to has been really impressed. They appreciate something that's exceptional when it's put in front of them.'

'Nothing's exceptional in here, except perhaps your faith in me.'

'Do you want me to take a swipe at you right in the middle of all this, because I will if you keep running yourself down. Why don't you tell yourself a few home truths? It's not that you have no ability, it's that you've got no guts. If you'd had some fire and spirit you'd have done something like this years ago, and wouldn't have relied on a liar like me to sneak around your room searching out your secret passion.'

Never had she been so forthright with him before, and that shook him. He stood there, stung by her words, finding no answer, before she was swept away by a reporter from the

San Francisco Times. Everyone in the room knew the woman with the compelling jade-coloured dress, and the wary eyes that were downcast one moment and then shining the next, had arranged the event, but none had noticed the retiring, white-faced young man near the door who was the actual artist. Suzannah was so afraid her attack on him would frighten Billy away that she decided to take another gamble just in case he did disappear completely, and guided the journalist, who was so full of praise and bursting with questions, over to the painter himself.

After that there was no hiding place for the Cornishman. With Suzannah beside him, prompting him all the way, he opened up enough for a short interview, then found himself surrounded by strangers who wanted to shake his hand, and discuss the first canvas that he had finished in New Mexico, the stamping grounds of Billy the Kid and Geronimo, and then the sketch he had made of the Paiute Indians in Nevada and their Ghost Dance, which he had been privileged to be able to watch.

There was a period when he felt completely under siege, though at the same time a splash of self-assurance began to surface which carried him through the rest of the day with almost consummate ease. Such was the gentle influx of optimism that when the doors were closed, and the crush had dispersed, he had regained enough equilibrium and hope to realise that the day had maybe held promise after all.

By then, Suzannah was so drained she couldn't manage to mask her exhaustion any more. Even Billy, who was usually so bound up in himself that everything else passed him by in a haze, was able to recognise that she had given her all in the cause. He sidled up to her.

'You may be a scheming woman, Suzannah, but I've got to be grateful to you. Without you I'd never have been here, and those paintings would still be rotting underneath my bed. It may have taken me a painfully long time to come to terms with it, but thanks for trying to drag me out of my shell. The trouble is I don't quite understand why you've bothered. You were talking about guts earlier on. It must have taken something for you to try and enlist Henry's help in all this, the way he feels about you.'

At that moment he wanted only to rest, to lie down and not have to move again for days.

'To be blunt Billy I'm not sure why I did it. Basically, I knew you wanted a push along the way. You saw yourself as a failure when you're not and that annoyed me. I'm the failure, not you.'

'Suzannah . . '

'Don't Suzannah me. It's true. Maybe I thought a bit of your success would reflect on me a little. Perhaps I was being purely selfish.'

'Whatever you were being, I can't express how grateful I am. Do you know at least three quarters of my work has been sold already? At this rate I'll never need to rely on hardware again.'

'I suppose you're right. Who wants a store when they can make money through beauty? Sell up Billy. Move here, to San Francisco. Find yourself a decent home. Here you'll be in the centre of things.'

At the thought, he shivered. He didn't like to

tell her that crowds worried him, scared him even, in case she questioned his courage again.

'No, I'm not going to let one good day steer me off course. I intend to stay just where I am for a while, but I might consider giving you the store. You're the expert where trading is concerned.'

'Isn't giving it away a little over-generous?'

'Not really,' he said softly. 'How long will Tombstone last? One day it will stand empty and abandoned. When its riches have gone the adventurers will just melt away like thin frost on Cornish fields when a spring sun rises. It'll be a dusty memory, little else.'

She stared around at the gallery.

'But your paintings will live on, won't they? The gold will be dug out and the silver, the fortunes will be squandered and the longhorn and the cattlemen will maybe fade into the past, but these will still be hung on differing walls, telling the story of what happened there.'

'That's a romantic notion, most unlike you.'

'It's nearer a fact.'

He studied the painting behind her, as if seeing it anew. It was of Wheal Bethany, and he had captured her in her prime. Men were gathered around the engine house and smaller figures of children and bal maidens were detectable scurrying around in the distance. In his mind's eye he saw her as she had become, crumbling and idle on the other side of the Atlantic, with nothing happening around or underneath her, with her engines rusting and finished, the waters rising in her workings, and the wind whipping through her assorted, lonely buildings.

Then he averted his gaze to the portrait of Ben

Northey, from Pelynt, who had befriended him during his first months in Tombstone. He was now dead, killed by an underground explosion that had blown away ten lives. Maybe, he thought, just maybe she's right.

Printed in Great Britain
by Amazon